GENEALOGY

GENEALOGY

A NOVEL

MAUD CASEY

HARPER PERENNIAL

NEW YORK • LONDON • TORONTO • SYDNEY

HARPER ● PERENNIAL

Permissions appear following page 260.

P.S.™ is a trademark of HarperCollins Publishers.

HarperCollins books may be purchased for educational, business, or sales promotional use. For information please write: Special Markets Department, HarperCollins Publishers, 10 East 53rd Street, New York, NY 10022.

FIRST EDITION

Designed by Phil Mazzone

Library of Congress Cataloging-in-Publication Data

Casey, Maud.
    Genealogy : a novel / Maud Casey.—1st Harper Perennial ed.
        p.   cm.
    ISBN-10: 0-06-074089-2
    ISBN-13: 978-0-06-074089-4
    1. Mentally ill—Family relationships—Fiction.   I. Title.

    PS3553.A79338G46   2006
    813'.6—dc22
                                                        2005052688

06 07 08 09 10 WBC/RRDH 10 9 8 7 6 5 4 3 2 1

For my sisters, Clare, Julia, and Nell

The brain provides us with wondrous things,
from mathematical theories to symphonies,
from automobiles and airplanes to trips to the moon.
But when it goes awry, we are undone.

    —from **Creating Mind** *by John E. Dowling*

—O remember
In your narrowing dark hours
That more things move
Than blood in the heart

    —from "Night" by Louise Bogan

GENEALOGY

GENEALOGY

Humble, Then, Your Wisdom

For forty-three years, the one-and-a-half centimeter berrylike sac has been nestled in Samantha Hennart's brain, like an exclamation point curled into a comma waiting for the end of the sentence.

Everyone is gone: her husband, her son, and since yesterday afternoon, without any warning, her daughter has disappeared too. As Sam waits for Marguerite to return—because she *will* return, because, really, there is no other option—her eyelid flutters. Flutter, flutter. It's been fluttering all morning. From nerves, she assumes. To calm herself, she looks out the window to what she calls the lifesaving view, the stubbly Rhode Island fields and fields and fields that lead to the distant sliver that is the ocean. The farmer's son and another boy are out in one of the fields baling hay and they look up to where Sam leans out of the window. In adulthood, she has emerged from a mousy girl shell to be the kind of woman who stops the wandering gaze of men and with her hair pulled back what her husband once called her revelatory forehead is revealed. A revelation of beauty, he said, placing his palm there delicately, deliberately, as if her forehead was a holy relic and Bernard was divining something, but that was years and years ago.

Sam appreciates that the farmer's son, upon seeing her, raises a hand in hello as if she were a normal woman.

Sam's daughter, Marguerite Hennart, will not be back today. She is searching for her heart in Queens. She believes her eighteen-year-old heart, strong enough, tough enough, is in a jar somewhere—she can hear it thump-thumping—against thick jelly jar glass. Up and down, up and down the up and down hall she shuffles, searching for her thump-thump heart, pressing her ear into door after door though the mourning women have told her not to. The mourning women whom Marguerite first met in the morning but then there they were in the afternoon and the evening too and so she knew they were not women who came in the morning but mourning women.

The mourning women tell Marguerite not to lean her ear against the doors because there are germs. According to the shorter mourning woman there are germs everywhere, which is kind of funny. Germs in a hospital.

"Germs on the doors, germs on the floor, germs on the walls," the shorter mourning woman says. "Germs everywhere."

"And in *this* kind of hospital," Marguerite's roommate, Regina, says, skating by on legs bruised from kicking herself, "there are germs on the mind."

But if finding her heart means getting ear germs then Marguerite will get germs in her ears because above all, at the very top of the musty pile of musts, she must find her heart and have it ready for her brother when he comes to carry it to its final resting place. Suddenly, in the overhead sky of the indoor world: *paging Dr. Goodman* (florid mania, Dr. Goodman says, is like a flower bursting), *paging Dr. Good Man*, and Marguerite is hopeful. Up and down, up and down, an ear pressed to every door.

Marguerite's brother, Ryan Hennart, isn't on his way to find her heart because he doesn't know it's missing. He doesn't even know Marguerite is missing because he has been gone three weeks, longer than anyone. He is in San Francisco, sitting at a wobbly thrift store table, one of its legs propped up by the Yellow Pages. He is in an apartment not his own in the Mission, across from a woman elaborate with tattoos—lines and squiggles that were indecipherable when he was having sex with her in the dark last night. With his second cup of coffee, the tattoos become more legible: thorns with drops of blood, an anchor, Jesus on a cross wearing a dress.

"Where did you say you were from?" the woman asks. The woman's pointed question threatens to turn a perfectly enjoyable one-night stand into an interrogation and Ryan is late for his job as a long-term temp.

"Are you going to answer me?" The woman puts her toes in the cuff of Ryan's pants and jiggles her foot. "What are you, mute?" She kicks him.

"Something like that." People should be tattooed by love, Ryan thinks as this woman waits for an answer, although Ryan suspects that no answer will satisfy her. Love should leave a mark on the body, carve itself into different shapes, but he isn't thinking of this woman, he is thinking of Marguerite whose love has tattooed his heart with something that Ryan imagines looks like the snake that winds its way up this woman's arm. The snake that is right now reaching out across the worn, scratched surface of the wobbling table for a carton of milk whose expiration date is a week ago.

"Whatever," the woman says finally, standing to readjust her robe, opening it briefly to reveal a tattooed flower over her left breast. And then, shit, Ryan remembers that all of this love tattoo bullshit is something his mother once said to him and, Jesus, was he so pathetic that he was recycling thoughts of his mother's? A woman who the last time he spoke to her was touting the benefits of some freaky Quaker medicinal treatment that involved taking baths all day long? A woman who was using this freaky antiquated quack treatment to cure whatever it was she thought ailed his sister? If she had asked Ryan, and no one ever did, the longterm effects of parents like she and Bernard weren't going to be washed away by any bath, no matter how long you soaked.

Ryan pulls the woman's calf rough with razor stubble up onto his leg and traces the anchor. He lets his relief at being states and states and states away from his parents run through his finger to this calf in front of him. He can see in this woman's eyes the way relief is being interpreted as something deeper.

How did Bernard Hennart end up in a dark diner somewhere on a back road in Virginia, shades drawn to keep the bright light of noon from mocking the dinginess? He's lost track, driving and driving for the last three days, ever since he walked in on Sam with that pseudo-Benedictine, hippy porn carpenter who came to make the bathroom over according to some Quaker code of bathtub ritual. Sam, perched on the rim of that continuous bathtub of hers, legs spread, bracing herself with one arm against the wall and the hippy porn carpenter on his knees, his limp blond head of hair between Sam's thighs while their daughter slept, waterlogged in a nearby room.

Bernard's been driving from one small town to the next trying to shake that image, staring out the windows of dark motel rooms that smell of stale cigarette smoke. In the morning, he wakes up with quilts scarred with tiny round cigarette-burned holes scratching his face. He's been trying to abandon not only that image but time itself—the weeks, the months, the years, and the rest of the calendar. He keeps the shades drawn in an effort to outsmart time, but it refuses to be outsmarted and eventually he remembers he's fifty-nine and his wife is having an affair, his son left home and it's Bernard's fault, and his daughter's skin, which used to glow from the inside out, grows prunier and prunier by the day. He's fifty-nine and not only are all of these things lost to him, he's abandoned the material for the research project that has meant more to him than anything in years—an essay by a German doctor on the stigmata and ecstasy of the nineteenth-century Belgian mystic, Louise Lateau— on the back of a rest-stop toilet.

No matter how quickly Bernard drives or how much bad TV he watches, there's also no shaking his wife's voice rattling in his head since he left Rhode Island. Sometimes Sam's voice rails against the way he has disappeared into his research. *If it makes you feel better to keep calling her* research, *more power to you, but I prefer to call the bleeding Belgian what she is: a reality substitute.* Sometimes her voice rails against his leaving. *Here's the part where, after everything that's happened, you take off into the wild blue yonder.* In rarer moments, Sam's voice waxes nostalgic. For this version of her voice, Bernard would endure any number of rants. *"Humble, then, your wisdom, which is based on reason, and place all your fidelity in those things which are given by love, and illuminated through faith,"* Sam says, quoting Marguerite's namesake, Marguerite Porette. Bernard's head is in his hands as he studies a mustard stain on the tabletop, waiting for the waitress to come take his order.

Remember that? Sam asks. The kindness in her voice is like a star's light arriving from years and years ago. For this version of Sam, Bernard would give anything.

You Were Only Waiting for This Moment to Arise

The day the Hennarts discovered the secluded beach, the sky was an inscrutable blue, the air thick with ocean salt. Seagulls hovered just above the sand, riding the wind as it pushed them backward, flapping their wings only occasionally to stab their beaks into a stray piece of sandwich from a leftover picnic. In the distance, a sailboat slid quickly along the top of the water. From the shore the sailboat was the size of five-year-old Marguerite's thumb held up to measure it the way twelve-year-old Ryan showed her.

"Look how that huge boat seems so tiny," Ryan said solemnly to his sister, who looked up at her brother and nodded with equal solemnity, still holding up her sailboat-size thumb. Down the beach, Bernard and Sam stood ankle-deep in the water, their shoes dangling from the tips of their fingers.

Up in the tall grass of the dunes, local teenagers, two sets of recently established summer couples, huddled in a circle in the tall beach grass passing a collective joint and laughing. They had gone swimming earlier, and both the hair on their heads and their pubic hair were tangled with the red weed that filled the water all the way out to the deceptively slow, almost invisible swell of water, the beginning of the waves.

"Catch," the tallest teenager said. He wore a paisley handkerchief that matched the sky, in part to keep his long hair out of his eyes, in part to accentuate his long hair, of which he was quite proud. He reached down his swim trunks and pulled out a seemingly endless string of weed and threw it at the nearest girl who had been out in the sun all day the day before in a different bathing suit. Now there were two white strips that looked drawn on above her strapless bikini top. Last summer, the teenagers made up a game—throw-the-weed—when the configuration of the couples was different.

"Asshole," the girl said, but she laughed and caught the weed and wrapped it around and around her neck like an elaborate scarf. "I think that kid was the one who came down and skinny-dipped with us the other night." She pointed to Ryan who kept shaking his floppy brown hair out of his eyes so it fell back over them in exactly the same place. He had made it a point not to look in the teenagers' direction.

Ryan *had* snuck down to the beach several nights ago. He'd seen the huddle of smoking, shirtless long-haired teenage boys during the day, one of whom he recognized from when he'd watched from the window as the boy rode the tractor around the fields. Ryan had seen their bikinied girlfriends too, a crescent of secret flesh escaping their bikini bottoms. The night he snuck down to the beach, he found them all gathered around a bonfire stoked with cardboard cases that once carried the beer tossed into the sand.

The bikinied girls had ruffled Ryan's floppy hair when he arrived and offered him a joint, which he smoked though he'd never smoked before. He held the smoke in his expanding lungs and they grew large and beautiful until he felt each grain of sand between his toes, each separate grain as he followed the teenagers who tore off their clothes and headed for the water. As he tore off his own clothes, Ryan, named for his mother's long-dead father whom he'd never met, felt his body distinct and cutting through the air, separate from his parents, separate even from his sister who he loved most of all.

Being naked on the beach that night felt like the word *freedom*, and that word echoed in Ryan's head as he ran after the teenagers, down to the water with his large and beautiful lungs and the rest of his body growing large and beautiful too. Each hair on his arm was a loner, exquisite in its lonerdom. As Ryan's torso in the warm air grew colder than his legs in the frigid ocean water, his body felt soulful and his soul felt real, like something he could touch, like the way his father said the girls from the Middle Ages could feel their souls, and the way his mother said the line from the Elizabeth Bishop poem—"The art of losing . . ." (he couldn't remember the rest of it)—made her feel as though she could feel *her* soul.

One of the bikinied girls, the one, if Ryan had to choose, with the more beautiful breasts, had linked her arm through his and one of her soft, beautiful breasts pressed against his hand for a moment. "You have beautiful hands," the beautiful-breasted girl said, taking his hand in her hand, so smooth, and all of him collapsed into that web of crisscrossed lines, into the tiny thump of her pulse. In the pitch-black of the night, they stood holding hands with the rest of the group, a quiet, still line, braced for the waves, swelling slow and invisible out there somewhere, to break against their bodies.

"The boy's embarrassed," the girl, the one who wasn't wearing the weed boa, said. She was busy fashioning an anklet out of weed. "That's cute."

"Look how sweet he is with his sister," the girl with the weed boa said, lifting it momentarily to look at yesterday's tan lines.

Both of the teenage boys pouted their lips and said "Awwwww" like crying clowns. "He's so sweet!"

Ryan held Marguerite's hand tightly. Pale and freckled, Marguerite was a peculiar-looking child really. Her skin shone bright white, as if she had swallowed a phosphorescent light bulb that lit her up from the inside. She held her brother's hand, standing apart from their parents as if they'd never in their life met their tall beauty of a mother—her hair pulled back in a bun held together by a stick

snapped off a tree on the way down the rocky path to the beach—
or their shorter, squatter father with his wandering eye.

Ryan made a V with his thumb and index finger that matched
the V of birds making their way through the sky so blue it seemed
transparent, like it might reveal another secret sky behind this one at
any moment. Marguerite copied him, making the same V, but with
her whole hand and her thumb sticking out. She imitated the slow
movement of the seagull's wings, opening her mouth and caw-
cawing. "That's not the sound of a seagull," Ryan said. "That's the
sound of a crow!" and Marguerite laughed so hard she fell down,
plunk, on her butt in the sand. She tried to make the sound of the
wind caught in the seagull wings, a sound like sheets snapped open
over a bed, but she was laughing too hard. Ryan slid his arms under
her armpits, clasping his hands against her flat chest, and spun her
around and around while she pretended to mind. "Stop!" she
shouted, though it sounded as though she meant *faster*.

After Ryan relented and put her down, after she made a big production of falling backward onto the sand again, she lay still and
studied the tip of her brother's nose. It started high up on his forehead and cut a line through the air like a miracle. Marguerite liked
to think about miracles because she had been named for a mystic
from the Middle Ages (only recently had she gotten it straight that
this was a long, long time ago, a time that her father studied, and not
the age of her parents who talked endlessly about their own Middle
Ages). "Humble, then, your wisdom, which is based on reason and
place all your fidelity in those things which are given by love," her
father would say, quoting Marguerite Porette from *The Mirror of
Simple Souls*. Marguerite Porette, her father told her, had been
burned at the stake for her beliefs. "And illuminated through faith!"
her mother would add, as she had done just this morning. "You forgot that on purpose!" she exclaimed, laughing. "It's not such a dirty
word. Faith, faith, faith. I've said it, now we can all say it."

"You're not *that* dizzy," Ryan said, pulling Marguerite's hand
while she let her body go slack. "You're faking. You could stand up
if you really tried." Marguerite watched the tip of her brother's nose
bob as he spoke to her.

"Oh no I couldn't," Marguerite said, trying and then falling again. "See!"

She liked to think about placing all of her fidelity (which meant faithfulness and loyalty to the millionth degree, her father had explained to her) into Ryan's nose, which she was sure had been given to her by capital *L-O-V-E*. She believed she was the only one who could see the gentle movement of her brother's nose as he talked, that her powerful love for him was like a pair of glasses that allowed her to see things about him that nobody else could. For instance, the secret language of his bobbing, miraculous nose. I love you the most, it said.

"*So cute*," the girl with the weed boa said, nudging her friend with the weed anklet, pointing to the little girl, now flat on her back in the sand, her brother using a big stick to draw a big circle around her.

"*So cute*," the boys sing-songed. They reached their hands deep down into the depths of their swim trunks to pull out more strands of weed to throw at their girlfriends.

Dirty, yellow foam floated on the top of the shallow, brackish water in which Bernard stood now. He'd walked down the beach from Sam to talk to the man in tall rubber boots wading between the giant rocks underneath the pier just at the shoreline. The rocks were huge, looming over the men, casting shadows on the beach. The man in tall rubber boots threw imaginary sticks for his dog running in frantic circles, occasionally biting his own tail and then barking as if he was surprised.

"Is the pier safe?" Bernard asked.

"There's a stash of life preservers up there," the man said pointing toward the dunes.

Bernard tugged at his beard and headed in the direction of the teenagers. "The guy down there says there are some life preservers up here I can borrow," he called as he headed in their direction.

"We like to call them pillows," the boy wearing the paisley handkerchief called back. "For kicking back around the bonfire." He relit a joint and took a long toke while the other teenagers laughed and laughed.

"There's only one," Bernard said, holding up the life preserver he salvaged from under a stack of empty beer cans. "Oh, well, Margue'll use it." He shrugged, then tugged his beard again as if mulling something over. "We bought the house up the way," he said to the teenagers. He pointed up the hill, away from the beach, toward the pine forest. "Up the rocky path. The train depot," he said, putting the life preserver around his neck. The train-depot-turned-house was a place all of the teenagers were familiar with; they'd spent nights there when their parents thought they were elsewhere.

"That's super," the shorter teenage boy said in an exaggeratedly nerdy voice.

"Look I don't care about the joint," Bernard said, holding up his hands as if the teenagers were arresting him. His wandering eye floated slightly, giving him the appearance of looking in two different directions.

The boy with the handkerchief pulled it from his head and snapped it at the shorter teenage boy because, even though they were stoned, it seemed rude to make fun of the guy.

"Ow, man," the boy said. "Look what you did." He pointed to the red mark on his leg.

"Pot smoking doesn't bother me," Bernard said, unaware that he had been made fun of. He had been a college professor for so long he had grown immune to the derision of young people.

The Hennarts were a family who enjoyed its own in-jokes and Bernard began to relate a family joke he'd started when they'd first moved into the train depot a month ago.

"You see," Bernard began, while the teenagers avoided looking at one another in an effort not to start laughing and never stop, "there's this original bench from the lobby, now in our foyer, where people waited for their trains. Whenever we sit on it, one of us says, 'Where's my fucking train?'" Even though the teenagers made it a point not to look one another in the eye, they began to laugh in a way that made it clear, even to Bernard, that they were laughing at him. Still, when in doubt, Bernard explained. "As if we were waiting for a train, you know, in our own house."

As the teenagers' barely muffled laughter grew increasingly hysterical, one of them beginning to cough, Bernard didn't tell them that his family stumbled onto the train depot while they were just tooling around on an afternoon drive during a not very well planned vacation that had ended up being a lot more driving than vacation. Until they stumbled upon the depot, things had been going very badly—the kids were whining and Sam complained that this is what he got for never planning for anything and here they were, without a plan and stuck in the car. But when they decided to get out of the car to wander—unplanned, Bernard pointed out—down a road, they saw the For Sale sign. Confusing perhaps the overwhelming relief of being freed from the car with the spirit of spontaneity, Bernard and Sam decided to leave the life to which they'd grown accustomed: the university town where they'd met, where they'd married, where they had Ryan and Marguerite, a town which, while not quite a big city, was a place where Bernard was recognized by students when he stopped for coffee on his way to the office in the department where he had a stable and rising career, a place where there were rambling dinners with other professors and the occasional artist, dinners that lasted late into the night at each other's houses. Their life there had become, in Bernard's mind, dangerously familiar and comfortable.

Bernard didn't tell the teenagers that, in an unspoken effort to keep love and family alive, and in the interest of fresh air and avoiding road rage, he and Sam made an impulsive decision to move to the country, to see what effect a new landscape might have on their lives. He didn't tell them he had decided to quit the good job for a position at a community college.

"You'll start writing again," he'd said to Sam.

"You can't expect this to change everything," Sam said, a warning. "You can't expect this to make you, or us, happy every single day." He didn't tell the teenagers it was as if she'd read his mind, and even though he agreed—"Of course not," he said as though she was being ridiculous—he *had* been thinking that maybe the move would make extraordinary happiness *possible*.

Years later, when Bernard found himself sleeping in a hotel

room dreaming of the former train depot's kitchen where he reached automatically for the silverware, when he woke up and realized that he wasn't in anything like his own home and might never be again, he would have an epiphany different from the one that told him a new landscape would mean a new life. He would realize that at various times in one's life, it was entirely possible to feel as though one had sprung full-blown from the ether, to consider the possibility of extraordinary happiness a ridiculous luxury. A shameful aspiration.

But today Sam looked beautiful with her smooth, elegant, revelatory forehead, standing ankle-deep in the water. She had taken off her shirt and was standing there in her jeans and what was, in fact, her bra. This gave her husband a rush of the kind of extraordinary happiness he'd hoped for as he held the life preserver above his head to show her.

"It's a *black* bra," Sam insisted when Ryan, and then Marguerite copying Ryan, protested.

"It's *embarrassing*," they whispered.

"It looks just like a bathing suit," she said. As she scooped water on to her shins exposed by her rolled-up jeans, and then her arms, the wind teased her hair, strand by strand, from its bun fashioned out of the stick.

"Wouldn't kick her out of bed," both of the teenage boys had muttered when she first stumbled onto the beach with the rest of her family. The boys would insist later that what she wore was definitely a bra. The girls would say *in their dreams* and that anyone who wasn't a *pervert* could see it was a bikini top.

Sam was a poet, though she denied the title having had a stretch of writer's block that had kept her from writing anything for the length of Marguerite's life, and not much for seven years before that. She had been young, eighteen, when Ryan was born. Then Marguerite was a bit of an accident seven years later. "Happy! Happy!" Sam and Bernard would always say quickly if it ever came up, which it did from time to time, disguised like most things as a joke.

After what was about to happen happened, after Marguerite was not, in fact, lost to them, Sam would realize that for a moment that wasn't even a second she had wished her daughter *had* been stolen from her. It was fleeting, only a flash—blink and it was gone—but the flash was enough. No, no, she would argue with Bernard, because theirs was a family that thrived on pretending to argue, unlike Sam's long-dead parents who, midwestern-style, would avoid an argument if it killed them both. No, no, Sam would say when Bernard made fun of her for reengaging with the long-gone faith of her long-gone parents—not the automatic pilot faith of her parents talking to George the preacher after church on Sundays, more like the stirrings of a belief in *something*. Sam would never, ever, tell Bernard about that flash, the not-even-a-second of wishing their daughter gone.

When Bernard rolled his eyes at what he called her convenient belief in God, when he argued that what happened that day was, for him, confirmation of the awe of the natural world, that "those rocks caught our daughter in their rocky arms," all she could say was, "Rocky arms? That's all you've got?" What she would mean but would never, ever be able to say, was what she'd feared all along: *I am not a mother.*

"You know," the handkerchief-snapping taller boy began, interrupting Bernard now wearing the tiny life preserver which barely fit around his neck as he launched into an explanation of a game the Hennarts played called "Who is the most?" Bernard might have recognized the beginning of the kind of lie one of his students told him if he hadn't been so busy describing how much fun it was to be a Hennart. "We just saw a family of dolphins," the boy continued, "and if you and your family hurry up the ladder, you should be able to catch them."

"Hurry, hurry," the shorter teenage boy said. As Bernard scurried off, the boy made an exaggerated show of wiping his brow with one hand and used his other hand to form a beak that opened and closed, opened and closed, like Bernard talking on and on.

The teenagers watched as Bernard took the orange life preserver, bleached yellow in places by the sun, from around his neck and gave it to Ryan to put around the thin neck of pale, freckled Marguerite. They watched as the Hennarts clattered one by one up the metal ladder to the top of the rickety pier that the township had been threatening to tear down for years. They watched them go in search of the blissful dolphin family the teenagers alleged was out there.

The Hennarts heaved themselves one by one onto the wood dark from ocean spray, and walked out to the very end. Below was the place where the waves began their invisible swell and the red weed the teenage girls wore like fantastic accessories ended. Bernard and Sam fell deep into conversation, gesturing wildly at each other in a way that the teenagers hoped meant a fight. Occasionally a phrase was carried by the wind to the teenagers up in the dunes. "Chopin's heart!" and "Did too!" and "Who is the most?"

"They don't look at all alike," the teenage girl with the weed anklet said, nodding at Ryan still holding his sister's hand. "Do you think her husband knows she was doing someone on the side?"

"But just look at the way he watches out for his sister," the teenage girl with the weed boa said.

"You want to *do him*," her boyfriend for the summer said, having retied the paisley handkerchief around his head. The girl kicked sand at him and he wrestled her to the ground, rolling her around so she screamed. The teenagers didn't notice as Sam paused in the throes of her conversation with Bernard, turned to Ryan and said something to him, her face suddenly stern.

The teenagers didn't see as he led his sister away from their parents, back toward the rickety ladder, or as he suddenly let go of her hand and used his freed hands to gather pebbles and throw them one at a time off the pier into the choppy water. The teenagers looked up only as the little girl wandered toward the edge of the pier. They watched her stumble and go right over, falling, and then disappearing just as quickly in between the giant rocks.

Just like that, it was no longer a regular blue sky getting-stoned-at-the-beach day and the hovering seagulls became frightening, monstrous creatures as the teenagers watched Ryan scream. It was almost a growl and it wasn't until later, when they learned the girl's name was Marguerite, that they were able, in their memory of the event, to hear what he was screaming. Margritte! Margritte! Margritte! When Marguerite disappeared from sight, the shorter teenage boy said, "She's a goner," and the one with the paisley handkerchief imagined that the monstrous seagulls would become the backdrop of the story they would all tell about the girl's death the day they were just hanging out at the beach as usual. The girl with the weed boa grabbed and snapped the weed so it fell from her throat. It seemed wrong to be wearing something so frivolous.

The teenagers wouldn't know for minutes that seemed like hours, until after they'd all concocted their version of the story to tell later, that Marguerite had fallen into the space between the two giant rocks, that the life preserver she wore snagged and held her there, snug. The man in the rubber boots stopped throwing imaginary sticks for his dog and climbed up one of the giant rock faces to help Bernard, who had scrambled down the rattling metal ladder and up the face of the other giant rock to pull his daughter out. Sam remained trembling on the pier while Ryan continued to growl "Margritte!" Then they all—the man in the rubber boots, the teenagers, Bernard, Sam, and Ryan—gathered around Marguerite's small body, paler still against the sand where Bernard had laid her out like a fish he'd just caught.

The man in the rubber boots, his dog barking excitedly at his heels, said, incredulous, "The life preserver preserved her life. The life preserver preserved her life." Over and over, like a tongue twister: "The life preserver preserved her life. The life preserver preserved her life." The teenage boy with the paisley handkerchief turned quickly to the man in the rubber boots. He meant to snap at him, though he was still stoned and his words came out slow and smooth. "Yeah, man, we get it," he said. "We got it. She's preserved. She's preserved."

Firefly Flash

It becomes one of those family stories, the kind the family is so good at telling, a story more real than the event itself. *See, look, this explains everything.*

That night, the family still trembles with adrenaline from dodging death, death who has stepped out of the shadows where it's been lurking all along, foolishly forgotten. In honor of the event, Sam institutes *mandatory family dinner*. She announces this in what Bernard calls her inimitable midwestern way (he calls it this because it annoys her but also because it makes her feel known)—*Let's fix an existential crisis, but quick, with something practical*, he drawls until she throws something substantial but not dangerous, a spoon, a breadbasket, tonight a flip-flop.

"No more drifting in and out. No more eating in front of the television. No more blah, blah, blah, fuzzy around the edges," Sam says from where she leans into a stuck window with her shoulder. The sleeves of the loose blouse she put back on after the accident flutters in the breeze coming in the window on the other side of the room, the one she has succeeded in opening. Through the window, stony Rhode Island fields and fields and more fields filled with mountain laurel, Hollow Joe-Pye Weed, jeweled forget-me-nots, eggs-and-butter, Queen Anne's lace, mullein, goldenrod. The gray bark on the trees, trunks entwined with the vines of wild grapes, turns rose with the setting sun, and in the distance the ocean is a quivering blue line. This new place is paradise. Before they went to the beach this afternoon, Sam took the children to pick blackberries from the bushes just outside the front door. The children stained their hands purple despite her best efforts to keep them from eating all of the berries so there would be enough for a pie. There's not, but she doesn't care. They can do whatever they want. The life preserver snagged on the rocks, held their daughter aloft. They are a lucky, lucky family. She is a lucky, lucky woman, and she will do whatever it takes to prove she never wanted to be anything else, that there never was a moment, a flash, a blink, a not-even-a-second when she didn't want Marguerite to be alive and well, when a tragedy might have suited her.

"Why does it have to sound like a punishment?" Bernard teases. He's in a great mood. *"Mandatory family dinner."* He leans over what used to be the train depot's ticket counter, now serving as the entrance to the kitchen, hands in the lobster-claw pot holders Marguerite loves. He twirls a fork around his ear: cuckoo, cuckoo.

"Where is your italicist?" Sam asks, grunting as she still tries to open the window. "You know that little man who jumps up and down behind you whenever you make a really important point?" This is a new family joke, one Sam is especially proud of because the first time she made it, Bernard spit the water he was drinking onto his plate. "By the way," Sam says, laughing despite herself at her own joke, "if I ever get this window open, I'm throwing myself out of it."

Bernard sticks his head out over the ticket counter again, this time with a spice bottle in each lobster-claw. "Wait until we've had dinner."

And suddenly the window flies open and there is the smell of the blooming flowers of late spring, and the warm, salty breeze off the ocean, and the underlying rich odor of cow manure. The original giant clock from the train depot hangs over Sam's head, in between the bay windows. Its second hand sweeps through time as if dismissing it: out of my way!

"We'll eat together like those families we've only heard about and we'll enjoy it!" Sam shouts. She collapses in an armchair stuffed with dolls bought at a thrift store, a doll foot poking out of a hole in the back. "Sort of like shabby chic," the store owner had said, "but different. Creepy chic." There is laughter underneath Sam's words and she fights to suppress the smile around the corners of her mouth, a full-lipped mouth even fuller after Bernard pulled her into the bathroom on their way to the kitchen just before dinner. He pressed her against the bathroom wall feverishly, as if their lives had started all over again and they were strangers beginning an affair.

Ryan shuffles in wearing a Flying Burrito Brothers tee shirt that Conrad at the record store in Providence recently bestowed upon him in exchange for helping him with his deliveries. "A summer job will be good for him," Bernard insisted when Sam began to protest that Providence was too far for a twelve-year-old to travel, though Conrad gives Ryan rides back and forth. "It will keep him out of trouble," Bernard said, as if he was the kind of parent who said that kind of thing. "Are you kidding me?" Sam said. "Who *are* you?" "I'm your brand-new husband," Bernard had said, and pulled her laughing onto the couch stuffed with dolls.

Ryan's worn what seems like the same pair of jeans for years, though he insists, on days Sam is pretending to be the kind of parent who asks, that he changes his pants every day. Long-limbed, lithe, he heads for the couch. Never one to stay vertical for long, he wraps his long-and-getting-longer arms around a pillow, one long-and-getting-longer leg draped over the side of the couch, the other sprawled out onto the floor. Marguerite trails behind him, especially close tonight, sitting on the floor at his feet, though Ryan can barely look at her. That she continues to follow him around as if nothing is different, as if what happened this afternoon wasn't all his fault, only makes it worse. He feels like an almost-murderer, though no one seems to know he let go of his sister's hand. Or worse, no one is mentioning it.

"Where is my fucking train?" he says, hoping to piss someone off. "The service around here sucks."

"Where is *my* fucking train?" Marguerite asks, hoping to make her brother laugh because he hasn't since what happened at the beach.

"Like I said," Ryan says, making fart sounds with one hand under an armpit. Marguerite trying to make him laugh is also making everything worse. "The service sucks."

"Hey, hey" is all Sam says, while Marguerite creates a breeze with her flapping arm in imitation of her brother.

That Ryan has managed to be in trouble most of his young life is an achievement in this family. He skips school to the point of suspension, he stows away in the back of Conrad's van as he did two weeks ago, huddled between broken-down amps and sleeping on the towels stuffed into the drum kit, and though no one noticed when he snuck out late, late that skinny-dipping night, he has been reprimanded for staying out late with the farmer's son and his friends, though, as Ryan is the first to point out, it was Bernard who suggested Ryan help the farmer's son bale hay in the first place so it's his fault if his son has gotten caught up in a sticky web of teenage corruption.

"How did this become my life?" Sam stage-whispers to the air. It's a call-and-response routine she and Bernard have worked up over the years. She pulls at the doll's foot poking out of the couch until the doll comes too, thick eyelashes over drawn-on blue eyes. "Eew," Sam says, dangling the doll by the toe.

"How did you become my wife?" Bernard calls back, carrying a big pot of stew with his lobster-clawed mitts. The stew is made from vegetables the farmer's wife dropped off. "Look! Fresh, fresh . . . ," Bernard stammered to Sam. "Fresh everything!"

The train depot creaks and shifts and crickets chirp outside in the summer evening, and then a train (maybe a train that once stopped here before it never came back?) whistles through the nearest town miles away. Since this afternoon, Marguerite can hear the grass growing in the fields with the lowing cows, even as the cows, whom she likes to go visit to see if they will let her touch their big bony heads, eat the grass with their strange multi-stomachs, even as the strange, multi-stomached cows give the grass a haircut as Ryan likes to say, at which point Bernard will quote Walt Whitman about the grass needing a haircut and Ryan will roll his eyes. She's escaped the fall from the pier without even a bruise. "Like her namesake, she defies all that is logical," Bernard said. Still, Ryan has put a few Band-Aid strips on the tiny scratches on her face because Marguerite insisted. She hopes that Ryan will play the blackbird song for her later, the one about you were only waiting for this moment to arise, the one that when he first learned on the guitar he practiced for days and days and days on end until Sam and Bernard begged him to stop. "I used to like Paul McCartney!" Sam cried with her hands over her ears. Now when he plays it, the song is a skeleton of itself. Marguerite thinks that asking Ryan to play the song will cheer him up, though she's not sure what has made him so sad. She tugs at the cuffs of his jeans and smiles at him, studying the miracle, given by L-O-V-E, that is the tip of his nose.

"Where's my fucking train?" Ryan whispers in her ear so that his miraculous nose touches her cheek. Then he puts a pillow on Marguerite's head and she holds it to her face and walks into a wall to make him laugh.

Who loves Marguerite the most? Ryan does. He loves her so much that even laughing teenagers wouldn't keep him from holding her hand. No one has argued with this (even in jest) since the day she was born and they brought her home from the hospital and Ryan made a bed out of napkins in a shoe box beside his own bed for her.

Ryan never told anyone about the night he heard his mother yell over Marguerite's crying, "If you don't like it here on earth so much, go back! Who invited you anyway? Not me!" "Pull yourself together!" Ryan heard Bernard shout and then, "You're tired. It's okay, let her cry. Kids are supposed to cry." Seven-year-old Ryan went to Marguerite and picked her up, perched her on his shoulder, her giant baby head resting against a towel he expertly slung there. Late at night, in an unspoken arrangement, Marguerite became Ryan's child. At first Sam showed him how to warm the bottles of milk in the fridge, and then, one night, Sam turned it over to him. She let Ryan carry Marguerite around the house while she slept, when Bernard thought she was taking care of things, and then, when he realized she wasn't, it was too late. By that time, Ryan was the only one who could console Marguerite. While he carried her, he sang songs he made up: *Be careful of the souls in the soles of your shoes,* he sang. *Walk lightly, walk lightly. Don't squash them.*

"Okay, okay, enough," Sam says now. She tosses the doll out the window, then stands up and takes the pillow away from Marguerite. She turns her in the direction of the dining room table where Bernard is doling out the stew. The dining room is actually one corner of the big open room that used to be the train depot lobby and now serves as the family's living room and dining room, with high vaulted ceilings and the tremendous bay windows with a view to the sea. Marguerite's love for her brother pricks Sam like a pin tonight and she puts one hand on each of Marguerite's shoulders and pretends to drive her like a car to the table. This morning, she reminds herself, she made Marguerite laugh by pretending she was looking for poetic inspiration in the linen closet. "Is it under the towels? Under the pillows?" As Marguerite laughed harder, Sam grew more frenzied. "Is it up your nose?" she said, checking each of Marguerite's nostrils.

"Ryan," Bernard says, and Ryan walks the slow way around the couch to the table, taking the time to study one of Sam's seashell collection on the coffee table, though he's never been interested in seashells in his life. This afternoon on the walk down to the beach, he *had* put his ear to Marguerite's tiny shell of an ear and swore he could hear the ocean. "The clouds are moving that fast just for you," he told her, pointing at the sky with her tiny hand in his. "They're showing off the only way they know how. Imagine how hard it would be to show off if you were transparent and wordless."

Marguerite, her palm sweaty with the tight hold she had on her brother's hand, considered this because this was exactly how she felt sometimes, as if she were a cloud, wordless and racing transparent through the sky. But she didn't know the words to say this, so instead she looked up at the sky where a Vof birds chop, chopped their way through the blue and smiled to show her brother her appreciation for the racing clouds trying their best.

"I think we should have a toast," Sam says, holding up a wineglass, and indicating with a nod of her head that Ryan and Marguerite should hold up their milk glasses. "To the miracle of Marguerite."

"And thanks to you, Marguerite," Bernard says, holding his wineglass up to Sam, "your mother found God."

"All I was saying," Sam says, pointing a fork at her husband, "is that there was something miraculous, spiritual, or whatever you want to call it, about the day—the fog on the path down to the beach, those seagulls flapping in place against the wind." And then a story comes to her on the spot, so quickly it doesn't even seem like a story. "And the fact that I remembered to ask for that life jacket for Marguerite and the life jacket saved her life."

Ryan begins to cough dramatically. "What did you use to ask for it—sign language?" he coughs under his breath.

"All I'm saying," Bernard says, putting his wineglass down but still standing, "is that you can't just all of a sudden have faith when something horrible happens. It doesn't work that way." That afternoon, Bernard felt the refracted light of winter give way to a more direct beam of spring sunshine through the mist. It shone pleasantly on his growing bald spot as he walked side by side with his wife down to the beach. Their heads were bent in conversation that he wasn't paying attention to because his focus was on the gentle, less and less accidental, collision of their shoulders that had him shivering like a teenager. All he could think was how glad he was that they'd taken this risk and bought this place on a whim, about how he couldn't wait until he and Sam were alone. The return now to her hokey religious roots annoys him.

"Well, maybe it works that way for me," Sam says.

Ryan, still coughing, puts his hands to his throat and falls out of his chair, while Marguerite looks on, delighted.

"Since when did an intelligent, educated woman like you believe in God?" Bernard holds up his spoon to Marguerite and mouths, *eat*.

"I'm not a baby!" Marguerite says, looking under the table to watch Ryan roll around, clutching his throat, as if he were in the throes of death.

"Is that supposed to be a compliment, Bernard? Because if there's one hiding in that sentence, I'm still looking for it," Sam says. She gets up and tucks a napkin into Marguerite's tee shirt.

This is happiness, Sam thought this afternoon on the way down to the beach. *This is happiness happening right now. Maybe Bernard was right: extraordinary happiness is possible here.* Even the kids' complaints sounded sweeter. "How long will this walk take?" Ryan had yelled to her and Bernard from a few paces back where he walked with Marguerite. Sam and Bernard were almost invisible the fog was so thick. Anonymous dogs barked somewhere down the stony path, and cows lowed on the other side of the stone walls that marked the boundaries of the fields. "We're almost there," she and Bernard had shouted back in unison. "How stupid do you think we are?" Ryan shouted, and Marguerite echoed him, "Yeah! How stupid?" They had all laughed and the day felt so easy.

"And I never said the *G-O-D* word," Sam says now. "I said spirituality, faith in *something*, though while you're on the subject, how could an intelligent, educated *G-O-D* believe in you?"

"And here we go again," Ryan says, back in his chair, holding his bowl up to his face and slurping. He preferred his parents arguing to going over the events of the afternoon, to the moment just after he began to throw pebbles into the froth around the pier's tall legs reaching into the ocean. Plunk, plunk, the pebbles sunk deep and he focused on them and the sun-glittered surface of the water rather than looking at his mother who had dared to turn around and tell him to be sure to hold on to his sister's hand. "Be sure to hold Marguerite's hand," she said, as if Ryan wasn't already. He preferred getting in trouble to thinking about the look of fake concern on his mother's face, to thinking about the way he tempted a splinter with his big toe he was so mad.

"I don't think God had anything to do with how hard those teenagers were laughing at you," Ryan says. "You told them our whole life story."

"That's not true," Bernard says, his voice breaking on 'not.' He takes a sip of wine to keep from protesting too much, but still, they hadn't been laughing only at him, had they? Ryan always manages to embarrass him just when Bernard is starting to have a good time. It's as if Bernard has been transported back in the evilest of time machines to high school, where he is the bookish kid with Coke-bottle glasses (which he, in fact, was) being bullied by the cool kid, in this case, his son. Still, Bernard tries to rise above, to give as good as he gets. "At least I wasn't torturing jellyfish with a stick."

"How would *you* like to be poked with a stick?" Ryan says, in a falsetto voice meant to be Sam's.

"I'd like it a lot!" Marguerite chimes in, imitating her brother's answer.

Bernard pokes Marguerite in the stomach with his butter knife and she squeals the way she had when the man in the rubber boots had stopped throwing imaginary sticks for his barking dog and showed them how to throw a rock to make the clams underneath the mud flats spray water.

"Well, what were we supposed to do? We weren't *allowed* to go swimming," Ryan says. "There was all that red weed. And the waves were too big, Sam said." That was the first and second thing his mother did to make him angry. And he was already embarrassed that his father had talked on and on to the teenagers, one of them the beautiful-breasted girl who had held Ryan's hand in hers, the girl whose pulse he'd become in the water the other night. Then Sam had looked at him as if she was the kind of mother who gave a shit and said, "Ryan, be sure to hold your sister's hand." As if he hadn't been Marguerite's whole life.

·"Come on, Ryan," Bernard says.

"Come where?"

"Just ignore him," Sam says. "Margue, would you like some more?"

But Marguerite doesn't hear her mother the way she didn't hear her parents' conversation on the path up ahead on their way down to the beach this afternoon, only the music of their voices, no words, the music that was the soundtrack for her brother's love for her shimmering through the fog. "There are seeds," Ryan said when he handed her the tiny red fruit he pulled off a bush. The seeds were crowded together where Ryan exposed them with his teeth. "Rose hips," he said, and wiggled his own hips.

"Well, it *was* Bernard who wanted to climb up onto the pier to look for the dolphin family those smoking teenagers up in the dunes claimed they saw," Sam says to distract her husband from her son. "And he *did* believe them."

"Now who needs an italicist?" Bernard asks.

"It's only funny when I say it," Sam says. "Now if you don't mind, why don't we focus on the good news of the day."

Marguerite smiles because she knows she is the good news her mother is talking about. She held Ryan's hand tight and looked up into the sky at the clouds still racing through the marble sky and at the V of birds chop, chopping. She tried to make a V like Ryan showed her and put it over the V of the chop, chopping birds. She had been worrying because she heard her parents talking the other night about something called the aging process. This meant people got older and that meant Ryan would get older and then he would eventually die, something Marguerite hadn't gotten a straight answer on yet, but it involved disappearing forever. And just as she thought this, Ryan let go of her hand to throw rocks into the water, and it was as if he was disappearing right then.

"Firefly flash," Bernard says. "That's what remembering is like. Someday each of us will be walking down the street and—firefly flash—we'll remember this day."

"Firefly flash," Ryan says, tilting his glass so the milk comes almost to the edge. "The life preserver preserved her, the life preserver preserved her, the life preserver preserved her . . ."

"We got it, Ryan." Bernard extends his hand to Marguerite for her to pass him her bowl.

"We were looking for those imaginary dolphins," Sam says, "and firefly flash, Bernard began that argument about Chopin's heart again."

The argument over Chopin's heart is a long-running one, one neither of them even cares about anymore. It's the pleasure from the tension it creates that fuels it. The window Sam worked so hard to open falls shut suddenly with a bang.

"Oh, Christ," Sam says.

"Oh, Christ," Marguerite says.

"Oh, Christ," Bernard says. "But it's not really an argument if I'm right. He was half French. George Sand left him there to die of tuberculosis."

Sam jumps up from the table to lean her shoulder into the window again. "The smell was so nice—those flowers, the ocean, the manure. I have to open it again! But first, you are absolutely wrong. After Chopin died, they put his heart in a glass jar and buried it in Poland. His sister carried it to Warsaw. You can insist that they buried it in Paris all you want, but it doesn't make it true. Look it up."

Ryan mimes cutting Marguerite's heart out. "Don't!" she squeals, though it's tradition by now, and her protesting sounds like, "More!" Ryan puts Marguerite's imaginary heart in his water glass and marches it around the table.

"And if I'm remembering correctly," he says, "one of you shouted, 'I'm not through with this conversation' and the other shouted, 'Who is the most argumentative?' and then the other one shouted, 'You're not ignoring me, I'm ignoring you,' Something really mature like that."

"And that's when it happened," Marguerite says suddenly, and they all look at her as the window Sam has been leaning into flies open again. Whoosh, until the rocks caught her life preserver in their giant rocky arms and she was lodged there deep in the crevice, the life preserver that preserved her life snagged on the rough edges, her arms sandwiched at her sides, suspended in the dark. Turning her head up to the sky, she saw the clouds, still transparent, still racing, still wordless, still showing off. Suspended there, for once, she, a born worrier (that was her role, her father says)—What if the fog off the ocean came and swallowed her family while she was at school and they were lost forever? What if a kitchen appliance exploded in the middle of the night when they were all sleeping? What if the farm cat that sometimes wandered up to their house wasn't warm enough? What about nuclear war?—wasn't worried. The silence lodged in her cells and eternity was in that lack of sound and everything was still and calm.

"Margrrrite! Margrrrite! Margrrrite!" That's what Marguerite remembers most of all. Three times, Ryan growled her name as if he was casting a spell, as if he was making her magic. His voice called her back to earth. The sound carved out the loss of her, something she wasn't meant to hear because it was the anguish of her already gone. In that awful, wonderful moment, she was alive and dead. Like the mystic she was named for, she became the sea below and the sky above. She was both once. *Divine*, that's what her father called it. From where she was lodged, she was *divine* and the birds chop, chopping through the sky above her and her brother's voice calling her name became all of the world and that world was all she needed, so she didn't cry out.

"Yes," Sam says. "That's when it happened." She watches as her daughter watches her son as if he is a wizard as he returns to preparing to spill his milk on purpose. Marguerite's first word was her brother's name. "Ry," Marguerite said when she was nine months old. Ryan was playing with Marguerite in his room in the old house, with the playing cards with the trains on the back that Ryan later said predicted their future in a train depot. Sam, taking a break from trying to write—she was forever trying to write but never writing—was wandering around the house and heard her say it. "Ry," Marguerite said again. When Sam heard Ryan coming to find her to tell her, she hid in the bathroom. She didn't want to hear it. Before she began her wandering, she'd closed her study door because she didn't want

Bernard to know that she wasn't working. She knew Ryan wouldn't go in if the door was closed. *Don't disturb us while we work* was the one rule she and Bernard had succeeded in implementing, so Sam knew Ryan wouldn't interrupt Bernard either. At dinner that night, Ryan tried to coax Marguerite to say his name again at dinner, but she wouldn't, and Sam continued to pretend she hadn't heard her say it at all. "She's still a little young, sweetie," Sam said and she hoped no one else heard the hardness in her voice when she said "sweetie." Still, Marguerite had spoken Ryan's name first. Sam just couldn't bear to admit it. Soon after, Marguerite was saying "bzz" for fly and "caw, caw" for bird and then one day, it was as if Marguerite realized that there were millions of words out there waiting to be learned and spoken, millions of words with which to name the world. She stopped talking altogether. "She'll talk soon," Sam reassured him when Ryan told her, alarmed. "You have to be patient." Secretly, she was grateful that Marguerite had fallen silent, that there was still an opportunity for her to say "mama" or "papa" before she returned to "Ry." And she had, with Sam's coaching. The way Marguerite loves her brother sometimes makes it hard for Sam to control how she says things, and, every once in a while, what she says.

"Right after I told Ryan not to let her get too close to the edge, Marguerite fell." She laughs as if it is a joke.

"Jesus, Sam," Bernard says. "Lay off."

Ryan gives his mother a look he's perfected: one eyebrow raised, his mouth ruler-straight. When they came home from the beach, and Marguerite was in bed resting with the Band-Aid strips she'd insisted Ryan put on her face, he said, "You look like one big Band-Aid." He tried to make her laugh though he trembled still. "I'm just cold," he said, though Marguerite hadn't asked why. "Sing the *don't squash the souls* song," Marguerite asked. *Watch out for the souls in the soles of your feet*, Ryan began, but his heart wasn't in it. He wasn't sure where his heart went since Sam turned around and told him to watch his sister and he felt like he would strangle everyone on the pier, including his sister whom he loved more than anyone.

"How about this instead?" he asked Marguerite. "A train came to the house today," he sang to the same vague soul-squashing tune, "while we were gone, and we all missed it. Another train came later and I got on and rode it for a while, but then I missed you and came back."

Ryan swings his long-limbs-growing-longer out of his chair and strides over to the stereo. "It's time to dance," he says to Marguerite on his way past her and she slides down off her chair, readjusts one of her Band-Aid strips, and leaves her parents at the dinner table to follow him.

That's all right.

There will be nights and nights and nights like this. *That's all right*. After mandatory family dinner, Marguerite's body will already be moving against the beat—*that's all right*—jerking just behind the drums, as Ryan puts on *Exile on Main Street*. It's his secret message to himself: his family is Main Street and he is in exile. *Don't want to walk*. Ryan will sing it so hard he sometimes spits by accident. He'll sing it so hard—*don't want to walk or talk*—he can feel the tendons in his neck strain—*about Jesus*—and his throat hurts and he feels like the guys with the long hair and the gruff voices who hang out at Conrad's store jamming on guitars they can't afford to buy, the ones he wants to be someday. *I want to*—yes, yes, yes— *see his face*.

Bernard and Sam will fall silent as they watch Marguerite's lurching limbs talk back to the music—a flailing arm, a shaking leg—as Ryan eggs her on. "Go, Margue!" She's loved to dance since she was a child, since she first said "Ry," and Ryan would hold her up by her hands and twist her back and forth to the beat. Dancing is the thing that allows her to give *L-O-V-E* back to her brother, Marguerite thinks whenever she is doing her after-dinner dance.

Tonight her spasming hips, twisting, snaking arms, shimmying shoulders, move faster and faster until the throw of her hips and the swirl of her torso is so fast she feels featureless, limbless, quick and indecipherable, the whoosh of falling lodged in her muscles like a message she was meant to carry into the future. *Relax your mind, yeah, yeah, relax your mind*.

Marguerite's limbs whir like a windmill in a storm. She shakes her head as if she wants to shake her brains right out of it.

"Hang on, sweetie," Sam says, beginning to get up from her chair. "You've got to be careful. You had a close call today."

Ryan takes Marguerite's arm and twirls her in a circle away from their approaching mother, then dips her, giving her an exaggerated smack of a kiss on the cheek.

"She's okay," Bernard says, getting up to stand behind his wife, pressing her back down into her chair. He puts his hand on her shoulders and stoops to kiss her neck. "The life preserver preserved her, remember?"

"We got it, man," Sam says, imitating the teenage boy with the sky blue paisley handkerchief around his hair. She laughs, relieved at the prospect of this afternoon's becoming another routine. She puts a hand on Bernard's face, tugs his beard. "She's preserved. She's preserved."

Good Mourning in the Queen's County, Part I

Germs, germs, and still, up and down the up and down hallway Marguerite presses her ears against doors, so close she can see the lumpy texture of the paint.

"Forget about the germs jumping off the doors into your ears, don't disturb the privacy of the other patients," the shorter mourning woman with her scary mask face of cheerfulness says, rolling back and forth in her chair on wheels. Marguerite's roommate Regina told her the shorter mourning woman is barely 3 percent, using her percentage system to assess the world. A system as precise as any, Regina says.

Hello how are you god mourning god mourning fine fine high high, the shorter mourning woman says as Marguerite shuffles by the front desk. She smiles hard to anyone who walks by.

"September all day long," says the taller mourning woman who Marguerite likes best. "And tomorrow too." Sometimes the taller mourning woman can even hear the question in Marguerite's mind. What month? Though the taller mourning woman's forehead is no revelation like Marguerite's mother's, though her forehead is not even a revel, her big-featured face is pliant with a smile and she never looks down to notice no shoes because she understands that Marguerite doesn't like to walk on souls.

"Lots of .traffic," the taller mourning woman says out loud, quick and gentle hands on Marguerite's shoulders as she slides by. She knock-knocks on the doors of those not already upping and downing, backing and forthing. "Get up, get up," and *get up get up* is a song moving through the dull hallway air. Who is the so-called taller mourning woman in real life? "That woman is one hundred percent real," Regina told Marguerite. "No so-called about her."

In the up and down hallway, there are posters of small tri-umphant animals performing human feats. A panda at the office! A snail—someone's drawn a mustache on what appears to be an upper lip, though really who's to say what a snail's upper lip is? He's on the phone, perhaps calling someone about his new mustache. Come see, a snail first! Marguerite ups and downs, backs and forths her way past him and his miraculous mustache.

In the heel of Marguerite's sock, a tiny hole has begun unravel-ing and unraveling like the story of her life which walking helps to ravel back up. And finally, there it is, what she's been waiting for all mourning or eternity, a firefly flash lights up the dark of her mind: Marguerite's parents on the pier down at the beach where the thin line of ocean on the horizon is revealed to be—presto chango!—an eternity of magnificent water. A V of birds chop chopping through the inscrutably blue sky. Her mined mind holds time tight like a fist so the past is present, like her brother's fist with her hand squeezed tight inside before he let it go.

"Chopin's heart was carried by his sister all the way to Warsaw Cathedral," her mother said.

"Was not," said her father.

"Was too," her mother said. "It was a love beyond love. Or have you forgotten what that's like?"

Was not was too was not was too while Ryan plunk plunk plunked pebbles into the eternity filled with red weed, but Mar-guerite stopped hearing the words because she was five and had re-cently been informed that sisters couldn't marry their brothers and really, Marguerite, you're a little old to be having those fantasies, aren't you? Just kidding, just kidding, they said when she began to cry, just like forgetting that love beyond love was just kidding, just kidding. What Marguerite heard instead was that her brother would someday carry her heart in a jar for miles and miles and miles to a land beyond love. She hears it now, years later, miles and miles and miles away, if she can only find it.

Regina appears in the hospital hallway, where the optimistic bright light of noon is muted by drawn shades and fewer windows. Regina is tall and thin like the half-naked tree outside the window at the end of the hall, but she prefers "resplendent" even though, she admits, it's not exactly a direct translation. She has bruises like secret maps to almost countries along her long legs. "See? It's almost Chile," she says, pointing to a long thin one gone yellow around its edges, or "Right there, almost China."

"Maps to my heart?" Marguerite asked her when she arrived yesterday or the day before. It's hard to tell when time loops-the-loop. Sometimes, Regina tells her, a night lasts all day and sometimes there are days from years ago that take over for weeks that last only minutes. "Maps to my own secrets, selfish girl," Regina had said, brushing her leg and the constellation of almost countries with long fingers.

"Thump thump," Regina says now, laughter in her voice, but the kind that means I'm with you, and she taps her chest twice with a closed fist. "I've decided. I'll help you find it after all," she says. "But first a cigarette," and she heads toward the room full of people with smoke rising from their brains like a fire of an idea that's just been put out.

"Anna Karenina!" the girl who drowns in her sweatshirt day in and day out shouts after Regina as the door to the smoking brains swings shut behind her. "No train's going to mow me down" all day long since the lending library van stopped by the hospital and lent her *Anna Karenina,* which she devoured, and then devoured, tearing the first ten pages into tiny balls which she swallowed. "That's one way to digest a book," the taller mourning woman said, laughing, while the shorter mourning woman, rolling, rolling, shook her scary mask face and said, "That's destruction, plain and simple."

"How many times do I have to tell you and it's my real name, thank you very much! And you're not welcome! No thank you either!" The flesh on Anna's skeleton face is drawn tight from no sleep.

The never-sleeping man with the wide-awake shouting face and the falling-down pants doesn't sleep either. "I'll smoke all of you!" he shouts, pulling up his beltless pants and lighting another cigarette in the no-smoking up and down hall because he likes to watch the mourning women run.

No sleeping for the flabby-armed pot-smasher either, lurking silent, his jiggling flesh a quiet ripple, waiting for someone to replace the last smashed potted plant, the same plant that the day before yesterday or the day before that he aimed right at the poster of the small kitten cooking dinner. He's partial to the snail so he never throws in that direction. "I drew that mustache," he whispers as Marguerite ups and downs her way past him. He stares at the space where the old pot used to be, waiting for the next one so he can smash it too. He never asks the questions the mourning women ask that Marguerite refuses to answer: Where are you from? Where is your family? Or the questions they don't ask but Marguerite hears: Who do you love the most? (Her brother.)

Instead, pure dirt explosion! "High!" the pot-smasher shouts as he mimes doing it, followed by the aftermath jiggle of his arm.

Outside the window at the end of the up and down hall, a plastic bag snagged on the half-naked tree expands like a lung, beautiful and filled with wind that sets the tentative, crackly brown leaves at the end of the bony branches trembling. They tremble with the wind. They tremble at Marguerite. Tremble, tremble, they say.

She leans her germ-filled ear against the smudged cold of the window as an ambulance sings by, like the one that brought her here from the so-called shelter where Seedsucker, a friend of her brother's, called Seedsucker because he sucks the salt off of seeds, dropped her off instead of taking her all the way to Ryan the way he said he would. Seedsucker stood in the stubbly-grassed field outside her bedroom window in his *The Song Remains the Same* tee shirt, just like the one Ryan had given her before he left home, the one she slept in every night since then, and it was a sign. She climbed out her window and took the hand Seedsucker offered her once he'd tossed the sucked-clean seeds he held into the grass, spitting one out of his mouth at the same time.

"I always liked you, Marguerite," he said. With her eyes, she said to him: there is life and death inside of me. She thought he understood. They got in his car to the quick glint of plastic bag between Seedsucker's tearing teeth, the dashboard a pile of sunflower seeds already sucked clean and soon, down the road, Marguerite too was a sunflower seed sucked clean in a bathroom stall miraculous with graffiti. On the inside of the stall, two handprints from hands dipped in ecstatic red, and, underneath, written in splotchy blue ink: Presto chango! God doesn't give a shit!

And then, presto chango! Seedsucker had to see some friends. He curled Marguerite's fingers tight around a fistful of dollars. "Your brother's too far away. He's all the way across the country, and all of your swish, swish, whispering blood shit is making me crazy," he said. He left her at a so-called shelter where there were other women who had been kicked out of love. "I'll call your mother and tell her to come get you," he promised, sucking, sucking on those seeds. Marguerite could tell he wouldn't, but that was fine with her—it was her brother she was looking to retrieve.

At the so-called shelter, before day had even turned to night, different mourning women told Marguerite she tried to hurt herself though she tried to explain (though maybe not out loud?) how she scraped her arm against the bed's metal frame by accident when she tried to rise from where a god she hadn't invited, not any god she recognized, not the god of her mother or her father, flattened her to the floor. Her hands didn't yet yearn to bleed then; she was not dead to all earthly objects, only to Seedsucker, and to her mother and to her father. Her mind was so fast and glittering it was getting harder and harder to decipher the signs. Seedsucker's tee shirt: The song *does* remain the same. Her brother's singing: *Blackbird, fly* (away from home), *into the light of the dark black night*. But the graffiti: God doesn't give a shit so presto chango, make your own god? And when Marguerite first arrived here in the charcoal air of late September, Regina's long mapped legs were a mystery too.

Is it still September?

"All day long, and soon it'll be October," the taller mourning woman says now, continuous like the so-called continuous baths Marguerite's mother gave her that lasted beyond time. Firefly flash: amine neurotransmitter and hypothalamic-pituitary-adrenal-axis system, her mother would say, her shirtsleeve rolled up to the weary elbow of her weary arm to test the bathwater. This will heal you. Her mother's words like a poem she was trying to write whenever Marguerite shut her eyes and saw, against the back of her eyelids, her brother and her father each in a different lonely room and then gone.

Outside, the ambulance croons through the traffic waiting at the light, sending crumpled, food-stained wrappers, another plastic bag up into the bony tree, breathing in and out, sending a hairnet up into the air that smells like burned leaves and exhaust.

"Good mourning here in the Queen's County," Dr. so-called Con says, and once again Marguerite is suspicious. Sixty-five percent real, Regina says. Always talking about persistently elevated, expansive, irritated moods, talking about persistence, persistence in elevation, moods so dogged and persistent they fly like potted plants against the wall in order to express themselves. Regina told Marguerite to tell him that she didn't fuck that god when it rose up in that place full of women kicked out of love, she only fooled around with him. "Where are your shoes?" Dr. so-called Con asks her. "You're not in Kansas anymore."

Marguerite curtsies because you never know who might help you find your heart here in the Queen's County.

Keep Death Daily Before Your Eyes

Everyone is gone. Most of all her daughter Marguerite with her fierce pointed nose like a command in the center of her face. On a patch of kitchen linoleum warmed by the sun, Samantha Hennart stands in bare feet gnarled with calluses from walking outside with no shoes. The gnarled feet, the warm linoleum, the blackberry bushes that have grown around the periphery of the former train depot—all once a sign of abundance—now only confuse her. She lays the flyswatter on the kitchen table—the same flyswatter she uses to kill flies and bat her gone husband's high-pitched frequency of disdain out of the air—in order to open the window and let in the familiar sharp mingled smell of ocean salt and cow manure.

"Let it be said," Sam says out loud. She doesn't bother to finish the sentence. She's forgotten how it ends or if it ever had an ending. There is nothing to be said; there is only the silence of her entire absent family. No more footsteps in rooms above her or on the stairs, footsteps that lately were always on their way to other rooms. No more rush of pee in the toilet, no more muffled coughs or stifled sneezes. No more of her son's plaintive guitar playing from under his closed door. No more rattling pans in the kitchen as her husband warms milk for himself and Marguerite as he prepares to read aloud to her, when he thought Sam wasn't listening, from that so-called sacred text of his about the ecstatic nineteenth-century Belgian girl who bled for God.

But Sam was always listening to the things Bernard was deaf to. "Do you hear the blood rush and swirl?" Marguerite asked yesterday morning before she disappeared. She said it matter-of-factly, as if she was asking what time it was or wondering about the weather. She pinned Sam's ear with her wrist. That wrist at the end of the slender branch of her arm, her elbow like a giant knob on that slender branch. "Do you hear the blood rush and swirl? Begging me?"

"What is it begging you?"

"Begging to be let out."

"Let it be said," Sam says again now. Still nothing occurs to her, so instead she looks out toward the water. This view could save a life. It is that beautiful. The stony fields, fences, and fields, and fences, and fields leased by local Rhode Island farmers, empty space made cozy by the lowing cows swinging their big dumb heads, and finally, just beyond, that quivering line of ocean on the horizon, the allure of all that mysterious water always within sight. The view is saving her life right now.

She said this to Bernard when they first bought the former train depot thirteen years ago and decided to make it their home. The man who had sold the place to them said that before it had been converted into a home the bedrooms for the children were once luggage rooms, the kitchen the ticket office. He'd told them the bench in the foyer was from the train depot's original waiting room, and when the man went outside to take a call on his cell phone, Bernard sat down and demanded, "Where's my fucking train?" Sam repeated it, and then twelve-year-old Ryan did too. Each time it was funnier and funnier until finally Bernard was rolling around on the floor, shouting: I'll give up my recently tenured appointment in that fucking navel-gazing English Department! We'll start over in the countryside that smells like a manure-filed ocean! It will be good for the kids! It will be good for Sam's poetry! Sestinas about manure and the ocean! He leaped to his feet, smothering Sam with dusty kisses, and when the owner returned, Bernard shouted, "Sold!"

"Where's my fucking train?" five-year-old Marguerite said out of the blue, shrugging her tiny shoulders in fake disgust, and the owner looked to Sam to explain her daughter's behavior. They were all laughing so hard the owner, frowning with concern, said, "I'll leave you all to look around then." They laughed their way up the creaking stairs, but the laughter that had hold of Sam's body like violent hiccups stopped abruptly when she looked out the window. "This view could save a life," she said.

"Yes." Bernard was no longer laughing either. One word, so sweet and unfettered. It was all Sam had ever wanted. Yes, the word felt as durable as love felt then; yes, as if it were leaving a visible mark on Sam's skin.

"Yes," Bernard had said, and placed his hand against what he then called Sam's revelatory forehead, as if she had a fever but not one he wanted to cure her of, one he wanted to catch. It was a forehead, she notices now in her shadowy-eyed reflection in the window, that could hardly be called revelatory anymore. No revel there at all. Her right eyelid flutters again—it's been doing this all morning, a tic from nerves? She rubs her eye with the back of her hand, pouring the rest of the coffee out in the sink, then digs a chopstick out of a drawer to put her hair up in a bun.

Samantha wore her hair up the first day of Topics in Medieval Literature: Vision and Heresy in the Hagiography of the Beguines, stuck through with two pencils because she thought it made her look older than her sixteen years, capable of either vision or heresy, or maybe both. Her mother begged her to take a year off before she "left her mother and her father all alone on the farm."

"You skipped a year of high school. What's your rush?" Belinda asked, standing there in a flour-dusted apron. Behind her, Ryan kicked back in his Lazy Boy recliner, eyes closed, drinking a beer. Both of them looked a thousand years old, and Samantha was out of there. She changed out of what Belinda called her "dress-up slacks" into a plaid miniskirt in the cramped bus depot bathroom.

She was in such a hurry she knocked her elbow against the rim of the sink so it rang with pain and it seemed to her that this was the feeling of going out into the world. She banged her elbow again to make sure and, yes, it was. She felt this same painful but pleasurable ringing through her entire body when Professor Bernard Hennart walked into the classroom the first day. He was the exact opposite of the big, strapping, Nordic farm boys her mother always encouraged her to pursue, boys who never looked at her twice because she was bookish and quiet, never making the most of her looks.

"Curlers are miracle workers, Samantha," her mother said to her over the phone, as if she could intuit the knot in Samantha's tangled hair. "And a few strokes of the brush never hurt."

Professor Hennart was shorter and much slighter than her father, with a scruffy beard and startled eyes set far apart, but then he began to speak about the Beguines, single women who for centuries made a life for themselves in communities of other single women in towns with names like Liège, Willambroux, and Oignies, the g effortlessly soft, gentle, and unpretentious in Professor Hennart's mouth hidden deep like a secret in his beard. He spoke of women who chose to lead lives of prayer and contemplation in communities that, unlike the convent, allowed them freedom to come and go. "To be involved with the world and the world beyond this world," Professor Hennart said. "To lay chaste hands on lepers and the dead." It was then Samantha understood the reason the other girls on her college hall giggled about his *intensity* when she told them she was taking this class.

"Independent women who embodied an ecstatic kind of holiness so powerful it wasn't meant to be imitated," Professor Hennart said. Though he stood awkwardly in front of the class, one of his hands gestured wildly as if he were playing that kid's game Samantha used to play with her father where she would stand behind him and operate his arms to make her mother laugh. Samantha saw the potential lurking underneath the franticness for more deliberate, calculated movement. "Rather," Professor Hennart continued, "they saw their bodies as vessels, opportunities for God to break through into the mortal world."

One of Professor Hennart's eyes wandered slightly as he leaned back against the desk, folding his arms across his thin chest as if to contain his flailing, gesturing hand. Samantha wasn't sure if he was looking at her or beyond her, but still her body rang and rang like her elbow in the bus depot bathroom. As he began to list the names of the women whose *vitae* they would be reading over the course of the class—Mary of Oignies, Odilia of Liège, Christina Mirabilis, Margaret of Ypres, Lutgard of Aywieres—Samantha yearned for Professor Hennart to see clearly the bold girl who sat before him, a girl who had left her family behind to venture out into the world and receive wisdom the way the Beguines received God.

"Mary of Oignies," Professor Hennart said, that *g* as gentle as his hand in hers would be, "tasted honey whenever she was at mass." He spoke of women who for months ate nothing but the tiny flowers off of lime trees, who craved only the Eucharist, whose fingers exuded healing oil. Samantha could hear Professor Hennart's admiration in the soft, tender sound of the consonants as he described these women whose breasts filled with milk in imitation of Mary on the night of the Nativity when Christ was born, whose hair bled when cut, and Samantha wanted her own breasts to swell with milk, for blood to run freely from her own cut hair.

Under the skittish gaze of Professor Hennart, filled with the mystery and intelligence of all of the books she'd yet to read, Samantha resolved to tell him her name was Sam. She'd never been called Sam, but she always wanted a nickname and her parents, who never, ever, told her there were men like this out in the world, had always insisted on Samantha.

Flutter, flutter goes Sam's left eyelid now as she stares out onto the lifesaving view.

Sam had been her parents' baby, and she would remain their baby. When she was eighteen, their Nebraska farm burned to the ground, the result of faulty wiring. There were other fires on other farms, but the local electric company refused to take responsibility. They knew that the struggling, middle-class families whose houses were destroyed would never fight back, especially when the farmers themselves were turned to ash. This was essentially what George, the Lutheran minister whom Sam had known since birth, said at the service about her parents, but in a kinder, gentler way.

And then there he was with his wandering eye and his learned beard: Bernard.

"It's like Marguerite Porette," Professor Hennart said when she went to his office to show him a poem from the book-length collection that won her the university's prestigious poetry prize. No undergraduate had ever won the prize, and certainly never a sixteen-year-old. "'Humble, then, your wisdom,'" Professor Hennart said, "'which is based on reason and place all your fidelity in those things which are given by love, illuminated through faith.'" He stared off into two versions of the distance. "It's from the only work of hers that exists. She was accused of being a *pseudo-mulier*. Killed in 1310, during the Paris Inquisition. Burned at the stake."

Sam couldn't help it. *Pseudo-mulier*, though she didn't even know what it meant, was the sexiest thing she'd ever heard a man say. *Burned at the stake* was the second sexiest. Sam nodded and smiled the smile she had perfected to indicate of course, of course in the face of one more thing she didn't know. After she left his office, she would rush out and discover that *pseudo-mulier* meant "fake woman" and that Marguerite meant "pearl" in Old French. She loved that. It was as though through her very name, Marguerite fought back. Sam would find Marguerite Porette's book, *The Mirror of Simple Souls*, and pore over its pages for a message from Professor Hennart to her. *You who would read this book if you indeed wish to grasp it*, it began. She wanted to grasp it all as she thought of Professor Hennart's eye upon her in the office, wandering especially far afield that day.

Flutter flutter, the sun coming through the kitchen window is sharper now, like little flecks of glass.

Everyone expected Sam to go on to great things after the poetry

prize. She hasn't. Every morning she attempts to leave her body and
float out into this lifesaving view—the fields and fields and fields so
beautiful it's as if they're creating themselves over again each morning just for her. She wills herself to float out the window into the
field speckled with those dumb, lowing cows, like the ones she grew
up with so long ago in that part of her life that seems like a dream.
She wills herself to float in order to dodge the boulder that rolls
down the hill on top of her whenever she sits down to write.

Earlier this morning she went to her study in an effort to distract
herself from counting the minutes that made up the hours she had
been instructed to wait by the police before calling back to file a
missing persons report for Marguerite, the only member of her family she currently wanted to find. She likes to imagine her study was
the room where the depot agents played poker. When they first
moved in, she found a few packs of cards and a calendar of pinup
girls underneath a stack of train schedules, though Bernard insisted
the guy who owned the place previously had bought them and put
them out for show. This morning, she tried to make something out
of "agonists" and "antagonists," neurological words she's come
across in her research in order to help Marguerite. Sam prefers not to
consider it an illness; she didn't like the idea of lumping her daughter
in with the millions of aspirers to mental illness. Agonists and antagonists had something to do with receptors in the brain, activating and
blocking receptor-mediated events, but who was she kidding? "No
one is here," from Robert Lowell's "Skunk Hour," filled her mind
until she had no words of her own. She herself was hell.

She took out her notebook and tried to flush the poison out by
rewriting the words that she came across in her frantic research on
her way to the discovery of Edward Strecker's continuous bath
(okay, so giving her daughter warm baths wasn't exactly modern
medicine, true, but it was friendly, kind, invented by the Quakers
for Christ's sake, and it had seemed, until yesterday, to have a calming
effect on her daughter). *Morbid, externalizing disorders, reuptake inhibitors, single-blind placebo, psychotropic, rapid dose escalation protocol.*
Words spawned by the guidance counselor's premature suggestion

that they might need to put Marguerite on medication. The counselor called to tell Sam that her daughter had been crying in the bathroom every day the entire first week of school, her daughter who had never had trouble at school. Yes, Sam said, she'd always had problems making friends because she was shy, but she had always gotten good grades. And that on this particular day, there had been an incident in Marguerite's physics classroom in which Marguerite appeared "distressed," was how the counselor put it. At first Sam enjoyed talking to the guidance counselor, inhabiting fully since Ryan was gone the role of mother to her daughter whom she still felt flickers of guilt over for imagining her (and that's how she described it to herself now, *imagining*, not *wishing*) her daughter gone for that split second on the pier. But then, the counselor started talking about medication. "Have you even met my daughter?" Sam had said, outraged by this woman who sounded like the plastic smile Sam imagined her to be wearing. "What is this rush to diagnose?" Sam felt outraged and the outrage felt good, *maternal*. "Why are you such a lemming?" Sam had asked. Perhaps she had been abrupt and nasty, but when Bernard told her she might have been rude when she recounted the conversation, she slammed a door in his face.

Open naturalistic examination, mood lability, neuroleptics, rates of refusal, noncompliance, rapid loading strategy, lithium carbonate, valproate acid, carbamazepine. These words backfired, bringing the poison back, and she ended up rewriting the sentence that had been echoing in her head for months now: *A woman who once spoke poetry and now speaks only in frogs.*

And there was that boulder, on top of her before she even began, there since yesterday when the police came armed with questions about Marguerite after Sam called them to report her missing yesterday. They came after Sam's frantic search up and down the road to the beach, after she interviewed the latest crew of lanky teenagers smoking in a huddle up in the beach grass of the dunes. The wind blew the beach grass into pretty arcs that nicked Sam's bare thighs with sharp tips. The teenagers knew nothing, but offered her a cigarette, which she gladly smoked though she had quit years before.

"Was your daughter unhappy?" the police officer asked. He stood in the kitchen with a small notepad not unlike the notebook Sam threw against the wall of her study this morning.

"She's eighteen," Sam said. "Eighteen," she repeated dumbly, and she found herself wanting to ask this police officer if he thought she was a good mother. What could he say anyway? He would never tell her the truth. It was one of those questions you could never get to the bottom of. And here she was, thinking of herself when her daughter was gone.

"Was she suicidal?" the police officer asked, his face so still it was as if it was paralyzed. Her gratitude for the interruption of her own thoughts almost diluted the awfulness of the question.

"No," she said and then wondered if she said it too quickly and if she had did that mean she didn't believe what she was saying? Sam attempted to still her own face. *Do you hear my blood begging to be let out?*

The photographs of Marguerite Sam could locate most quickly were a series of black-and-white pictures Ryan had taken: Marguerite, slim and wearing one of Ryan's tattered tee shirts, brown hair recently cut short by Sam herself. Sam thought it must have been exhaustion that made her wonder as she took the scissors to Marguerite's hair, as Marguerite had asked her to, whether her hair would bleed like Bernard's Beguines. She looks like a boy in the pictures, dancing wildly as was still tradition after dinner to *Exile on Main Street*. Sam had asked Ryan to play other things, but until he left Ryan had been boss of the CD player. In the picture, Marguerite's arms are flung outward and blurred like wings.

The look on the police officer's still, still face told Sam that these pictures only confirmed that her daughter was out of her mind. He touched Sam's shoulder. Why was the shoulder always the default area of comfort? People were forever touching her shoulder. Even one of those stoned teenagers at the beach had touched her shoulder.

"Check in with me after twenty-four hours," the police officer said, handing her his card, which now lies on the kitchen table next to the flyswatter.

With two more hours to go, Sam pours more coffee into the mug she just emptied and opens the window, sticks her face farther out into the day.

Maybe Marguerite has disappeared into the fields, where she often goes for walks with the cows whose big bony faces she's loved to touch since she was a child. Sam pours her coffee into the sink again, reties her robe, and rushes out into the stubble of the fields on the calluses of her oblivious bare feet. She puts one hand over her shut left eye to prevent the flutter, shielding both her eyes from the the sharp light of the sun. She leaps over piles of cow shit and then stands on a rock and looks around like the gophers that come up out of their holes and sniff the air. All she sees are fields and cows. She rushes up to the herd of cows who swing their big heads up from the stubbly grass and gallumph awkwardly away.

"Stupid fucking cows!" she yells.

Let it be said, Ryan's leaving was Bernard's fault. Let it be said, Bernard kicked him out. Bernard was always mysterious about the exact nature of the fight itself, but Bernard never had known what to do with a son who didn't love books, who, at the age of twenty-five, preferred rock and roll and hanging out and smoking dope and was never going to go to college no matter how much Bernard wished it to happen. Still, Bernard should have considered Marguerite, who was devastated when Ryan left. Bernard's departure, *that* Sam is willing to take some responsibility for. Let it be said, she fucked the carpenter who came to redo the bathroom. As she walks back up to the house, she has a feeling Thompson, the carpenter, might suggest, "Run into the light of God!," according to St. Benedict. "You've got to be willing to keep death daily before your eyes," he said just before he left for his weekend retreat. Thompson referred to himself as her boyfriend, though they've slept together only twice—three days ago when Bernard walked in on them, and once more since Bernard left. Each time Sam made sure Marguerite was sleeping after a bath.

She's not sure what running into the light of God entails, but it's strangely comforting to her because it reminds her of church in Grand Island, Nebraska, where her other long-gone family would drive every Sunday from the farm and speak to George the Lutheran minister after the services. George knew everyone by name so it seemed to Sam as a young girl that he probably was also on a first-name basis with God, which was a relief because Sam had a hard time feeling God even then. She's always wanted to feel God, but when she tries it's like she's constipated. Nothing will come out. Sam has decided to nod and smiles enthusiastically at Thompson whenever he tells her to run into the light of God because she wants to believe in his version of God, or any version really. *Yes, Bernard,* she thinks, remembering the way Bernard mocked her mercilessly for attributing the fact that Marguerite didn't die when she fell off the pier that day to something spiritual, *I want to believe in God.* She also smiles at Thompson with as much enthusiasm as she can muster whenever he suggests *running into the light of God* because she wants to prevent one more person from disappearing.

Back in the kitchen, Sam pours herself yet another cup of coffee. She uses the flyswatter to push a few dead flies off the windowsill. In an attempt to still her rapidly fluttering eyelid, she looks for an inanimate object on which to focus and settles on the rocks shouldering their way to the surface of the soil in the backyard. The backyard is actually just one more stubbly field with a fence that Sam and Bernard built around it. The rocks come from underground, pushing their dumb rock faces against the dirt until they split the earth. Recently, Sam's been harvesting the rocks, pulling up what's left underground from the dirt, but lately it depresses her, this constant battle with the mute rocks who don't even thank her.

"But why should they thank you?" Bernard teased her when she first began harvesting them, after the call from the guidance counselor.

"Well, more likely them than you, right?" she said because she knew it would start a fight. Flutter, flutter, flutter, faster now, and she closes her eyes against the sun's jagged light.

The wind whistling through the window has grown louder, sirenlike, though the curtains don't rustle. Sam lets the ocean salt and manure smell fill her former Midwestern girl lungs, her former poet lungs, and soon-to-be former wife lungs, and then shuts the window. She doesn't even think "former mother lungs" but, there, she's thought it. There's a sweet aluminum ping of pain in her ears, the wind's siren growing louder, the sort of sweet aluminum ping of pain that, if she still wrote poems, would make her want to write a poem.

"Run into the light of God, my ass!" she shouts out the window. The farmer's son, still baling hay, doesn't look up. Sam shuts the window.

It is noon and when the clock in the front hall chimes it's as if Sam is inside a bell. Flutter, flutter, flutter, and even though she closes her eyes against the tic, the flutter becomes a needle through the back of her eye. She steps away from the window and the fields and fields and the sweet ocean salt and manure smell disappear as her rebellious blood forces itself against the arterial wall, spilling into the area around her brain.

Though Sam won't live to learn this, she has known the berry-like sac, resting in the now dilating, bifurcated vessel, longer than she has known anyone. They are intimates; she and it are one and the same. It's been there since the day she was born, part of her body's plan all along, adhered to the weak muscle layer of the blood vessel wall. A similar blood-berry sac was lodged in the brain of a great uncle who died before she was born and in the brain of an aunt on her father's side of the family, someone he never spoke of because of a long-standing family grudge having to do with her father's mother's will, though no one could remember who exactly did what. Their blood courses through her veins the way her blood courses through her children's veins, wherever they are, whether they like it or not.

The Shutting Off of Sound Communication with the Outside World

I've found something that might help," Sam said to Bernard, riffling through papers on her desk. "Let me find it." The sweet, milky tone in her voice reminded him suddenly of the sweet, milky tone in her voice that day in his office all those years ago, when they had talked about Marguerite Porette, before Sam became so familiar that she turned into a stranger all over again, this time not one he would necessarily want to know better.

"Bernard?" The sweet milkiness turned to sour irritation.

First, Ryan left ("Let it be said," Sam said, "kicked out!") and Marguerite was devastated no matter which tack her parents took with her. He'll be back for a visit soon and he can't stay mad forever (Sam) or he's twenty-five and it was about time that he left home, working at an amusement park in a mini-basketball booth and living with his parents couldn't last forever (Bernard). Then school began and at the end of the first week, there was the call from the guidance counselor. Since then, Sam had decided to give Marguerite a week off of school. "A chance to rest and recover from her brother's sudden departure," she said pointedly to Bernard.

Bernard was currently distracted by the walls of his wife's study, which seemed to have grown a thick skin of paper. Pages torn from books and pinned to the wall with thumbtacks fluttered in the breeze coming through the open window. "What *is* all this stuff?"

"It's *research*," Sam said, folding herself into a chair. Sam could make herself remarkably compact for a woman of her height, her long legs folded underneath her. "I'm looking at a few books. Trying to help my daughter."

"*Our* daughter," Bernard said. "And I don't think she needs help. She's sensitive. She misses her brother. She's a teenager. There's no help for that." In fact, Bernard had been watching Marguerite at the dinner table since Ryan left. She was sad, yes, skittish maybe, but she seemed, well, knowledgeable. It was as though the light underneath her skin had been turned up, as bright as it had been when she was a kid, and Bernard wondered whether she might be able to help *him*, here, a quarter century into his marriage, as he wondered what came next. As he looked at what remained of her childhood freckles, a Jackson Pollack splatter across her nose, Marguerite moved her lips but no sound came out.

"What did you say?" he'd asked and he'd been as disturbed by his own desperation to know as Sam seemed to be by his asking.

"Lay off," Sam had said.

"I didn't say anything," Marguerite said, though still her mouth moved. Bernard found himself thinking of something he'd read about her namesake, Marguerite Porette, that reason had to be sacrificed in order to inhabit the plenitude of life. And then, of Louise Lateau, another young girl who seemed to know a thing or two about the plenitude of life.

Bernard had recently come across an article in an 1879 edition of *The Catholic Review* about this Louise, the Belgian mystic. A slight tangent from the book he was working on, having to do with one of his medieval visionaries, but not so far off course.

Like them, Louise fasted for extraordinary stretches of time, twelve years to be exact. The bleeding Belgian, as Sam called her, did, it appeared, bleed for God. In effect, her body became a battleground for the God in which she believed as the villagers in her small town of Bois d'Haine (the Forest of Hate!) caught wind of the miracle and began to gather at the windows of her family's cottage to watch. She became the physical manifestation of God, one they could see and touch. A professor from the Belgian Royal Academy of Medicine arrived to poke and prod her in an effort to get to the bottom of the mysterious bleeding. It was an era that gave credence to hysteria—Louise had even been the subject of a study by a disciple of Charcot, and been dismissed by Freud as ridiculous and delusional.

The essay centered on Louise's teenage years in her small village of Bois d'Haine. After years of caring for the sick of the village, after losing her father to smallpox, after surviving a cholera epidemic, the stigmatas appeared and Louise became a spectacle, a phenomenon. Not only with the villagers of Bois d'Haine but with scientists and clergy. This was all of interest to Bernard, but he found himself less interested in the evident struggle between psychology, the science of the time, and the effort of the German doctor who had written the essay to prove God lived in this girl. It wasn't even the stigmata themselves that most fascinated Bernard. It was the ecstasies that accompanied them. It was in these descriptions that he heard, and he knew he was being melodramatic, her voice, well, *calling* to him.

The first time Louise called to him, Marguerite was sleeping because Sam insisted she needed rest more than anything and the silence in the depot was heavy, filled with the potency of Marguerite's invisible dreams. Sam was puttering around in her study, looking for answers on the Internet to questions that hadn't been asked as far as Bernard was concerned, and when the Amazon package containing the Rohling essay arrived at the door, Bernard shut himself away in his study. It was stiflingly hot after a blast of late, muggy summer weather and the backs of Bernard's thighs stuck to the leather of the chair as he flipped through the essay and came upon the description of the first day of the ecstasies. One day, sitting in a chair (and here he was, sitting in a chair, Bernard found himself thinking, childishly, he knew, but it had been a while since he'd felt a connection to anything so he allowed himself this indulgence) . . . One day, sitting in her chair, Louise fell utterly still. Her eyes were motionless and her face stony. "Dead to all earthly objects," Rohling wrote, "she is absorbed in the contemplation of some spectacle, which she seems to behold above the region of the earth." It wasn't Rohling's voice Bernard heard as he read these words but Louise's, a teenage girl's, wise beyond her years, calling to him across the centuries. The train depot creaked and groaned, as it always did in the late afternoon, but Louise's voice was louder: *I am dead to all earthly objects, beholding a spectacle above the region of the earth*. A spectacle! Above the region of the earth! Dead, but completely alive!

What did she behold? It didn't matter. Her yearning reached Bernard in his study where the air was so close it was hard to breathe, reached him where he sat, his sweaty thighs stuck to the chair, and the fact of the spectacle was enough.

Again and again, with villagers and scientists and clergy looking on, Louise was washed in a sea of light as she bled from a crown around her forehead and her side and her hands and her feet. Again and again, she fell down on her knees with the force of it, the spectacle, the wonder of the spectacle. The act of faith was a kind of faith in and of itself. As the farmer's son rolled by on his tractor outside the train depot window, the grind of the tractor accompanying the chirring of summer insects, Bernard felt Louise's yearning for something bigger than herself, for a sign of something greater. He felt it so keenly it made his chest ache. For this ache, he fell down on his knees with gratitude. He was so overwhelmed with the feeling of *being overwhelmed* that the tear that fell onto the back of his hand startled him. Had he hoped for blood? He suddenly felt like the ridiculous man that he was, on his knees on the floor of his study, and he picked himself up off the floor, his knees cracking. He pulled himself together and went to dinner and there it was again, that same kind of yearning in the light behind Marguerite's eyes, the light beneath her skin, shining outward.

"Look, why *not* cry in the bathroom?" Bernard said suddenly to Sam now, startling her out of her effort to ignore him. "Why must everyone always be getting to the bottom of things? Why not let the mystery of life have its place? We should all be so lucky to be crying

in the bathroom for Christ's sake. *No one is here.* You are hell. Remember that?" Bernard knew there was a bit of arguing for arguing's sake in his outburst, but if it broke through the static roar of
family life, it was worth it. And really, if anyone tried to get to the
bottom of him, he'd go cry in a bathroom too.

"That's helpful," Sam said flatly, continuing to sort through
stacks of papers on her desk. "Be quiet and let me find this thing."

At least Marguerite felt *something*, thought Bernard. What happened to Sam's love of the Beguines whose hair cut when bled?
What happened to her own yearning for breasts swollen with milk
to nurse Jesus? Did Sam even remember the time she threw herself
into a thorn bush, in part to make him laugh, but then startled him
into loving her?

It had been over a year since she'd taken his class, and she caught
up with him on his way out of the English department. She was
only kidding around, pretending to throw herself like one of the
Beguines into a rosebush, but then she really fell and he took her
home because, he told himself, it was nearby. Had he even told himself it was the responsible thing to do? He cleaned her scratches
with hydrogen peroxide, stuck little bits of toilet paper to her face as
if she was a teenage boy who had just learned how to shave. He had
been good. He sent her home. Later that night, she came back to
him, the toilet paper still stuck to her face streaked with tears. She'd
gone home to a message that her parents had died. She never left
Bernard's again. Arrangements were made, she would stay at school
as she had nowhere else to go. She was just eighteen, an adult she
kept insisting. She continued to go to classes until they could no
longer hide the fact that she was pregnant.

Now, Bernard studied Sam's long neck bending over the article,
"The Continuous Bath in Mental Disease" by Edward Strecker,
M.D., as she ignored him and for an instant he forgot that they no
longer had play arguments, that they only had the real thing over
and over. Still, he longed to kiss that neck the way he had longed to
kiss it that day she went face-first into the rosebush, before their
lives together really began.

"The guidance counselor said something about getting her eval-
uated, but before we do that, I want to try something else," Sam
said. "She needs rest. She seems exhausted. I don't want them
pumping her full of medication—the guidance counselor was already off on a pharmaceutical tear. She was talking about the possibility of bipolar disorder and depression even after I told her her
brother recently left home. It was ridiculous and, before any of that,
there are better ways."

"A bath?" Bernard said with more disgust in his voice than he'd
intended. He was angry at her. For what exactly, he wasn't sure. For
not being a girl anymore?

Sam ignored him again and read aloud from the article by Dr.
Edward Strecker. "The value of the prolonged neutral bath for pro-
ducing quiet and sleep in certain nervous conditions, hysteria, mild
excitements and anxiety states has long been recognized."

"Did you get this off the Internet?" Now that he'd started, he
couldn't stop himself.

"At first, but then, believe it or not, professor, this college
dropout went to a real live library," Sam said.

"Did you say hysteria?" If Bernard couldn't blame time for its
too-quick passing, he would blame Sam. "That's helpful. This article is from 1917, yes?"

She swatted at her face as if Bernard's voice was a bug, and went
on. "Kraepelin noticed that confused, restless, and debilitated patients were greatly benefited by several hours spent in a warm bath."

"Marguerite is not debilitated," Bernard said. He inched toward
the door because he could feel his vague anger starting to take aim
and he might need to make a fast escape. "I think this has more to
do with the fact that you haven't written a poem in over twenty
years."

Sam didn't even look up, and Bernard thought she might not
have heard him. "The chief requisites for the treatment room are
ample space, sufficient light and air, and mechanical facilities for the
shutting off of sound communication with the outside world," she
read. She looked suddenly less like a swan and more like a praying

mantis, her long legs folded up underneath her in the chair stiff and buggy. She read as if Bernard didn't exist at all, which is what he tells himself drove him to say what he said next.

"Or maybe it has to do with some residual guilt over what happened when Marguerite was born?"

The paper Sam threw at him fluttered to the floor like a feather, but the book she hurled reached its mark.

The next day, the carpenter, Thompson, and a small crew arrived to redo the bathroom. They tore down the wall to the adjacent closet to make the bathroom bigger (ample space), stretched the existing window in either direction so it opened wide onto the fields and fields and fields that lead down to the thin line of ocean (sufficient light and air), and they soundproofed the walls (shutting off sound communication with the outside world). "Too bad they couldn't have soundproofed the soundproofing," Bernard said more than once, but Sam was usually a room or two away.

Thompson and his crew painted the walls periwinkle blue, bluer than the sky on bright days, bluer than the ocean, so blue it felt to Sam as though she was underwater the first time she walked in. By the giant window, they placed the slightly battered red divan Sam bought at the same thrift store where she found the doll-stuffed couch. She and Thompson—"the hippy carpenter" Bernard called him, though Sam secretly liked his thin, blond ponytail, and the way he often had to push strands of hair that had fallen out of the rubber band behind his ear off his forehead—tried different spots for the divan. They finally situated it so that it looked out onto the back pasture with the weeping willow, its drooping greenery sweeping the ground like a plea, and the occasional groundhog popping its head lazily out of a hole and then darting back underground.

"That's a lovely view," Thompson said, and Sam hoped Bernard heard him. As she looked at the side of Thompson's suntanned face, cows gathered at the fence as if to admire the handiwork, and Sam felt for the first time in a long, long time that she was accomplishing something.

"Yes, it is lovely," she said.

Along the far wall, far from the window for privacy's sake,
Thompson and his crew installed the giant, claw-footed bathtub,
something Sam discovered at an estate sale. "In other words, a
dead person's bathtub?" Bernard asked when he wandered in.
Thompson gave him a funny sideways glance and looked at Sam,
who only shrugged as if she didn't know who that guy posing as
her husband was.

Thompson told Sam she could begin using the bathroom almost
immediately once the plumbing was done. "As long as you don't
mind if I'm around, tinkering," he said and he gave her a slight variation of his funny sideways glance causing Sam to blush. "No, tinker away," she said, and then cringed as she hurried out of the room.
Only a woman ten years older than he is says tinker away, you idiot, she
thought, quickly exiting the bathroom. She went to the kitchen and
swatted herself with the flyswatter she usually reserved for swatting
at Bernard at dinner whenever he brought up the "dead person's
bathtub" or suggested "soundproofing the soundproofing."

Before Sam gave Marguerite her first continuous bath, she
placed a pile of the plushest towels she could find, towels whose col-
ors Sam imagined were especially soothing; sunset vermillion; coral
(to go with the underwater theme); royal purple. Near the tub went
the bookshelf filled with Marguerite's favorite childhood books
("The introduction of books, magazines, a few games and puzzles,
and possibly a picture or two on the walls, will perhaps help its monotonous appearance," wrote Dr. Edward Strecker): *Where the Wild
Things Are, In the Night Kitchen, Pierre: A Continuous Tale in Five
Chapters and a Prologue*, as much Beatrix Potter as Sam could get
her hands on, *The Phantom Tollbooth, Mother Goose, Charlotte's
Web, The Little Prince*. She was still mad enough at Bernard that she
left out Grimm's *Fairy Tales*, which included that scary story he
read over and over again to Marguerite when she was a little girl,
about the kid who wanted to know what fear was. It was one of the
few things she and Ryan could agree on. Ryan disapproved too,
though Bernard insisted it was only because Ryan didn't like to be
read to in the first place and that Ryan was only jealous of his sister.

Over the tub, against the periwinkle-blue wall, went the framed illustrations from the books: Max walking ashore to tame the Wild Things ("Be still!"); the Little Prince with his lone flower on Trafalgador; the naked boy, his *In the Night Kitchen* dough costume melting away as he sinks in the bottle of milk while the giant chefs with their giant faces look on (Oh, that Mickey. That racket in the night.)

When they are done, though she would never admit this to Bernard or to Ryan, Sam did feel more maternal, as if she'd created this beautiful place just for her daughter. She would never have admitted it because admitting it would have meant admitting that she hadn't felt it before, that there had been years after she quit school that she felt more resentment than anything else, that she had felt nothing but relief the first night seven-year-old Ryan walked crying Marguerite so Sam didn't have to. But now, Sam was able to offer her daughter *this*. So when Marguerite stood on the lip of the bathroom door that first time in her brother's Led Zeppelin tee shirt, the same one she'd worn almost every day since he left and which Sam suspected had never seen a washing machine, Sam said, "This is for you. It's all for you."

Marguerite hesitated, her quick green eyes becoming quicker still. She looked around at the blue walls as if they were starting to close in on her. Sam tried to keep her voice quiet, quiet like the periwinkle-blue walls, quiet as if she and Sara were actually underwater. Then Marguerite stepped inside, and Sam was surprised at how quickly Marguerite peeled off the filthy tee shirt. "The Song Remains the Same" and Sam thought no longer, no longer, she would show Bernard and Ryan what a good mother she could be and though she tried to hide it, there was a twinge of anger like sand in her shoes mixed in with her strong maternal desire.

Then there was her daughter, naked: Her breasts perfect little cups covered in gooseflesh, her small, dark nipples tight from the cold air. The skin on her eighteen-year-old angular hips was smooth like Sam's when she and Bernard first met. There was a birthmark on the back of her upper thigh that Sam had never noticed before. Why hadn't she noticed? Down the hall, she heard music coming from Marguerite's room where Marguerite had left the CD playing, a Graham Parson's song, Marguerite told her, one of Ryan's favorites about a heart that is strong enough, tough enough. So Sam hadn't noticed the birthmark before, still what a gift this was, to see her daughter's body, a body that was once inside her own, and to feel finally, after so many years, that she was this body's mother.

Sam watched Marguerite dip her long toes like Sam's own into the bath, the bath which Sam tested again and again with her hand to ensure it was the perfect continuous bath temperature, and as Marguerite slid into the water, Sam felt the soft water on her own body, the relief of it. When Marguerite leaned her head back against the rim of the tub, eyes closed, breathing peacefully, Sam lay down on the divan. While this might not be a solution to whatever was going on with Marguerite—And who was to say? What did that guidance counselor know really? She wasn't her *mother*— why not try this for a while? Let Marguerite skip a week of school; let her stay home and rest. "After five or six hours in the tubs the majority of such patients became quiet and drowsy, and often fell into a sound slumber shortly after being placed in bed," said Dr. Edward Strecker, and though five or six hours sounded a bit excessive (Sam would start off with an hour tops), Marguerite fell into a deep sleep. Sam turned her back on the lifesaving view to kneel beside the tub and watch her daughter breathe softly. She listened to her breath moving in and out and thought: *This could save her too*.

Into the Light of the Dark Black Night

Marguerite was eighteen and she was a neuron, filled with resting potential. "Resting potential," said Mr. Roberts, her Biology II teacher who had a reputation among the other teachers at the high school for being "eccentric."

It was the first week of school and Ryan was gone, disappeared in the middle of the night. The next morning, Marguerite's blood began to sing to her. Swish-swish, like Mr. Roberts swooshing by Marguerite on his way around the room on the roller skates he pulled from behind the podium he hadn't yet stood behind except to read a preview of "The Raven," which he promised he would read in full on Halloween. He used a voice that echoed down the hallways so that the physics teacher next door stood outside the door with his hands on his hips until Mr. Roberts lowered his voice, though once the physics teacher had gone back inside his own classroom, Mr. Roberts returned to his original volume. Now, he turned off the buzzing, fluorescent lights and pulled the shades, all while doing a quick pirouette.

"I've decided to talk about something that's been on my mind," Mr. Roberts said. "Or rather, *in* my mind. Resting potential." He poured ethyl alcohol along the lab tables, lighting the trail of liquid so it burst into triumphant blue flame like the flames that rose from the mouths of drunk peasants passed out on the side of the road in the seventeenth century, the ones Ryan told Marguerite about on nights when he got home from his mini-basketball booth at Playland, after she begged him to tell her again about spontaneous combustion because even though it scared her, she liked to be scared. "The fiery death," Ryan called it.

Before he left, Ryan had been reading a book of essays by doctors about particularly bizarre medical cases and though she didn't really believe them and could tell he didn't really believe them either (mostly, he liked to make Bernard angry—succeeding one night in getting Bernard to call the book pseudo-academic garbage because it made reference to incidents of spontaneous combustion in Gogol's *Dead Souls* and Dickens's *Bleak House*), these days the stories of the drunk peasants and their fiery deaths kept Marguerite from lying in her bed and worrying about being too far away from Ryan, who called occasionally from the road where he was traveling with his band, and though he only ever wanted to talk to her, he rarely wanted to talk for very long. Thinking about the fiery deaths kept Marguerite from feeling so far away from Ryan that he might not be able to call her back to earth.

"I'm putting today's lesson plan aside for a minute," Mr. Roberts said, leaning into a corner like a speed skater.

"In case we hadn't noticed," scoffed Kevin. He was an older boy who had been held back twice and called Marguerite a zombie freak to her face because Marguerite didn't talk much at school. When he realized Ryan was her brother, he started saying "zombie freak" only under his breath to the wall just above her head. "Zombie freak," he whispered now, but Marguerite was concentrating on her neuron-ness, her zip-zapping potential. Tommy, Kevin's sidekick whom everyone called Seedsucker, sucked the salt off one more sunflower seed and put it on top of the pile of slick sucked-clean seeds on the table where he and Kevin sat. Everyone said Tommy got held back because he couldn't stand to be without Kevin, though no one would say that to his face. Still, Marguerite always liked Tommy a little bit because the sunflower seed sucking seemed like a kind of nervousness she could understand.

Whoosh, whoosh, swoosh, swoosh. Mr. Robert's whooshing was like the swirling Marguerite sometimes heard inside herself, a sound that had grown louder. Swish-swish, a wish for Ryan to come back. But was it only a wish for Ryan? She wasn't sure, but it was so loud sometimes it made her cry because she wanted to know so badly what it was this wish wanted from her. As Mr. Robert's skated around the room, the triumphant blue flame lit the way. "On each side of a cell's membrane there are different numbers of positively and negatively charged ions. An imbalance. This imbalance creates a resting potential across the membrane of all cells, and there's power in that resting potential." He stopped short, his hands exploding into the air like voltage no longer at rest. "Power waiting to happen."

Even Kevin lifted his head as the triumphant blue flame grew, surrounding them on all sides, a fence of fire. He wiped the drool from the corner of his mouth, and stopped carving "this school SUCKS" into his desk with the sharp end of a protractor he stole from someone that afternoon. "Roberts is going to get so fired," he said. Tommy nodded appreciatively, sucked the salt off another sunflower seed and added it to the pile.

The flames danced along the lab stations and in the shadows Mr. Roberts ghosted by, waving a lit sparkler through the darkness so the sparks showered down on them like falling stars. Under those falling stars, Marguerite's vision was getting sharper. So sharp, it was as if her mind had gotten glasses. She could see inside Kevin's rage, his stomach drenched in neon orange; Tommy's desperation was a fluorescent yellow stain on his ribs, like the ads on TV where the dirty dentures got dropped into the fizzing liquid to be made clean again. The glistening whites of the eyes of all the other students in the dark of the dead frog-smelling science room were little firefly illuminations.

Flash, flash, and inside her, Marguerite's blood whispered, *You are a neuron with resting potential.* Power waiting to happen; power that refused to wait one minute longer. Last night at mandatory dinner, Bernard mentioned Marguerite's going to college and Marguerite nodded instead of telling them that she wanted to follow Ryan instead. She told them less and less. For instance, she didn't tell them about the whisper of her blood: *Swish-swish, the fall was a miracle akin to the tip of Ryan's miraculous nose bobbing only for her. The fall was the story of the miracle of life and death inside her at once, her rise from inside the dark turban of almost-dead into the snake-charming light of her brother's voice.*

Mr. Roberts was a trail of glittering light zooming around the room. "Power waiting to happen," he said.

"Jesus, what a fag," Kevin said.

"Total homo," Tommy said.

The word *POWER* wrote itself across Marguerite's mind, striking it like a match upon a hard surface, seeking out the trail of fire-making liquid. A triumphant blue flame rose up inside her, a bright heat that started low in her belly, licking at her soft insides and she was a neuron whose power was no longer waiting to happen but *happening*. The fire rose in her throat, climbing its way up into her mind, and there it was, her brain, illuminated, lit on fire, a harsh and burning light. She could smell the salt of the ocean though her school was nowhere near the ocean, and the grass growing up and around the mute rocks that pushed their faces against the earth in order to be reborn outside in the air. She saw through the dark to the clock on the wall. She felt time happening, springing free of the hands that moved through hours and minutes and seconds to move through her.

She'd never raised her hand in class, never wanted to call that kind of attention to herself. Her heart banged in her chest and she imagined it bursting out of her skin onto the floor and Ryan coming back to collect it in a jar like Chopin's sister did with his heart, carrying it all the way to Warsaw.

Where would Ryan carry her heart? Suddenly Marguerite was worried. Would he have to carry it all the way to Poland?

At the blackboard, Mr. Roberts made sketches of neurons with long squiggly axons and delicate tree-branch dendrites. He wrote *axons* and *dendrites* on the board next to the squiggles. "There are billions and billions inside your mind," Mr. Roberts said. "Imagine that."

Marguerite was beyond imagining. Looking at Mr. Roberts's drawing, she was no longer worried about where Ryan would take her heart. Her blood whispered that he would take it where it needed to go and if it needed to go to Warsaw, then he would carry it to Warsaw. Looking at Mr. Roberts's squiggle drawings, she felt the neurons, each with its own delicate configuration of thin branches and squiggles, firing and firing and firing inside her.

"There are scientists in Maryland—you know the kind, white lab coats, hair on end, frizzy with brilliance and discovery"—Mr. Roberts pulled his own limp hair above his head—"who've turned bladder cells into neurons."

Marguerite scraped her wooden chair back from the table for two she shared with no one. She stood on her tiptoes because the heat in her brain was rising, pulling her heavenward. She clasped her hands together and moved her lips, panting, not like a dog, like a girl with something inside her, like a girl with something to say. Kevin and Tommy looked at her in silence as if the heat and light and fire inside her were burning their way out, ready to burn them. The rest of the class, their eyes shining in the dark, was silent too.

"Marguerite?" Mr. Roberts said. Marguerite could see right inside to his kindness, red and clear like his gently beating heart. He put a hand on her shoulder.

"I think I'm dying," she whispered, though it might have been her blood's swish-swishing that made these words. It was the sound not of someone who was dying but of someone who had never felt so alive in her life. She looked Mr. Roberts in the eye to make sure he understood that what she meant was life and death inside her together and that this wasn't so bad. In fact, it wasn't bad at all. It was everything, everything at once.

Who Is the Most?

Where are those children with Sam's blood running through their veins as she falls to her knees in the kitchen in the bright light of noon, the gentle, oblivious ocean salt and manure smell breezing in through the open window, riffling her hair, becoming a discordant screech as the exclamation point disguised as a harmless comma stretches itself long and shouts?

"So you're not going to tell me where you're from?" the woman asks, sliding her leg off Ryan's lap.

"No, I'm not." Ryan is really late for work now, and work is the only thing he cares about these days. Since the band broke up upon arriving on the west coast, Ryan spends his days as a "long-term temp" wheeling X-rays of children's brains with hydrocephalus and spina bifida around a local hospital where he has befriended Hyuen, a morgue technician in the whole-body donation clinic. As Hyuen pumps bodies full of formaldehyde and prepares them for the med students he tells Ryan random facts about embalming. "Alexander the Great was embalmed in honey," Hyuen said yesterday, his gloved hand massaging a corpse's thigh.

"Don't be like that," the woman says. "Do you want more coffee?"

Ryan shakes his head no. Maybe the answer to this woman's earlier question is he *is* mute. Maybe it began when Marguerite called the day before yesterday. "The song remains the same," she said. He felt guilty for rolling his eyes at her crazy cryptic rock speak, then guilty for being the one who gave her the Led Zeppelin tee shirt in the first place, then even guiltier for being relieved that after twenty-five years he is all the way across the country, far away from the sister he claimed to love more than anyone.

"Suit yourself," the woman says, rolling her eyes and refilling her own coffee cup.

Sam took the phone from Marguerite and without even saying hello began to read to him as if trying to convince herself. *Kraepelin noticed that confused, restless and debilitated patients were greatly benefited by several hours spent in a warm bath. He gradually increased the treatment time to an entire day, and finally the unsatisfactory condition of his excited patients during the untreated or night period led him to attempt the experiment of a really continuous or* Dauer-bad. *Patients are now frequently kept in the baths for weeks, or even months, without any untoward results.* "It's from Edward Strecker's article on the benefits of the continuous bath."

"Are you kidding?" Ryan had asked, once he found his voice again.

"Well, since you don't seem to care," Sam started to say, but Ryan hung up. It was Marguerite who told him about the carpenter tearing down the walls in the bathroom and how she heard him mumbling about wearing clothes at night in order to get up in the morning and pray more quickly, something to do with St. Benedict. "It's in a book that Mom said was saved in the fire that killed the first Ryan and Belinda," Marguerite said before she asked again when he was coming home.

Ryan was glad he was long gone at that point. "You're okay, right, Marguerite?" he asked, and she had said yes, she just missed him, but he remembered her face when he told her about the book on spontaneous combustion he'd been reading—smoke rising from the thighs and stomach of a man as recently as the 1990s, the skull and a few fingertips left in a pile of soot. She looked frightened in a way that made him want to protect her. That's the way her voice sounded now, like her frightened face. He decided not to answer his phone anymore.

Ryan shares an apartment with an artist, a former prep-schooler named Sebastian who calls himself Bat, whom Ryan connected with via a flyer in a coffee shop. Bat's current interactive sculpture is a pumpkin left to rot with a concrete block at its core. The rotting is part of the art piece, creating negative space, man, Bat claims. Their living room, apparently, is also part of the art piece. It's filled with a dead meat smell, and fruit flies swarm around Ryan's head as soon as he walks through the door.

"They're attracted to dirt," Bat said yesterday. "Maybe you should bathe."

Ryan no longer responds to Bat. It's gotten so he no longer responds to anyone except Hyuen the morgue technician. Ryan treats Bat as if he is another concrete block beginning to peek out of the corner of a particularly fetid part of a pumpkin.

"Where? Are? You? From?" the woman asks, bouncing her foot on his thigh in time with the words. "Come on. Is it really such a mystery?"

"I come from nowhere."

"Why are you such an asshole?" The woman pulls her leg off Ryan's lap and the table wobbles and coffee sloshes out of their mugs.

Ryan thought his offhand answer suggested to this woman: let's drink our coffee and I'll trace the anchor on your calf and we'll call it a day. And suddenly the woman is more trouble than she's worth. The woman's name is Cathy, an artist friend of Bat's who aspires to one day create rotting pumpkins of her own and even last night Ryan knew that it was Bat whom Cathy wanted to sleep with and maybe this pissed him off when all he wanted to think about was the relief of not having to sleep in his apartment and the relief of getting laid. He takes another sip of the dregs of his sour milk coffee. Why was everything rotting and fetid? He stands suddenly, and the table wobbles and the coffee sloshes again.

"Oh, Jesus Christ," Cathy says, standing too, shaking her head in disgust, putting her hand on the table to steady it. And suddenly, like all the women he sleeps with and never calls again, she looks alarmingly like his sister, thin and boyish, protruding tendons at her neck. *Tried him in the morning. Tried him in the noontime. I tried him in the midnight hour.* The night he left threatens to fight its way into his consciousness; he has to get out of here.

"Trust me," Ryan says. He is irritating himself now. "I come from nowhere."

"Oh, that's *fascinating*," Cathy says. "So *intriguing* and *mysterious*. Oh, wait, I think I'm going to come *right now*."

"Glad I could oblige," and he's out the door. As much as Ryan dislikes this version of himself, it's effective.

"And by the way, it's rude not to kiss someone when you fuck them," Cathy calls after him. "Just so you know." But Ryan is already headed for the train that will take him to the hospital where he hopes Hyuen will tell him more about the slow, sweet honey moving through Alexander the Great's veins.

The rupture in Sam's brain is aggressive, violent: take this! It's as if it was punishing her, but the sac, beautiful and ripe and red, ready to be picked from the posterior circulation of her brain, bears her no ill will. If speech, if language, if thought were still possible, Sam would say to the pan on the stove, with its skinlike layer of milk along the bottom, to the whisk leaning against the side of the pan: here I am, beyond reason and self-control. She would ask the singed lobster-claw pot holder hanging from the nail by the stove and the pan in the sink with its crusted burned layer of last night's red pepper and artichoke frittata: Is this a state of exhilaration? Is this what rapturous delight is all about? She would shout at the recycling: I am on my way to profound calm! To the boxes and boxes and boxes of Bernard's books spilling out of the alcove by the refrigerator, boxes Sam has promised herself she will put in storage, she would say: this is it, the trance state accompanied by loss of sense perception and voluntary control, you fuckers.

Bernard taped the definition of ecstasy to his study door sometime during the first week Sam kept Marguerite home from school. "Why can't you have a normal midlife crisis?" Sam asked him. "Go out and find yourself a nice young blonde? Enough with the bleeding Belgian. Buy a sports car!" Bernard responded by taping the definition on his door. At mandatory dinner, he looked out over the dinner table, one eye on Sam, the other wandering toward Marguerite, and asked, "Who is the most ecstatic?"

From the start, Sam thought "Who Is the Most?" was a terrible game. Sam couldn't remember when they first played it (it seemed the question was always hovering in the air, even before it was spoken), but she remembered the first question: Who is the most secretive? Each of them had written furtively in confident all-caps on tiny scraps of torn paper napkin: ME. Shouldn't they have realized then that it was a bad idea? Shouldn't they have stopped there? But no, always, Who Is the Most? Who Is the Most? The night of "Who Is the Most Ecstatic?" no one offered up their answer. Since Ryan's departure, everything seemed like an effort. Sam didn't feel like playing, and she suspected Bernard and Marguerite of writing Louise Lateau because Bernard had started reading aloud to Marguerite from that article about the bleeding Belgian as if it were another fairy tale.

Earlier this morning, when Sam discovered once again that she couldn't flush the poison from her system long enough to write poetry, she found herself, transfixed by rage in front of the only scrap of paper—two pieces taped together actually—taped to Bernard's study wall, staring at the description of one of Louise Lateau's ecstasies, translated from the German:

During almost the entire duration of the ecstasy, Louise remains seated in her chair, inclined somewhat forward, and motionless as a statue. Her bleeding hands rest on her lap. Her eyes are motionless. Her countenance indicates rapt attention: dead to all earthly objects, she is absorbed in the contemplation of some spectacle, which she seems to behold above the region of the earth . . .

No spectacle could be more impressive than that which is now presented. The bleeding coronet on her forehead; the blood trickling down her face and falling on her dress; her hands, the blood from which is dropping on the floor where it lies in large patches; the circle of bystanders of every rank and condition grouped around, speechless from awe and wonder, and many of them weeping with emotion—all this combines to form a scene which irresistibly forces upon the beholder the conclusion that it is the work of God.

This was not the first copy of this fragment Bernard had made. One day during one of Marguerite's baths, as Sam folded Marguerite's jeans, she found a copy in one of the pockets, the paper rubbed thin with eager fingers as if the ink itself held sacred power.

Bernard, king of "Who Is the Most?" is still waiting for the waitress. He is in the middle of an argument in his head with Sam's voice.

I'm not saying what I did was right, Sam's voice says, *but you were practically having an affair with the bleeding Belgian. The truth (as long as we're on the subject of the divine, and truth is divine, isn't it?) is, she would spurn you if she met you. She'd look at you with her eyes glazed over with ecstasy and laugh at you.*

Don't bring Louise into this, Bernard thinks. Don't mock what you don't understand. Who knows, you might be soaking the possibility of ecstasy out of my daughter with those everlasting baths? And now that you're too busy getting it on in the everlasting bathroom, how would you even know? You don't even notice the light shining through Marguerite. You never did.

Our *daughter. And why don't you fuck off and run into the light of God?*

Don't talk to me in the privacy of my own mind about that hippy porn carpenter's bullshit, Bernard thinks as loudly as he can.

"Where are *you* from?" The waitress appears like a mirage in this diner that appeared like a mirage on the highway this morning. She towers over Bernard's table, a very, very tall mirage with curly red hair that explodes from her headband. She has a large Roman nose and eyes a little too close together. The question she asks is rote, saccharine sweet. She's not using her real voice, which Bernard imagines to be sweetened with cynicism. She puts a hand bejewelled with colorful oversized plastic rings on her hip and opens her close-together eyes wide as if to say: I'm vaguely interested in your answer, but I don't have all day.

She's beautiful, Bernard realizes, as she refills his coffee with one hand and passes a rag over the milk he's spilled. *Don't cry over that.* No wonder he has a headache. The waitress is beautiful in the way he is handsome, not at-first-glance-beautiful, but if you took the time to look closer, there it was, beauty a more subtle secret in his face, his eyes too far apart as the waitress's are close together. Beauty for those who took the time to look.

Oh, please.

"Hellooo?"

The waitress's hand is back on her hip and she continues to look at him expectantly with those eyes that make him feel slightly cross-eyed. Had he spoken out loud? Had he answered her? How much time has passed since she first asked him the question? It was getting harder and harder for him to tell.

"I'm not from here," he says. It occurs to him that he, a man who has slept with only one woman for the past twenty-six years, wants to sleep with this woman he doesn't know, this beautiful-at-a-second-glance stranger. He wants it with such urgency it feels like an emergency.

You and your emergencies, always your emergencies. Louise Lateau is an emergency. Ecstasy is an emergency. Who is the most? Who is the most? Sex as an emergency. Yawn.

"Well, it's obvious you're not from here," the waitress says grouchily, nodding her head out the window at the scraggly woods that divide the diner from the trucks roaring by on the highway. "I could have told you that. I'll come back when you make up your mind." Clearly, he didn't respond to the beautiful-at-a-second-glance waitress as kindly or invitingly as he thought. But, wait, how could Sam dare say there weren't emergencies? How about the emergency of her screwing the hippy porn carpenter while his daughter slept in the next room? How about that?

Our daughter!

With whom he sometimes dreams he's sailing away on Foucault's Ship of Fools, one of the ships from the Hieronymus Bosch painting that Foucault claimed really existed, madmen driven out of villages in the Middle Ages to sail the ocean.

If you start quoting Foucault, I'll barf right here in your mind.

"I'm sorry," Bernard says to the waitress's back, but she doesn't hear him or, more likely, she doesn't care. She keeps walking. The table smells like dirty, wet rag where she's mopped up the milk. It's a grim end-of-the-line kind of smell.

That's right, nurse those wounds. There's not a trace of guilt in Sam's voice for betraying Bernard with the hippy porn carpenter, for leaving the image of the hippy porn carpenter's head of greasy hair in her lap burned into Bernard's mind.

Look, if you want guilt, conjure guilt.

The legs of the dead flies swept from the windowsill stand straight up in the air as Sam's berry blood seeps between her dura, the tough membrane separating her brain from her skull. It seeps and clots and clots, the blood clot disrupting the circulation of her cerebral spinal fluid like a dam. The blood seems filled with intention but it is devoid of intention. Still, it creates a dam, an obstacle, as if it was doing something constructive, actually constructing, creating death. Her ventricles, her brain's open spaces, balloon, the fluid building. The blood presses against brain cells it's never met. So forward really. Her blood, which for forty-three years has sustained her with oxygen and nutrients without asking her whether she wanted to be sustained or not, leaks and seeps, pressing and pressing, fast and loose, a neurological one-night stand.

Out in the middle of one of the fields, the farmer's son lights a joint as he maneuvers the tractor around a rock, heading in the direction of the ocean.

At least the birds that have been flap, flapping in Bernard's chest are quiet now as he plays with his napkin, twisting it until it shreds. He tears off tiny pieces and makes a pile in front of his coffee cup as he waits for the waitress to return to his table that smells like the end of the world, or at least the part of the apocalypse where things begin to rot. An early lunch crowd begins to trickle into the diner and a man wearing a Red Man baseball cap carries a small barefoot boy wearing only shorts who whines, "I've got to go bad." They pass Bernard's booth on the way to the bathroom. Bernard chose a booth way in the back in an effort to hide, though the diner was empty when he arrived. "Why is that man tearing up his napkin?" the boy says to his father in a loud whisper. "That's bad table manners."

"Don't point, honey," the man says, grabbing the child's hand and tipping his baseball cap sympathetically at Bernard.

Red Man's sympathy makes Bernard feel more desperately alone than ever, and suddenly he wants to make amends with the beautiful waitress and ask for a hamburger in the most tender voice he can muster. He meant to answer her question tenderly, the way he meant what happened with his advisee as a tender gesture.

At the end of the spring semester, during the last week of the colloquium he co-taught, he and his colleague, a man squinty and hunched like a cane, had been doing a section on visionaries. Bernard had felt a tiny flapping in his chest that day, and though he told himself it was probably heartburn and he was making too much of it, he couldn't deny he felt strange, as if he might do *something*. He wasn't quite sure what. He and the cane were in the midst of discussing *The Oresteia* when Bernard found himself thumbing the creases of a paper airplane he had been working on during the first half of class. The cane shot him that pull-it-together look.

"At first, Cassandra denies fate," Bernard's advisee, another underappreciated beauty with buckteeth and a deliciously raucous laugh, said. She looked to Bernard for approval, not at the cane or any of the other students in the colloquium. Bernard, who had been intent on his paper airplane, was surprised.

He'd never been one of those lecherous professors who cultivate pretty young followers. When Sam began coming to his office hours all those years ago, he'd tried to turn her away. He *had*. But she had startled him with her poetry, filled with the erotic images of the Beguines. One in particular had made him blush as he read it, even though he was alone. The poem made use of Lutgard of Aywieres' vision in which she saw John the Evangelist take the form of an eagle and nurse from Christ's breast. The eagle then flew to Lutgard and fed her soul by placing his beak in between her parted lips. The image in Sam's poem was a metaphor for sex, and Bernard found himself thinking about the curve of Sam's armpit, exposed when she raised her hand while wearing a sleeveless dress in class the other day. But still, since then, he'd *always* been the guy who made fun of those kinds of professors, graying and pathetic, clinging to somebody else's vestiges of youth, clinging to somebody, to some body.

"Before I die, I'll tread on you," the bucktooth advisee beauty read, still looking Bernard's way. At that moment, the tiny flap, flapping, like tiny birds trapped underneath the bars of his rib cage, became more forceful, as if the birds were trying to beat their way out.

"Yes, and . . . ," his cane colleague trailed off, encouraging Bernard's advisee to continue, but Bernard didn't hear the rest because he launched the paper airplane. Did that crashing sound come from Bernard's mouth as the airplane hit the wall? There was a hum of fluorescent silence as everyone turned and watched the airplane sway back and forth, like a feather as it rode the puff, puff of the air conditioner to the floor. The hum was so loud that it frightened the birds in Bernard's chest and they flew haphazardly, then settled, the thump of their wings echoing relentlessly in Bernard's eardrums.

"Ah, a visual aid," the cane said, not even bothering to shoot Bernard the look. The students, including the beautiful buck-toothed advisee, stared at the paper airplane as if it might speak, as if it were, at any moment, about to explain Bernard's actions to them. He excused himself and stumbled into the men's bathroom as the birds flapped. He tried to convince himself he was having a heart attack—this seemed eminently more reasonable than tiny birds flying around in his chest—and he lay facedown on the cool tiles of the bathroom, pressed his cheek to the floor, and waited (hoped? wished?) for the relief of death.

He had no idea how much wicked time passed before he gave up on the false promise of sudden death in the bathroom and got to his feet to go hide in his office where he ate the fresh tomatoes from the garden outside his study at home. The tomatoes had been thriving from the cow manure he and Sam used as fertilizer. Juice dribbled down his chin, the way it had dribbled down his and Sam's chins when the very first tomatoes ripened thirteen years before. He ate the tomato quickly, furiously, as if eating it faster might take him back to that time. He watched the juice drip onto the student papers piled on his desk, wondering how he and Sam had arrived at this place, so far away from those first ripe tomatoes.

"And yet she knows, she's screwed: *Oh men, your destiny*," the beautiful bucktoothed advisee said as she walked into his office without knocking, as if she and Bernard were in the midst of a conversation. She stared at Bernard without blinking, unschooled in the ways of subtle flirtation. What had he done? Had he said something to her that he didn't remember saying?

"*When all is well a shadow can overturn it. When trouble comes a stroke of the wet sponge, and the picture's blotted out. And that, I think that breaks the heart.*"

What could he do? He wiped the juice from his chin with his shirtsleeve and offered her a tomato. There were no napkins in the desk drawers he never used, though he banged a few open and shut for good measure and found a packet of honey, a few straws, paper clips, last semester's grade books. The bucktoothed beauty ate the tomato eagerly, without blinking. How did she do that? Her eyes were wide open. *Why* did she do that? Bernard started to feel dizzy again, as if he might fall out of his chair, the flapping of the bird wings growing louder, so he leaned over and licked the juice dribbling down the advisee's face. She seemed flattered by this tender gesture, but the department secretary walked in, alarmed. "Oh, oh," she said, and then "Oh" again. She took her glasses off and put them back on again. She cleaned them on her blouse, as if that is what she meant to do the first time, before backing out of Bernard's office.

The chairman called it a "series of events." That, and frankly, no one was really sure what Bernard was working on these days. What happened to that book he'd been working on about Lutgard? His last book on asceticism and its representations in the Beguinages was so well received. Why didn't Bernard take a leave of absence in the fall? The birds flapped their agreement.

Now, the tiny birds (he imagines them as finches) are quiet as the pile of shredded napkin grows on the apocalyptic-smelling table. Bernard never told Sam about the chairman's recommendation for a leave of absence. First he finished up the semester, and then summer drifted in and wafted along, and then there was the fight with Ryan that Bernard has become expert in not thinking about. And then school was supposed to begin, and when Sam asked him his schedule, he made one up. On those days he was supposed to be at school, he went to a Providence coffee shop where they made the perfect espresso the minute he walked in the door. He'd always wanted to be a regular somewhere. The longer he hadn't told Sam about the "series of events" and the leave of absence, the easier it became not to tell. And when Marguerite started staying home from school, Sam was distracted anyhow.

When all is well a shadow can overturn it. Where is your italicist? What are *you doing?* And as quickly as her voice disappeared from his head, it's back. Bernard wonders if Sam's reading his mind, and then he wonders what it looks like in there. Could he ask her?

We were so happy, don't you remember? When we first moved into the train depot and it seemed like the beginning of everything? And the tomatoes were riper than any tomatoes we'd ever eaten? We'd never tasted anything like it. Where is that fucking train? Don't you remember when you wanted to disappear into my kiss but you also wanted to surface again like those crazy stones in the yard so that we could look at the world together, a pair of eyes? Sam's voice isn't a hammer anymore; it's quieter now, tap, tapping like the rain that's just started outside, tapping against the windows of the diner.

Swallow me up, oh please, swallow me up, Bernard begs the earth, or the closest thing to the earth, the cracked linoleum floor of the diner. The barefoot, shirtless little boy runs past Bernard's booth carrying a roll of toilet paper, unfurling it as he goes, his father close on his heels. "Johnny," the father says, tipping his Red Man cap at Bernard, "I told you about messing with the toilet paper."

The beautiful cross-eyed waitress seems to have disappeared into the kitchen, never to return and Bernard resigns himself to never ordering a meal. He doesn't deserve one. The apocalyptic wet rag smell has ruined his appetite anyway, or maybe it's his life that's ruined his appetite?

Bernard thinks about waking up in the dark hotel room tomorrow morning with the quilt scarred with tiny round cigarette-burned holes scratchy against his face. The shades will be drawn in an effort to outsmart time, which refuses to be outsmarted, and inevitably he'll remember he's fifty-nine and Sam is having an affair, and Ryan left home and it's his fault, and Marguerite's skin, far from glowing, is even prunier than the day before.

"Are you all right?" It seems Bernard has begun to fall out of his booth and there is the beautiful-at-a-second-glance waitress, righting him with strong hands as he begins to fall. Her close-together eyes are so close to his own that he goes a little cross-eyed. The birds are back, nose-diving for the floor. The waitress is humming a tune, never pausing in her humming as she settles him again in his seat. It's as if she is merely wiping that grimy rag over a table instead of lifting a man off the floor. Then she sings a snippet of what she's been humming. "What you're missing."

"Very funny," Bernard says, recognizing the song as one of the
few exceptions to the polling stones on nights Ryan put on music so
that he and Marguerite could dance after mandatory family dinners.
The waitress's strong hands linger under his armpits now that he's
been righted and the feel of them there is better even than the song
and, coming from those lips, the song is pretty good.

Nowhere man, Sam sings along. Da Da Da. *At your command?*

Lying on the kitchen floor, Sam no longer feels the sun-warmed
linoleum pressed against her face, or against her thighs where her
skirt rose up as she struggled against the sunlight broadcasting pain
across her skin. The warm manure and ocean salt breeze blows a
few more dead flies, tiny legs stiff with death, off the windowsill
and onto the floor next to Sam's vomit.

No time for anything else but this; no such thing as time anymore. It has ceased to exist, forty-three years shrunk to the twisted
shape of Sam's body on the floor. Waves of nausea crash through
her like the magnificent, mysterious, quavery suggestion of the
ocean. Weak and watery, her muscles no longer respond; her body
has lost its outline. Its hard physical container has sprung a leak. She
is as diffuse as the ocean itself. Her neck stiffens and the violence in
her head is the sound of Thompson and his crew tearing down
walls to make the continuous bathroom. A demolition headache, as
if Thompson was taking a wrecking ball to her brain.

There is another wave of nausea and Sam presses her cheek to
the floor until she can feel the bones in her face and then the bones
dissolve into flesh and the flesh dissolves too. There never was a pan
on the stove, a whisk, a singed lobster-claw pot holder, recycling,
never boxes and boxes and boxes and boxes of books. Did you hear
that Mickey? That racket in the night?

It isn't until her arms go numb that the distant ocean sings
through her in words that aren't words that she might be dying.
The blank afternoon sun burns her eyes that no longer see. Bring
on the wild rumpus! She's the most wild thing! The most wild of

all! The flutter, flutter in her left eyelid gone now that the eyelid droops. The siren manure and ocean salt breeze is years and years ago.

Her blood is agony circulating. There is a lurch toward stillness. Is that lurch what Marguerite feels when her blood is clambering to get out? "Life and death together inside me," Marguerite said once.

This part is electric. Is this what you feel, my girl, wherever you are?

Her girl, gone but still there, a firefly flashing, iridescent in Sam's mind already on fire. Sam's berry blood, without intention, but fierce with something akin to purpose, presses and presses, presses life and death together until they are indistinguishable.

Miracles of No Ordinary Kind:
An Event That Concerns the Whole Human Race

The day it arrived, Bernard placed the dusty rose manuscript at the center of the captain's desk in his study and by midnight its pages were marked by a flurry of yellow Post-its, each with a note written in red pen, the color of emergency: Diagnosis of ecstasy! The so-called science of the times versus the good doctor's Catholic agenda! Shrunken imagination—ha!

A nearby bookshelf sagged under the weight of books dusty with disuse, books detailing the lives of those "lusty low country women," the "almost nuns," as Sam used to call them when she was still in the mood to be playful. Vitae of women like Ida of Nivelles, Alice the Leper, and Lutgard of Aywieres.

"How did you discover Louise Lateau?" Sam would ask, playfully at first. Whenever Sam asked Bernard this question, unspeakable thoughts pressed themselves against his forehead as if it was a screen. *Who are you? How is it I know you less and less? If you do that thing where you wipe the hair off your fucking forehead one more time, I'm going to scream.* Sometimes Sam looked at his face with such intensity, he felt sure she was reading the thoughts right there.

"And how did you discover Louise Lateau?" Sam would ask again, when Bernard wouldn't answer.

It had, in fact, been Sam who led him to her. One day, she pressed a book into his hands, and when her pinky grazed his wrist, Bernard remembered the way his and Sam's shoulders tenderly collided as they made their way down the rocky path to the beach the day Marguerite fell from the pier. That tender collision reminded him of another one, his and Sam's shoulder bumping as they walked down the hallway together toward his classroom. Sam was younger than Marguerite then, wearing one of those sleeveless shirts that had allowed him a glimpse of the beautiful curve of her armpit. Bernard had felt the warmth of her skin against his. He remembered thinking how strange it was, how, in that moment, his attention was devoted entirely to her shoulder. There was nothing else in the world. How strange the way the memory took over, such absolute focus, and then how it disappeared and there they were, in the same bodies but years and years later, him with the book in his hand.

"Take it," Sam had said. "I think you'll find it interesting." Bernard had appreciated her effort to find common ground. There'd been very little in the weeks since Ryan left, but when he read the book Bernard couldn't help wondering if she was trying to tell him something. The book was about the first diagnosed fugueur, a Frenchman in the nineteenth century who wandered as far as Algiers and Constantinople in a semiconscious state. He would arrive somewhere else, far from home, having abandoned his family, and not understand how he got there. This man who wandered the earth in a daze reminded Bernard of himself, arriving in this moment of his life with very little idea how he'd gotten there.

Still, he read the book Sam gave him dutifully, and it was in this dutiful reading that he stumbled across the footnote about Louise. Bernard ordered what he thought was a book and instead the flimsily bound manuscript with the dusty rose cover arrived.

"She is intelligent, but almost totally devoid of imagination," Dr. Rohling, the author of the article, wrote. "She speaks only French, reads with some difficulty, and writes badly. Her disposition is gentle and calm; she is singularly modest, simple, and upright, and her candor is such that she has been described as transparent as crystal."

Simple?! Upright?! Bernard read and reread these lines until the words came apart.

There was something decidedly defiant, not simple or upright at all, about Louise. For example, Bernard would argue to an invisible audience in his head (an audience that often included Sam), one Thursday evening, in order to test the authenticity of the stigmata, the curate of Bois d'Haine and another doctor fitted her with thick leather gloves, wrapping the gloves around and around with a wrist-band and using melted sealing-wax to keep the contraption secure. When they returned Friday morning, the ritual day of her stigmata, the gloves were filled with blood and her hands marked by stigmata wounds, just as they had been every other Friday. To Bernard, it was as if her blood was saying: You doubt me? Take that!

"Ha!" he cried, delighted, when he reached this part of Rohling's essay. He found himself rooting for her. "See?"

"What?" Sam called from her study, and from then on Bernard railed in a whisper against the scrutiny of this girl by scientists and clergy and Dr. Rohling. He wanted to protect Louise from anyone else's prying eyes. He didn't want to talk about it with Sam the way he had his other projects. He wanted Louise to himself. He was not, he decided in another argument with Sam in his head, going to think about the fact that he had abandoned the suffering girls of one era for a suffering girl of another. He was a fugueur after all. Wasn't that what Sam had been trying to tell him with that book? He would arrive where he arrived unselfconsciously, blissfully, defiantly, willfully ignorant.

"To the facts . . ." wafted down the hall from the study late that first night the manuscript arrived, on the lower-pitched waves of Bernard's baritone voice. Though he tried to whisper, he found himself almost singing. When you sing, you pray twice, St. Augustine once said, and as he read, he felt lifted above the silence that yelled through the house that night with Marguerite back in her bedroom and Sam in her study.

"Infidels war against the Gospel," Bernard hummed, reading. "Because they are unwilling to make the sacrifice of the passions, which submission to its precepts involves. With such men we are scarcely concerned here. But God grant that they may weigh well the story of Bois d'Haine, and reflect that through this simple peasant girl on whom God has bestowed such wondrous favors, they, too, perhaps are called by him to take part in the really glorious war against vice and crime."

"Glorious war," Sam said, walking by Bernard's study on the way to the bathroom. "I'll give you glorious war. I got your glorious war right here." The silence that followed yelled even louder.

Over the course of the next week, the Post-its stuck on the pages of the flimsy manuscript became crumpled, the ink blurred from the oil from Bernard's frantic fingers. The ends of the Post-its curled, like feathers shed from a small, yellow bird, fluttering whenever the wind came through the window, as if the manuscript might take flight at any moment.

On the bulletin board above the desk, a pushpin now held two pieces of paper, their edges dark with Xerox shadow. To Bernard, it seemed as if darkness was closing in on this, the beginning of Louise's story:

Louise Lateau:

Her Stigmas and Ecstasy

An Essay Addressed to Jews and Christians

of Every Denomination

by Dr. Augustus Rohling

Translated from the German for the "Catholic Review," and furnished with notes, by the Rev. W. J. Walsh, professor of Theology in St. Patrick's College, Maynooth, Ireland.

To Catholics, Protestants, and Jews.

———————————————

To the facts which I am about to describe in the following pages, miracles as they plainly are of no ordinary kind, I invite the earnest attention of Catholics, of Protestants, and of Jews. For, surely, the occurrence of a series of miracles such as these, the reality of which is demonstrated by the strongest scientific evidence, is an event which concerns the whole human race.

One day, with the bathroom underway, and Marguerite in the bath, Sam came looking for Bernard in his study. She read from the scrap, "Human race?" She smoothed her hand over the piece of paper and Bernard inched forward in his chair, not wanting her to touch it. "The human race is something you seem to have forgotten about," she said. "And the fact that it happens to include your family. Or do you prefer the long dead who suffer only on the page?"

Bernard didn't bother to argue as Sam started to look wildly around the room. He could tell she was looking for the dusty rose manuscript itself and he had to perform several elaborate contortions to slip it underneath the desk so she wouldn't destroy it.

"'Human race' just *happened*—thank you, my italicist—to be the end of the opening of the essay," Bernard said. "Let it be said," he continued, in an effort to tease his wife. "Who led me to discover Louise Lateau in the first place?" By the stillness of her face, he had utterly failed in the endeavor.

Bernard tried again at mandatory family dinner that night, where Marguerite sat, speechless, not eating. Did she look a little puffy from the water? Was the light behind her eyes a little dimmer?

"So your mother tells me you're having a hard time at school," Bernard ventured, as Sam frowned at him.

"I want Ryan to come back," Marguerite said, tapping the tines of her fork against her plate.

"You need to eat, honey," Sam said. "Ryan called this afternoon, remember?"

"I'm sure Ryan will come back," Bernard said, helplessly, "He will. I bet he'll come back and get his old job back and everything will be like it was." He wasn't even sure what he meant, but Sam was smiling. It was as if she had taken over his mind, drawing these words out against his will. Bernard found himself wishing that Louise was here, that it was she who sat with him here at dinner. That he might introduce her to Marguerite. She would appreciate

her imagination while Bernard would praise her capacity for finding a way to tremble amidst the banality of life.

"He was the game operator at a mini-basketball game booth at
Playland," Marguerite scoffed. "Do you think he wants to go
back?"

Bernard had an idea. "Margue, I want to show you something,"
Bernard whispered when Sam stacked the dinner plates and took
them into the kitchen. When Marguerite allowed Bernard to take
her hand in his, it made more and more sense to him, this thing he
might offer to her. "I think it will remind you of the fairy tale you
loved so much. It's a story with *realness*."

Marguerite smiled. "Read! Read!" she said, laughing, and
Bernard was relieved to hear she remembered too.

The Story of the Young Boy Who Went Forth to Learn What Fear Was

"Storytellers would tell these stories originally as a form of entertainment when the light began to fade," Bernard would say to the top of Marguerite's tiny head tucked into the crook of his arm. Bernard would marvel at the tininess of that head. How could a head be so tiny? How was it that it was ever smaller than that? "Before TV," he would say, "in the dark ages. You know, when things were *dark*." He pulled the words out of the air, articulating the forever shifting night, carving out the rhythm of the dark with his voice.

It wasn't long before he didn't need the thick book of Grimm's fairy tales whose binding had cracked because over the years, four-, five-, six-, seven-, eight-year-old Marguerite was stubbornly determined to hear this particular story and only this story. Ryan never enjoyed Bernard's reading aloud to him, but for Marguerite, for a while, nothing else would do.

"This story has *realness*," she said, and Bernard knew she meant truth. There were moments, looking at the top of Marguerite's head, her soft child's hair pulled into a high ponytail with a rubber band, when he felt overwhelmed with a love for this tiny creature that felt dangerous, almost violent in its awesomeness.

Bernard had the story memorized and when he began to tell it, the shapes of the objects in Marguerite's room—the wooden horse on the bureau; her clothes hanging in her closet; the papier-mâché musical note that Ryan made for her birthday one year—grew starker, their outlines more evident. It seemed to Marguerite that the telling of this story would invite the night, not the other way around, and everything she thought she knew was suddenly not itself but something strange and unfamiliar and therefore more beautiful.

Some nights, Bernard would change a detail—the red-eyed cat that came to the haunted house to eat the boy would have blue eyes instead. "No!" Marguerite would shout, tugging at Bernard's shirt. "Red eyes! Red eyes!" Or he would forget the part when a villager says, "Now there's a boy who will give his father some trouble!" and Marguerite would turn her bird head and look up at Bernard. "Stop!" she would squeal, and then she would say the line for him. "Okay, now go."

At first Sam had objected to the story. "It's too scary," she said. Bernard thought she was being ridiculous. This was a story about longing, and, well, longing *was* scary. Bernard thought Sam was just jealous that Marguerite insisted Bernard read to her. Still, Bernard did make some changes that he didn't tell Marguerite about. He made the younger son rebellious and wily as opposed to "stupid" because Marguerite so fiercely identified with this wandering child and, really, Bernard thought, the story was wrong, the kid was anything but stupid. He was adventurous and eccentric but not dumb.

"Read! Read!" Marguerite would chant in the beginning and then, when Bernard had it memorized, "Tell! Tell!" And Bernard would begin: A farmer had a younger son who wasn't afraid of anything. But it wasn't a good thing—the son wanted to know what it was like to shudder the way his older brother did whenever he was in the dark or in a graveyard or any other grim or dismal place. "Grim," Marguerite would say with delight. "Dismal," and it always alarmed Bernard how frighteningly at home these words were in the mouth of his young daughter.

When the older brother got old enough, he became a farmer like his father, but the younger brother wasn't sure how he wanted to earn his living.

"He just didn't know?" Marguerite would always ask.

"He just didn't know," Bernard would always say.

When his father asked him how he expected to survive, the younger son said, "Before I decide how to make my way in the world, I would like to learn how to shudder."

"There's a fellow who will give his father some trouble!" Marguerite would shout at this point because Bernard would forget on purpose.

Luckily, the villager agreed to teach the youngest son how to shudder. In the middle of the night, he pretended to be a ghost, but the boy wasn't afraid. In fact, the boy challenged the so-called ghost and threw him down the stairs. In the morning, when the villager's wife asked the boy if he had learned how to be scared, the boy said no, but a ghost had bothered him and he'd thrown *him* down the stairs.

"EEK!" Marguerite would exclaim, pretending to be the wife exclaiming in horror because it made Bernard laugh. And then the wife rushed to find her husband with a broken leg at the bottom of the stairs. With despair, the father sent the boy out into the world because he was no longer welcome in the village, having broken the villager's leg and brought shame on his father's home.

"He's in trouble, right?" Marguerite would say giddily.

"And how," Bernard would answer. "Hold on. There's more."

The boy wanders out into the world and comes upon a king and his haunted castle. The king tells the boy that if he is able to stay in the haunted castle for three nights without leaving, then the king will allow him to marry his beautiful daughter, the princess. Other men have tried, but none of them succeeded because they were too scared. Well, this was exactly what the boy was looking for, a chance to learn what fear was.

"A chance to shudder!"

"Yes, that too."

So the boy agreed to stay in the haunted castle. The first night, two enormous black cats with fiery red eyes ("Red not blue!") tried to eat the boy, but he fought them off with a hot poker; the second night, the boy's bed moved across the room and instead of being afraid, the boy said, "Faster!" ("Faster! Faster! Read! Read! Tell! Tell!"); and the third night, a dead man who had been cut in two fell down the chimney in two pieces, which sewed themselves together once he landed on his feet and the half-man-turned-whole tried to strangle the boy, but the boy took a hatchet and cut the man in half again and the two parts of the man skulked out of the castle. At this point, Marguerite always scrunched her pointy little nose into what she considered a skulking expression, which involved holding up hands like claws and waving them around in Bernard's face.

"Okay, enough skulking," Bernard would say. When the king returned and found the boy unscathed, he offered him his daughter's hand in marriage. The boy accepted because the daughter was very beautiful, but still, the boy didn't know what it was to shudder. He didn't know what fear was. After several weeks of listening to her new husband complain about this, the princess decided to teach him a lesson. She went to a nearby river and filled a bucket with tiny, flickering fish. When she returned to the castle, she snuck into their dark bedroom and poured the fish down the back of her husband's nightshirt.

"A nightshirt is like a nightgown, right?" Marguerite loved to hear about the boy dressed in a nightgown.

"Yes," Bernard would say, showing Marguerite the illustration.

"Oh what makes me shudder so?" the young-boy-turned-husband shouted after his wife poured the fish down the back of his nightgown nightshirt, jumping from the bed (at this point, Marguerite would jump from the bed and run in circles as if her nightgown nightshirt was filled with tiny, flickering fish). The tiny, flickering fish swam out of the bottom of the young-boy-turned-husband's nightgown nightshirt as the imaginary fish, flickery, flickery, swam out the bottom of Marguerite's nightgown.

"Ah, wife," the young-boy-turned-husband said.

"Ah, wife," Marguerite would say in a pirate's voice because this, too, made Bernard laugh.

"Aye, matey," Bernard would say and then he'd switch his voice back from pirate to fairy-tale teller and continue with the young-boy-turned-husband's words. "You have taught me what it is to be afraid. And for that, I am forever grateful."

Marguerite thought Bernard's fairy-tale voice was a little scary and by the time he got to the end of the story, to the part where the young-boy-turned-husband was forever grateful she worried that his voice might be forever fairy-tale-ish, forever deep and ghostly. At the same time, she wished in a way that made her feel as though tiny, flickering fish were flickery, flickering up and down her spine, that his voice would get stuck and he would be forced to read this story over and over again. This boy who wanted nothing more in life than to shudder made her own fear seem important, something that would someday lead her to wisdom and gratitude.

"It's about how sometimes the smaller things are the scariest," Bernard said the first time he read it, not quite sure he was right, but feeling a professorial need to end with an explanation.

"But it's mysterious too," Marguerite said, and Bernard was proud that his daughter appreciated at such a young age the joy in a story's ability to continue to exist just out of reach.

Attend to Them with the Ear of Your Heart

Why don't you go lie down upstairs?" the beautiful-at-a-second-glance waitress says to Bernard, dropping a set of keys on the table. The feeling of her hands in his armpits, righting him moments ago, lingers. "I'll wake you up when I get off." *Nowhere man.* She turns, smiling with her close-together eyes as she walks away, still humming. *Please, listen.*

He's too tired to consider anything but the generosity of this gesture, too tired to thank her, and he hopes that the arrangement of the trembling muscles in his face translates into a smile of gratitude. Her keys are attached to a ring which is attached to a small red plastic frame with a picture of Marlon Brando, cut from a magazine, inside. Marlon stares at Bernard with a surly look that says: with these keys, you can postpone the search for yet another dark, smoky motel room; the scramble to get underneath another scratchy quilt as the roar of the highway reminds you that elsewhere people are going on with their lives; and the moment when you'll squeeze your eyes closed and wish for sleep to swallow you whole.

Here's the part where you disappear, again. Sam's voice seems to be coming out of Marlon Brando's mouth. "My chance to learn how to shudder?" Bernard asks Marlon's sneer. *Going, going, gone.*

• • •

In San Francisco, Hyuen makes a small incision in a dead man's neck. Ryan has stolen a few moments after dropping off the last X-ray (a tumor in the brain of a three-year-old child, inoperable) on the hospital mail route to sneak his usual visit to Hyuen in the morgue.

"Barber surgeons in nineteenth-century England called embalming ripping the corpse," Hyuen offers now. He is teaching Ryan the language of death and embalming.

Though no one was there to hear it, Ryan taught Marguerite to say his name when she was nine months old. It was her first word— "Ryan"—sitting there on the floor of Ryan's room, chewing on the soggy corner of one of Ryan's playing cards with different kinds of trains on the back. Later, when they moved into the former train depot, Ryan would hold up the cards and say, "Where's my fucking train?" for a laugh until all he needed to do was hold up the cards and Sam would frown at him and shake her head. "Enough," she would say. Ryan had been trying to get Marguerite to say his name for days, tickling her, making goofy faces, singing her the songs he would continue to sing to her to comfort her in the middle of the night. *Don't walk on the souls of your shoes.* He'd given up trying to get her to say his name, had returned to dealing himself a new hand of solitaire, and when she said it, he wasn't sure if he really heard it or not. Then, "Ry," she said it again, and he looked into her baby face to make sure she was looking his way, to make sure she knew what she was saying. He pointed to himself, mouthing his own name. "Ry," she said again, laughing until she toppled over.

He grabbed her up in his arms and hurried up the stairs to get his parents, but both study doors were closed, the one family rule *Don't disturb us while we work.* He waited for dinner. He thought he would get her to say it before he even told them, to show them, so he coaxed Marguerite for Sam and Bernard, but she just laughed. "She's still a little young, sweetie," Sam said, and Ryan, even at seven, heard the hint of anger in that "sweetie," something she never called him, and later he would hear the hint of relief, as if she was glad it wasn't true that Marguerite's first word was her brother's name and not *mama* or *papa*. But Marguerite had spoken, Ryan knew it. She spoke his name. Soon after, she said "bzz" for fly and "caw, caw" for bird in front of their parents. But she only said "Ry" in front of him so no one ever believed him, and when Marguerite learned to say "mama" and "papa" before she ever said "Ry" in front of Sam and Bernard, Ryan learned for the first time to be content for a thing in and of itself and not in the sharing of it.

Then one day Marguerite stopped talking altogether. "She'll talk again soon," Sam reassured him when Ryan told her, alarmed. "You have to be patient." Her parental tone, one she seemed to slip over her voice like a costume, made Ryan so angry he went into his room and punched a small dent in the wall. Bernard came down and tried to read him that young boy who wanted to learn what fear was bullshit, but only succeeded in making Ryan hide his head farther under the pillows. "Well," Bernard said, laughing so that Ryan burrowed deeper under the pillows, "there's a fellow who will give his father some trouble."

Ryan watches as Hyuen connects the tubes to the incision in the dead man's neck and the gallons of embalming fluid begin to find their way into his artery. The language Hyuen is teaching Ryan is somehow comforting, even "ripping the corpse." But Ryan's favorite so far is the honey running through Alexander the Great's veins. He imagines honey in his own veins, slow and thick and sweet.

"You don't look so good," Hyuen says, his voice cutting through the honey.

"Hangover," Ryan says, and it's mostly true.

Ryan dreads getting home later and shooing the fruit flies from his face, holding his nose to keep the dead-meat smell at bay. The pumpkin has nearly rotted through; the gray concrete laid almost bare.

When he calls for his messages from the pay phone in the hall, there are two hang-ups on his machine, and when the third message kicks in, he realizes he was hoping for his sister's voice saying his name. It's Cathy. "For the one who isn't busy watching pumpkins rot: Want to take a quick trip to L.A. and do a tour of the cemeteries—the Hollywood Forever Cemetery? Charlie Chaplin and Mel Blanc? The Calvary with Lou Costello and John Barrymore? There's a marble angel holding up her hand—you can't see what I'm doing, but it's like this: not so fast. Where you're from might be a mystery, but where you're going, well, you know what I mean."

She's about to say something else, but it's so painful, Ryan deletes it, along with the two hang-ups, reminding himself as he does that he's quit the pot so he shouldn't go in search of Bat's not-so-secret secret stash later. He comforts himself by planning to grab a stool at the bar on the corner, downing a few quick beers to kill his mind, before he heads back to the land of rotting pumpkins.

In Queens, thump, thump, the search for the heart continues. *Tried him in the morning!*

"You're some serious kind of strange," Regina, says, on her way past Marguerite in the up and down hall, more like a breeze than a person breezing by.

"Ear germs, that's what the ladies say," Regina says, still moving on her long bruised-from-kicking-herself legs, touching long spidery fingers to her own ears.

Tried him in the noontime. Marguerite presses her ear against another door. Thump, thump, each time she thinks she's found it, the sound disappears. *Tried him in the midnight hour!* Marguerite rests for a minute, her ear squashed against the door. There's a ticklish skittering as the germs make the leap, find their way into the warmth of her ear. *Think, sister, think*, they sing to her and firefly flash, she is dancing for Ryan, dancing on the bed to *Think, sister, think*, to show him how big her heart is, how worthy of being carried for miles and miles. Someone is at the door, watching her dance, watching Ryan watch her dance, but she doesn't know it until it is too late, until she has already walked toward Ryan not like a sister but like someone asking him to dance. *Humble, then, your wisdom*, she begins to say, and then the music is gone and the firefly flash too, faded like the sound of her heart thump-thumping its way away and away and away.

The Assignment of Impossible Tasks
While Saying Alleluia

Before he is formally introduced to grief, Thompson the carpenter meets confusion. Thompson has worked hard all of his thirty years to be a spiritual man, a passionate man, a patient man. Now he tries to harness a lifetime's worth of this effort. He tries his damnedest to listen with the ear of his heart, according to *The Rule of Saint Benedict* but nothing has prepared him for this and, though he concentrates until his chest aches, he has to admit, when it comes right down to it, he's not sure whether his heart has an ear.

Standing in Sam's kitchen where he found her—over there on the floor by the window where he will not look even now that her body is gone—he stares at the skin of boiled milk in the pan on the stove, poking a finger through the singed end of the lobster-claw pot holder. This afternoon, he sped back from the retreat in his battered truck into the bright red light of the setting sun. He sped back from the retreat that would give Sam the time she wanted with her daughter, the retreat he knew next to nothing about based on the description Sam read him from the flyer she found. It promised no electricity, no running water, modesty and humility. He sped in order to return to Sam as quickly as possible, to tell her how serious he was, to tell her yes, they had made love only twice, but they had a miraculous connection. They had St. Benedict.

"Sex!" Sam insisted, laughing. She has a great laugh. Had? He wasn't sure how this went. It was only the day before yesterday he had watched her undress fully for the first time, and it seemed too early for the past tense. She had a great laugh. It burst forth, trumping everything else. She laughed her great, bursting laugh and said, "It was sex. I mean, come on, the first time it was in the bathroom!"

Still, Thompson was serious as religion. Serious as God, goddamnit. His plan was to return to Sam and say, Listen, my lover. The singed end of the lobster-claw pot holder tears and white fluff spills out. He pulls at the white fluff, concentrating on the texture. Soft, airy, disappearing. *Listen, my lover*, Thompson thinks or does he say it out loud? *Listen, my lover, to the master's instruction, and attend to them with the ear of your heart*, he planned to say to Sam when he walked in the door. *Listen, my lover* was a variation on the first line of *The Rule of Saint Benedicts*'s prologue. St. Benedict, a man who renounced his world in the sixth century while the Roman empire disintegrated all around him, emperors being deposed in the midst of constant war. St. Benedict had retreated to a cave thirty miles east of Rome in search of structure, security, and stability. St. Benedict, the sixth-century miracle man had brought Thompson and Sam together.

Now, his finger pulling at the fluff coming out of the singed end of the lobster-claw pot holder, Thompson speaks these words— *Listen, my lover*—in order to fill his mind with anything else than what might come next. *Listen, my lover*. Thompson had been practicing when he found Sam on the kitchen floor. *Listen, my lover*, as he pulled her hair back and then pushed her heavy, stiffening body away from the vomit and the pile of dead flies. Why were there so many dead flies? Here is where confusion saved him, set him to counting the dead flies and wondering why there were so many instead of wondering why this body, which all weekend he had imagined underneath him, on top of him, beside him, above all, warm and soft and alive, when he should have been listening to the ear of his heart, was dead on the floor.

Listen, my lover, as he tried to remember CPR from a high school gym class while he waited for the ambulance, though he knew it was too late as he pushed his mouth against her lips that didn't push back. Was he supposed to hold her nose while he blew into her mouth? He gave up and washed her face with a damp cloth he found under the sink. After he toweled up the vomit, he lay her head back down against the linoleum, parts of it still warm from the afternoon sun. When the ambulance came, one of the guys who put Sam on the stretcher put his hand on Thompson's shoulder in a way that said, *She's dead*, at the same time as he spoke words out loud that suggested there was more, "Follow us."

Listen, my lover, while a doctor explained to Thompson in a gentled doctor voice the idea of a spontaneous subarachnoid hemorrhage, a massive brain injury with a 40 percent mortality rate suffered by three point six to six percent of the general population, and women were more at risk. Was she on the pill? A smoker? Any family members who'd experienced intracranial aneurysms? Thompson hadn't known if she was on the pill, or if she ever smoked. All he knew was that her parents were killed in a fire, so he made stuff up. "Yes, she was on the pill. Yes," he said, gathering steam, "she smoked, but she quit recently because I asked her to." He knew about the fire, but his ignorance about the smaller details hurt more. Are you her husband? "Yes, yes, her second husband," desperate to connect himself to her. And then, "Her parents were killed in a fire." He offered this because, though he loved her with the deaf ear of his heart, it was all he truly knew.

Thompson's finger pulls at the fluff (wispier and wispier strands, it was almost gone at this point) at the singed end of the lobster-claw pot holder. His finger feels detached from his hand, as if it is floating. When he gives up on the fluff and tries to scrub the skin of milk out of the pan on the stove, his hand, too, feels detached as if it has nothing to do with the rest of his body. He stands as still as he can for a moment, waiting for his body to piece itself back together before he sets about the arduous task of figuring out what to do next.

The hospital told him they could put him in touch with a funeral parlor, but Thompson said he would do it, that he needed to go home and find his daughter, "daughter" tripping off his tongue as naturally as "second husband" had. Thompson wasn't sure where Marguerite was, but he felt a certain responsibility since he was, in part, the cause of her father's running off. He waits for her now, though he's not at all sure what he'll say to her once she arrives. "We'll hold the body in the morgue until you decide what to do next," the people at the hospital told him. The body? When had Sam become "the body"? And where had the rest of her gone? Run into the light of God, he told her, but he hadn't meant it.

Thompson gives up on the pan and puts it back on top of the stove. He twists the thick rope bracelet around his wrist, given to him by a buddy of his he traveled around the country with, a buddy who died in a rock-climbing accident, and even though Thompson wasn't particularly close to him, the fact of his death has made the bracelet somehow important. It was white originally; now it's gray, dirty from years of never taking it off. He tried once when he tried to give it to Sam, but she wouldn't take it. "You'll regret it," she said, touching her hand to his wrist, to the bracelet, as if to keep it in place. He could tell she meant, "I'll regret it." *Listen, my lover*.

"We've known each other for *two and a half weeks*. There's no *love* involved," Sam said, but she was laughing as she spoke. "We've had sex *twice*. Don't you know that love is a selfish thing? Don't you know that this is more about you than me? You don't even know me." She was still laughing, that loud, explosive laugh, and even though she was laughing at him, Thompson could tell she appreciated his reckless affection.

Now, Thompson wills his arm no longer connected to his hand no longer connected to his finger no longer poking through the singed hole of the lobster-claw pot holder to shut the window that looks out onto the fields that lead down to the water. He slips a little on a lone spot of linoleum that hasn't yet dried. When he told Sam she was beautiful, she said, "No," and pointed to the view out the window. "*This* is beautiful. So beautiful it could save your life."

St. Benedict had saved Thompson's life. He had been really, really lost for a while there, drinking too much when he wasn't at work, lonely after his wife left him because, well, he drank too much, though to be honest, he wasn't sure which had come first, the loneliness or the leaving. He felt loneliness like a disease, like something inside him, lodged inside his liver and his spleen. He sometimes pictured it as the rough edges of two broken cement slabs grinding together, making a rough noise that hurt his teeth when he thought about it so he tried not to think about it, which meant drinking. Then one day he was walking along the streets of Providence, heading for a bar, and on his way he stopped at a sale bin outside a bookstore. There was a dog-eared, second-hand copy of *The Rule of Saint Benedict*. The buddy who died had mentioned St. Benedict once, so Thompson picked it up.

He and Sam had talked about St. Benedict the first day he began his work on the bathroom. Her forehead was marked with lines that looked less the product of age than of worry. She couldn't be more than forty, though she never told him how old she was. The lines looked real, earned. Thompson was a sucker for someone who had been through something. Confusion is useful here too, focusing on how old Sam is (was?). He had wanted to understand her worries, to read those lines on her forehead like braille. *Speak to me with the ear of your heart.*

Thompson pulls his thin blond hair away from his face into a loose ponytail, remembering the way she saw the thin book, *The Rule*, sticking out of his back pocket, the way she slid it out. "This book!" she said, and he almost touched that forehead but stopped himself.

He goes into the bathroom in order to remember that moment better. It's beautiful work he's done here, he thinks, as he looks around the light, airy room, and it was a rush job too. "Can you do it in a week?" Sam asked, and even though there was no way, after the St. Benedict connection, after seeing the lovely lines on her forehead, he said he would and he did.

"This book," Sam said, "was one of the only things that survived when my parents' house burned down. It survived their death, and somehow that made it meaningful. Silly, right?" Sam's eyes, a dulled and tired green when Thompson arrived earlier that day, grew vibrant and loud. "I wonder if Edward Strecker read him," she said, and though Thompson had no idea who Edward Strecker was, it didn't matter, he was willing to listen. "There's a feeling of searching for structure there," she said, and he saw the opportunity for rescuing her with the rescued words of St. Benedict. He hoped that his solemn silence suggested he'd been familiar with St. Benedict for years. As she went on about Edward Strecker and a bathroom that was more like a living space, *light and airy*, he imagined pulling the chopsticks slowly out of her hair one by one. *Run into the light of God*, he reminded himself. She is (was) a married woman.

Thompson sits on the rim of the tub, remembering how *run into the light of God* became *run into the light of God with me*. Every day, Sam came into the bathroom to talk about St. Benedict. "I'm so glad you reminded me of the book," she said, bringing him and the guys who worked for him iced tea. "I'd forgotten about it really, though it's always been there on my bedside table." She blushed when she said "bedside table." *Run into the light of me*. Thompson runs his hand along the smooth edges of the claw-foot tub's rim.

The next day they talked about Benedict's rules of obedience, humility, and contemplation. "Contemplation's my favorite," Sam said. "What he says about contemplative reading. Reading as meditation, not reading for information or entertainment. With 'attention to beauty and form.' I'm trying to write a poem about it."

"You write poetry," Thompson said. "That's cool." He blushed because he'd wanted to find another word for the surprise he felt each time Sam spoke.

"Yeah," she said. "It was cool." He could tell she was making fun of him a little, but she stayed longer that day and longer still the next and the next, and each day she revealed a little bit more. She told him how it had been hard for her to write, for years now, and about her concern for her daughter—it was for her that the bathroom was being built. She was having some kind of trouble, Sam didn't explain, at school. "My husband thinks I'm overreacting," Sam said. "And I have a son. Really, he was too old to be living at home, twenty-five, and working at a dead-end job, but it was the *way* he left. Something to do with my husband," and again Sam trailed off and Thompson didn't want to push her.

At first, he recognized the phenomenon of people telling him their stories because he was a stranger passing through their lives, someone who would be gone eventually, to whom they wouldn't be accountable. Still, he was so grateful for Sam's conversation, for whatever he wanted to tell her—the cement slabs of loneliness were still there inside him but they no longer rubbed against each other, making that rough noise. He didn't want to scare her off, and he tried never to push her or ask too much. Even when he thought she was a little nuts, with this continuous bath stuff—"This isn't some yuppie renovation," she said, when she explained what she wanted him to do, "I'm talking transformation for the purposes of moral medicinal treatment"—her authority and that loud laugh won him over. When the bathroom was still dusty and the place where they'd knocked a wall down still fresh, she asked the men to clear out in the afternoon and she began to give her teenage daughter hour-long baths in the afternoon. Afterward, she wrapped Marguerite in a towel and ushered her off to her bedroom where she put her to sleep.

"That is some crazy shit," Frank, one of Thompson's men, said while they sat on one of the giant rocks in the backyard eating sandwiches.

"Don't criticize what you don't know. It's a moral medicinal treatment," Thompson found himself saying.

"Yeah, I bet you'd like a piece of that treatment," Frank said, and the rest of the guys laughed. Thompson threw what was left of his sandwich at Frank and stormed back inside, realizing as he did it that he'd just proved Frank's point.

Confusion conspires with memory, which offers itself up to replace the image of Sam on the kitchen floor. A week and a half later, the bathroom was almost finished and Thompson sent everyone home early, claiming he could clean up on his own. "You guys have really busted your asses. You deserve a break," he said. He ignored Frank's raising his eyebrows hubba-hubba style.

"Never give a hollow greeting of peace or turn away when someone needs your love. . . . Speak the truth with your heart and tongue," Thompson said when Sam appeared, and he blushed again, the second time in his life. "I love that part," Sam said. She slid a hand under the curve of her ass to keep her wraparound denim skirt from riding up as she took a seat on the rim of the bathtub where Thompson sits now.

"My daughter's asleep. She really needs rest. That's the main thing. These baths seem to be working," she said, pushing a wisp of hair off her face revealing those lines on her forehead that Thompson found himself thinking about when he drove home at night. She took the fold of her skirt and opened it a bit in order to wrap it tighter, and Thompson got a glimpse of her thigh. He'd thought about that too. "My husband doesn't care," she said suddenly. "We don't even talk anymore."

Thompson's face was a question and her face was an answer as she nodded and took his hand and then he kneeled down in front of her. He unwrapped her denim skirt and lay his face against the cleavage of her thighs. *The celebration of vigils on Sundays,* he whispered. *The celebration of the solemnity of lauds. The celebration of lauds on ordinary days.* "Keep going," Sam whispered back and Thompson did. *The discipline of psalmody,* and he looked up at her as he undid the tie at her waist and then unwrapped her skirt as if she was a gift. "Keep going," she said, running her fingers through his hair. *Reverence in prayer,* and then he kept going without language but with an honest tongue that longed to celebrate vigils with this woman who tasted like the sea across the fields. He longed to laud on ordinary days and to be reverent in prayer with her. *Let me remind you of the times for saying alleluia and you are one of them.* Both of them so reverent that neither of them noticed when Bernard walked in.

"Clearly it's you who needed the restorative bath," Bernard said in a voice so calm it was as if he was saying, "Nice work." He stood there, not moving, as Thompson and Sam jumped away from each other. His stillness scared Thompson so much that he hid in the closet and listened from there as Bernard ran (the stillness didn't last long) down the hall and Sam ran after him. The way Bernard's eyes looked everywhere at once scared Thompson too. And there was the night Thompson stayed late and overheard them all at the dinner table, shouting. Bernard was the loudest. Who is the most? Who is the most? The guy was strange.

From the closet, where he found himself standing among many plush bathrobes that smelled a little like Sam, he didn't hear Bernard back into the tree or shout "That's your fault too!" as he peeled out of the driveway. Sam told him that later.

He isn't exactly listening with the ear of his heart, Thompson thinks, standing up and rearranging the erection in his jeans. He doesn't deserve to even *think* alleluia. He walks to the window. Where is Marguerite? He looks out into the fields where Sam told him Marguerite sometimes went to walk with the cows, but all he sees is a weeping willow and a groundhog perched on a rock sniffing the air.

Marguerite wandered through the bathroom one evening just as Thompson was getting ready to head out. She surprised him. He'd never seen her up close before, and her face was sharp with cheekbones and her eyes were green like her mother's but slanted, like a cat's. Sam had told him she was eighteen and she did have the creamy smooth look of an eighteen-year-old girl, but standing there in her oversized Led Zeppelin tee shirt and cutoffs, she looked as if she was shrinking, the way old people do.

"Do you know where my mother is?" she asked. Was she trembling? There was something charged about her, as if she'd just come from putting her finger in an electric socket.

"I haven't seen her," Thompson said. But he didn't want her to leave right away, this girl who was a part of Sam. It made him feel closer to Sam. "Do you like Led Zeppelin?" he asked, realizing as he asked it just how stupid it sounded.

"Yeah." Marguerite said dully and pointed at her tee shirt.

"Me too," Thompson said meekly.

"Do you know if the song remains the same?" Marguerite leaned against the windowsill, suddenly intent, as if Thompson might be able to tell her something.

"I like that song," he said, wondering whether his awkward question had prompted this awkward question in return.

"No," she said. "Do you know if it *stays* the same?" Fortunately for Thompson, Marguerite looked him up and down and then slipped out as easily as she had slipped in and he didn't have to figure out what the hell she was talking about. The truth was, she frightened him.

Looking out the window now, he's not sure what he'll do if Marguerite appears but he's decided that if it was important enough for him to rush back to tell Sam he loved her, then it's important for him to stand by that feeling because if he loved all of her then he loved this subarachnoid hemorrhage too and he will find a way to tell her daughter what's happened.

When he goes into the kitchen, he finds more dead flies lining the windowsill though he felt sure he swept them all up and again his arms threaten to separate themselves from his body and float away so he leaves the kitchen too and his legs take over, carrying him down the hall to the room Sam has never allowed him inside though he asked more than once to see where she worked.

"Where I *try* to work," Sam corrected him. "And the study is the opposite of Benedictine order."

" 'Whoever humbles himself shall be exalted.' " Thompson said, pulling the book out of his back pocket and holding it up to her.

"Hey, no fair. Throwing St. Benedict's words at me like that." The ice cubes at the bottom of his empty iced-tea glass rattled as she took the glass from his hand and turned to walk out of the bathroom. Thompson felt worried that he might have genuinely offended her, but then he caught the corner of her smile just before she disappeared through the doorway.

And even now, in the midst of the confusion that is keeping him on his feet, he still wants to know everything about her. Still, when he opens the study door, he is startled. There is no furniture except for a lone desk and a chair. It's as if the room itself is in mourning.

Then there are the walls. The walls are as crowded as the room is empty. Thompson counts two, three, four bulletin boards, before he gets to the paper tacked directly to the walls themselves. Why hadn't she asked him to cork-board the walls? There was so much he would have done for her, but then confusion skitters back in to save him. It pushes him forward, insisting that it's important to read these scraps as a way of honoring Sam. An act of contemplation. Reading so that the soul is the center of attention. Here is the source of the beautiful lines on Sam's forehead.

This mass of torn ragged-edged papers covered in a heart-attack scrawl, wallpapering the study is a collage of Sam's mind. It is a work of art, Thompson thinks. He feels greedy all of a sudden. There is so much here to investigate, to look at, to study and learn. He pauses for a moment, wondering if looking around Sam's study is a selfish act, something he should turn away from, but then confusion pushes Thompson forward. Read, it says to him. Reading is an act of contemplation, he repeats in his mind. He walks the room as if it were a room in a museum, his hands clasped behind his back in deference.

On the first bulletin board, a small scrap of paper. Notes Sam took while talking to a guidance counselor, Thompson gathers from the nature of the notes in red pen in the heart-attack scrawl. Thompson has never seen Sam's handwriting before and it is so intimate it's as if he is seeing yet another part of her naked body. *Possible bipolar disorder?* the notes read. *Just a hunch. So says the trigger-happy guidance counselor (if that is her real job) with a plastic smile I can hear over the phone. Not diagnosing, Ms. so-called guidance counselor claims. So what are you doing?*

Thompson's eye lands next on a string of sentences scrawled on a scrap of paper. Read, an act of contemplation: 1854, Falret described *la folie circulaire*. "This succession of mania and melancholia manifests itself with continuity and in a manner almost regular."

Madness is to delirium what walking in sleep is to dreaming. In blue ink, heart-attack style: *Diseases of the Mind*, Benjamin Rush, 1812, the same guy who thinks madness originated in the liver.

In the corner of a photocopied page of text (Pascal: "Men are so necessarily mad, that not to be mad would amount to another form of madness"), Sam's hand has been captured too, emerging from the shadows. Thompson almost asked her if he could read her palm one day when she brought him iced tea, though he had never read anyone's palm before in his life. He had wanted to trace that lifeline off the map, up her wrist and her arm. Sam's watch, always turned to the inside of her wrist, is copied too. Nine twenty-five. Thompson rests his cheek against Sam's photocopied palm, though he keeps his eyes wide open for fear of what he might see if he closed them.

Read, an act of contemplation with Sam's soul as the center of attention.

On the most central bulletin board is a sentence that overshadows all the others, each letter blown up to the size of Thompson's pinky: "The efficacy of mood stabilizers in children and adolescents has not been studied adequately." Heart-attack red: From *Mood Stabilizers in Children and Adolescents*—Ryan, Neal D.M.D.; Bhatara, Vinod S. M.D.; Perel, James M. Ph.D., American Academy of Child and Adolescent Psychiatry, Volume 38(5), May 1999, pp. 529–536.

Underneath this scrap, SIDE EFFECTS scrawled at the top of a list: drowsiness, dizziness, blurred vision, stomach upset, loss of appetite, changes in vision, muscle aches, and restlessness. Notify your doctor if you develop: sore throat, fever, chills, unusual bleeding or bruising, yellowing of the skin or eyes, dark urine, nightmares, hair loss, mouth sores, ringing in the ears, sensitivity to sunlight. Symptoms of an allergic reaction include: rash, itching, swelling, dizziness, trouble breathing, severe headache, tremor, hallucinations, anxiety, nervousness, agitation, confusion, restlessness, seizures, eating disorders, vomiting, stomach/abdominal pain, ringing in the ears, fainting, unusual weight loss or gain, trouble breathing, decreased sex drive, and painful and prolonged erection.

Thompson returns to Sam's photocopied palm, presses his cheek against nine twenty-five, and imagines he hears tick tock, tick tock.

In red marker on a big strip of butcher paper taped along the full length of an entire wall:

Further experiments and observations confirmed his suspicions; and led him to the painful conclusion (painful alike to our pride and our humanity) ... medicine as yet possesses very inadequate means to relieve the most grievous of human disease. Samuel Tukes, *Description of the Retreat, nine-teenth century.*

On top of the desk, the 1917 article by Edward Strecker on the continuous bath in *The Journal of the American Medical Association*, Sam's notes scrawled in the margin: Bath serves as a mild hypnotic agent, a means of inducing fatigue and calm—even pleasure?—in manic patients.

"She's so quiet in the water," Sam said to Thompson on that same afternoon he had yearned to read her palm, to trace her wrist and her arm. "I lie on the divan and she lies in the bath, and I'm grateful. I feel like, finally, I'm doing something right. While we're there, together and quiet, I think, this is all I need. This stillness."

"You *are* doing something right," he said. What he meant but couldn't say was: You make me feel still. You make the grinding stop.

Portions of the article are highlighted in pink:

The continuous bath room of the future will probably be developed along somewhat more esthetic lines. Since certain patients are under treatment for many hours, days and sometimes weeks, the room must necessarily be used not only as a bath, but also as a living apartment. The introduction of books, magazines, a few games and puzzles, and possibly a picture or two on the walls, will perhaps help to modify its rather monotonous appearance. Edward A. Strecker, M.D., "The Continuous Bath in Mental Disease," 1917.

At the bottom, in the familiar heart-attack handwriting: *Call that carpenter.*

That carpenter. Thompson *was* that carpenter, that person without a name. Before Sam knew him, he was nothing but ink on a page to her. As that ink on the page, that idea and nothing more, he is able to walk out of the study. As an idea and nothing more, he is able to shut the door, confusion still his faithful guide. From *The Rule of St. Benedict*, Thompson has memorized most of chapter 68, "Assignment of Impossible Tasks to a Brother." *A brother may be assigned a burdensome task or something he cannot do. If so, he should, with complete gentleness and obedience, accept the order given him.* Thompson hurries, an idea of a man, in order to make the calls to the numbers on the wall above the phone in the kitchen, Sam's husband's office, her son, before grief arrives to muscle confusion out of the way.

Should he see, however, that the weight of the burden is altogether too much for his strength, then he should choose the appropriate moment and explain patiently to his superior the reasons why he cannot perform the task. Who was that superior and where was he? He walks on legs that seem to be somebody else's, back to the kitchen. He wishes he could run into the light of God and never look back but the words cast no shadow.

He plays with the dirty rope bracelet around his wrist and then takes a knife out of a drawer, saws it off and tosses it in the trash can. *If after the explanation the superior is still determined to hold to his original order, then the junior must recognize that this is best for him.* Out the window, a herd of cows has gathered at the back fence. It is as if they are watching Thompson and he draws the curtains. He picks up the flyswatter and then forgets what he meant to do with it.

He leans his head against the window and practices what he will say to the husband, to the son. *This is Thompson,* he says, over and over again until he can't feel his lips anymore and he begins to wonder whether it's true or not. How did he, Thompson—*call the carpenter*—end up in this moment? *Trusting in God's help, he must in love obey.* This is Thompson the carpenter, he practices. This is Thompson the carpenter, this is Thompson the carpenter, this is Thompson the carpenter.

Good Mourning in the Queen's County, Part II

Marguerite is on the verge of arrival. She will rise above and above, like Louise Lateau. Up and down the up and down hallway, Marguerite will make the heel of her sock unravel for the love of something big. Once Ryan comes to find her heart, like Louise Lateau there will be a bleeding coronet on Marguerite's forehead; the blood will trickle down her face and drop on the floor where it will lie in large extraordinary patches.

"No train's going to mow me down," the shrinking woman (Anna Karenina! Anna Karenina!), drowning in her sweatshirt, says. She blocks Marguerite's shuffling path in the up and down hallway, standing just outside the room where the extinguished brain fire smokes and smokes. More and more, people can see inside Marguerite's head as if it is an aquarium, her thoughts tropical fish sparking with light. Watch me, their tails, flickery flickering, say. Firefly flash: "Well hello, Dolly" her mother sang while Marguerite climbed into the bath, until Marguerite said, "No, play Graham Parsons." A heart strong enough, tough enough, one of her brother's songs that remains always the same.

"Where is *my* fucking train?" Marguerite asks Anna Karenina in her shrinking fairy-sized sneakers, which are good and right, smaller and smaller so fewer souls crushed. "What do you know about *my* fucking train?"

Outside, another ambulance croons through the traffic waiting at the light, sending crumpled, food-stained wrappers, another plastic bag up into the bony tree to breathe in and out. A hairnet flies up into the air that smells like burned leaves and exhaust and the charcoal of still September because the taller mourning woman says so.

"Not you! Not anyone!" Anna Karenina shouts. "No train's going to mow me down!" She flops the long sleeves of her sweatshirt, as if she had no arms at all, in Marguerite's face.

"Ease off," Regina says, emerging from the room with the brain fire, a cigarette hanging from her lips, though there is no smoking in the up and down hallway. She does an almost-split in her borrowed nightgown she insists is a dress. "A nightshirt?" Marguerite asked her, but Regina didn't know what she was talking about and then Marguerite didn't know what she was talking about either as the firefly flash went dark again.

The thump-thump remorse code of Marguerite's heart calls to her: Who loves you the most? Who loves you the most? Firefly flash: her mother in the blue bathroom, and her father in the late night kitchen with Louise Lateau who is not blue but orange-red fire like the sun close up. In the night kitchen, the naked boy tumbling into the giant jug of milk and she wonders if this is what her so-called mother had in store for her, drowning her in mother's milk. Her mother gestured come in, come in, the water's ready, just the right temperature, splashing weary fingers along the surface until the water rippled. Marguerite slid into the warm tub for her mother because this is what her mother wanted the most, and she imagined that she was immune to hot and cold like Louise Lateau. She practiced not feeling anything in order to feel everything, and when she closed her eyes, she saw the millions of stars in the night kitchen with the roly-poly chef laughing and laughing his roly-poly laugh and her body felt the heat because she was not Louise Lateau yet, but slowly, slowly her blood was moving faster.

Overhead in the sky of the up and down hallway: Dr. Goodman, Dr. Good Man, and again she is hopeful.

Regina is taller than Anna Karenina and Anna Karenina flaps
her long shirtsleeves and takes flight down the up and down hallway. Regina is taller than Marguerite too, and her voice taller still.
She spins on her long legs with their secret map bruises. "Uzbekistan," she says, pointing to a dark shape that looks like any other
country to Marguerite.

"Regina," the scary mask face, at the front desk pumping another patient's arm tighter and tighter, calls over. "No cigarettes outside the smoking lounge."

"Don't give me your three percent God nonsense," Regina
whispers. Earlier, the scary mask face pumped Marguerite's and
Regina's arms tighter and tighter too, taking their so-called blood
pressure like a punishment for not receiving her capital *G* God,
Regina said. Regina nods to Marguerite, her we'll-find-your-heart-
in-a-minute nod.

"What are you?" Regina asks, steering Marguerite toward the
room filled with brain fire. "A shark? Going to die if you stop
walking up and down? Don't make me do a split." She starts to
slide her feet farther apart. "You know I will." And though Marguerite has never seen so-called Regina do a split, the fact that
Regina knows that a split is what Marguerite is thinking makes so-
called Regina seem like she might just do one after all.

"No train's going to mow me down, not even where-is-my-
fucking train," Anna Karenina says to Regina's chest, darting past
her and through the door toward a magic ashtray where someone
has pulled the silver lever so the cigarette is about to disappear into
the abyss but not before Anna Karenina rescues the butt for her
own purposes. Marguerite walks through the swinging door after
Regina, whose 100 percent voice like music tattoos her mind, telling
her it will seek out Marguerite's heart. *You were only waiting for this
moment to arise.*

"And don't you so-called me. I'm one hundred percent Regina,"
Regina says, and once again Marguerite doesn't know what she's spoken out loud. But with Regina it doesn't matter. In the beginning, a

day ago that lasted a year, when Marguerite first arrived here—when the flabby-armed pot-smasher, pot in midair, first shouted, "Cracking up! I'll show you cracking up!" and then pure dirt explosion—in the dark of their room with the clanking radiator, Regina whispered, "I know what it is to bury the dead." It was then Marguerite understood that Regina knew Marguerite before they'd ever met, that Regina could hear the swish-swish of Marguerite's blood inside her, that she understood the serious nature of Marguerite's quest for her thump-thump heart.

"Come on, shark lady," Regina says, her long sliding legs not sliding anymore but standing tall and straight in front of the chairs filled with smoking brains.

Regina lifts her nightgown dress nightshirt and flashes her belly with the long scar up the middle, a Caesarean scar, Regina explained. Translation: a baby disappears after she's born, when she's more than a thump-thump on a moonscape screen. In their room where the radiator clank clanks like another relentless god desperate to get out, Regina told the story to Marguerite:

A girl lives in a city where it's hard to see any birds at all never mind a V of birds chop-chopping through the air and the birds she does see peck trash from the streets. She is a long, long way from the ocean and any mysterious red weed. This girl falls in love with a man who loved her mother first and must keep the love secret (Marguerite doesn't interrupt to tell her about her secret love for her brother because flickery, flickery, she feels sure Regina has seen it flicker across her aquarium mind already). The girl lives with her mother and she doesn't want to break her heart, but she also has her own heart and its longings to consider. And then one day, the girl is filled with this man's so-called love, cells dividing and dividing inside her until they've divided so much there is no hiding the division as it grows so evident it mutes the beating of the girl's mother's heart until the girl thinks it has stopped altogether.

In the mother's confusion, she throws the girl out into the streets with the trash-pecking birds where the girl thought the man she loved who loved her mother first would take care of her and the dividing cells inside her, but instead he loves her mother again and they leave her and her cells to divide and divide on their own. The cells dividing become a baby and the girl has the baby alone. There's a lot that happens in between but the 100 percent music that is Regina's voice sang that it would skip that part because some things aren't meant to be sung.

Instead, she said she would skip ahead to the parts that most needed to be sung. The girl finds a place of her own. On the first day in the new place, she needs to go to the store for milk. She looks—a look that hears and tastes and smells and suddenly there are other senses too, ones that didn't exist until now because the baby brought the new senses into the world with her—at her baby, the sum of the cells dividing and dividing, a sweet-smelling creature whose face is neither hers nor the man who no longer loves her but loves her mother instead, whose face is a new face filled with wonder and love that the girl likes to imagine her mother must have seen in the girl's face when she looked at her long, long ago when she was her mother's sweet-smelling creature.

The girl, said Regina, over the clank, clank of the radiator, whispers to the wondrous, loving face that she will be right back, down the stairs to the deli for a carton of milk, maybe some eggs, quick and back up again, back before the wondrous, loving face has opened her eyes again. So the girl goes, hurrying and still not fast enough. While she is gone someone comes, sent by her mother who is still loving the man who loved the girl once, to check on her and the baby and finds only the baby sound asleep and in the fifteen minutes that the girl is gone, the sweet smell and the taste and the touch and the wonder are taken from her. Years and years go by (and in those years, Regina said, the girl has done things that also aren't meant to be sung) and during one of those years there were papers that claim to terminate her mother love. So, there it is, Regina said to Marguerite, in their room where the air smelled of unwashed pillowcases and sweaty nightmare hair. There it is, she said, in the darkness like Marguerite's mind before a firefly flash. That is *my* lost heart, Regina said. It's so long gone I can't even hear it anymore.

Regina turned away from Marguerite, curling toward the wall so that her spine showed through her nightgown nightshirt. In that dark that floated outside of time, Marguerite let the words LIFE AND DEATH INSIDE ME TOO swim across her aquarium mind for Regina to see. And then, from the dusty rose manuscript with the border of marching insects: *Present therefore in their daily celebration of the Eucharist and at the saying of their offices is this reminder that death is part of life.*

Now, with her own brain smoking from a butt retrieved from the magic ashtray, Anna Karenina shouts at Regina, "Get dressed! Move your cut-open belly!"

Regina pulls her nightgown nightshirt dress up higher and then pulls it down again.

Through the brain smoke, the TV sings about hearts broken, stolen, bruised, abandoned, lost. "Say my name" it sings. Firefly flash: Marguerite's brother's voice of anguish, *Margritte, Margritte, Margritte,* into the inscrutable blue sky where the V of birds chop, chops through salty ocean air.

"Say my name" Anna Karenina sings from the corner where she perches on a chair, waiting, just waiting, with her thin blue river veins traveling her fragile arms for a tall or a short mourning woman to tell her to put her feet on the ground.

"Why don't you get down from there and while you're at it, shut the fuck up," a brain fresh from the world shouts.

"You're just mad because you weren't the first Jesus to walk into a rest stop on the New Jersey Turnpike," Anna Karenina says. She turns to Marguerite and looks straight into her eyes in a way that makes Marguerite worry that she is stealing percentages from her, that Marguerite's percentage is slipping: 98 percent, 85 percent, 74 percent . . . "That's not Destiny, Child. That's Destiny's Child."

"For your information, there is no train up in here," Regina says to Anna Karenina, taking a long drag on her cigarette and staring her right in the eye, as if she is smoking *her.* She presses the TV's POWER button off, then presses it on again, then changes the channel to a lady and a man with lots of makeup talking about a terror drill to gauge coordination in the area. "Off the charts of negative percentage!"

"Terror! Gauge!" the never-sleeping man shouts.

Regina changes the channel back to the song about hearts broken, stolen, bruised, abandoned, lost and Marguerite hears the moist blood-red thump of her own heart somewhere off in the distance. She tugs at Regina's sleeve.

"Happier?" Regina says to the never-sleeping man, shaking Marguerite off.

"More and more," he shouts.

"Then why are you shouting?" Regina asks.

"Let's go," Marguerite says, touching her chest to indicate it is time to go look now.

The never-sleeping man follows them out into the hall, calling after them, "I'm smoking you where you stand." Then, "I'm smoking you in your tracks," to the flabby-armed pot-smasher, though he is making no tracks at all.

The so-called nurse who is really Carol Channing with her big-tooth smile, friendly shining teeth stuck to her thin upper lip, beckons Marguerite to the nurse's depot where there are the pills that demolish time, smash it like the pot-smasher smashes pots.

The broad back of the so-called psychiatrist goes by. "Dr. Good Man?" Marguerite says, hopeful.

"No," he says, turning around, no good man at all.

"Seventy-four percent," says Regina.

Still, Marguerite curtsies because you never know.

"Stop with that crazy curtseying and come rest," the so-called nurse Carol Channing says. No one's told her that nurses are never this kind in real life or the movies. They would never reach out and take your hand and give you a giant-toothed smile and tell you that the rolling of the hospital carts probably doesn't mean there's a revolution afoot although wouldn't it be kind of fun? Regina, who slips into their room with the clanking radiator says Carol Channing is 111 percent. "It's complicated. Not necessarily better if you're surrounded by lesser percented so-calleds."

"Maybe you and I should start our own revolution," Carol says now, winking her fake eyelashes. "But for now you should swallow these."

"The time of my parents' trial began with me," Marguerite thinks across her mind.

"No, my dear girl," Carol Channing says. Evidently the words escaped Marguerite's mouth. "You are a young girl. Oh, excuse me, an adult!" When Marguerite arrived, they tried to make her a child, but she said no, eighteen, two years older than Louise at the height of her powers!

Carol takes Marguerite's hand and puts the miniature pleated cup like a trick cupcake wrapper (Look: no cupcake!) right there in the center of Marguerite's palm where she imagines the blisters will rise up, rise up like a cupcake of ecstasy.

"Take these while you stand here."

"This is no cupcake," Marguerite says, and Carol laughs a friendly laugh different from Regina's I'm on-your-side-laugh but still as genuinely friendly as Carol's big, friendly teeth.

"Everything is going to be all right, definitely going to be all right," Carol says. Wink-wink, eyelashes so thick, Marguerite imagines tiny brushes of 111 percent gentle against her cheek. "All right."

"Everything right at once?" The words rush out of Marguerite's mouth, lured by Carol Channing's kind, white teeth. "That seems like the most and is the most possible?" Somewhere down the hall, thump-thump, thump-thump. Who loves Marguerite the most?

Carol smiles bigger than anyone has ever smiled before. She says, "Yes, yes it is. The most is possible."

Marguerite hears the chop-chop of bird wings outside, their chop-chopping louder than the song of the ambulance. The ocean salt is deep in her nose and in a flash that's not a firefly flash but a flash into the future of fireflies, there are her brother's hands, his guitar blisters their own kind of ecstatic, carefully, carefully carrying a jelly jar with her thump-thump heart all the way to the cathedral in Warsaw. Marguerite turns on her bare heel, unraveling and unraveling, and heads for the room where Regina waits. Marguerite's hands fisted tight, the pulse at the center of each palm yearning, yearning more than ever to learn how to shudder.

"You better put that thing out," the taller mourning woman says to the never-sleeping man, tapping his ash, inhaling deeply, outside the small round window that looks onto the room with the smoking brains. "A window on a ship," he says. "A ship of fools."

The taller mourning woman begins to walk toward him. "Put it out," she says, and he does, on the front desk, and the mourning women busy themselves with something on the verge of fire.

In the clank clank room, Regina lies on her bed, her borrowed nightgown nightshirt spread out around her like a body halo. In the corner by the muted brown bureau, edges dulled as if worn down by a nail file, are Marguerite's shoes, tongues swollen and awkward in their laces, but she will not be tricked like the trick cupcake by her shoes' desire to squash souls.

Outside, the ambulance sings its emergency song through the bright air, singing by the time-telling bus stop. When Regina isn't sleeping as she is now, a rare and gentle snuffle, she teaches Marguerite to keep track of time using the ever-changing people waiting for the bus to come and swallow them up. The people are ever-changing and time is never the same. This afternoon, almost the noontime meal: Presto chango! A little boy holding a magic wand, casting spells on a mother who ignored him as she tried to read the bus route on the inside of the bus shelter. Firefly flash: Marguerite's littlest self turned into a tiny cat by Ryan's magic wand, casting spells until her huge awkward paws were splayed with tiger love for him.

Now o'clock, a woman stands at the bus stop, not a woman Marguerite knows, but she is accustomed to not knowing. The sun sinks in a brisk, clear sky and the woman paces the length of the bus shelter, dipping her foot into the gutter near the crackly brown leaf-covered drain. The woman, her outline carving a place in the air of the outside world, turns in the direction of Marguerite's window and Marguerite is sure she sees inside and then inside and inside, beyond

Marguerite's aquarium mind, past her flicker fish thoughts to the blood that courses through her. The now o'clock woman reaches up out of herself to touch the pompom on the top of her wool hat as if she has just remembered something from long ago that will explain everything.

The Time of Trial Begins

By the time Bernard began to read to Marguerite from the dusty rose manuscript, the original fragment taped above the captain's desk in his study was surrounded by a flurry of fragments. The wrinkled knuckle of his thumb lurked in the photocopied shadow of one, holding down the page as he made the copies at school when he'd gone to clean out his office. Though Bernard had packed his books into boxes, the chair had said space was tight, and Bernard would need to take the boxes out of the office while he was on leave. Bernard had gone to school in the evening when it was relatively empty because he didn't want anyone to ask any questions about his leave. He especially wanted to avoid any more conversations with the chair about the paper airplane in class or his lying on the floor of the bathroom or the tomato incident with the student, never mind his lack of recent publications. He was beginning to worry that whomever occupied his office while he was on leave would be allowed to take up permanent residence. As he made copies of the passages to do with Louise's ecstasies so that he could write in the margins ("Who is the most ecstatic?"), instead of on the manuscript itself, a colleague leaned against the front desk in the main office to talk with one of the pretty graduate students who worked there.

"So who is this Eminem fellow really?" the colleague asked.

"A satirist, like Swift," the student said, and Bernard had snuck past them both.

"So what's this story that's like our fairy tale?" Marguerite asked, startling Bernard. Though Bernard had expected her, had in fact invited her that very night at dinner to his study so that he could share his secret Louise with her, it was becoming easier and easier to wander deep into his mind until he found himself, hours later, still holding the dusty rose manuscript, unsure for a moment of where he was or how he had gotten there.

Marguerite slid into the room, through the same shaft of lamplight illuminating each photocopied fragment of the Rohling essay one by one. She shut the door with her back, her arms folded across her chest. She was somehow much taller than Bernard remembered her looking at dinner and the rash of pimples on her chin alarmed him. When had she become a teenager? What land had he wandered off to when this happened? Still, she'd said *our* fairy tale" and it gave Bernard hope.

"One of those stories from the dark ages? When things were *dark?*" Marguerite asked.

Bernard's laugh was too loud, but he couldn't help it. He was relieved by the reminder of Marguerite's tiny head in the crook of his arm as he read to her in that fairy-tale voice, the reminder of a time when family life was, well, *familial*. He was relieved that Marguerite remembered. Yes, he had been a part of that family life. He had participated. Who was he defending himself against anyway?

"Marguerite, I know you don't have your shoes on," Sam called down the hall from the kitchen. "I can sense it. Your mother has these powers. She knows you're out there somewhere in this house ruining another good pair of socks: the loose thread at the heel of your sock, the beginning of the end, the end of civilization, kaput, sayonara sucker."

"It's probably best if your mother doesn't know about this," Bernard said, putting a finger to his lips.

Just yesterday Sam told Bernard that Marguerite had confided in her. She had in fact fled her English class to go hide in the bathroom and cry, just as the guidance counselor (who Sam referred to as plastic smile lady) had said. The teacher had been talking about Hamlet and suddenly, Marguerite told Sam, it was as if she could see the yammering skull of her teacher through her flesh. But more than that (and here Bernard thought Sam was embellishing) Marguerite said that when she got to the bathroom, her malaise—

"She used the word *malaise*?" Bernard had asked.

"Well, no," Sam said. "But something close to *malaise*. Do you always have to be so professorial? Jesus. Her *sadness* had more to do with the bright fall afternoon light and the smell of freshly cut grass outside."

Isn't that something you said to me once? Bernard wanted to ask her. He saw the reason for concern, he *did*, but he also thought that Sam was putting words in their daughter's mouth, that she was mistaking acute sensitivity for something more dangerous. He'd often seen the skull underneath the flesh of people who yammered on. In fact, he saw Sam's yammering skull as she explained to him she was going to give Marguerite some time off school.

But here Marguerite was now, with that filthy tee shirt of her brother's—"The Song Remains the Same"—there was something so obstinate about that, Bernard thought, but then his daughter smiled at him and he was grateful.

Marguerite rolled her eyes in the direction of her mother's voice and put her own finger to her lips. "Read me the story," she said. She moved a pile of books off a chair and scraped the chair across the wood floor toward her father. "I want to hear it."

"Well," Bernard said.

"Don't *describe* it," Marguerite said, folding her legs up under her. *"Read."*

Read! Read! Tell! Tell!

"Aye, matey," Bernard said.

"Exactly," Marguerite said.

" 'Louise's First Sixteen Years,' " and Bernard began at the beginning. Louise was born on the January 30, 1850, in Bois d'Haine, near Manago, in the diocese of Tournay in Belgium. An older sister, Rosina, and a younger sister, Adelina. Her father, Gregory, worked in the ironworks and from his savings and his wife's dowry he built the family a small cottage. " 'But, with the birth of Louise,' " Bernard read, " 'their time of trial began. For three weeks the mother was unable to leave her bed of sickness. When Louise was but six weeks old, her father died of smallpox.' " Bernard read to Marguerite about the cholera epidemic in Louise's village and how Louise, at the age of sixteen, tended to the sick, how she procured coffins and buried the dead when the families couldn't bear it. He told her how Louise herself almost died and then somehow didn't and appeared in the village church one day, a miracle for the other villagers to behold. How one fateful Friday, April 24, 1879, Louise found herself bleeding from her left side, and believed she was ill again, but then the next Friday, she bled from her right side and from the tops of both of her feet, and the following Friday, she bled not only from her sides and the tops of both of her feet but from her palms and the backs of her hands as well.

Bernard paused to look at his daughter. She pulled at a thread at the worn heel of one of her socks. Maybe he had been wrong. Maybe Marguerite wouldn't understand Louise Lateau. Maybe she wouldn't hear her voice calling to her across the years the way Bernard had.

Then Marguerite looked up and Bernard recognized the fierce slanted cat eyes of the little girl riveted by the fairy tale about the young boy who yearned to know what fear was. "Keep reading," she commanded. And Bernard did, skipping to the part that fascinated him most: After the commission was formed and the investigation began—the archbishops and the scientists arrived to make sure that Louise was the real deal—the villagers started to gather around the cottage. Every Friday they peered through the windows to witness their miraculous Louise bleed:

" 'His grace visited Louise in her mother's cottage, at three o'clock in the afternoon. He found her in an ecstasy, her hands covered with blood, but upon his simply mentioning her name, "Louise," she instantly recovered consciousness.' "

Bernard paused. Bernard hoped this wouldn't remind Marguerite of the way her esteemed brother, now touring the country with a band called I'd Rather Drink Bleach, called her name from the pier the day she fell. Bernard was so tired of that story. *He'd* rather drink bleach. He was ready for new stories, or new old stories, like Louise's, and he wanted Marguerite to hear them too.

Marguerite looked up from the unravelling thread at the heel of her sock and pushed her hair back from her face. Since Sam cut her hair into a choppy pageboy, Marguerite looked smaller. Or maybe it was those baths? Was she shrinking? Her skin was pale, more translucent than usual, and when Bernard reached out to circle his daughter's thin wrist with his hand, he felt her trembling.

"Let me close the window," he said. As he did, he looked out onto the garden rampant with weeds where he and Sam had planted those tomatoes that first week in the train depot. The evening air smelled like charcoal, like the beginning of fall. "Are you tired?" he asked his daughter, and felt that he himself could close his eyes and fall immediately to sleep.

"A little," she said. "But I like hearing this story, Please read."

" 'Upon his simply mentioning her name, "Louise," she instantly recovered consciousness,' " Bernard read again.

"That's so sad that her father died when she was so young," Marguerite said.

"It is sad," Bernard said, and he wanted to offer his daughter something. He pretended to be reading from the dusty rose manuscript, but this time he improvised. "Her father returns to her. In spirit. He returns and keeps her company on those Fridays when she has the stigmata. Her sisters tell her that it's God speaking to her, but Louise doesn't hear God. She hears her father." Maybe that was too much? "Faintly," Bernard added. "His voice is faint."

"Read about her ecstasies," Marguerite said. The shaft of lamp-

132

MAUD CASEY

light shone at the foot of her chair, illuminating the swirling dust motes at her feet as though she were an angel. Maybe Bernard was the one who was tired.

"Read! Read! Tell! Tell!" she shouted, laughing.

Her laughter brought color to her cheeks and Bernard began to read again from the manuscript. " 'The bleeding points around her head are the seat of the most excruciating pains. As described by herself, she feels as if a band of red-hot iron were bound around her head, pressing against it with enormous force. And the slightest touch upon her forehead redoubles her agony. The wound in her shoulder is so painful that she describes herself as feeling unable to sustain the weight of her head; it deprives her eyes of their wonted vivacity, and exhausts her strengths to such a degree that she is unable to recognize a person at the distance of a yard or two.' " Bernard looked up to see Marguerite looking past him, out the window into the night where the crickets chirped through the dark. Farther down the gravel road to the beach, a dog barked.

"When Louise's mind would wander away from her village to faraway cities," Bernard said, improvising again to bring Marguerite back, "she wondered how and why she was born into this particular family and what would have happened to her if she had been born into another. When her mind wandered and she felt such smallness that she would find herself on the brink of tears, just as she was about to fall into the deepest kind of despair, blacker than night, her father would speak to her and Louise would listen, letting her father's words fill her the way her sisters told her God filled them at church."

"Hey, why are *you* crying?" Marguerite asked.

"I'm not," Bernard said, though he had gotten carried away, imagining himself dead and Marguerite mourning him and then hearing his voice speaking to her.

"The scientists studied the blood, analyzed it," Bernard said.

"Hey, you're not reading," Marguerite said.

He was thrilled that she had caught him, thrilled that his daughter could still tell when a story had *realness* in it, and he returned to

the manuscript: " 'The blood is of the normal consistency, present-
ing, on several occasions when examined with the microscope, no
unusual appearance.' "

"They did tests?" Marguerite asked.

"They did tests."

"What kind of tests?"

"Tests to see if she was for real," Bernard said. He continued
reading. " 'On the 27th of November, 1868, Drs. Lefebvre, Lecrinier
and Severin endeavored to produce by artificial means a bleeding
surface like that of the stigmas. On that day the stigmas were bleeding copiously. The epidermis of the blister had burst and discharged
its fluid contents; the surface of the skin thus exposed had com-
menced to bleed. Dr. Lefebvre then applied liquid ammonia, a
powerful vesicant, to the back of the left hand, over a space equal in
size to the bleeding stigma, and close beside it, taking care, however,
to leave a small space between them. After twelve minutes a blister
was formed; it was filled, in the usual way, with a colorless fluid.
However, the blister thus formed did not burst of itself as the blisters of the stigmas do. Dr. Lefebvre at length cut it open, thus ex-
posing the surface of the skin beneath.' "

"What were they trying to prove?" Marguerite had stopped
pulling at the unraveling thread at the heel of her sock altogether.
She unfolded her legs and perched on the edge of her chair like the
most attentive student.

"Well," Bernard said, taking his time now that he had her full
attention. "This article is written by someone who was writing for
the Catholic Church, and the Church wanted to make her a martyr."

"What's a martyr again?" Marguerite asked.

"I'm one," Sam said, appearing in the doorway, hair disheveled,
wearing an apron stained with wet handprints. Bernard felt convinced she'd taken the time to tousle her own hair, that she'd put the
apron on for show. In fact, he didn't think he'd ever seen her wear
an apron. "Mandatory family dinner's ready," she said.

"Maybe if you didn't refer to it as mandatory, it might have a
chance of being fun," Bernard said.

"Oh, my sweet Jesus," Sam said, indicating Marguerite's socked feet with an ah-ha raise of her eyebrows, and ignoring Bernard altogether.

"You're welcome to him," Bernard said, standing up and replacing the dusty rose manuscript carefully in the center of the desk, smoothing its cover with careful hands.

"Keep the bleeding Belgian to yourself, Bernard," Sam said.

"I'm serious," Sam said again as Marguerite slid down the hall ahead of them.

Sliding down the hall toward mandatory family dinner, Marguerite still didn't know what a martyr was, but she liked the sound of the word in her mouth, all of those *rs*—the *ar* like Bernard's pirate's voice *ar*, the *yr* like a growl. The word reached out for something with that sound, the way her brother's voice had—*Margrrite, Margrrite, Margrrite*—lifting her name up above the sum of its letters to something that felt like God. Lately, she could feel her blood's movement, the push, push through her veins, the tug of it inside of her when she, lay still in her bed at night. She could hear it whispering its way through her body, urged on by her heart pumping with love for her brother, traveling, traveling, never asking for permission as it pressed against the walls of her blood vessels. It pushed at her skin, begging: Let me out. Let me out. Let me out.

Relax Your Mind

In the hospital morgue, Hyuen lifts the plastic from the girl's naked body with careful fingers, peeling it back like burned skin and then covering her face with a cloth. He runs a soapy cloth over her feet, between her long toes, then up her strong calves, and her thighs. He swipes the rag gently, efficiently, between her legs, leaving a trail of soap bubbles frothing along the dead skin of her belly.

"You still look like shit, Ryan," Hyuen says, looking up from the torso of the girl. His thick eyelashes betray the tenderness that his steady almond eyes hide. "You look worse than she does," and Ryan knows he must really look bad because Hyuen never makes fun of the bodies. He is, so to speak, deadly serious about the dead bodies.

Hyuen is tall and flexible. That first day, when Hyuen discovered Ryan flattened to the wall in a futile effort to hide as he spied, Hyuen had leaned sideways out of the door so that his face appeared to be suspended without a body. "Welcome to my castle," he said in a Dracula voice, beckoning with his index finger. When Ryan entered, Hyuen acted as though it was perfectly normal for Ryan to be spying on him as he worked. He never asked why. Ryan would soon learn that Hyuen was surprised by very little. No one at the Thai or-phanage where Hyuen's parents found him in the early seventies knew Hyuen's parentage, though his lankiness, and the hint of Cau-casian features, suggested his father might have been an American tourist passing through the red-light district. Hyuen said that his parents wanted to make up for U.S. imperialism, that they thought that adopting was a step toward redemption. "Are you feeling the love already?" Hyuen said to Ryan. Hyuen's parents gave him a Thai name as a way of empowering the prostitute they imagined his mother to be. "Do you feel the *power*?" Hyuen asked Ryan, holding up splayed hands as if he was performing a jazz dance move. Hyuen always looked as if he was about to break into dance.

"Ryan?" Hyuen says now. He puts a hand on his hip and Ryan imagines him launching into a do-si-do. "Did you hear me? You look like shit."

"Yeah, thanks," Ryan says from where he's propped up against his usual spot of the wall in the windowless, concrete room.

"Should I be worried?" Hyuen says, swiping at some invisible thing on his cheek with his latex-gloved hand.

With the sound of Hyuen's voice, the dead girl is just a dead girl to Ryan again; she no longer threatens to be Marguerite, which is a good thing because Hyuen is making an incision in the girl's taut neck, the mixture of hydrating agents (as Hyuen has explained to Ryan)—penetration-enhancers, alcohol, salts, dyes, formaldehyde—sliding through her body into her tissues' cells. Hyuen inserts the hollow needle into her belly, aspirating the gases and fluids from the center of her body, and then inserts another needle to disperse the disinfectant fluid. Her organs are like secrets revealed, pulled from where they've been hidden deep in her body by Hyuen's kind hands. Hyuen handles the kidney and spleen like newborns, seem-ing to bring life rather than to collude with death. He steeps the or-gans in the same mixture of alcohol, salts, and formaldehyde, dusted with preservative powder, then places them back inside the girl's husk exactly as they were.

The girl is no longer Marguerite to Ryan, but Marguerite is

everywhere, in the shifting—shiftier still from the whiskey—moonlit shadows of Cathy's face above Ryan last night in her curtainless bedroom filled with those half-finished clay busts she's been working on. During his restless half-sleep in Cathy's bed, Ryan dreamed it was Marguerite, not Cathy, lying next to him. She turned to him and offered to donate her body to science. "You have to be dead," he told her. "No amputations, no Creutzfeldt-Jakob disease, no infectious diseases." Matter-of-factly, he ran down the list of whole-body donation program's rules, as Hyuen had for him. When he woke up to Cathy's snake-tattooed arm draped over his stomach, he panicked because she wasn't Marguerite, and then panicked because in his dream, she had been. He woke up out of his dream to heads with no faces, faces with no eyes, one misshapen ear, lips so thin they seemed to be disappearing. The half-busts of Cathy's looked the way Ryan felt, so when she explained the half-finished look was the point, part of her artistic concept, Ryan understood.

"Ryan?" Hyuen asks.

"You shouldn't be worried," Ryan says now, surprised once again by how easy it is to be with Hyuen. "I'm the one who should worry. I'm a wreck. But you know I always try to look pretty for you."

"No need, my friend. You're pretty on the inside." Hyuen gives him a fake sentimental look, bats those eyelashes, and continues to maneuver his way around the woman's body. The movement of his long arms as he massages her thigh suggests tubes and the draining of blood but more than this, he and the body are in on this together, meeting in this place where living ends and death begins, moving toward each other.

"You're too good to me," Ryan says. He says it sarcastically, but he means it. It's not just that Hyuen is his only friend in San Francisco. Watching Hyuen is, well, *blissful*. He's not sure how else to describe it. Except for a few pot-induced revelations about the larger order of the universe—that first time he got stoned down at the beach and became part of the beautiful-breasted teenage girl's pulse at the center of her palm—he has never experienced anything like watching Hyuen work.

"Why don't you water the plants?" Hyuen gives a quick nod toward the lush ferns in the corner, flourishing from the formaldehyde.

Ryan finds the tin watering can in the industrial sink and heads
for the plants he's dubbed the *ferns morbiditus*.

"It's freaking *Little Shop of Horrors* over here," Ryan says.

"Don't hurt their feelings," Hyuen says. "Just water them." He
squeezes water from a sponge to let the soap run off the girl's body,
and the water trickling onto the concrete floor sounds like rain.
Ryan hopes Hyuen knows how grateful he is to have something to
do, how grateful he is to Hyuen for being the first welcoming person since Ryan ended up in San Francisco after the band broke up.
After two weeks on the road, the drummer ran off with the little
money they had and, as they crossed the California border, Jim, the
lead singer, finally emerged from the sleeping bag. He'd cocooned
himself in the back of the van in order to make maximum use of
the supersonic weed Ryan had gotten from one of the farmer's sons
before they left Rhode Island. There were spots all over his face that
turned out to be chicken pox, the final humiliating straw.

It took Ryan a while to find this job as a long-term floater de-
livering mail within the hospital. He knew from the beginning he
was hardly cut out for a job that entrusted him with the MRIs,
CAT scans, and X-rays of children's brains ripe with encephalitis or
spina bifida or blossoming tumors. The blue files go to Dr. Cogen,
the yellow ones to Dr. Edwards; be sure to check the Medical Records in the U-126 box; send unsigned Op reports to M787 (with a
Post-it asking for doctor's signature); all correspondence to the
Neuro-Onc box in right-hand-corner mailbox; all copies of the cen-
sus and corrections of the Op reports to Evelyn; make sure to give
discharge summaries to the secretaries; refer any calls you happen
to answer from concerned parents to Joyce who knows how to
speak to them with "efficient, time-maximizing compassion."
Didn't they realize Ryan was a stoner who had lived at home until
the age of twenty-five?

On his first day on the job, he rolled the mail cart around the
hospital, lost in the maze of echoing hallways. When he rolled the
mail cart past the morgue, the door was slightly ajar. Pinned against

the wall, he watched as a tall man in a lab coat danced around the top of an old man's skull with hair wispy like cotton candy. Though the body was still, the dancing man, his arms in constant motion, made the body look alive, and finally, there it was, a flutter of pleasure after years of trying to discover an ecstasy of his own.

Who is the most ecstatic? There was a long history of failing to find the kind of happiness his father insisted on: pleading with his parents to buy him drums when he was nine and instead getting shipped off for lessons at Sweetest Sounds Music Center, which smelled like a dusty old attic, where the guy tried to teach him to read music when all he wanted was to make the kind of feedback sound Lou Reed made on Metal Machine Music; then his parents relenting when he was twelve and buying him a nylon string guitar that was a piece of shit with the action too high and too hard to play so instead pretending to still go for lessons at Sweetest Sounds and then walking for miles to a music store with posters of local bands in the window where a long-haired, tattooed guy (the kind of guy Ryan aspired to be) named Conrad allowed him to make deliveries in exchange for letting him play every guitar in the place; finally, finally, after proving he could actually play, getting an electric guitar and sitting in his room waiting to play it for the first time, but then playing it didn't seem like enough, he wanted to climb inside of it, wanted to *be* the guitar so he licked the strings, sweaty and metallic, and they rang in his mouth like a sound; finally, finally, finally, playing an out-of-tune chord, playing it for hours, a wall of sound filling the air of the too-quiet train-depot-turned-house (Where was his fucking, fucking train?), and if he'd known then what Hyuen told him about Alexander the Great and the honey running through his veins, that's how he would have described it, sweet and slow and mellow, disappearing like the music into the air, like Marguerite's voice outside his room whenever he practiced. Ryan, the only lyric to the song she sang to herself.

The first day Ryan watched Hyuen swaying over a body, a shell offered up to feed science, was so intimate, so unlike anything Ryan had ever seen. He finally understood, watching Hyuen's dance, what his father explained at the mandatory family dinner table as the thing that the people during the Paleolithic Age, freaking 20,000 to 8,000 B.C., were after when they came up with mythologies to do with flight—a desire for the magic of the sky, for something bigger than their feet treading over the earth. Watching Hyuen was like hearing Jimi Hendrix for the first time: *Music sweet music*. Even now, almost a month later, it's like watching music.

"What are you staring at?" Hyuen throws the cloth covering the girl's face at Ryan's head, and bacteria that smells like ripe earth rises from the dead girl's mouth.

"Fuck you," Ryan says, swatting the cloth to the concrete floor, more embarrassed than disgusted. "That's gross." He puts his face in the ferns until he is overwhelmed by formaldehyde.

"So, I'm going to talk to the curator today about getting you a job in the whole-body donation program. I heard her new secretary's not working out." He fills the girl-not-Marguerite's skull with water in order to float the eyes up for extraction.

"Thanks, man," Ryan says, and he keeps his face in the ferns because all of a sudden, he's on the verge of tearing up from Hyuen's kindness. This morning on the train, looking out the window at the hills of prosperous Victorian houses in Haight-Ashbury, he suddenly saw himself standing there. Actually it was a guy who looked like him—unkempt hair falling over his eyes, a little extra flesh, a sideways smile like he was about to do something that no one would like but some would admire—standing in a park but it felt as if Ryan was looking at himself. Ryan used to stand outside Marguerite's room in the train depot late at night and stare at his reflection in the window looking in. Marguerite asleep inside and Ryan would stare at himself and think, she trusts *that* person, she depends on *that* person. He was happy to be separate from his family then, not lonely at all because he had a purpose. But this morning on the bus, seeing this grownup version of himself standing in that park, he felt separate from *himself* and it freaked him out.

"'Since I have wounded you to death by love. Now reason is dead,'" his father said to Ryan the night Ryan left home. "From *The Mirror of Simple Souls*. Marguerite Porette," he said, as if Ryan gave a shit where his bullshit quote came from at that point. As if Ryan hadn't heard his father, his mother, and moments before, that very night, his sister quote from that book as if it explained something. That his father couldn't even be bothered to come up with his own words made Ryan more angry than the words themselves. How dare Bernard dress himself up as a parent and spy on them that night? Bernard claimed it didn't matter if he was spying. "Lucky thing I was," he said in a voice so patronizing it made Ryan want to punch him more than he ever wanted to punch him before, and there had been plenty of times he'd wanted to. *What happened to the sweet Ryan from before Marguerite was born?* became the refrain when he began to get into trouble. As if there was such a time as *before*. There were no stories from before Marguerite was born. They had started over with her. And then, *Ryan, would it kill you to read a book? Ryan, you've got to look beyond the moment. Ryan, don't you want to set a good example for your sister?* Had Bernard even noticed the way Ryan took care of Marguerite? That Marguerite cried every time Ryan even mentioned leaving? What the fuck did Bernard know about anything except those crazy girls from the Middle Ages who threw themselves into thorn bushes? And that was some fucked-up shit by the way, that Sam, when she was a teenager, had thrown herself into her own thorn bush, as a way of flirting with Bernard. Who was Bernard trying to impress with his fake father act anyway?

"Stand up and be the audience and I'll do my whole routine," Marguerite said that last night. This was before the rhythm guitar and the steady drumbeat, and then Mavis Staples's voice, heaving and pitching. *Are you sure your prayers haven't been answered? Think, brother, think.*

Ryan's head is still deep in the ferns, and he forces himself now to think of anything, anything else, to keep that last night in the train depot from returning: the time seven-year-old Marguerite stubbed her toe and asked him if it was okay to say *shit* in her mind and his saying, yeah, that's fine, you can say anything you want in your mind and her saying, good because I just said *shit* a lot in my mind.

"Hyuen." It comes out a little choked up and Ryan clears his throat. "I really appreciate you talking to the curator. Helping me out."

"No problem. But you've got to quit staring at me while I work. It's freaking me out," Hyuen says. He raises a thin elegant eyebrow as he arranges the girl's eyes in a plastic bag and puts them in the refrigerator. "Hey, lay off the plants."

Ryan looks into his palm where there are a few leaves torn from the most thriving fern.

The girl's eye sockets are sunken in her face and Ryan stares at her for too long. "Who loves me the most?" she asks. It's the whiskey from last night talking, and the nicotine patch he's been wearing. Since he's been trying to quit smoking pot, the double whammy of the nicotine from the patch and the nicotine from cigarettes is as close as he can get to feeling stoned, but clearly it has side effects.

"Nothing to do but wait a while," Hyuen says, pointing to the tubes, filling and draining the girl on the table at the same time. Embalming fluid in, blood out. He peels off his latex gloves and throws them in the sink. "I'll be right back."

Ryan looks the girl straight in her sunken eye sockets. The only way to deal with hangover hallucinations, Ryan has learned over the years, is to face them head-on. *Who loves you the most? Who loves you the most? You know it was me. I love you the most, I always have, and no one's argued with that since the day you were born and they brought you home from the hospital and I made a bed out of napkins in a shoe box beside my own for you. It was me who heard you crying in the middle of the night when our parents didn't (or wouldn't). Seven years old and I made you* my *baby. Sam still feels guilty about that night she screamed and told you if you didn't like it here on earth so much, you should go back. Who invited you anyway? she asked you. Bernard was horrified. Pull yourself together. Who's the most hysterical? Who's the most accusatory? Who's the most? Who's the most? Late at night, you were my child. I learned to warm the bottles of milk Sam left in the fridge, and they were only too glad that someone stepped in. I carried you around the house and sang those songs: Be careful of the souls in the soles of your shoes. Walk lightly, walk lightly. Don't squash them.*

So why'd you leave? the girl on the table asks.

That last night, Marguerite, dancing to Mavis Staples, pointed her finger at Ryan, then raised her hands skyward, the direction of prayers. *Are you sure your prayers haven't been answered? Think, sister, think.* She gestured to herself, then back to the sky, with an abandon uncharacteristic of eighteen-year-old girls and Ryan can admit it with a whole country between them, she was beautiful that night like the beautiful-breasted girl in the ocean, but was that so crazy?

"You're a husk," Ryan says to the girl on the table. She is a nameless girl, a dead girl.

"Talking to our friend?" Hyuen asks, slipping back into the room and into his lab coat that hangs on a coatrack next to the IV drip.

"To the plants," Ryan says.

"See? They're very friendly once you get to know them." Ryan appreciates the way Hyuen treats everything as if it was as normal as a corpse on a table. He's never asked Ryan any questions, but always makes him feel welcome as he performs the private, humble art of preparing bodies for dissection by the medical students.

"The Egyptian embalming god Anubis thought hearts were the seat of intelligence," Hyuen says. "That's who I was trying to remember the other day. He had the head of a jackal and scavenged graveyards harvesting hearts. The brains he considered useless and he'd pry them out with a hook and toss them aside."

Every move you make; every wiggle of your head; every wink of your eye. Marguerite's whole body gyrated, her head wiggled, she winked. Her body filled with the sound of the tambourine, Mavis Staples's voice, the guitar, the drums. This dance wasn't like her usual after-dinner dancing. There was something aggressive about it. Her body filled with the music until she was unable to contain it, until it seemed she might explode.

"What is that tool that pierces the heart?" Ryan asks Hyuen, trying to stamp out the images with words. He fingers a cigarette he's dipped in formaldehyde. The formaldehyde tip has a pleasant numbing effect on his lips and he wishes that he could smoke it with his brain.

"Trocar," Hyuen says.

With *trocar* written across her forehead, Marguerite jumps higher and higher, higher than she's ever jumped in Ryan's memory, reaching to the ceiling, up to some version of heaven. *Raise your voices high and the Lord will hear you.* Marguerite jumps still higher, her body ringing from the inside out, her head almost touching the ceiling. *Tried him in the morning. Tried him in the noonday.*

"I've got to get back to work and then I'm going to go grab a smoke," Ryan says. "I'll see you later."

"Don't bother donating that smoky body to science, my friend," Hyuen says, but Ryan is already out the door, feeling as lush and weepy as the formaldehyde ferns. He pushes his cart (emptied of the MRIs, CAT scans, X-rays, and Op reports signed and unsigned, the fate of children's brains hanging in the balance) down the hall, past the neighboring Pediatric Oncology unit, past the bulletin board with its notices for brown bag lunch lectures, past a woman crying silently into a pay phone. Near the bank of elevators at the end of the hall a huddle of hospital workers in green scrubs on their breaks smoke furiously out on the firescape.

Marguerite went down on her knees on the bed and Ryan saw the woman's face Marguerite's teenage face would one day become as she sang along with the same growly passion as Mavis Staples. *Tried him in the midnight hour!* And when she jumped off the bed, she collapsed in Ryan's arms. "Humble, then, your wisdom which is based in reason?" she asked. He's not sure it was a question, but there was a question in Marguerite's face. Shutting down the memory is, like so many things it turns out, an act of will.

Ryan leaves the mail cart in the elevator. He won't go back to work. Not today. He's not sure what he'll do. He's given up the religion of pot—the sweet ache has gotten less sweet, now it's just pure ache, not to mention it once convinced him he was a guitar player. Then one afternoon on the way across the country, before the chicken pox fiasco, he woke up in the van on the side of the road, viscously hung over but finally sober. He woke up to the sound of a a church choir in a broken-down bus practicing outside their window. The voices rose like a fountain, up and up from the earth and Ryan, his mouth like a whiskey and cigarette ashtray, realized that not only was he nothing like them, but he'd never be able to play like that, and all he'd achieved in the end was long hair and late nights.

When the elevator arrives on the ground floor, Ryan rushes out, then faster and faster down the brightly lit halls of the hospital, past doctors interpreting the X-rays he's delivered, past families waiting, past people with a purpose even if it was waiting for someone to die so they could mourn him. Ryan wishes that Anubis would come along and pry his brain from his skull with a hook. He imagines a hook like the one used in vaudeville routines: get this brain off the stage.

Back on the train headed for his apartment reeking of dead fruit and swarming with fruit flies, Ryan is afraid to look out the window for fear he'll see himself out there again, watching himself go by. Still, he tests himself as the train makes a stop just before his own in the Mission. A quick glimpse, but instead of himself, he sees another beast, a cat run over by the train and tossed to the side of the tracks and there goes his brain, back and back (where was Anubis when he needed him?) to the dead barn cat and its splattered brains.

Eight-year-old Marguerite ran to him, calling his name the way they'd called each other—always in threes—since she almost fell off the pier: Ryan, Ryan, Ryan! The farmer's son and his younger brother called Seedsucker with his handful of sucked-clean sunflower seeds, took off across the field, having gotten Ryan really high behind the shed. Marguerite clutched a fistful of the eggs and butter flowers picked from the field where she went every day to visit her favorite cow, the one she claimed followed her around, although Ryan never actually saw it. She held the flowers to his chin to see if his chin shone yellow (it did), which meant he was good or bad or loved someone, Marguerite couldn't remember which. And then she stepped on a bee and Ryan picked her up and carried her on his back, twirling her around to distract her from crying before he could get her back to the house and dress the sting with baking soda.

One of Marguerite's flip-flops flew off, her legs sticking straight out and she tilted her head back, forgetting about the bee sting as Ryan hoped she would, her long, dark, straight hair flying behind her as they headed for the train depot. And suddenly, right there in the driveway in front of them on the hot black asphalt, head smashed open, gray brain leaking out, the barn cat who had wandered in and out of their lives for years, wandering over from the farm next door because Marguerite insisted on giving it a bowl of milk. "Don't do it," Ryan warned her because he was worried about bringing something into her life that might die and break her heart, but then he relented because she was his little girl after all, and helped her to get the bowl down from the too-high kitchen cabinet.

"I thought cats landed on all fours," Marguerite said, and Ryan shivered. For a second there, for the first time ever, he forgot she was on his back. He forgot Marguerite was there. Even when he let go of her hand and let her fall off the pier, he knew she was there.

"What kind of dumb cat is this?" Marguerite kicked her legs into Ryan's sides, furious.

Ryan was entranced, hypnotized with revulsion and fascination by the cat's brain on the pavement, that secret thing right there in front of them. Marguerite kicked him again. "Hey, I know it's sad, but don't kick me. I'm not your horse," Ryan said. He'd been thinking a lot lately about how you live all your life in your body but you never really get acquainted with your organs and how strange that was and here was the most secret organ of all, spilled out on the asphalt for them to see. Ryan wondered what it would be like to hold his own brain in his hands. What if he could have a conversation with it as he held it?

"I don't believe it's dead," Marguerite said.

Ryan pinched himself in an effort to become less stoned. "I think you're right," he said. "That cat is definitely not dead. Let's leave it alone to come back to life." He spun them both around and with Marguerite clinging to his neck he cantered like a horse toward the house where her rage turned to guilt.

"I knew I should have protected it better," she said. "What if it was really hurt when it died?"

Ryan tried to distract her with his favorite Dylan song, which had become her favorite Dylan song, "Positively Fourth Street," changing the words as he took her inside and caked her bee sting with baking soda. *Marguerite comes bee-sting foot/Face full of black soot/Talking that the dead cat/Is alive, imagine that.*

"Sing the cat back to life!" Marguerite shouted so loud that Bernard and Sam in their respective studies heard her and stomped their feet on the floor. Keep it down! Keep it down! *Don't disturb us while we work.*

"Where's my train already?" Marguerite shouted back.

The amazing thing was, until his parents started their stamping, Ryan had forgotten for a moment that *they* existed.

"Dude, wake up," says a teenage girl with jeans slung so low that Ryan can see the bones of her hip as he scrambles past her in order not to miss his stop. The girl smells like pot and cinnamon gum and Ryan wonders whether sticking to the three weeks-one-day-ten-hours-and-twelve-minute-but-who-was-counting?-long boycott was such a great idea after all. He barely squeezes through the train door as its rubber stoppers jam against his sides. He jogs home, down a hill, through a park where nouveau hippy kids play footbag, then up the familiar hill so steep that by the time he's reached his front door out of breath, he's decided to reward himself with some of Bat's stash.

Bat isn't home, a good sign, and the pumpkin is gone too, an even better sign. The cement block sits exposed on the chair and only a few stragglers from the swarm of fruit flies remain. The signs are everywhere: smoke, smoke, smoke. On his way to Bat's allegedly secret stash under the kitchen sink, Ryan hits the blinking message button on the answering machine.

"So," Cathy's voice says with such studied casualness it pains Ryan. "If the L.A. cemetery tour is not of interest, how about another fuck?" Ryan imagines her spending hours crafting the perfect message and doesn't even hate himself as he begins to figure out

how to avoid ever seeing her again. For once, he's glad he can't afford a cell phone—he's less accountable. Anubis would be welcome
to his heart as well, although he might find it even more useless than
his brain.

He's groping around underneath the sink, finding only damp
spiderwebs and something that feels like recently discarded chewing gum, when a guy who sounds like he might have smoked the
rest of Bat's stash leaves a message for Bat about a "mind-blowing"
art opening tonight in a "mind-blowing" gallery, so if Bat wanted to
"get blown, dude, dumb joke, right?" he better show up. And then
two hangups in a row, the second one a little bit more delayed. It
sounds like monks are chanting in the background.

Ryan pulls his hand sticky with cobwebs out from under the sink
just as there's a third hangup on the machine, this one even more delayed than the last. In the background, he hears, "I'll smoke you
where you stand! then "You just try it, and I'll send all the trains in
the world to run you down!" The wail of a siren. Ryan checks the
caller ID: Queens, New York. He scrolls through the other caller ID
numbers and the hangups are from the train depot—Marguerite and
Marguerite, Ryan assumes. Sam and Bernard never call. It has to be
Margue who has been leaving messages, including a strange one yesterday, something about "life and death inside me" which Ryan
guessed was a lyric from something he wasn't able to remember because he'd smoked too much pot in his life, which was why he gave it
up in the first place. He hated not returning her calls, but the day he
landed in San Francisco he found himself standing in front of an
open refrigerator, stoned and eating capers out of a jar, and all of a
sudden he caught a glimpse of his reflection in the window and he
swore he would change his life. That vow included a little less Marguerite, at least for now. This was not his problem now. He's trying
to be his own person, trying to make his life work in a different way,
trying to turn over a whole new leaf, his very own new leaf.

When the phone rings, the train depot number flashes on the
caller ID box and Ryan picks it up immediately. What whole new
leaf? What was all this leaf bullshit? Who needed new leaves? He's
kept his distance from his sister long enough.

"Margue?"

"This is Thompson, the carpenter," Thompson says. "You don't know me."

"Who?"

"The carpenter," Thompson says. Thompson hasn't practiced what happens after he says his own name.

"What carpenter?"

"Your mother hired me?"

"Oh, Jesus."

"To redo the bathroom? Thompson?" Thompson says again.

"Where is my sister?" Ryan should never have left her alone in that house. He'll get on a bus. His first paycheck at the hospital went to rent and he has no money, but he can afford the bus. He'll get on a bus and go to Rhode Island.

"This is Thompson," Thompson says again.

"You mentioned that," Ryan says, frantically searching for Bat's stash, slamming drawers, opening the refrigerator. Nothing is making any sense anymore. All Ryan knows is he needs to get stoned and fast. He turns on the stove.

"It's your mother."

"What?" Ryan turns the stove off.

"She's dead," he says. "There was a blood berry sac, a subarachnoid hemorrhage."

Sam's leaning into the perpetually stuck window in the train depot's living room/dining room. If I ever get this thing open, I'm going to throw myself out. Is this my life? Are you my wife? Bernard wearing the lobster-claw pot holders. They were both mad at Ryan for something—skipping school, smoking cigarettes with the farmer's son, playing his guitar when they told him not to—and he wished his mother would throw herself out the window.

"Where the fuck is my sister?" It seems easier to move on to the next question than to respond. Better to find Bat's stash before he allows himself a thought. It's as if his entire head has been dipped in formaldehyde.

"I don't know," Thompson says. "Gone. I can't find her. I've looked and looked."

"Where is my father?" Better to keep asking questions, question after question, until he can find what he's looking for, until he can tranquilize his mind.

There is silence on the other end of the line. "It's a longer story. He's gone too. He took off and hasn't come back. It's a much longer story."

"Longer story? Were you fucking my mother?" Keep asking questions, no matter which questions, just keep asking. The longer story can mean only one thing—it doesn't matter, ask anyway.

"I loved your mother with the ear of my heart." Thompson's voice cracks on the word *ear*.

Ryan hangs up and then he hangs up again and again and again until the sound of hanging up fills his mind. He looks out the window to see his neighbor, one of the nouveau hippy footbag players, tripping out the back door to fire up a grill. Thompson loved his mother with the ear of his what? And how could this guy next door be getting ready for dinner, wearing his droopy cargo pants, as if nothing has happened? How is it possible that Ryan is in his kitchen finding out that his entire family has disappeared and this guy is walking out of his apartment with nothing on his mind but what to have for dinner? Ryan bangs on the window and when the cargo pant–wearing footbag player turns, Ryan gives him the finger. "Fuck you," he shouts, and the cargo pant–wearing footbag player gives him the peace sign and grins.

Ryan meant to put some distance between himself and his crazy family; he didn't mean for everyone to disappear. He was the one who was supposed to move; they were supposed to stay still. They were supposed to remain the fixed point around which he orbited.

Bat's stash turns out to be in a kitchen drawer Ryan has never opened before, filled with screwdrivers, rubber bands, expired coupons for oil changes (though as far as Ryan knows neither Bat or any of Bat's former roommates has ever owned a car), receipts, and several thumbtacks, one of which sticks into Ryan's palm. He leaves it there as he finds his one-hitter under Bat's bed (he asked Bat to hide it from him and then watched him do it) and takes a long toke.

The grinning cargo pant–wearing footbag player next door

tends the coals, but he still looks around. Yes, you should look around, Ryan thinks. You fucker. Look around, be wary. Ryan decides then that he isn't going home to stand outside the train depot to look in on a family that isn't even there anymore. He is through with that. That version of himself is over.

His mother is over. His mother is over. His mother is over. The sentence runs through his head like a little man with a hammer, smashing any feeling. Smash, smash, smash. If she wasn't even going to be there to ignore him while she pretended to take care of his sister, if all that was there to see was the nothingness, then he didn't want it. It's not even that he doesn't love his mother; it's just that she's done. His mother is over. His mother is over. His mother is over. He's grateful to the little man and his little hammer. He exhales a stream of delicious skunky pot smoke and walks through it, letting it surround his head, letting it be everything for a second. He pushes the thumb tack a little farther into his palm so that it will stay there. The main thing now was to find Marguerite.

He turns on the TV with the hand that doesn't have the tack in it and there's a news story about the discovery of 160,000-year-old fossilized skulls buried under volcanic ash near the village of Herto in Ethiopia, and as he takes another long toke, he imagines his own brow ridge and cranial vault as stark as the Ethiopian skulls crumbling to dust in the desert. Marguerite recently left a message on his answering machine saying that as she sat in her English class, her teacher's flesh fell from her skull. Ryan exhales and steps into the fog of sweet smoke again, and then he's got it, the hangup from Queens, New York. Margue is in Queens, and he's back to the bus idea.

He pulls the tack out of his palm slowly, amazed at how little blood there is, just a pinpoint hole and a small dot and he thinks about the berry sac in his mother's brain hiding out there for all those years and wonders whether it's hereditary and whether there's a blood sac about to burst in his brain right now. He takes another tack out of the drawer and sticks this one in a little deeper in order to focus, focus. Then he begins to clean out this drawer he's never opened until tonight because there's change in the bottom of it, quarters, dimes, and nickels. Bus fare.

The talking head on the TV says that anthropologists have discovered ancient Ethiopian skulls severed from their bodies, that the heads may have been removed from their bodies as part of an ancient mortuary practice and Ryan thinks of the sloping shape of Margue's head (he used to roll an egg off it and let it crack on the ground to make her laugh) and he realizes the person he most wants to talk to right now is Hyuen. He pulls the second tack out of his palm slowly, the dot of red blooming and rising to the surface, in order to dial the phone. Focus, focus.

Not only does he not know Hyuen's number at work, he doesn't know Hyuen's last name. Up until now, their friendship hasn't required phone numbers, or last names. He calls hospital information and a woman whose voice sounds as if it's coming through a tunnel answers. "Yes?" she says again, and there's an echo: Yes? Yes?

"Oh, Jesus," Ryan says, staring at the pumpkin-smelling cement, the so-called negative space, sitting on the chair in the corner of the living room. He begins to feel that gray, that grainy and useless.

"Don't Jesus me," the woman's voice says through the tunnel. Jesus. Jesus.

"Hyuen," Ryan says. "I don't know his last name."

"Look, we've got three Hyuens." Hyuens. Hyuens. "Which one do you want?" Want. Want.

"Hyuen the morgue technician," Ryan says, considering putting another tack in his palm.

"Why didn't you just say so?" So? So? and the operator puts the call through.

"Hey, what's up?" Hyuen's voice is such a relief on the end of the line that Ryan closes his eyes and considers taking a nap. Though they have never spoken on the phone. Hyuen doesn't sound surprised that Ryan is calling him.

"Do you know about these 160,000-year-old fossilized skulls severed from their bodies as part of some ancient mortuary practice?"

"Nope," Hyuen says.

"It's very Anubis-y," Ryan says. He turns on the faucet in the sink and then turns it off again.

"What's going on, Ryan? Stop fiddling with the sink."

"My sister ran away," Ryan says. He's already decided he'll skip the part about his mother dropping dead. He wills it into the past for now. "I kind of raised her. She hasn't been doing very well since I left. She once heard birds flying around the house. She thought she was a neuron for a day or two. Then this guy in my band set up a gig for us through a friend in Ohio and another one in Arizona, and it seemed like a good enough reason to go on tour because my father was mad at me, but that's another story. It was better than lying in the dark feeling bad about myself, worrying about Marguerite, so I left her there." He's not sure he's making sense. He's not even sure he's speaking in full sentences anymore. Was he even speaking English?

When Marguerite was fourteen, Ryan found someone to cover the last part of his shift at Playland and took her to see *The Last Waltz*. That night, he taught her that "Stage Fright" was about Bob Dylan, and pointed out Neil Young's cocaine booger, but all Margue could talk about when they left was Robbie Robertson's eyes. "They're like he just woke up," she said. "Like yours," she said to Ryan. He denied it but he loved it. It was as though she knew what he had been waiting for all of his life and then said it. He wanted to be Robbie Robertson more than anything on nights he was playing with I'd Rather Drink Bleach in some Providence nightclub, never the headliner, always the band people drank their way through to get to the band they really wanted to see. Squeezed into a back room, the walls plastered with stickers of bands, crammed in there with amps and guitar cases, Jim the lead singer always pitching some last-minute fit about the order of songs or Ryan's guitar playing drowning out his vocals and then insisting like the diva he was that he have a moment to himself before they went on. Finally, climbing blind into the harsh stage lights, up rickety wooden stairs while the band before them scrambled offstage, inevitably leaving behind guitar cables so they had to jump back onstage in the middle of a set. The sound guy turning off the music so that they stood there like idiots tuning up in silence and Sarge the drummer putting his

beer without fail on the corner of an amp and spilling it so Jim
pitched another fit while Ryan distracted himself by reading the set
list of the band before them taped to the floor: Killing Me Harshly,
Amnesiacattack, The United States of Go Fuck Yourself. But then,
one two three four, Sarge counted off, and suddenly they were inside the music and Ryan would always imagine himself as Robbie
Robertson, his eyelids growing heavier and Robbie's slouch stretching Ryan's body longer, leaner. Always, he imagined Margue watching him because it was her watching him that transformed him.
Where the fuck was his sister?

"Hyuen?"

"Yes." Hyuen's voice calms Ryan's turbulent organs. It removes
Ryan's spleen, his kidneys, his lungs, washes them gently, puts them
back clean.

"Would you come with me on the bus to find Marguerite? She's
in Queens, I think. I can't go alone," Ryan finishes. His newly
rinsed organs feel raw, exposed.

"I can't take a bus," Hyuen says, and Ryan thinks that his next
step will be to take the concrete negative space left from the rotting
pumpkin and smash it over his head. He considers putting all of the
tacks into his palm at once.

"I can't take that much time off work," Hyuen is saying. "but
look, I've got so many frequent-flyer miles from my parents flying
me over to Thailand so that I can get in touch with my true self that
you and I could fly to Queens."

Ryan sits down on the couch and closes his eyes. Attention is the
natural prayer of the soul, Bernard said to him once, quoting Paul
Celan quoting Malebranche. Ryan's not sure what Bernard was really trying to say to him, but this line returns to him, makes sense
finally in this context. Hyuen's attention is like a prayer, the way,
one night after mandatory family dinner, just before Ryan left,
Margue not only danced her after-dinner dance of the whirling
arms and gyrating hips, but sang along to the Rolling Stones song.
Relax your Mind. She sang right into Ryan's Robbie Robertson's
eyes. *Just want to. . .* Her attention was like a prayer too. *See his face*.

"Hyuen, man," Ryan says. "I don't know how . . ."

"I'll be over after work." Once again, Hyuen steps in to save Ryan from being too grateful in a way that might embarrass them both. "We'll take the red-eye."

"Two brothers and their nephew in eighteenth-century France discovered this particular embalming method," Hyuen says as the plane hurtles down the runway. "More aesthetically pleasing, preservative ingredients: lavender, chamomile, and vermilion injected into the femoral artery. But a Dutch guy in the seventeenth century, Frederick Ruysch, was the first one to think of injecting preservative solutions into blood vessels."

Ryan has his eyes closed, listening intently not so much to the words but to the steady rhythm of Hyuen's voice. After Hyuen convinced the man sitting in the middle seat to move over one so Hyuen and Ryan could sit side by side—"Not near the window, not near the window," Ryan said, suddenly frantic—Ryan told Hyuen the thing he'd been too stoned to say on the phone. He's deathly afraid of flying, always has been. As soon as the seat belt sign was turned on, Hyuen began reciting embalming facts. Ryan focuses so intently on the cadence of each word as Hyuen speaks it that the sentences they belong to don't make sense, but it doesn't matter.

As the plane takes off, "Formaldehyde, discovered 1867." As they begin their ascent, "During the Civil War to preserve the bodies of dead soldiers so they could send them home. They rode dead, embalmed Lincoln approximately seventeen hundred miles on a train, touring the country, stopping in each town. Seven million people had seen his body by the time the train reached Springfield—a one-corpse rolling advertisement for embalming."

The plane reaches cruising altitude and stops climbing into the sky like a rocket. The seat belt light goes off.

"You okay?" Hyuen asks. "They're going to show the movie soon."

"Fuck the movie," Ryan says.

"Egyptians embalmed cats and other sacred animals. Let's see, Juan Perón asked an anatomy professor to preserve Evita with layers of plastic and wax for one hundred thousand dollars so he could bring her with him as he traveled. She followed him, stuffed, into exile and allegedly sat at the dining room table with him and his wives after her."

"And?"

"You want more? I got more. Vladimir Lenin, 1924, big debate by Soviet officials over how best to preserve the body."

As the plane shudders through the air, Ryan fights to keep Evita Perón's and Lenin's bodies from becoming his mother dead on the kitchen floor, the mystery in her brain exploded. She called a week ago to tell Ryan that Marguerite wasn't doing well, that he should come home, and somehow ended up telling him that Bernard was spending most of the time in his study researching some teenage girl with stigmata. Ryan was feeling particularly mean and told her her marriage would end in perfect flameout fashion, like the Sex Pistols. In his best Johnny Rotten voice, he asked her "Do you ever feel like you've been cheated?" Of course she hadn't recognized the quote. "No," she said earnestly. "Do you, Ryan? I'm worried you do." He laughed at her.

"While they were fighting," Hyuen continues, "a committee got together and put Lenin in a refrigerator. They didn't realize that freezing accelerates the decomposition process. Big mistake."

Ryan lets Hyuen's words fill his head as he keeps up the mantra: *Margrrite, Margrrite, Margrrite*, calling his sister back from wherever she's gone.

Learning to Shudder

Marguerite slip-slided in her socks down the hall on her way to her brother's room after mandatory family dinner, after Ryan and her father fought over what Ryan was doing with his life. It was the end of the summer and Bernard insisted that, come fall, it was time for Ryan to stop behaving as if every season was summer. "Marguerite's going back to school. Your mother has her writing. I'm going back to school." Bernard paused. "Playland isn't a place you want to be forever. Consider the name: *Play*land."

"Bernard," Sam said sharply.

Even so, Ryan had told them both to go fuck themselves. As a result, there was no dancing after dinner, but Marguerite still wanted to hear Ryan's music. If he played her some music, she felt sure he would feel better. Maybe she would tell him he looked like Robbie Robertson.

"Marguerite, shoes on," Sam called from the dining room.

"Why does she care so fucking much about your socks? Shouldn't that train of mine be here by now?" Ryan said, sticking his head out of his bedroom door. He wore the same MC5 tee shirt he wore last night and the night before and the same soft tattered jeans with the late night smoky bar smell. He gestured with his hands and his sleepy eyes: Come quick, before the parents see you. "Hours! Months! I've been waiting for this train for years." His mouth was wide open, pretending to shout but whispering instead.

Marguerite laughed and slid inside, pitching herself onto Ryan's bed so she landed on her stomach.

Who loved Marguerite the most? Marguerite knew it was Ryan. She loved to hear the stories of how he walked her to sleep when he was a child and she was a baby. How he made a bed of napkins to put near his own bed for her when she was just born and home from the hospital. Lately, Ryan doesn't like to tell those stories, and so Marguerite finds herself going in search of him. Down the dirt road, where the fog rolled up from the ocean in the morning and threatened to swallow them all, dogs barked anonymously.

Back in the dining room, Sam read aloud from that book about monks, saved from the fire that killed Marguerite's grandparents before she ever got a chance to meet them. Something about the shepherd bearing the blame wherever the father of the household finds that the sheep have yielded no profit.

"Please," Bernard said. "No more shepherd talk tonight."

"I've only just got started with the shepherds," Sam said. "This is only the beginning of these shepherds and their sheep!"

"Play 'Blackbird,'" Marguerite said to her brother.

"Again? Aren't you tired of that song?" Ryan said, the miraculous tip of his nose bobbing only for her, but he smiled in a way that told Marguerite she'd said the right thing, that she was making up for Bernard's behavior at the dinner table. "I mean it's beautiful, but Jesus."

"Please, no more Jesus talk tonight," Marguerite said, imitating her father.

"You can say that again," Ryan said. He opened his guitar case and sat down on his bed.

"Please no more Jesus talk tonight," Marguerite said again. Ryan held his guitar over his head, as if he was going to clock her, and Marguerite poured herself off the bed and onto the floor at his feet. She closed her eyes as he played a few random notes, tuning up.

She listened to the random notes and tried not to dread the

beginning of school. She was shy around everyone except Ryan, and when she was at school she often found herself hiding in the bathroom between classes or pretending to read a book at lunch. Or imagining a year or two from now when she and Ryan might live together on their own. They would be a family. They would find a house away from their parents and their arguments about God, maybe one down by the beach and they could make pies out of rose hips and go swimming in the ocean whenever they wanted. Every night, after they'd eaten their rose hip pie, Ryan would play "Blackbird." It was silly, something she would never, ever tell Ryan.

Blackbird, singing in the dead of night.

Ryan stopped and put his guitar pick in his mouth so he could tuck a strand of his floppy hair behind his ear. "Paul McCartney wrote this about the Civil Rights movement."

"That was really interesting the first five hundred thousand times you told me. Sing!"

Ryan rolled his heavy-lidded eyes, which Marguerite tonight thought looked especially like Robbie Robertson's, but suddenly she was too shy to say so. "All right already," Ryan says now. "I'm singing. I'm singing."

Take these sunken eyes and learn to see. All your life. You were only waiting for this moment to be free. Ryan singing these words always carved out an ache inside of Marguerite, the one she felt when her father read her the fairy tale all those years ago about the boy who wanted to learn how to shudder.

As the melody tattooed her heart, Marguerite imagined the tattoo to be the shape of a blackbird. And then, in the dark of her mind, darker than any night, she heard them. The same chop, chop of the V of birds that Ryan matched with his thumb and forefinger the day she fell, but louder and getting louder by the second. The sound of them flying with broken wings was the whooshing sound of her mother shaking out a blanket in the yard. Whoosh, whoosh. The blackbirds, a whole flock of them, were passing through every room in the house, taking a tour. Into the dining room where Sam and Bernard were having their after-dinner drink and arguing over shepherds, but they didn't notice them because the birds were there for Marguerite. They came for her. Her blood whispered for the first time that night, though she couldn't yet make out the words. Swish-swish. Her blood's whisper called to the birds, calling them to her, a girl with life and death inside her.

When they whoosh, whooshed into Ryan's bedroom Marguerite kept her eyes shut because she didn't want to scare them away. The electricity in her wrinkled gray brain sang along: *Blackbird, fly. Into the light of the dark black night.* And the light of the dark black night made perfect sense the way it always did with Ryan, lying like this with her eyes closed on the floor of his room while he played this song over and over and over. She hovered on the edge of the world, imagining the song now as the music to the last waltz if the last waltz was a real dance. She hovered somewhere between life and death, life and death inside her at once, inside the song, deep into the light of the dark black night.

A Light Which Flashes on the Soul

Bernard lay on his back beside the captain's desk in a tee shirt and underwear. He had taken to spending nights in his study now, believing at first what he told Sam, that the carpenter working day in and day out on the bathroom was akin to having his head bulldozed.

"He's almost done," Sam insisted, but she didn't say it in a way that indicated she cared very much whether Bernard stayed in their bedroom or not. He wondered whether she would even notice if he stopped pretending to go to class. He was beginning to wonder whether she noticed him at all. Sam didn't even look up when he said he was going to sleep in the study, so he just went to the linen closet. The early September nights were still hot, so a single sheet and a pillow was really all he needed. It was better this way, he convinced himself, lying there at eleven o'clock, still not dressed, staring at the fragments copied from the dusty rose manuscript above him on the wall. One seemed to be missing, perhaps it fell? He wasn't sure. He turned his head and looked underneath the desk, but there was nothing there but frightening balls of dust the size of tumbleweed. He turned his head in the other direction and there was the pile of dusty, abandoned books on the sagging bookshelf—young women from the Middle Ages throwing themselves into rosebushes, eating their own scabs, beside themselves with a kind of agony for God. For so long, Bernard had wanted some approximation of God to make him feel something as endless and enormous as Sam's lifesaving beautiful view of the fields and fields and fields and the sliver of ocean.

Sam was reading *The Rule of Saint Benedict* again. In the interest of keeping a version of the peace, Bernard didn't tell her what he thought: her interest in the book had more to do with it as an object that survived her parents than anything else. Who was he to say that anyway? Maybe it didn't matter how she'd become interested in it again. Didn't William James say that "religious love is only man's natural emotion of love directed to a religious object"? That religious awe was related, possibly even the same thing, as the thrill we feel, for instance, looking at the lifesaving view? What bothered him so much about Sam's interest in St. Benedict anyway? Was it that the object of her religious love wasn't him anymore?

He looked at his stomach spilling over his underwear; even while he was lying flat on the ground, it pushed at his waistband. There was a long wild hair just above his left nipple and the hair on his head was unruly and thinning. His wandering eye had started to look just plain crazy, without the intrigue. Even if this was the midlife crisis Sam said he was having, did knowing he was having it make any difference? He tugged at the wild hair around his nipple, but it apparently had deeper roots and he succeeded only in making the skin around it pucker and turn red.

The old fan he brought in here sputtered now and then kicked in, whoosh-whooshing all of a sudden, and then sputtered again. It seemed always to be on the verge of dying. When it sputtered, it made a sound like the static of the baby monitor his father had used in the house when his mother was dying. His father was a good Catholic, ashamed and confused by his son's atheistic leanings, particularly in the moment of his mother's death when faith was all that was left—how else was his father to bear his wife's death? He and his father would wander the house listening to his mother's breathing through the monitor. They listened to every variety of it, snoring, wheezing, rattling, and, every once in a while, suddenly, there would be nothing, and he and his father would stop whatever they were doing and listen as hard as they could as if the intensity of their listening might bring the breath back and, often, it did.

One night, he and his father sat on the edge of his mother's bed in the dark. The moon outside was a single bulb in a lonely room, and his father asked his mother if she needed to go to the bathroom, wanted an extra blanket. Was she hot? Was she cold? Did she want some yogurt? "No thanks," she said matter-of-factly. "I'm going home."

Later that night, Bernard had heard his father singing Dvořák's "Going Home" quietly to himself in the kitchen. And later still, years later, one late night in the bed he no longer slept in with Sam, unable to sleep, he watched a movie in which the asylum inmates, led by Olivia de Havilland, sang the same song. Once again someone, this time Sam instead of his daughter, turned to him and asked him if he was crying and he said, no, no, no and got up to go to the bathroom to cry privately.

Was that a tear slipping sideways down his face now? He was really falling apart. He felt like a stranger in his own home, that's what it was. His son gone, stowed away in the back of a dirty van, now wheeling a mail cart around a hospital (or so Sam told him— the few times Ryan called, he didn't ask to speak to Bernard). His wife conferring with the hippy carpenter or holed up with their daughter in the bathroom. Were they both starting to look somewhat pruny or was it his imagination? Bernard felt as if he wasn't in his own home, as if he was waiting to go home, as if he'd wandered far, far away from any version of home. Maybe Sam was right, he *was* a fugueur, but he was worse than a fugueur because he hadn't even wandered anywhere and he was still lost.

He stood up and ran his hand over the sagging back of his underwear. He pulled his pants on and fastened his belt, clanking at his waist. Rather than risk looking in the mirror, he licked his fingers and smoothed his hair down. He kicked the sheet into a corner by a stack of papers he no longer recognized, and went over to read the fragments he'd copied from the dusty rose manuscript. Louise was the one person these days who made him feel as though he was arriving somewhere new, a place he had begun to recognize.

The crash and bang of the carpenter threatened to undo him, but Bernard persevered. He leaned against the wall and leaned right into Fragment number one, the paper rubbed soft by other days of leaning in and laying his palm against it. One day, Canon Hallez, the president of the Episcopal Seminary of Tournay, was commissioned to interrogate Louise on the subject of her ecstasies. "It fills me," she answered, "with such a lively sense of the presence of God, that, from the contemplation of his greatness of my own littleness, I feel at a loss whither to turn that I may hide myself." The fan sputtered, whooshwhooshed, and out the window, the farmer's son on his tractor waved at someone else standing in another room of the train depot. Bernard looked down and noticed an unfamiliar stain on his tee shirt.

Bernard's own littleness was huge. But this was where Louise helped Bernard. She reveled in her own littleness, believed in it even as it was tested and tested again. She rose above and above. She was her own person, at eighteen! Like Sam had been, Bernard realized, but even as he realized that he was, in part, searching for a substitute, some other part of him understood simultaneously that you could know too much about yourself, that being aware of your mistakes sometimes didn't make you stop committing them. This part of his mind often wrestled the aware part to the ground, pinned it, and knocked it out.

Fragment number two, its surface also rubbed soft by the oil from Bernard's eager palms pressed against it:

> Dr. Lefebvre endeavored in a variety of ways to produce such reflex motions in the ecstatica; he irritated with a feather the most sensitive of the mucous membranes, those of the nostrils and of the ear; he also applied liquid ammonia to the nostrils, but Louise remained as motionless as a corpse. He also pricked her face and hands with sharp needles, he gathered up a fold of the skin of her arm and pierced it with a stout pin, in doing which

he was obliged to work the pin about in order to drive it
through. But, under all these tests, not a muscle moved,
nor was the slightest trace of sensibility to be observed.
Another time he drove the point of a penknife into her
flesh, deep enough to draw blood. Sometimes, standing
behind Louise in order to apply the tests, so that they
should be altogether unexpected, he suddenly drove a
penknife into the flesh at the back of her neck.

Bernard felt his ears once again grow hot with fury at Dr. Lefebvre. He would never have treated Louise this way; he would have
understood that her natural emotion of love was merely searching for
an object. He would have understood that she was experiencing her
own littleness and it was huge. Sputter, sputter, the fan died, but
Bernard didn't even notice the stillness of the air. He didn't see the
cows gathering near the fence closest to his office window. It was as if
they were watching him. It was as if they were waiting for him to do
something miraculous.

His ears still burning red, Bernard allowed himself his recent
daily indulgence, fantasizing that he and Louise were bound by
blood, that her blood, simmering with a desire to be plunged into a
sea of light, ran through his veins. Through some wild accident of
ancestry, Bernard was a cousin removed many, many times, but a
cousin nonetheless, a man who understood what it was like for her
as she withstood the scrutiny of the Dr. Lefebvres of the world.

Bernard lay his palm on Fragment number three too, as if he
was absorbing the Louiseness of it.

Louise's father was a man of robust and vigorous constitution; he died, at the age of twenty-eight, of a disease
which had suddenly broken out in the neighborhood. He
had never suffered from any description of nervous afflic-
tion or of hemorrhage. He was a man of quiet disposition

and good character. His mental capacity was of an average type; he had received but a poor education.

Her mother, also, is a person of robust constitution; with the exception of a prolonged illness which followed Louise's birth, and a subsequent attack of inflammation (pleuro-pneumonia), she has been singularly free from sickness. She is of somewhat bilious temperament . . .

Directly outside his study, he heard Sam talking with the carpenter. Bernard felt sure that she had chosen her location expressly to annoy him.

"The bath," she said, "and I'm quoting, 'approximates the physiologic steps between the production and onset of normal fatigue and sleep.'"

"So it's gradual?" the hippy carpenter asked.

"Exactly!" Sam exclaimed and her delight was like a thorn in Bernard's side. "Gradual rather than 'rapid and hypnotic,' it says here in the article by Edward Strecker. Exactly!"

Though the voices were right outside his study, still, the knock on Bernard's door startled him and he jumped away from the wall, ran around the captain's desk and was pretending to rearrange some of the dusty, abandoned books on his bookshelf when Sam walked in without waiting for an invitation.

"I have something I want to show you," she said.

Bernard pulled at the bottom of his stained tee shirt, suddenly self-conscious in front of his wife, and then feigned disinterest, holding a book up to his face. In the midst of his effort to look as though he was deep in thought, there was a spasm in his eyebrow.

"Reading upside down these days?" Sam asked.

"I've written a note to myself upside down in the margin," Bernard said, putting the book down. "Can I help you?"

When he turned, he saw just how awful Sam looked. The puffy circles under her eyes made her look as old as he did. "You look awful," he said, and he was genuinely surprised when instead of looking grateful for noticing, she gave him the finger.

"If Marguerite wasn't asleep, I'd bother yelling at you. Just follow me," Sam said. She swivelled on her heels and headed for her own study across the hall.

"Do you need another bulletin board?" he asked when he saw the walls of her study, which had become even thicker with paper and thumbtacks. .

"You're one to talk," Sam said. "Read this." She pointed to a page torn from a book with the tiniest print Bernard had ever seen. He put on his glasses and made a big production of squinting and pursing his lips. His eyebrow spasmed again as he read the highlighted section.

> The hypothesis that manic-depressive illness is transmitted through a gene on the X chromosome was first proposed by Rosanoff and associates (1935) over fifty years ago. Two decades ago, Winokur and colleagues (1969) reported the first evidence for X linkage using genetic marker data as well as family study results. In their family study data, the morbid risk for female first-degree relatives of bipolar probands was greater than that for male first-degree relatives, and male to male transmission was not apparent. Both findings were suggestive of a dominant X-linked disease. They also presented data on two bipolar pedigrees in which color blindness (CB) segregated with affective disorder. Since this publication, numerous reports concerning possible X linkage in manic-depressive illness have been published. Mendlewicz and Fleiss (1974) reported close linkage of protan (CBP) and deutan (CBD) color blindness to 17 bipolar pedigrees, and linkage to the CB loci in 14 unipolar pedigrees was excluded. They also reported that loose linkage [recombination fraction (theta) of 19 percent] of the Xg blood group to bipolar disease was present in 23 pedigrees. The large genetic distance between these two X chromosome markers makes these two findings inconsistent, however.

Subsequently, reports of additional manic-depressive pedigrees, consistent with linkage to CB or to glucose-6-phosphate dehydrogenase (G6PD) deficiency (another X chromosome marker located 3 centimorgans from CBD and CBP), appeared in the literature over the next ten years. Evidence of clear male to male transmission in some bipolar pedigrees and family studies, together with a report of five pedigrees in which color blindness was not linked to bipolar disease (Gershon et al., 1979), leads to the conclusion that bipolar disease is genetically heterogeneous (Baron 1977; Risch and Baron, 1982) and that only a fraction of bipolar pedigrees could be linked to these Xq28 markers, that is, markers of the terminal fragment (28) of the long arm (q) of the X chromosome.

"Do you even understand what this means?" Bernard asked.

"It means what it means," Sam said. "Your great uncle, for example." Bernard noticed several gray hairs in the bun she had fashioned with a spoon. Was everyone aging exponentially behind his back? Even himself?

"He was a little off, right? Didn't he spend some time in one of those homes for the alchoholically insane?"

"Your point? I thought you weren't interested in diagnosing Marguerite. I think you've been surfing the Web too much. So my uncle drank too much. Are you accusing me of having a 'bipolar pedigree'?"

"Read this," Sam said, and pointed at another torn page tacked to the wall, its print as minute as the last.

Mood disorders have also been classified according to at least four different conceptual models. First, the endogenous *versus reactive model* considers endogenous depression to be a strictly biological event unrelated to any environmental forces, whereas *reactive* depression must be psychosocially triggered and devoid of any biological factors. This distinction unjustifiably assumes that a depression's etiology is (a) known and (b) either biological *or* psychosocial.

"Your point is what?" Bernard said.

"*Reactive?*"

"Is that supposed to mean something?"

"Reactive means us. There's something we're doing."

"Is this because of what Marguerite said about seeing her English teacher's yammering skull?"

"Look, it means what it means," Sam said. "I think you should stop filling Marguerite's head with stories of Louise. It riles her up. It undoes the effects of the baths."

"Do you want me to tell you what *you* think is wrong Marguerite, though let me state here for the record that I don't think there is anything wrong with her that isn't wrong with anybody trying to grow up in a world where people are poked and pricked and prodded for their beliefs, for the way they behave. . . ." Bernard lost his train of thought. "Are you saying this is my fault?"

"You said it, not me." Sam pushed her hair off her forehead in that way Bernard used to find endearing.

"Are you sure this is about Marguerite?" He regretted it as soon as he said it, but once it was spoken, once the words formed themselves on his tongue, her blaming him for whatever she was trying to pin on their daughter launched a series of regrettable sentences from his mouth. "What about the fact that you've stopped writing altogether? You never did answer the question that you've turned our daughter into your latest project. The *mother* project."

It would have been so much better if she had yelled, if she had said anything. Instead, she walked out of the room, as if he hadn't spoken at all, as if he never existed. He was relieved when she slammed her own study door behind her.

After a few seconds, she poked her head back in. The spoon was tangled in a rat's nest at the end of her hair.

"Get out of my study," she said.

• • •

Later that afternoon, when Marguerite went for a walk with the cows, and the carpenter took a break, Bernard would go in search of his wife to apologize. He would look and look until he heard something in the closet of the bathroom where Sam bathed their daughter. There, he would discover Sam, her face hidden amidst the lush robes, rocking and rocking, her arms around her drawn-up knees. For a moment, it would make Bernard happy. He would feel as though their connection wasn't lost after all because he knew what she was imitating: infant rhesus monkeys.

When she had walked out of her study, slamming her own door behind her, he saw an article on her desk about an experiment in which these monkeys had been separated from their mothers. Some of the monkeys were raised in isolation in wire cages and permitted only visual and auditory contact with other animals. These isolated monkeys, this newspaper article said, showed a despair response that simulates clinical depression. At the top of the article, in Sam's frantic handwriting, she had written: Reasons why M. should stay at home with her mother.

Sam would continue to rock and Bernard would realize that, while the fact that he knew what it was she was imitating spoke to some kind of connection between them, the fact that his wife was rocking back and forth in the back of a closet was too disturbing for the connection to make any difference. Bernard would wonder if a doctor was to measure the level of norepinephrine in Sam's cerebral spinal fluid, the way the scientists did with the infant rhesus monkeys, there would be a noticeable drop.

"Let's not fight," Bernard would say instead.

But Sam wasn't fighting, she was rocking like an infant rhesus monkey. She didn't say anything.

When Bernard left the room, she pointed this out to him. "I'm not fighting!" she shouted but he would be halfway down the long hall where Marguerite slipped and slid, wearing holes in every pair of socks. He would be rooms and rooms away.

That Fruitless Expanse Between
Two Countries

Confined on the ship, from which there is no escape, the madman is delivered to the river with its thousand arms, the sea with its thousand roads, to that great uncertainty external to everything. He is a prisoner in the midst of what is the freest, the openest of routes: bound fast at the infinite crossroads. He is the Passenger par excellence: *that is, the prisoner of passage. And the land he will come to is unknown—as is, once he disembarks, the land from which he comes. He has his truth and his homeland only in that fruitless expanse between two countries that cannot belong to him.*

—**Michel Foucault,** *Madness and Civilization*

Bernard dreams that he and Marguerite are in a rowboat, drifting on the water. Neither of them uses the one oar that sits in the brackish water filled with strands of red weed at their feet. Their sneakers are soaked through. What little waves there are roll gently underneath them as Marguerite reads from the dusty rose manuscript in a language that consists mostly of consonants.

"What language?" he asks, and she looks up with her big brown eyes, beautiful like her favorite cow's, the one she never named, though it followed her through the fields outside the train depot.

"The cows have their own language, you just have to wait for them to speak to you," she reminds Bernard now, as if he is ridiculous beyond belief. "Shh," she says, and suddenly she's five again, though growing more and more cow-like by the minute. "Moo, dummy," she says. "It's the secret language of my blood."

"Careful, honey," he says as her fingers become a hoof. This seems like something Sam wouldn't like very much, so Bernard stands up, which instead of making the boat rock renders it strangely, pleasantly still.

"Careful is for sissies," Marguerite says, tossing the dusty rose manuscript overboard. The stillness of the boat fills Bernard's chest. His chest has been filled with the kind of sunset light that clarifies the smallest object. Bernard doesn't even care about the manuscript. He watches it warp as it sinks down and down and down and finally disappears altogether.

And suddenly there is Sam standing on the pier, pregnant, radiating a sepia-drenched love for him, the way she did when she was sixteen and she thought he was wonderful. "You know Foucault never got his facts right!" she shouts, genuinely playful. "There is only one fool in that ship, and it sure isn't that cow!"

The phone rings on the boat and Bernard answers it, expecting it to be Sam, because she is playing that new trick of hers where she is in many places at once. She is on the pier and back at the train depot; she is at the train depot and in his mind. He loves this quality of hers, and there she goes, no longer on the pier but a silver fish flickering underneath the water near the boat.

"Hello?" The sound of his own voice and the weight of the phone in his hand startle Bernard awake.

Sam hangs up, but it's not Sam's heavy breathing Bernard hears before he returns the receiver to its cradle on a bedside table, which is actually a fruit crate, piled high with paperbacks, and Bernard isn't on a boat, or in the train depot, as he sits up in a bed that smells like someone else's lemony soap and sweet shampoo and aggressively fresh-scented laundry detergent. Still, it takes him a minute to return from the dream. How dare Sam accuse him of being a cow! Even in a dream! A sheet draped over the one window diffuses the hard bright light of a streetlamp. It's nighttime and this is not a motel with brownish beige flower patterned curtains and there is not a scratchy quilt irritating his chin. Bernard tries to linger in this moment between dream life and waking, before anything is real, but as soon as he feels himself trying it's too late. How dare his wife, an adulteress with her daughter sleeping in the next room, accuse him of being a fool. Especially in a dream! Now he is wide awake.

He sits up and throws the covers off. In the folds of the wrinkled pants he's still wearing, he finds half a cashew and a raisin from the trail mix he was eating in the car yesterday and pops them in his mouth along with some lint. And then, flap-flap, the tiny fragile birds are back, in the pulse at his wrist, pushing at his skin. Rising slowly from the bed, he strokes his own wrists, pets his own heart in an effort to replace it with the dream light stillness. "Shh, shh," he says to himself. "Don't make a racket" *Did you ever hear that Mickey? Making a racket in the night?*

The beautiful-at-a-second-glance waitress's apartment is small and barely furnished, except for the bed and a TV and lots of fruit crates used as tables and as hampers for the few clothes that aren't strewn around the room as if the place has recently been searched, but for what?

Bernard leans down to pick up something that looks like a petticoat and discovers that it is, in fact, a petticoat. On his way to the sheet-draped window, he discovers several crumpled dresses that, when he uncrumples them, seem to be from another era. And then he picks up something off the floor that it would be within the realm of possibility to call a bonnet.

This is the last bonnet he'll ever pick up off the floor of a beautiful-at-a-second-glance waitress whose bed he just took a nap in, Bernard thinks, playing the "This is the last . . ." game he used to play with Sam when they first met and he teased her about how much older he was than she. This is the last car he'd ever buy, he'd say in a quavery voice as if he was about to drop dead right then and there. The last time he'd ever be at the secluded beach, its dunes grown wild with cord grass. He said this the day they discovered it accidentally on the walk they took after they stumbled across the train depot in an effort to get out of the car and away from each other. "Because you'll never find it again," Sam had said. The last time he'd ever be in Nebraska when they'd gone to visit the site of Sam's childhood home after it burned. "No fair," she said. "*Neither of us* will ever be here again."

By the light of the lone streetlamp on this back road and the glow of the nearby highway, the very one he was traveling intent and purposeless until he arrived here just in time for his humiliating collapse in front of the beautiful-at-a-second-glance waitress, Bernard can see the parking lot of the diner. There are only a few cars, and he is relieved to see his car and its crumpled trunk from where he backed into the tree in a rage after discovering the fucking hippy porn carpenter and Sam perched on the dead man's bathtub.

That wasn't funny the first time. Despite the headache she gave him yesterday, Bernard is relieved that Sam's voice is back. *And I can hear what you're thinking, but the continuous bath wasn't an idea I plucked out of nowhere. Emil Kraepelin, ever heard of him? The French guy who coined the term manic-depression in the nineteenth century? Big believer in the continuous bath, so don't make me out to be some kind of quack mother.*

Hippy porn carpenter, that's all he was saying. And that bathtub did come from a dead man.

Louise the bleeding Belgian. Who is the most ecstatic?

At least I didn't fuck her. He wasn't going to have this argument with his wife's voice or himself or whoever it was he was arguing with. It was too late at night, though when he checked the heart-shaped alarm clock on the fruit crate by the beautiful-at-a-second-glance waitress's bed, it was only nine-thirty. This may be the last time he was an old man checking a pretty waitress's alarm clock to realize . . .

You're right. You didn't fuck her, but you might as well have. No more of "this is the last"? It's as bad as "who is the most." I never liked either one of those games.

Bernard lets the sheet fall back over the window and pats the back pocket of his pants to find his wallet remarkably still there, but where are his keys? After a quick check under the pile of crumpled petticoats, and a quick look under the bonnet, he heads for what must be the bathroom. When Bernard flips on the light, it is, indeed, a bathroom, decorated with more discarded petticoats and sundry underwear from another era. But of course.

No ventilation means the air is thick with the steam from all the showers the beautiful-at-a-second-glance waitress has ever taken. Strands of her long red hair are curled in the sink, coiled as if alive and ready to spring. Bernard looks at himself in the mirror only to discover that out of the context of academia, his unkempt beard and soft pale body look crazy and weak. He has become a ridiculous person. The only thing to do is to make himself even more ridiculous, so he takes off his clothes and slips on a pair of bloomers he picks up off the linoleum floor, its corners crumbling to reveal raw wood. He pulls the bloomers up over the unfortunate paunch which appeared, determined and proud, around his fiftieth birthday, refusing to be vanquished by any number of sit-ups (okay, so he stopped doing them after the first week—they hurt, for Christ's sake) and takes a closer look in the mirror.

His younger face—high cheekbones like Ryan's and those wandering eyes, one of which wandered toward Sam when she walked into his classroom—has disappeared over the years into softer flesh, the pillows and wrinkles of this older unfamiliar version of himself. He looks maniacal rather than mysterious. He always used to think of himself as looking mysterious.

You did *look mysterious.* He can't tell if that's Sam talking or him, though Sam did say that he looked mysterious several times before they slept together the first time. She was so young, how did she know to say that? How did she know that's what he needed to hear? He can't remember the day that younger version of his face refused to emerge from this face, which reminds him of an article he once read which described the phenomenon of people noticing the presence of things more than the absence of them. People, the article said, notice when a man grows a beard, but are less likely to notice when he shaves it off. It was true, Sam hadn't noticed for an entire day when the scraggly beard first came off. When he finally pointed it out, she planted a hundred tiny kisses on his tender, raw face to make up for her inattentiveness.

But now, here he is, a grown man in women's underwear, *bloomers*, what remains of the hair on his head and another beard .peppered with stiff, gray, wiry hairs, but what he notices about his life is precisely the absence of things, what is gone rather than what is still here. More and more of him exists in the past; so much of him has already happened.

Which is why it's so important to keep death daily before your eyes. Bernard knows it's probably something that hippy porn carpenter told Sam (he should have known when he overheard the two of them singing the praises of St. Benedict that it could only lead to adultery); still, though he hates to admit it, she's got a point. The phone rings again and this time he ignores it. As is only proper when one is in a beautiful-at-a-second-glance waitress's home for the last time in one's life. He hoped that was Sam groaning in disgust he heard.

He turns off the light in the bathroom, puts the toilet seat down, and has a seat. Before Marguerite was born, Ryan, just a little boy, used to call it the "throne of the dumped" and Bernard and Sam cooed over this. Sam even used it in a poem, back when she was still writing. Then Marguerite was born, an accident (Happy! they both exclaimed, perhaps too vehemently), and Ryan no longer said little-boy things anymore. All he wanted to do was carry Marguerite around the house as if he was her father. Bernard had let himself believe it was a good thing, that it was part of Ryans adjusting to the new baby, but there was one night he poked his head out into the hall where Ryan sang to Marguerite as he walked her up and down. Ryan looked at him severely, held a finger to his lips, and his little-boy face had vanished into sharp edges of worry. Bernard hadn't noticed the absence of Ryan's boy self enough.

Sitting there on the toilet listening to the foreign tick-ticking of the pretty waitress's apartment, his stomach hanging over the top of a pair of bloomers, Bernard wonders where he and Sam went wrong.

Foucault wrote madness was the *"déjà là"* of death. When a person loses his mind, it's like a preview of death. Maybe if Bernard went crazy, it would be a version of keeping death daily before his eyes?

Puh-lease. Oh, wait, maybe now you'll show some interest in that great-uncle of yours?

When had Sam gotten so mean? Right before Bernard discovered her and the hippy porn carpenter, she left an article about a Siberian dwarf hamster on the bathroom floor as if by accident, though it was clearly there for Bernard to find.

I am sorry about that one. That was uncalled for.

The Siberian dwarf hamster, said the scientist in the article, forms intense male-female bonds and when the mates are separated from each other, the male ventures out to explore his surroundings less and less and, the crowning glory, he gains a lot of weight.

You haven't gained that much weight.

Bernard is growing accustomed to sitting in the thick air of the dark bathroom. This might be just the place for him. Finally, he's found his home. Maybe he'll embrace his Siberian dwarf-hamster self and stay here forever. The clattering of pans downstairs in the diner and a loud, "Shit!" startles Bernard to his feet and he flees the bathroom.

"Cute," the beautiful-at-a-second-glance waitress says, opening the door to discover Bernard stuffed into her bloomers standing in the middle of her apartment. She puts her purse down on a fruit crate that says 100% FLORIDA ORANGES on its side. Was there an orange that was, say, 78 percent Florida orange and 22 percent something else? Bernard wonders. The pretty waitress undoes the knot of hair at the back of her head. "Real cute."

The phone rings again, and Bernard, feeling at home after all his time in the bathroom, walks over to the bedside fruit crate and answers it.

"Who is this?" a nervous male voice bursts forth on the other end of the line.

"Come on," Bernard says. What a question. He adjusts the waistband of the bloomers. "Is that all you've got?"

"What the hell are you talking about?" the voice says. The beautiful-at-a-second-glance waitress slips the phone gently out of Bernard's hand, giving him a stern look as she shakes out her red hair with her fingers.

"That's my phone, you know," she says softly, touching Bernard's bare shoulder so lightly he isn't sure if it really happened, only that suddenly gravity has been called into question again. The birds threaten another nosedive—flap, flap, flap—and he sits down on the bed to keep from falling again. In the diner *was* the last time in his life that he would collapse in front of a pretty waitress, he would make sure of it.

"Is this Ralph?" the beautiful-at-a-second-glance waitress asks the phone in the same tender voice she told Bernard that the phone was hers. Then, suddenly, the tender voice grows thorns and she shouts, "Ralph, fuck off, you fuck!" She slams the phone down, continuing to shake out the red hair whose strands Bernard fingered where they lay curled in the bathroom sink, and, with the birds beating against the cage of his heart, Bernard finds himself thinking about the beautiful-at-a-second-glance waitress's pubic hair against his face.

"I'll go change," he says.

"You didn't have to do that," the beautiful-at-a-second-glance waitress says when he reemerges from the bathroom. "I meant it when I said you look cute. Better than I do when I wear that stuff." She gestures toward a fruit crate where Bernard might sit and flops down on her bed, kicking off her sneakers. "When I'm not down-stairs, I do Civil War reenactment. Part of my lucrative acting ca-reer. But that's all about to change. Wait, are you crying?"

"No," Bernard says indignantly, "I'm not crying." He thought he wiped his eyes sufficiently in the bathroom.

"Do you want to know my name?" the beautiful-at-a-second-glance waitress asks, running her thumb over the arch of her long, lovely nose.

"I'm Bernard," Bernard says. After twenty-five years, the closest he's come to sleeping with anyone besides Sam was when he licked the bucktoothed advisee's face in his office and he's not sure how this goes. Now that it looks as if this might be heading in that direction, introductions feel somehow awkward. He wonders fleetingly if Sam felt embarrassed with the hippy porn carpenter, but puts it out of his mind lest it invite her voice back, because as embarrassing as this feels, her voice in his head would be the end of it all.

"Bella," the pretty waitress says with a smirk. "My parents didn't take into consideration how it might force the issue in an unfortunate way." She gestures to her face as if it was evidence of the "issue."

"But you are bella," Bernard says before he is aware that he's speaking. "I mean beautiful." Clearly, this whole situation is going to get more and more embarrassing before it isn't anymore.

"Come here," she says.

Or maybe not. Bernard moves toward her and she turns away from him, as if she is about to take a nap, but she reaches underneath the bed and pulls out a condom and hands it to him as she closes her eyes and begins to undress. "I like to pretend I'm asleep. I'm an actress," she says, eyes still closed.

The phone rings again and Bella knocks the receiver off the hook. When the phone begins its off-the-hook beeping, Bernard thinks: Exactly. Sex is an emergency. For Ralph, for Bella, for me. Entering somebody else's body must leave a person changed or more knowledgeable.

Here's the part where you're full of shit.

But touching Bella was the only way he could keep from floating away at the moment. He undresses quickly before he loses his nerve.

Here's the part where you have an epiphany about your life. Here's the part where you look at the wreckage and make something good out of it. Please, Bernard.

Bernard pulls out of Bella, who's still pretending to be asleep. He reaches over her and puts the phone back on the hook. She turns and looks at him incredulously.

"Like I said, that's my phone."

"Okay, okay."

Please, give me this, Bernard thinks, happy to ignore the phone. Here, now, this, the immediacy of sex, the ghost that hovers over two bodies, a ghost but a ghost with strong bones and teeth. A ghost that will help me muscle my way out of the past and into the present. Bella turns her head slightly so he can see her mouth open, as she reaches her strong arms behind her and then behind him to wrap around his lower back, pushing him more deeply into her. For a moment, most of Bernard hasn't already happened, most of Bernard is right here.

"Do you mind if we sleep now?" Bernard asks when she finishes shuddering.

"You mean for real?" Moist and naked, Bella rolls over, pulling the tangle of covers with her.

"Yes, sleep for real."

Bernard's sleep is jagged—words marching across his mind: 65 percent Florida oranges. The lifesaving view. Where is my fucking train? When he gives up on sleep, he thinks of a day Sam went to the library to do more research into Marguerite's alleged illness. This was about the time she had decided that Bernard's lineage was responsible for it all. The hippy porn carpenter and his crew were on a break, and Bernard snuck into the bathroom and looked at the red divan where Sam, when she had still been talking to him, told him she lay while Marguerite took her baths. He was tired and wanted to rest, but was afraid that if he lay on it he might find the exact shape of her body with his, locate the exact shape of her absence, so instead he lay on the floor with his eyes open. To be mocked by the sky blue walls was preferable to what he might see if he closed his eyes. He swept his arm under the divan and pulled out a notebook, apparently the part of Sam's brain that hadn't been blown out all over the walls of her study. He convinced himself it was his duty as her husband to read it, to discover for both of their sakes what was wrong, what was festering at the heart of their marriage. Even as he dreaded the pages filled with diatribes about what a monster he was, he told himself it was in the best interest of their future together.

Instead, there was a list in what looked to be the form of a poem with line breaks: morbid externalizing disorders/reuptake inhibitors single-blind placebo psychotropic, rapid dose escalation protocol/ open naturalistic examination mood lability/neuroleptics rates of refusals noncompliance rapid loading strategy/lithium carbonate valproate acid carbamazepine. The last line, a question: poem? A few blank pages. Nothing about him, not a word. It was so much worse than a diatribe, he almost didn't read on, but what else could he do? On the next page were these lines. Fairy tale in reverse: a woman who once spoke poetry and now speaks only frogs. Lying in Bella's bed, Bernard wonders whether hating himself even more than he already does is possible when he hates himself the most? Who hates Bernard the most?

"Get the fucking dog off the bed," Bella says and pulls the covers off Bernard, bunching them up over her head so there's no hope of retrieving them. Bernard's ready to give up on this half-sleep anyway, and sits up in the dark bedroom, listening to the grinding gears of trucks on the highway.

Somewhere in a rest stop along that highway, the dusty rose manuscript sits on the top of a paper towel dispenser by a soap streaked mirror. Bernard left it there this road trip, strange that at the beginning of somehow his rage at Sam led him to do the very thing she'd been asking him to do all along. Abandon the bleeding girl. As he hurtled south along the highway in his car with the freshly crumpled trunk, Sam's voice began.

That's right, go off into your bleeding girl world; I'll stay here in the land of real people. And he began to wonder if Sam was right. The day before the hippy porn carpenter incident, he found himself at a Mormon Web site looking into the genealogy of his family to see if there was any way he might be related to Louise. He couldn't find anything, and he realized it had become more than an indulgent fantasy. He had hoped it was true more than he cared to admit, believed there actually might be a familial connection to her, this girl who knew ecstasy firsthand.

And enough with the ecstasy. You win, okay? He knew he'd never convince Sam, but he had posted the definition of ecstasy on his study door as encouragement to them all, the whole family, to aspire to this feeling, this thing beyond the everyday. At the time he hadn't meant it as a competition, but now he wasn't so sure. He was pleased when Marguerite loved the story of Louise, but then he worried that she was closer to Louise than he would ever be, and then there was that night when he felt such a flash of jealousy that he may have pushed things a little too far, but as with the night Ryan left, he doesn't allow his mind to wander there.

That day on the road, he wanted to prove Sam wrong, but it was more than that. Hurtling down the highway, getting there and getting there but never getting there, Bernard felt more powerfully than ever that he didn't have a home. The flap-flapping began and gravity lost its meaning again, so he pulled off the road at the next rest stop and lifted the dusty rose manuscript out of the backseat of the car where he'd thrown it next to a potted plant he grabbed on the way out the door of the depot in an effort to take *something*. It was as if he was lifting a heavy object from a sinking ship though it was practically weightless. He slammed the door of the car, and the license plate, barely attached since he backed into the tree, clattered to the pavement in the parking lot, but he didn't stop because if he stopped he felt sure he would turn to stone, crumble to dust.

What he was about to do, he told himself, had a kind of divinity to it. As he strode through the bathroom door, glancing at the guy at the urinal with some affection (he was, after all, part of this divine moment), he felt something beyond himself guiding him as he lay the dusty rose manuscript on top of the paper towel dispenser. He avoided his own reflection in the soap streaked mirror because this wasn't about him; this was about exerting a deep and lasting and altruistic influence on some other person, whoever that might be. Some guy who, after taking a leak and washing his hands, happened to look up and, out of curiosity, because of fate, because of destiny (*Oh men, your destiny. When all is well a shadow can overturn it. When trouble comes a stroke of the wet sponge, and the picture's blotted out. And that, I think that breaks the heart.*), would pick up the dusty rose manuscript and read the story of Louise for himself.

Once again, you're perfectly willing to give if it has to do with another person, preferably a person you will never see again. Sam's voice here in Bella's apartment is brighter than the muted lights of the highway trucks or the fuzzy diffuse light coming through the sheet. Her voice is a nuclear yellow, a bright orange highway cone, a computerized emergency billboard on the highway: Congestion ahead! Turn back!

Bernard has had enough. Sam is even interfering with his effort to efface himself, to disappear from the earth. It's too much. "Shut up!"

"I didn't say anything," Bella says indignantly, bolting upright, casting those pretty, slightly crossed eyes around the room— looking for the fucking dog?—tangled in covers as wild as her hair.

"Not you," Bernard says, awkward and scared again now that she's awake, or worse, just acting.

"Who, me? Couldn't be," Bella says, rubbing her eyes with the flat of her hand. "Then who?" She laughs, a terrific cackle. "Who stole the cookie from cookie jar?"

"Do you mind if I read?" Bernard runs his finger along the pile of paperbacks by Bella's bed. Her electric laugh has a calming effect on him. The birds are still, wings folded, sleeping in his heart cage.

Bella yawns. "Go for it." She turns away from him. "I'm really sleeping this time," she says. "Oh, and my born-again mother sent me the ones on top. Don't worry, I'm not a crazy Jesus freak. Although, what do you care, right?"

Bernard switches on the light on top of the fruit crate. Bella still has all the covers, so he retrieves the blanket at the end of the bed and wraps it around his knees. At the bottom of the pile of books: Stanislavsky's *An Actor Prepares*, Lee Strasberg's autobiography, a history of the Group Theater. The books on top have names like *Final Dawn Over Jerusalem, Soul Harvest*, and *Prosperity and the Coming Apocalypse* and the images on the front covers all seem to include some version of a giant sun and people in profile looking heavenward. Bernard picks up one called *Left Behind* and reads about a 747 airline pilot named Raymond Steele, a skeptic, whose family has been taken by the Rapture, and who must gradually learn to accept Christ so that he may be vaporized as well.

"Bella?" Bernard tugs on the covers. Over the past week, he has been able to feel as blank and unused in the motel rooms as every wrapped bar of soap and tiny bottle of shampoo. Sometimes he felt as blissfully inanimate as the comforting brown strips of paper that sealed the toilets shut. But when Bernard presses his nose into Bella's shoulder moving up and down as she breathes, there is a sharp, tangy scent beneath soap and shampoo, reminding him he is alive too. "Bella?" He tugs again on the covers.

"Are you reading about the Apocalypse?" She turns over quickly so that the blankets pull tight around her and she is a pretty red-haired mummy. "It's not good to read about the Apocalypse in the middle of the night." She begins to peel the blankets from her. The blue light of early morning lurks just behind the window's sheet and in between the highway traffic, Bernard hears the caw-caw of a crow and a gentler bird's morning song. He marvels to think these birds, and their bird friends and relatives, have made these sounds for Bella on other mornings before he ever knew her.

"Let's go downstairs," Bella says, touching his face, tugging on his beard. She is out of the bed and already half-dressed before he can thank her. With a rubber band in her mouth, she re-knots her hair at the back of her head, mumbling, "I have to be back at work in a couple of hours anyway."

In the diner, they head toward a booth next to two men drinking coffee and eating baklava. "I don't want to talk about the Knicks," one of them says. "They're not talking about me."

"Hey, Bella," the one not talking about the Knicks says. "Who's this one?"

"Shut up, jealous," Bella says. "Bernard this is Cook and Dish-washer. They don't deserve names. I'll be back in a minute."

"Hey, man," Cook says, extending his hand.

"Good to meet you," Dishwasher says, and Bernard takes his hand too. He stands there holding each of their hands as if they were kids in a kindergarten class getting ready to sing a song.

"Why don't you have a seat, man," Cook says. "Looks like you could use a cup of coffee."

"Or two," Dishwasher says.

Bernard slides into the booth behind them.

"Sometimes coffee solves everything," Cook says, patting Bernard's shoulder and suddenly Bernard feels like he might cry again.

Bella returns, wipes the table off with the same grimy sponge from yesterday, and then sloshes two cups of coffee on the table.

"You're not a very good waitress," Bernard says. "I noticed that yesterday."

"Yeah, yeah, yeah." Bella swats his head. "Let's try something this doctor I met once told me about. The one who recommended all of those theater books."

"So you do this all the time?" Bernard imagines other men listening to the caw-caw of the crows and the song of the gentler morning birds from Bella's bed. He can't believe he's pouting and jealous, but he is.

"Don't be a baby. You think I've been waiting all my life for you to walk into this diner? This guy really helped me out. I told him about the Civil War reenactment gig, and he told me I should apply to the Eugene O'Neill Theater School in Connecticut. He knew somebody, and talked me up as this raw talent, the whole waitress-from-the-backwoods number. I don't care what he said about me or what they think as long as they pay. So I got a scholarship. I'm going next week."

"Oh," Bernard says. Had he really thought that this would go on for longer than a night? His innocence, his naïveté, surprises even him. But more than that, his inability to think beyond the next hour. In some ways, he's achieved the thing that has always eluded him, the ability to live in the present moment. But why did it have to involve feeling like a weepy idiot?

"Come on," Bella says, pouring cream in both of the cups. Though Bernard takes his black, he doesn't say anything. "You're like those rats those researchers shocked until they learned helplessness—zap! Where is your hope, man?" She throws the grimy sponge at him. *When trouble comes a stroke of the wet sponge, and the picture's blotted out.* "This will be fun."

Out the window, the cars rushing by on the nearby highway sound like a river. "Whatever," Bernard says.

"Don't be such a fuck-and-run type. Humor me a little."

"All right, all right," Bernard says, touching her crooked nose.

Here's the part where I marry you and then have your children.
Here's the part where one of our beautiful children, filled with the po-
tential of all children who have not lived long in the world, presses her
tender, pulsing veins to my ear to let me hear the blood rush and swirl,
begging to be let out. Here's the part where I tell her it's supposed to
rush and swirl, but she says no, her blood yearns to fill her bedroom,
sloshing against the walls. It yearns (one yearns) to drown her.

"Imagine the weight of the mug, the smell of the coffee, the bitter taste," Bella says.

"But my real coffee is right here," and he reaches for it, but Bella
swats his hand away.

"Use your imagination," she says, untying and tying again the
knot in her red hair.

"Imagination was never my strong suit," Bernard says, lifting
his cup in the air between them as if she wouldn't be able to see it
otherwise.

"Aren't you an English professor?"

"Was," Bernard says, experimenting with the past tense.

"Give a girl a break," Bella says. She lifts the cup out of his
hands and puts it on the table. "If you'd just focus."

Here's the part where a bad mother makes good. Here's the part
where I search and search for a way to help our daughter. Here's the
part of your life where you hide yourself away in your study with the
bleeding Belgian.

Was it possible Bernard felt too much, that if he recognized the
furious rush of Marguerite's blood that the tiny birds would beat
their way out of his heart? *There are parts you are leaving out. Parts*
of you in her, your blood furious in her veins. It was true, Bernard has
always longed to press the tender, pulsing veins of his own wrist to
someone else's ear, to anyone's ear; he pressed his wrist to Bella's ear
last night, but she didn't wake up, which seemed to him a good
sign, a sign that his blood was not yet clamoring to be let out, because this is what he is afraid of—the possibility that he's inherited
in reverse this rushing and swirling from his daughter.

"I'm focusing," Bernard says. "I'm focusing."

"I'm telling you, nerve tissue remembers things." Bella presses a hand over Bernard's eyes, and though he tries to think of coffee cups, any coffee cup, all the coffee cups he's ever lifted to his lips, there it is, Marguerite on Ryan's bed, jumping up and down, shaking her hips to a woman's voice that heaves and pitches. *Are you sure your prayers haven't been answered? Think, brother, think.* The Staple Singers. Ryan played them during mandatory family dinner one night. "Jerry Wexler, the producer for Atlantic records who produced Aretha Franklin, Ruth Brown, Ray Charles, Willie Nelson, Bob Dylan, said, 'Black music is my religion,'" Ryan said. "Vicarious religion," Sam said. Who is the most? Who can feel it the most? And there is Ryan, cheering his sister on at the foot of the bed. Neither of them knows Bernard is watching. Sent by Sam to find the children who aren't children anymore. Marguerite is eighteen and Ryan is twenty-five. Bernard is spying, looking through the crack in the door as Marguerite points at her brother and then raises her hands skyward, the direction of prayer. *Are you sure your prayers haven't been answered? Think, sister, think.*

Marguerite sings with abandon, dancing just behind the rhythm of the guitar and the steady drumbeat, in that jerky, funny way of hers. *Every move you make; every wiggle of your head; every wink of your eye.* She wiggles her head and winks at her brother, her body filled with the jangle of the tambourine. Her body fills with the music until it seems on the verge of exploding, ringing from the inside out.

Bernard stands there, wishing he could feel the way his daughter looks right now; instead, he realizes that he's made a terrible mistake in thinking that his children's lives were stories he could understand from afar, that their lives were stories at all. *You may not know how to pray, but He loves you when you try.* He regrets the argument he and Sam had last night in the car on their way home from a rare outing to a party where Sam had engaged her dinner partner in a long conversation about St. Benedict in his sixth-century cave, thirty miles outside Rome, at Subiaco while all around him the Roman Empire fell, war and chaos, and how nice it would be to find a cave like that, not a real cave, but a mental cave, a cave like a big membrane-y mind?

"A big membrane-y mind," Bernard teased her when they got in the car, though he knew it would piss her off and it did.

"You just don't like the idea that I might be interested in something that you don't know everything about. Our family might be salvaged by a dose of monastic structure."

"Salvaged? You think our family could be *salvaged* by behaving as if we lived in Italy at the fall of the Roman Empire?" He nearly hit a possum ambling across the road, its eyes laser red from the headlights, but he swerved just in time. It was then that he should have turned back. Even then, before the hippy porn carpenter or her obsession with the continuous bath, he should have seen that his wife was asking him to see her.

Sam's silence was longer and louder that night than any of her silences in the past year. Her silence that night carved a sculpture of hatred between them, and there was no unmaking it. There was only smashing it. "Reading as an act of prayer," she said, as if she was telling him to die. "An act of deep thought and consideration. Not a prescription, an idea, as in pattern, as in model, as in alternative to living like separate loud, crazy islands, as in a way of refocusing, living a more contemplative life where people 'speak the truth with heart and tongue,' where people try never to 'speak hollow words of affection to each other, never turned away when someone needed an expression of love.'"

"So," Bernard said. "Would that make you the abbot?"

In the daytime! In the midnight hour! Standing there watching his daughter dance, he has decided he will go to Sam, after he tells the kids to come to dinner. He'll apologize for it all; he'll tell her he wanted her to be abbot, or maybe better not to bring up the abbot thing at all.

Marguerite steps off the bed, and puts her hand over Ryan's eyes. Guess who? The gesture in reverse, all things in reverse, everything flowing backward. "Humble, then, your wisdom," she says, "which is based on reason and place all your fidelity in those things which are given by love, illuminated through faith." For a minute, Bernard feels proud that his daughter has memorized these words spoken to her by her namesake, spoken by a father to his daughter, but then, Marguerite takes her hand away from Ryan's eyes. She moves closer to him as if she is about to ask him to dance, not like someone who wants to dance but like someone who wants to get inside of him. When she kisses her brother, the flicker of her tongue is like a surgeon's instrument claiming his body for her own.

When Bernard shows Ryan to the door, he says, "Why did it take so long, this death?" Quoting chapter 87 of Marguerite Porette, Marguerite's namesake, from *The Mirror of Simple Souls*, "But now I can receive it freely, since I have wounded you to death by love."

What an asshole he was, no words of his own.

"Where are you?" Bella asks now. Bernard opens his eyes into the flesh of Bella's hand and sees the rocks in the fields outside the train depot butting their dumb, smooth heads against the surface of the earth, breaking it open, asking to be harvested like souls during the Rapture.

"Here," Bernard says, wishing it was ever true. "Right here."

Who Is the Most Ecstatic?

By the end of Marguerite's first week home from school, Bernard and Marguerite and Louise Lateau had become outlaws in the night kitchen. That's what Marguerite called them the night that Bernard regrets the most.

"Like the kid's book, *In the Night Kitchen*," Marguerite said when Bernard gave her a blank look. She sat at the kitchen table, her chin propped in her hands. The light from the moon came through the window and illuminated an approximation of Sam's tauter, thinner face in the depths of Marguerite's. It was the face of the girl who lost both her parents suddenly, a face sorrow had swept clean when Bernard first met her. "You ever hear of Mickey?" Marguerite asked, dancing her fingers like teeny tiny legs around the sugar bowl and then around the salt and pepper. She picked up the flyswatter Sam had left on the table and swatted invisible flies from the air. "That racket in the night?"

"Well, don't make a racket, whatever you do," Bernard said. Marguerite *did* seem better, more energetic, especially late at night. Tonight her usually pale, freckly complexion was flushed. Maybe from the baths? *I'll give you that*, he said to his wife in the imaginary ongoing fight he had with her in his head. Staring at his daughter as she flapped the flyswatter against her knee, Bernard didn't notice the milk beginning to boil over the sides of the saucepan. "Shit." He lifted the pan and milk foamed over the side, gathering in the well of the burner. "Now I've got to start all over. Boiled milk constipates you and we're trying to go to sleep, right?"

Marguerite had been sleeping so much during the days after her baths that at night she slipped out of her room and wandered the train depot and, even when Bernard lay on the thickest part of the rug, the study floor was still hard and he found himself up late and wandering too. For the past several nights, Bernard and his daughter met in the quiet of the night kitchen, ostensibly for a sedative of warm milk but also for a forbidden reading from the dusty rose manuscript.

Bernard poured fresh milk—*Healthy, calming milk, for Christ's sake,* he pointed out to the phantom Sam—into the saucepan. The milk grew a thick skin, and he poured it into mugs Sam never used, mugs she wouldn't notice if he washed them afterward and pushed them to the back of the cabinet. If Sam hadn't forbidden it, would it have been less appealing? Bernard was willing to admit that there was a pleasure in the furtiveness of the endeavor, but Marguerite also seemed to genuinely enjoy it.

"Very, very hot," he said, putting one of the mugs in front of his daughter. He slipped into the chair beside hers. Outside the kitchen window, there was no lifesaving view, only the pitch-black hum of deep, dark night.

"Read from the part about the tests again," Marguerite said, and she danced her tiny leg fingers up the side of Bernard's arm. "The part where the doctor pricks her with needles to see if she's for real." She rubbed the hair on her arm briskly and then held her hand above it to make the hair stand on end.

Yesterday afternoon when Bernard left his wife rocking in the back of the bathroom closet, he'd returned from rooms and rooms to sit next to her on the floor. "This is not fighting," he told her. He rubbed her arms the way Marguerite rubbed her own arms now, and felt the hair rise up to meet his palm. They sat together in the closet quietly, side by side, his arm around her shoulder, their thighs touching, two people who had once been in love. The ocean salt and manure breeze wafted through the room, that earthy, simple smell. Bernard looked at the deep purple paisley design of one of the robes hanging in the closet, and when it began to swirl, he looked up at his wife's face, to her forehead, and the paisley design swirled there too. For a minute it seemed like everything might be all right.

"I'm going to go wake Marguerite," Sam had said, getting to her feet, and the spell was broken. The paisley swirl disappeared from her forehead, revealing only worry lines. "And in case you're interested, she said something about her blood rushing and swirling today. I'm thinking about taking her to a psychiatrist. I just want to do the right thing. The baths seem right, but I need help, and you're not helping."

"Dad," Marguerite said now, and Bernard imagined his daughter's blood underneath her pale skin, rushing and swirling. "I changed my mind. Not the tests. I want to hear about her ecstasies."

"Louise had postponed her sewing," Bernard began, making it up as he went along. Marguerite was the only one who understood him; she deserved to hear Louise's story no matter what Sam said. He put the dusty rose manuscript aside and told this part in his own words. "It was unlike her to fall behind, but she wanted to watch the sun rise. She watched the light change, the subtle shadows on the foothills, her blood practically boiling with anticipation, but for what? She didn't know. She felt on the verge of arrival. The rising red and yellow and orange wounded her with its beauty because her body couldn't contain it, so much beautiful light. It rushed through her so quickly, she felt as if she were hovering on the edge of the world, about to fall off."

"Like when I fell off the pier?" Marguerite said.

Bernard nodded, not wanting to interrupt this story with another. Louise's story was theirs alone; the other story was the story of a family that no longer existed. "The big red sun burned Louise's blood, made it smoke. Her family was devout, but try as she might, she could never match their devotion. In fact, late at night, she wished for a sign, or an invitation, not quite a sign or an invitation but something from the outside and the inside both at once, something that would well up in her, big and woundingly beautiful as the sun." Bernard's voice became the fairy-tale voice from years ago.

The scrape of Marguerite's chair startled him, but not as much as her words. "During almost the entire duration of the ecstasy," she began, "Louise remains seated in her chair, inclined somewhat forward, and motionless as a statue." She stood. She didn't miss a syllable. She never paused. "Her bleeding hands rest on her lap. Her eyes are motionless. Her countenance indicates rapt attention: dead to all earthly objects, she is absorbed by the contemplation of some spectacle, which she seems to behold above the region of the earth. Her countenance and attitude undergo many changes."

Before Bernard's eyes, Marguerite's countenance and attitude changed too. Her eyes became luminous with moonlight and a vein at her temple pulsed. For a second Bernard wondered if the vein at Marguerite's temple would burst. Would there be a crown of blood?

Bernard didn't see the scrap of paper between Marguerite's fingers, stolen from the flurry of fragments above the captain's desk in his study. From the moment she began to speak the story of Louise back to him, Bernard believed utterly in the magic of his daughter. This was the light shining from the inside out. Behind her back Marguerite's fingers rubbed the thin and growing-thinner paper like a talisman, as if she was reading the stolen words through her fingertips. As he watched his glowing girl, Bernard didn't know that that very afternoon, after Marguerite watched Seedsucker lurking, lurking, outside her bedroom window, after Sam had dozed off on the divan, after Marguerite found herself finally alone, she had whispered Louise's words to herself.

Bernard didn't know that Marguerite's mind was clear as a giant chalkboard waiting to be written on. Write on this! That she had stared at her reflection in the mirror in the continuous bathroom, whispering the words so intently that she no longer believed it was she anymore. That even though she had never seen a picture of Louise Lateau, Marguerite, squinting her eyes, saw Louise herself in the mirror, her hair a brilliant, fiery ecstatic red like the afternoon sun, her cheeks flushed red too, and, there, a fierce pointed nose just like Marguerite's. Bernard didn't know that the glittering clarity in Marguerite's mind sparkled so bright that, standing in front of the mirror, Marguerite saw through Louise's eyes so that she too was transformed and, like Louise, made magnificent in the eyes of everyone around her. That his daughter leaned in to the reflection that was no longer her but Louise, as if telling it a secret, and whispered "magnificent." *Magnificent,* a word Bernard used frequently to describe Louise. He didn't know that Marguerite loved the silky sound of the *c* in magnificent and that she spoke it that very afternoon until she had no edges anymore, until she became the silky soft sound of it, softly, softly, so as not to wake her mother, in a voice so soft only the ocean down the rocky road could hear her.

Bernard didn't know that when Marguerite turned away from the mirror, she was still Louise, the words he had read to her writing themselves across Marguerite's chalkboard mind. The story of the priest who brought a silver vessel to test Louise. The kind of silver vessel the priest brought whenever he visited the dying, two separate compartments to this vessel carried in a special silken case—one for the holy oil for Extreme Unction, the other for the Eucharist blessed by the Church.

Bernard didn't know that Marguerite felt the same keenness of vision as Louise at the moment she outwitted the priest holding up a false relic: X-ray eyes looking through the silk, or maybe right into the mind of the priest, mining his mind. That Marguerite spoke the following words aloud: "But almost upon his entering the room, before he had come within two yards of the chair on which Louise was seated, she began to tremble . . ."

Bernard didn't know that Marguerite had trembled too as she continued to finger the worn piece of paper. That she held her own hand to stop the trembling because it frightened her a little, but she also wanted to know what fear was, she wanted to be a girl who know how to shudder. Her mind was not her own; it was filled with these words: . . . *as if under the influence of some extraordinary*

excitement, and then starting up with animation, as if beside herself
with joy, she immediately fell on her knees, stretching out her hands to-
ward the case in which the sacred vessel was enclosed, and remained in
that position, her countenance resembling that of a seraph absorbed in
adoration. The priest, still holding the sacred vessel toward her, moved a
step backward, and Louise, still retaining the same kneeling position,
was, as it were, drawn after him. He then went slowly around the room,
at times pausing for a few moments; raised from the ground and bent
forward, her hands still clasped in an attitude of adoration, continued to
follow his movements, falling on her knees each time that he stood still.
When the sacred vessel was brought out of the room, Louise resumed
her seat, and during the remainder of the ecstasy, everything went on as
usual. The bishop remarked that in all probability a small fragment of
the consecrated host was still remaining in the silver vessel; and when it
was opened in the church, such, in fact, was found to be the case.

All- Bernard knew was what he saw before him in the night
kitchen: his daughter standing beside her chair, her hands behind
her back, reciting words he didn't know she knew. "Her eyes
become moistened, a smile of joy plays around her half-opened
mouth; at another, her eyelids fall, her eyes partly close, her features
contract, and tears roll down her cheeks; again as she grows pale,
terror is depicted on her countenance, she shudders." Marguerite
shivered and because Bernard was looking at her arms, her ribs, her
forehead, expecting (or was he hoping for?) blood, he didn't see her
tears at first.

"No spectacle could be more impressive than that which is now
presented," Marguerite continued, her voice even stronger now, no
tremble, no quiver. "The bleeding coronet on her forehead; the blood
trickling down her face and falling on her dress; her hands, the
blood from which is dropping on the floor where it lies in large
patches; the circle of bystanders of every rank and condition
grouped around, speechless from awe and wonder, and many of
them weeping with emotion, all this combines to form a scene
which irresistibly forces upon the beholder the conclusion that it is
the work of God."

When Marguerite finished, when she sat down and began to cry in earnest, Bernard felt small. Tiny. It was as though he was shrinking. It wasn't until he realized he was shrinking out of jealousy that he felt ashamed.

"Bring yourself to the edge. Be willing to throw yourself over," he said, his mouth forming the words before he'd even decided to speak them out loud. He had wanted to see, just for a moment, his daughter's yearning blood, like Louise's own pressing at her skin, begging to be let out into the world. Later, he would insist to himself that he hadn't meant to speak these words. Later, when he could bear to return to this night, he would tell himself he meant no harm, that he was speaking to himself.

Good Mourning in the Queen's County, Part III

Get up, get up, the taller mourning woman sings the way Marguerite's blood doesn't anymore in the up and down hall where she is no longer up and downing, not because even the taller mourning woman has asked her not to put her ear against the germ-filled door of others, not because even Regina has told her that sometimes it's better to let your heart find you. "It's got the ring of the poster in the art therapy room: *If you love someone, set them free*," she said, "but what are you going to do?" Marguerite can't up and down this morning because she can't *get up, get up*, she can't get out of the bed with the covers tangled around her feet and her mind mined by Carol Channing's trick cupcake time-smashing pills.

"Love God with your lips not just your heart," the scary mask woman says to someone at the front desk, but loud enough so the whole inside world can hear it.

"My lips are without love, Mrs. Three percent," Regina says, lying on the bed across from Marguerite in another borrowed nightgown she claims is a dress. "What do I do about that? What do I do about my loveless lips?"

The shoe-scuffed radiator clank clanks, making the noise that

Marguerite would like to make in response, but her slack mouth is full of lumpy words like unmolded clay.

"Shark girl, they've got you knocked out," Regina says, rolling over on the bed and onto the floor in one swift motion to stand at Marguerite's bedside. "Look at yourself," she says. "You're drooling." With the beautiful skirt of her borrowed nightgown nightshirt, Regina gently wipes the saliva from Marguerite's mouth with a weary arm. Firefly flash: Marguerite's mother's weary arm, sleeve rolled up to test the bathwater, but then it disappears. The fireflies rustle their delicate paper-thin wings, but no flash, flash. Impossible to conjure the weary arm when Marguerite has become the weary arm.

Farther down the hall, the murmuring from the art therapy room, "Art practice makes art perfect."

"Don't be fooled," Regina says. She rolls over, props herself up so she's sitting against the wall, her legs with their secret maps curled underneath her. "That so-called art therapist, fifty-seven percent tops. Just one more parole officer of the mind."

Fifty-seven percent tops struggles to make art practice art perfect even with the never-sleeping man with his wide-awake shouting face and his falling-down pants, having returned to the hospital after being away for an amount of time, the length of which can be read on the inside of his forearms in the shape of stripes and star punctures.

"I'll smoke all of you where you stand," he shouts. "You don't know shit. The Department of Agriculture used phenothiazine compounds as insecticides to kill swine parasites. Gave it to rats to climb ropes to keep from getting shocked. And you all are taking it like candy, like some trained rats, like some swine parasites waiting to be offed." The shouting grows faint as an arm of muscle steers him into another room.

"Seventy-eight percent, but he is sometimes one hundred percent right," Regina says, falling sideways onto her pillow to begin her gentle snuffle of sleep.

It's still September all day long, the taller mourning woman says, interrupting her get up get up song to stick her head in Marguerite and Regina's room, and Marguerite looks to the bus stop to see if the now o'clock lady has returned with whatever she learned from the soft fuzz of her pompom, but there are different bus stop people, a crowd marching up into the mouth of a bus as an ambulance sings by and the wind blows the scarf off one of the ladies, who rushes after it. There are so many people, it's hard to tell what time it is, but it feels like years since Marguerite has heard her heart.

Just as she is about to give up, thump-thump, thump-thump, growing louder, at the front desk. Dr. Con, Dr. Con, Dr. Goodman, Dr. Goodman. The voice in the overhead indoor sky more and more urgent: Dr. Con, Dr. Con, Dr. Good Man, Dr. Good Man, and Regina sits up and then even the never-sleeping man with his shouting face is drowned out by the noise in the up and down hall. Marguerite turns to Regina, but Regina holds a finger to her lips. "Shh," she says, "listen."

"I don't care about a restraining order."

The voice out there is sucked clean too.

"Seedsucker." The word flickers across Marguerite's mind.

"That's no seedsucker, that's a man," Regina says, out of the bed, up on her toes, prancing, prancing. "Is that yours?"

"I'm a citizen and that's what being a citizen is all about, lady. Don't get me wrong, I'm smart like Einstein, bigger than Queens, bigger than all of New York. She called *me*. She said she needed me to find her fucking heart. Her brother's going to kill me, man. I just wanted to make sure she's okay. I don't know, she's *crazy*."

There was a phone call, but Marguerite is never sure when her words are out loud and time is loop the looping. "I don't know where your brother is," Seedsucker said when she called the number scribbled on a piece of paper, *in case of emergency,* she found in the toe of her soul-squashing shoes. "Maybe you could help me find him?" she whispered into the phone still warm with other people's coffee breath.

". . . want to see her," he says now, always in the middle of a sentence, and when Regina prances to the door to open it a sliver, Seedsucker lays his head on his rose tattoo. The tattoo is on the wrong side, the outside, inside out, not like the blackbird tattoo carved into Marguerite's heart, wherever that is. He mutters something to his inside-out tattooed arm about the failure of citizenship to guarantee his rights.

"Citizen?!" the scary mask face snorts. "A man who leaves a bite mark like that should be locked away."

Seedsucker lifts his head, slow, as if it's as heavy as the flabby-armed pot-smasher's planet head. "This is bullshit."

"How did you get in here?" Dr. Con arrives, with Dr. Good Man, giving the quick nod to the taller mourning woman and the security guard coming around the corner with the same hard arm of muscle he used to steer the never-sleeping shouting-faced man away. Everyone is banished—to your rooms!—even Anna drowning in another sweatshirt, singing "Train, Train."

"Someone downstairs made a mistake. Said he was her brother," says the taller mourning woman, and Seedsucker lifts his head from where he's let it fall again.

"I'm just trying to do the right thing here," he says. "I'm a friend of her brother's, okay, an acquaintance. Can't a guy do the right thing?"

Marguerite feels him look through Regina's borrowed night-gown dress, through Regina's body standing in front of her like an electric fence around the lowing cows. He looks through Marguerite, as the hard arm muscles him toward the elevator. "This is bullshit," he says again.

"He doesn't know anything about your heart," Regina says, still up on her toes. "He's useless to you," she says, and firefly flash, her voice becomes the whoosh of the wind outside the Seedsucker's car, his inside-out, rose-tattooed arm hanging out the window as he drove south, not west to the land of Ryan the way he promised. He tore a new plastic bag with his teeth, offered Marguerite the torn-open bag of sunflower seeds, but her electric fingers were wrapped around the crumpled piece of paper: *During almost the entire duration of the ecstasy, Louise remains seated in her chair, inclined somewhat forward, and motionless as a statue. Her bleeding hands rest on her lap. Her eyes are motionless. Her countenance indicates rapt attention* . . . She rubbed and rubbed that crumbling piece of paper because her singing blood told her to. *Rub and this will be you.* And it was her. There would be no more weary-armed baths, no more nights in the night kitchen.

It was time, her blood sang to her in the car with Seedsucker's inside-out tattoo hanging out the window. Her blood sang to her in the cleanest, clearest voice: *Marguerite, become the most.* Out the window, Travel Marts and highway scrub and highway scrub and exits lead to invisible cities, and Rhode Island disappeared far behind them, farther and farther. This was her fucking train and she was long gone. Underneath her electric skin, Marguerite's quick and glistening blood sang: You too are *dead to all earthly objects*, you too are *absorbed in the contemplation of a spectacle, which you seem to behold above the region of the earth.*

There was construction at the plaza with the fast food, the restrooms a makeshift trailer with a shutdown look, a face that said: *no way.* Inside the bathroom, her face was suddenly apparent in the bathroom mirror, apparent like the solution to a math equation that she could solve if she was given one, give her one right now and she'd solve it. Her features lit up, her eyes became moistened, a smile of joy played around her half-opened mouth. Then her eyelids fell over eyes partly closed, her features contracted, and tears rolled down her cheeks. A stifled cry escaped her lips.

The woman with her little boy who had to *go bad* scurried out without using the toilet because they didn't recognize epiphany when they heard it and in came Seedsucker. It was no longer the salt of seeds he was hungry for. He licked her blooming body as they stumbled their way into a stall, frantic with their mission. Marguerite ran her tongue along the inside-out rose tattoo to hear its music and understand with the taste that it was without song but still she kept searching for her brother the way she did that night he left, searching for something holy because everything including this sucker of seeds was a sign to be deciphered.

There on the bathroom stall: graffiti hands stamped on the wall in red ink. *Presto chango!* scrawled in blue next to the hands. This was a sign—with her newfound POWER striking her mind like a match and whoosh, whoosh, firefly flash, there was Mr. Roberts skating around the physics room—she would make her brother hers again. Seedsucker's tongue slid rough and urgent and her salt dissolved on his tongue until he was past the salt and she was a smooth seed licked clean, and after years of yearning for it, she shuddered and shimmered with love for her long-gone brother.

"Two percent if he's lucky," Regina says, steering Marguerite away from the door where Marguerite stands, watching Seedsucker disappear into the elevator. Regina lays her down and covers her up to her chin, careful to pull the sheet up farther so the scratchy blanket doesn't scratch at Marguerite's face as she rests because rest is what she needs and they will find her heart later. She lays her long spider fingers on Marguerite's face with a tenderness stowed away from long ago, when the wondrous sweet-smelling creature was still hers.

"Don't even think about picking that pot up, don't even think it," the scary mask face says out in the hall, and Marguerite can hear the pot-smasher smile, the bend in his rubbery face. Later, it says, I'll do it later, just you wait, one great big pure dirt explosion and everything will be clear.

"Let me tell you about this *G-O-D* of mine," Regina says, brushing the hair from Marguerite's forehead. She imitates all 3 percent of the scary mask face. "He is the king. He loves absolutely everything. He loves the dull broken pot that tells us nothing. He loves the ladies singing their songs on the TV about their abandoned, broken, no-good hearts. He even loves that so-called citizen pretending to be your boyfriend." And then she is Regina again, saying, "But he loves your heart more and we will find it." The long spider fingers of tenderness dance off Marguerite's forehead as Regina slips away to open drawers in the muted brown bureau and close them, open and close, open and close.

Marguerite's blood plods dutifully through her veins now. She is so tired. From where she lies in her bed, she uses all her strength to call to Regina. "What are you doing?"

"Rat torturers!" the never-sleeping man shouts.

"I'm helping you look for your heart, shark girl," Regina says. She shuts the door to the hall tight against the shout, and then returns to open and close.

"I'm worried I'm forgetting the language of my blood," Marguerite says. Her blood has stopped singing altogether.

Regina doesn't look up, her spider fingers still scurrying through a drawer, tossing Marguerite's heel-less socks onto the floor. She just nods like someone who knows the feeling.

The Harvester of Hearts

Hyuen picks a burned French fry from the grease-stained wax paper lining the bottom of the red plastic basket. Ryan is more accustomed to seeing Hyuen handling a scalpel; he's more accustomed to seeing Hyuen in the morgue dancing with the dead. This is all very confusing, which is probably good, because it means it's distracting him from the task at hand, which is leaving the airport and going in search of his sister.

Before he left his apartment to meet Hyuen last night, the phone rang again. Ryan rushed to pick it up and at first he didn't recognize the voice.

"Is this the fucking carpenter again?" Ryan said. "Look, I don't care if you fucked my mother, just leave me alone."

"Ryan, man," the voice said. "It's Tommy. You know, Seed-sucker. Listen, man, I'm glad I got you. I called your house and talked to some guy who was talking some shit about the ear of his heart."

"What?" Ryan asked. That was the only word available to him at the moment. He was too tired to be angry, too tired to be surprised.

"Listen, man, don't be angry."

He couldn't imagine what this guy wanted with him, but he was prepared for anything so when Tommy began to tell him that he had dropped Marguerite in New York at a domestic violence shelter, man, because she was acting really weird, talking all kinds of crazy shit about her blood talking to her, at first Ryan heard only the words, as if they were simply letters strung together to make sound, not meaning. The place was all women, man, it seemed safe, Tommy's voice continued, and Ryan turned the kitchen sink on and off as the letters and the sounds started to form words and the words began to make sense.

"Where the fuck is she?" Ryan said. He was so tired he was surprised that his voice sounded at all threatening, but once an older brother's friend, always an older brother's friend, and Tommy began to spew apologies.

"I told you, I fucked up. I'm sorry. She's not there anymore. They moved her."

Ryan took notes as Tommy told him where the hospital was, really an approximation because Tommy had been there only once. "Fuck you," Ryan said when Tommy was done, and then Ryan hung up and then he hung up again, and again, and again, waiting for the sound to drown everything else out. It hadn't worked with the carpenter, and it didn't work this time either.

Hyuen holds another burned French fry, really more like a piece of coal than anything else, out to Ryan. "You've got to eat."

"No," Ryan says. "But, really, that's sweet of you." They've been sitting in this sandwich hut/bar/coffee shop in the airport since their flight arrived in New York and Ryan realized he was unable to leave the timeless bubble of the airport.

"Anubis," Hyuen tried when Ryan stopped dead in his tracks on the other side of the tunnel that spit them out by the gate. Hyuen pulled Ryan aside to move him out of the way of a particularly impatient woman in a business suit who promptly rolled her suitcase over Ryan's foot, though Ryan didn't seem to notice. "Egyptian deity who was half jackal? Thought brains were useless? Hearts were the seat of all intelligence? Went to graveyards and dug up hearts and discarded the brains with a hook?"

"You've told me that one already," Ryan said. He hadn't told Hyuen that the reminder of Anubis conjured an image of Margue dead on a table in a morgue somewhere, side by side with his mother. Anubis had him picturing his mother's useless brain in a trash can and a jackal carving his sister's heart out.

"I'm sorry," he said as Hyuen took him by the hand and led him to the sandwich hut/bar/coffee shop. "I need to sit down and try to relax my mind." A Muzak version of "You're So Vain" was piped out of an invisible speaker above them as they sat down. "Oh, great, a message from on high?" Ryan said.

"You should eat," Hyuen says now. "Look, your sister's not going anywhere in the middle of the night. You called, she's safe." Hyuen has been eating steadily: one of the sandwiches wrapped in plastic, looking nuclear under the bright yellow heat lamps; two pretzels with melted Velveeta cheese; trail mix to go with the beer he ordered at the bar, the French fries. At first Ryan thought he was just eating to be polite, to buy time so that Ryan could pull himself together without feeling embarrassed as an endless rotation of people propped their luggage against their legs at the bar, had a drink, and then moved on. But Hyuen seems to be genuinely hungry and Ryan realizes that he doesn't know Hyuen well enough to know what kind of appetite he has, or what his eating habits usually are. Hyuen, it turns out, has the appetite of many men.

Here in the early hours of the morning in the sandwich hut/bar/coffee shop than at first there are only two people at the bar—a man and a woman in business suits, briefcases at their feet, sitting under an oversized American flag, talking to the bartender.

"Everything's changed," the bartender's saying, agreeing with them though he's shaking his head no. Along the fluorescent-lit hallways with no clocks—this fact has always annoyed Ryan about airports, but tonight it's working for him—the newsstand owners are beginning to lift the metal gates and sort the newly arrived stacks of today's papers.

"Look," Ryan says to Hyuen, who is running his finger through the puddle of grease in the wax paper now. "I don't know what's wrong with me." He actually has a clue, but he can't bear to say it.

Since he learned about his mother's death all alone in the kitchen of the train depot, he's felt robbed. Had he been imagining a court of law at the end of life where, finally, emotional justice would be served? On some level, yes. He's never admitted it before, but he expected his mother to come to him and apologize, to say, *I'm guilty. I'm sorry. Ryan, let me make it up to you.* What exactly would she be apologizing for? It is ridiculous, *embarrassing.* He is twenty-five, a grown-up, which is why he isn't going to burden this sweet man chowing down in front of him with this. He hasn't even told Hyuen his mother is dead.

"I don't know why I can't leave the airport," he says. "It's just too much. I'm so, so sorry. I'm sorry I got you into this. I'm sorry you have to deal with me. I'm just . . ."

"Do you want to call your parents? I know they're not exactly a cake walk, but maybe they can help out?" Hyuen hands him his cell phone and then turns the basket upside down and shakes it. He never looks at Ryan, but Ryan can tell he's keeping an eye on him.

"They're so stuck in the past, neither of them has a cell phone, and they never answer their regular phone," Ryan says. His parents have problems working a television set, so the part about their technological ineptitude is true—it's the implication that both of them are alive that's a little faulty.

The couple at the bar turn toward each other as the bartender points the remote control at the muted TV and clicks. The set blooms suddenly to life: an ad for a circus with clowns doing somersaults and kids riding ponies.

There was a night Ryan went to Playland so stoned he could barely see. When some knucklehead hit the light above the mini-basket and the glass shattered into a million pieces, some of which landed in Ryan's hair, it felt strangely right. "This game is a rip-off," the knucklehead yelled. "I want my two dollars back." Ryan gave it to him and left the glass in his hair to sparkle the rest of the night, even after someone came to fix the light. He feels like a version of that now, as though his body has shattered into a million pieces of glass that are barely held together and if he moves, it will shimmer brilliantly for a second and then crash to the floor.

"My mother died," Ryan says, holding the cell phone in the air like a wand.

Hyuen doesn't say anything, just holds up the hand that isn't digging in the red basket. *Stop*, the hand says. Then it offers Ryan a napkin.

The tears are utterly unfamiliar. Ryan might as well be having a heart attack, it feels that unnatural. He tries to remember the last time he cried and he can't. Has he ever cried?

Hyuen pushes the empty red plastic basket aside, and for a minute Ryan is afraid that he is going to say something or, worse still, hold his hand, but he doesn't. Hyuen told Ryan recently that the half-life of molecules is less than two weeks, the half-life of calcium in the bone is less than four years, and that every second, three million red blood cells are dying and being replaced. Inside Hyuen, matter and energy is never still. The vibrations from that constant movement reach Ryan across the table.

"I need to tell my sister," Ryan says. He takes a sugar packet from the bowl and pushes it around his side of the table sticky from other people's beer. "She's in a hospital somewhere in Queens."

"I'm pretty sure my mother died too," Hyuen says, taking the sugar packet from underneath Ryan's fingers and putting it back in the bowl. "In Thailand."

Ryan looks up into the swirling vortex of molecules that are Hyuen's eyes looking somewhere over Ryan's shoulder down the length of the airport hallway. Flight announcements crackle overhead. Hyuen's eyes are beautifully worn and soft like sea glass.

"Let's go to a hotel," he says, his soft sea-glass eyes suddenly sharp and focused. "It's the middle of the night. You're not going to be able to visit your sister until later anyhow, and we can't stay in this hellhole airport forever. We'll get some rest and go to the hospital later."

"I'd be sitting here for weeks if it wasn't for you," Ryan says.

Hyuen stands and the matter and energy in Ryan shifts, helps him to his feet, in imitation of Hyuen.

"Any idiot can face a crisis; it's the day-to-day living that wears you out," Hyuen says. When Ryan looks at him blankly, he adds, "Chekhov."

"Do you have to know everything?" Ryan says, but he is laughing, grateful. "Do you think you could limit it to one field?" Hyuen's knowledge is different from his father's. It doesn't make Ryan feel stupid; it made him feel as if he might learn something.

"Chekhov was a doctor."

With the thick drapes drawn, a false nighttime pervades the motel room. Ryan continues to follow Hyuen's lead. Ryan imitates Hyuen's steady breathing in the other bed in order to fall asleep, but he can't stop the music in his head. *Are you sure your prayers haven't been answered? Think, sister, think.* Marguerite on the bed, jumping higher and higher. There is that question again hovering between them as she jumps off the bed and walks toward him. *Why did you let go?*

Margritte. Margritte. Margritte. His voice growling her back to earth. That's what she's always thought, but it wasn't only the anguish of a boy who didn't want to be left behind, it was the anguish of a boy who wished in some awful, dusty corner of his mind, a corner he never visits except when he can't sleep at night and doesn't have pot to fill his lungs beautiful and big, that Marguerite might really be dead. Had he really wished for her tiny bones to be smashed on the rocks?

He was angry at his mother that day, but it wasn't only to be able to throw rocks off the pier into the air thick with sea salt, to hear the plunk, plunk, plunk, that he let go of his sister's hand? *You may not know how to pray, but He loves you when you try. So raise your voices high and the Lord will hear you, hear you.* Marguerite's first words were for him: *Ry. Are you sure your prayers haven't been answered? Think, brother, think.* Years later, Marguerite's lean body stepping off the bed and walking so close to him it took him by surprise, and all of a sudden, her tongue, not just curious but urgent in his mouth, seeking out the answer. *Why did you let go?* Her tongue trying to get inside and have a conversation with his brain. He would have explained this to his father if his father had given him a chance. But from where he stood at the door, spying, Bernard couldn't see Marguerite's intentions, didn't hear the question that her blood was whispering. *Do you hear my blood whispering?* she had asked the moment before she kissed him. *Does yours whisper too?* What he heard most of all was *Why? Why? Why?*

From where Bernard was standing, Ryan could imagine what it looked like. It looked like Ryan's betrayal, but, of course, always Ryan's. Bernard's hand on Ryan's arm steering him out of the room, leaving Marguerite standing there with her electric eyes, her electric tongue, her whole body electric.

"Go see your mother," Bernard said to her. Bernard maneuvering Ryan as if he was an inanimate object, a chair, no longer his flesh, his blood, pushing him into the foyer where he waited while Ryan went into his room to gather his things but Ryan wanted nothing from this place. He would leave it all.

"I won't tell your mother," Bernard said in a voice as even and steady as his hand on Ryan's arm.

"Right," Ryan said. "Why bother? Just start over—a whole new family."

"She can't handle it," Bernard said, as if Ryan hadn't spoken. "You are done here."

Ryan was a broken chair—why bother repairing him?

Even as he stood there in the foyer, Ryan was back in the room with Marguerite, replaying the moment from minutes ago. Had he pulled away fast enough? His mouth tingled with Marguerite's searching tongue. Had he encouraged it? He hadn't thought so until then.

Hyuen's breath washes over the images of the sea filled with mysterious red weed, the seagulls flapping their giant wings, hovering on the beach against the sky full of transparent, mute, clouds racing, racing, his sister's hand in his and then no. Ryan concentrates on Hyuen's chest rising and falling, rising and falling, rising and falling.

"We aren't victims of our genetic inheritance," Hyuen said one day in the morgue, as he danced his slow, elegant dance around a corpse. "Brain plasticity. The context of our lives, what happens to us along the way, how we react to those things that happen. These things make new pathways in our brains." Hyuen's chest rises and fall, rises and falls, and Ryan imagines Hyuen's breath is changing him, creating new pathways in his brain. Hyuen's breath, in and out, in and out, is the steadiest thing Ryan has ever seen. Ryan feels it tunnelling through the dark of his mind, creating a whole system of roads that will form a map he will read in the morning.

Good Mourning in the Queen's County, Part IV

Carol Channing, with her big strange teeth and thin-lipped smile, blinks all hundred of her eyelashes to indicate the revolution's on as soon as Marguerite takes these new cupcake pills. A flutter of firefly flash: Marguerite's arms whirling in a dance for Ryan after dinner. The pot-smasher nods his big planet head as if he hears Ryan singing the words too. *Enough walk, enough talk about Jesus. I only want to see that face.* They run across the front of her aquarium mind, as her bare heel scuffs the carpet, squashing no souls.

"Shoes, shoes!" scary mask says.

"With your lips, with your lips," the pot-smasher says, but still he nods and nods his big planet head at Marguerite as if she was loving God that way already. "The purest dirt explosion," he says.

Presto chango! God doesn't give a shit when time is a rubber band. Snap! Presto chango! Hours lost like sweaters, like brothers, and the magic cupcake pills, different from the first ones, Carol says, cause Marguerite's blood to sing again: *get up, get up.* Her blood is quick and glistening again. Friday all day long, the taller mourning woman said. Friday, the most important day of all, a holy day. It happens after the smallpox took Marguerite's brother, no, it wasn't smallpox, it was her love that took him away from her, and it is her love that will bring him back. She lacks the instinct for sacredness; she will never be a martyr—Martyr! Martyr! Martyr!—across the mysterious red weed sea. Like Louise, Marguerite stole her first breath from her mother's mouth. And her family's time of trial began, waiting and waiting for that train that wouldn't come to take them away so Marguerite slipped out the window and got in a car that took her to the place with the other women kicked out of love and then they brought her here and still she is searching for her brother.

It happens after eighteen years of yearning to shudder. Oh, for the glistening clarity. Oh, for the sea of light! On this Friday all day long, like any other Friday but like no Friday ever before, Marguerite finds herself back in her room looking out the window, searching for the now o'clock lady, the magic hour sunset lady, so she can tell Marguerite what she learned when she reached up out of herself to touch her pompom hat, but she's not there. Life and death inside Marguerite as she waits for this moment to arise.

A gust of wind fills the plastic bags in the naked trees and a bus stop lady, different from the now o'clock lady with her pompom, stands there waiting for the bus. She opens her long fuzzy sweater in order to pull it closer around herself and the parts she opens are like wings about to fly, chop, chop, away, and underneath the fuzzy sweater is the sign that Marguerite has been waiting for: a belly rising with life in a body destined for death. Life and death inside her all at once, everything at once. The big red sun in the outside sky burns Marguerite's blood until it boils in the pulse of her palms pressed hard against the mute bureau, telling her something louder than the wide-awake shouting man, louder than any smashing pot, louder than Anna drowning in her sweatshirt crying out for a train, any train. More powerful than God, the ambulance sings. More powerful than God. She knows what she has to do. There must be proof. She walks into the land of the smoking brains where she will achieve her magnificence.

"Hey sharky," Regina says, smoking in the middle of the smol-
dering, smoking brains. Marguerite reaches for the burning stick
Regina smokes. "Didn't know you smoked," she says. "Here you
can have one of your own."

Firefly flash: *A wiggle of your hips and a wink of the eye. It's his
laugh you're laughing, his tears you cry.* She jumped down off the
bed and walked toward Ryan as if she was asking him to dance, but
it was a dance unlike any other, a collision of their bodies so they
both might rise up and when she pressed her mouth against his, she
sought that rising thing out with her tongue.

She is no weary arm testing the bathwater. She is quieter now
than the eternity that embraced her between the rocks. She is quieter than the sizzle sound of the burning stick she presses into the
soft, secret place at the center of her palm, its web of lines that are
meant to tell a life but secretly yearn for something beyond the life it
tells. Marguerite presses the stick harder because at first there is no
shudder, at first there is nothing at all. And then she feels something.
Like a light in her palm, shining from the inside out. It's so bright it
makes a sound. The smoking brains, even Regina with her secret
map of bruises, hear it too, and here come the mourning women,
scrambling to put out another fire. All of the villagers are finally
amazed.

Living in a Nowhere Land

It feels as though the woman's hands are inside Bernard's body, massaging his liver and his spleen, handling his most secret organs, secret no longer. The birds in the cage of his heart are dead, their little necks wrung by the woman's hands in the first five minutes in this concrete room with no windows in the back of the truck stop.

"Softer," he gasps. He can barely catch his breath to make words. "Killing. Me."

"Deep massage," the woman says. "Supposed to kill you."

She moves on to his heart and his lungs, rolling them around until he can no longer speak, only surrender.

After they spent some more time "pretending to sleep" in her apartment, Bella decided they should hit the road. "We'll go to Connecticut," she announced. "We'll visit the theater school that's offered me the scholarship."

What could Bernard say? Hitting the road had become his specialty. He would become a scholar of hitting the road. He would study it until it became clear that it was the only last good option, like climbing aboard the Ship of Fools with the other fools and setting sail to whatever seaside town would take you in and treat you like a shaman for a while before deciding that you were only just a fool whose rantings were just words, not prophecy. And besides, it's been a bad year for Bella—an almost-marriage, a miscarriage that's kept her in bed with the shades drawn, reading the religious pro-life tracts and those apocalyptic novels her mother sends her because why do misery halfway? Why not do it right? When she thought he was really asleep, she told him, most days she leaves her apartment only to go to the acting class she's always secretly hoped would someday change her life.

This will be the last time you hit the road with a pretty waitress, and Bernard thought he detected a note of jealousy in Sam's voice. He didn't even bother to think *See how it feels?* though, there, he'd thought it. The hippy porn carpenter was miles and miles behind him.

So, in full hitting-the-road spirit, the new Bernard, the Bernard who intended to leave his life on the side of the road, didn't ask questions when Bella asked him to pull into the American Truck Stop off I-95 in Bethel, Pennsylvania. He didn't even pout when she said it was a trucker passing through the diner one night who had told her about this amazing massage parlor on the up-and-up, which all of his trucker friends swore by. Instead, Bernard simply maneuvered his car, its license plate now propped up in the rear window, through the sea of trucks in the enormous parking lot, pulling in next to one with COME FIND JESUS WITH ON THE ROAD MINISTRIES across its side in human-size lettering.

Why not? His life was an endless series of surprises now. He's wearing bloomers one night and then he's inside a building the size of Rhode Island, its interior like a mall, with shops that sold Bambi china figurines the shop must imagine a guy might bring home to the little woman as a gift when he's back from the road. The American Truck Stop has a corridor of video games and a room in the back devoted to gambling, a family-style restaurant, and a laundromat with a sign that promises ten minutes of shower for two quarters.

When Bella took his hand and started heading for the door that said "Chinese massage," Bernard didn't even hesitate. Not even when a guy wearing a baseball cap, his arm so frenetic with tattoos they were impossible to decipher said, "Happy ending, man! Happy fucking ending." Maybe it was time for Bernard to get a tattoo? It felt as though the flapping birds inside his chest had already scratched a tattoo on the flesh of his heart with their tiny, scrambling forked feet.

For a Siberian dwarf hamster, Sam said as Bernard followed Bella through the door, *you're pretty adventurous*.

"Your wife have massage with me," the man, who did in fact look Chinese, said, taking Bella's hand and leading her toward a table poking out from behind a thin rubber curtain hanging in the corner of the concrete massage room buzzing with fluorescent lights. "You have massage with my wife," he said, gesturing to the woman who at first pummeled Bernard not exactly into ecstasy, more like oblivion. She pounded his back so intensely that he couldn't even laugh when he heard Bella's humming "Nowhere Man" from behind the curtain.

"You . . . don't . . . know," she sings now, as if her voice was in a blender. "What . . . you're . . . missing."

"See?" the woman says, her hands having finished exploring his most secret organs. Though her hands are finally still, Bernard's body still vibrates from the inside out. "No happy ending," she says, slapping Bernard's arm. "Just happy."

"See, you feel great, right?" Bella says, poking her head around the rubber curtain. Her forehead is red from where it rested on the front of the massage table and Bernard touches his own forehead. He does feel great. Right now, at this very moment, he feels wonderful.

See, he says to Sam, *it is possible to seek out the extraordinary, to have it maybe not all of the time, but a lot of the time*.

The man with the frenetic tattoos is on the pay phone outside of the Chinese massage room. Still, he lifts his baseball hat in a salute to Bernard and smiles, mouthing, "Happy ending, right?" before he goes back to his conversation. "I'm in Florida. I'm in fucking Florida," he barks. "What do you want me to do?"

"Onward?" Bella asks, pulling a few greasy strands of her hair in front of her face to examine it before gathering it up to tie in the now-familiar knot. "Massage oil," she says.

"You don't want to spend the night here?" Bernard asks. His body still tingles and he doesn't want to move for fear it will stop, grow still enough for his life to take root again.

"In this dump?" Bella starts for the door, pausing only to slide a coin into a machine that prints the Lord's Prayer on the head of a penny. "A souvenir for my mother," she says.

Bernard follows her helplessly, the massage oil squishing between his toes, out to the parking lot where the On The Road Ministry truck is still parked by his poor dented car with the license plate propped forlornly in the window. On the back of the truck in smaller, calligraphic letters, is written: *When you get to your wits end, you'll find God lives there.* He grunts, not sure himself whether he's laughing or making some other sound that's not laughing at all, and if it's not laughing, what is it? Maybe the massage rearranged his emotions too? For a minute, he wants to drive back and rescue Louise and her dusty rose manuscript from where it sits on top of the paper towel dispenser, and then he realizes he doesn't remember which rest stop.

"What are you laughing at?" In the bright, brisk air, Bella stamps her feet impatiently, waiting for Bernard to unlock the passenger-side door.

"Nothing," Bernard says, noticing his breath in the air and the charcoal smell of fall for the first time. There's a girl leaning into a boy leaning into a car, huddled against the cold on the other side of Bella. It turns out Bernard is laughing at nothing in particular but everything at once.

Then they are back on the road, and Bella insists on another acting game, which involves saying only the words "Peanut Butter" to each other. "It's about subtext," she says. "You're saying 'peanut butter,' but, for example, you might really be saying 'get me the fuck out of here.' Get it?"

"Do you want to get the fuck out of here?" Bernard asks, suddenly panicked at the idea of her leaving him alone.

"Oh, Jesus, it was just an example," Bella says, putting a hand on Bernard's thigh. Bernard feels suddenly horrible that he's reduced their adventure to the normal insecurities of relationships. Was the sad truth that when it came down to it, he wasn't even up for the extraordinary?

"Okay, let's do it!" he says, a little too enthusiastically.

"Whatever," Bella says. "I thought that massage would relax you. Okay, so there's a slight variation to this game if you're on the road. You speak in road signs."

And so they begin. "E-Z pass," Bella says. "Eeeee-zeeee pass."

"Thru traffic, I mean, really, thru traffic," Bernard says.

"Road signs only!" Bella squeals. "No 'I mean' or 'really.' No other words at all."

"Kids eat and stay for free," she says, chidingly. "Travel Mart, Speed Limit 65, Open Joints on Bridge—ha ha—Cinnabon!"

"No laughing either," Bernard says. "Tag holder," he reads off the E-ZPass lane and means the way Louise Lateau, a footnote, was the best illustration of William James's theory that faith states were biological as well as psychological he'd found so far. She was proof of James's idea that "religion was not a mere illuminator of facts" but "a postulation of new facts." That religion didn't really exist in the form of a "dull habit," the way his parents wanted it to when they went dutifully to mass every Sunday, but as an "acute fever" burning with ecstasy.

"Hot Dog City," he says meaning the way Louise walked the fine line between religiousness and insanity. Here he was living on his own fine line and, real or unreal, it didn't matter—he was living.

"Guest Center!" Bernard proclaims, on a roll, meaning Louise, through it all, tried to continue to love something that might have been God but seemed more to Bernard to be life itself, to be something bigger than God altogether. He feels himself shrinking again. "Guest Center," he says again; this time he means the way he deserted Louise in that rest stop, the way he's deserted his wife and his daughter, the way he sent his son packing, the way he's walked out on it all.

"Rest stop," Bella says solemnly.

"Rest stop," Bernard agrees.

"No," Bella says, "I mean I really have to go to the bathroom."

Bernard pulls off, and Bella pats his leg again. "You're good at that game," she says.

While he's waiting for Bella, he wanders out into the parking lot that smells like the gas at the nearby Sunoco depot, being pumped by teenagers in gray jumpsuits, unlit cigarettes hanging from their mouths. It's dusk and the setting sun makes the woman yelling at her children to hurry up and get out of the road look not just fierce but fiercely beautiful. The magic hour, Ryan once told him—this hour of the day that was everybody's best light, the time for making movies. And, frankly, it was easier if Bernard thought of this as a movie and not his real life.

He pinches himself. See, doesn't even hurt. He feels nothing, except the sunset light making even his fifty-nine-year-old hand with its brown age spots and dry skin, seem fascinating, triumphant. How did that happen? A man in an orange hunting vest glowing like a beacon stares at Bernard as he passes him on the sidewalk and Bernard realizes he's stopped moving altogether, that he's standing next to a trash can whose fast-food smell reminds him to keep moving, keep moving, keep moving, or risk the magic-hour veil being lifted to reveal the world without good lighting.

He doesn't recognize his car at first, even with the license plate in the window and the now-familiar dent in the fender, because there's a man studying the license plate through the window. The man, who seems to be about ten years younger than Bernard, though with much less hair Bernard notes with some satisfaction, isn't just studying it, he's stamping his feet and pointing.

"I had a bad dream about Rhode Island!" the man shouts, pointing at the license plate through the back window. Bernard tries to quietly slip the key into the door.

"This is off the hook!" the man shouts. "Just last night."

Bernard nods, though he feels like he might start crying. He has no room for other people's bad dreams.

"I was up all *night*! Cookies and milk, that's all I could do, man.

This is a *sign*. This is speaking to me. Do you understand?" The man hops up and down on one foot.

"Uh-huh" is all Bernard can manage as he slips into the car. He locks the door and puts his seat belt on. He's missed so many signs. Not just missed them, but deliberately ignored them. No longer signs, but billboards. He's not sure he would recognize his own home anymore.

"Okay, so now *I'm* speaking to you," Bella is saying to the man still pointing at Bernard's license plate. "Get the fuck out of the way or we're going to back right over you." She bangs on the passenger-side window. "Hello! James Fenimore Cooper! Alert, alert! James Fenimore Cooper!"

Bella is taller than Bernard realized. He notices this as he leans over to unlock the passenger door, a gesture that has become as familiar as the walk in the middle of the night to find his daughter in the night kitchen, pouring the milk in the saucepan, the dusty rose manuscript.

"I finally got just the nuts," Bella says, holding up the bag. "This," she points to the floor where she's discarded the raisins and dried pineapple from trail mixes, "is disgusting and a big waste of money.

"Welcome to New Jersey," Bella says. "Hey, why aren't you driving? Let's get a move on."

"Governor Alfred Driscoll," Bernard says plaintively. His wife's voice has returned to him. *Remember that window that looked out over the stony Rhode Island fields and fields and more fields and remember that book of wildflowers guide I bought because the yard was filled with mountain laurel, Hollow Joe-Pye Weed, jeweled forget-me-nots, eggs-and-butter, Queen Anne's lace, mullein, goldenrod. Remember how hard I tried to remember the names of those flowers?*

"Shoulder closed," Bernard says, wanting to tell Bella about Sam, about everything. He wants to explain himself to her because he thinks she'll understand. *There in the distance, the ocean a quivering blue line. Remember the spring light that first time we went down to the beach, before our argument about Chopin's heart, the way it was*

*so different from the refracted light of winter? The way it was a more
direct beam of sun, warm on the top of our heads?*

"Fines doubled," Bernard says. *All of this possibility in our shoulders touching as we strolled down to the beach, the kids behind us.*

"Bella," he says.

Bella doesn't even look his way. "Don't, Bernard," she says
sternly, holding up a hand: *Stop.* "Really, don't. *Drive.*"

"I'm not going to say what you think I'm going to say." Bernard
reaches over and unties the knot in Bella's red hair so that it falls
over her shoulders.

"How do you know what I think you're going to say?" She
gathers her hair efficiently with two hands and reties the knot.

"I just want to talk," Bernard says. She seems so capable, the
way she ties and unties the knot in her red hair with her strong
hands. The way she handled the "off the hook" guy pointing at
Bernard's license plate as if it was a symbol telling him where he
should go next.

"I'm not interested in your talk," Bella says.

"I just want to explain." Bernard wonders if Sam's voice will
disappear if he tells Bella about it. He wants to find out.

"That's the thing." Bella looks out the window at the guy who is
no longer staring at Bernard's license plate but has moved on to another car. With a big fake smile on her face, she waves at him. "I'm
sure you're going through something really difficult, but, you know
what, welcome to the club. I mean, look at that guy."

The man on the sidewalk tugs at the sleeve of a woman heading
into the rest stop. "Off the hook!" he's shouting, pounding the air
with his fists as the woman shakes him loose and keeps walking.

The blush begins at Bernard's throat and spreads slowly, taking
its time as it makes its way up his face, into his cheeks, until he feels
as though he might have a fever. He wishes for the flap, flap, but the
birds, like Sam, have fallen silent. He feels his forehead with the
back of his hand, partly because he thinks he might have a fever and
partly to keep Bella from seeing his embarrassment. But she's looking out the window, showing him her lovely profile. Her nose cut-

ting through the air is the most beautiful thing he's ever seen, but he knows not to say that. He smells Sam's skin, a hint of rose and the ocean salt drifting up from the beach, a smell that's been lost to him since they stopped sleeping together months and months ago. His back aches from all the driving and there's a pain in his left buttock. He's way too old for this.

"Gas, food, lodging," he says decisively. He backs up, almost hitting a little girl holding an ice cream cone, and her mother shouts, "Are you blind? Can't you see there's a fucking kid here?" She takes the child's ice cream cone and hurls it at the back of the car and the child starts crying.

"Mom, that was mine," she squeals.

"It's not yours anymore," the mother says, taking the child by the hand and pulling her toward an SUV.

"That was useful," Bella says, but Bernard isn't listening as he pulls back out onto the tunnel-like highway. He is trying not to hear anything, especially the mantra in his head: *I want to go home, I want to see my wife, I want my family back*.

Miles and miles of silence down the road, the smear of ice cream still on the back window, the mantra continues. At the Grover Cleveland rest stop, Bernard pulls off again.

"Hey, what are you doing?" Bella shouts, throwing up her hands so that her bag of nuts explodes. Rolling her eyes, she rolls down her window. "You made me do that," she shouts after Bernard, who is already out of the car and headed for the building. She throws a nut after him.

But Bernard is through the door, on his way to the telephones. Bella has one of those cell phones he swore he would never resort to, but even if he took it out of the car, far away from her, it seems like the height of rudeness to use it to call his wife. He's dialing his home number and it rings and rings and rings. He's imagining Marguerite in the bath and Sam with her sleeves rolled up, lying on the red divan by the window. He's imagining them both asleep, then Sam waking up and starting to walk into the kitchen where the phone is ringing and ringing and ringing and ringing. He's imagining Sam cursing his name, refusing to answer the phone, swatting it with that flyswatter of hers.

He dials the number for messages and hears a mellifluous voice he doesn't recognize. "Mr. Hennart," it says. "I don't know you, but I'm a friend of your son's." Bernard's imagining Ryan dead, imagining tomorrow when he wakes up faced with the fact that his son is dead and he never apologized for the horrible way he threw him out of the house, for the horrible way he's handled everything. He's imagining years from now, living in a motel with a scratchy quilt, sticking his fingers through the perfectly round cigarette-burned holes and regretting his entire life. He remembers Ryan as a kid poking jellyfish with a stick on the beach and recognizing the look in his eye, barely visible under his floppy bangs, a look of hungry confusion that reminded Bernard of himself. He's thinking about how it's all too late, how he can never, ever go back when he hears the buttery voice saying, "He's unsure how to reach you." Ryan isn't dead. "But he felt it was important to try. Your daughter is in a psychiatric hospital in Queens." The voice leaves an address just as Bernard feels himself falling to the ground, no flapping birds, just the weight of the years doing its job, and there are Bella's hands in his armpits again. *See, it* wasn't *the last time a beautiful-at-a-second-glance waitress helped me as I fell*, he says to his wife, whom he once again blames for everything. It's clear to Bernard now: Sam's affair with that hippy porn carpenter has caused their daughter to run away from home, driven her states and states away, turned her into a *fugeur* just like her father, unsure of how she got where she is or how to get back.

Good Mourning in the Queen's County, Part V

Dr. Con turns out not to be a trick at all, not a trick like Carol Channing's trick cupcake that is no cupcake. In fact, even from this angle, sideways with her head turned on the gurney because the straps don't budge, he is George Harrison dressed up like a doctor. George Harrison, Ryan's favorite Beatle, a sign that tells Marguerite that Ryan is almost there, that he hears the thump, thump of the heart she no longer hears, that he is keeping track and that he will find it and carry it all the way to the cathedral by the beach.

"Do you know where you are?" George asks cleverly, and Marguerite knows it is time to show him her magnificence, soft and silky.

"I know it's the time when all your hopes have faded," she says, because he will understand the art of dying, life and death together inside one person. He will understand when things that once appeared so plain turn into an awful pain. He will understand the constant search for the truth amidst the lying. He will know this because these were his words first and she is only returning them to him. He nods his head, but it isn't a nod of recognition.

"Do you hear me?" she asks.

"You aren't speaking, Marguerite," he says, his shirt singing blue like the sea that left salt on their skin and Marguerite tastes it on her tongue. He undoes the strap and takes her hand, peels back the bandage he's used to hide her best work, and holds the bubbled stigmata up to her.

"You've hurt yourself," he says.

Carol Channing murmurs something about a change in the medication being the source of the problem and George murmurs yes, yes, a definite possibility, though Marguerite sees Carol's 110 percent eyelashes wink wink, and she knows this is code for *Look at the magnificence of the divine*.

"The life preserver preserved me," Marguerite shouts and she shouts it all day long because even though the taller mourning woman hasn't said so, Marguerite knows it's Friday and it's time for someone to hear about the miracle bestowed upon her all those years ago now that they have arrived in the moment she has been been waiting for all her life. All her life!

And at first, it seems as though George understands because he and the mourning women present her with a blessed object which she recognizes with a joyful smile.

"More powerful than God," Marguerite says because there is no need to shout now that she's gotten their attention.

They've brought the relic to her again, this pin with which to pierce her arm to see if she is 100 percent, if she will shudder with sacredness like the trembling leaves outside on the bony branches, and she does. But then she is still and, still, she is ready. She is so still that they no longer believe she is capable of movement, but with one swift twist, Marguerite turns against their thick pin, even as George and the mourning women try to steady her and then the blood does not flow from the opening of any former cut or wound but from the unbroken surface of her skin. The bleeding is not indifferent.

"I am the most," she says. Then, presto chango, the powerful silence has beckoned her, invited her to a place where her body may bleed and bleed, but her mind is stiller and stiller.

Outside the door, 100 percent Regina, no so-called about her, stands in the up and down hall. "I'll keep looking for your heart," she says into the door. "I'll use my secret maps," she says, pointing to Uzbekistan and the newly discovered Madagascar on her long legs. "I'll make new ones," she promises.

The pot-smasher silently nods his big planet head. No pure dirt explosion, he just nods in the direction of the snail with the mustache. Next to the snail, the panda at the office has a mustache now too. He wants to show Marguerite, but she cannot see.

Marguerite is so deep into the light of the dark black night that she becomes the dark black. She is so far outside of time that the night is neither here nor there, neither now nor then. It is everything at once.

That Unsharable Feeling or the Pinch of Individual Destiny

That unsharable feeling which each one of us has of the pinch of his in-dividual destiny as he privately feels it rolling out on fortune's wheel may be disparaged for its egotism, may be sneered at as unscientific, but it is the one thing that fills up the measure of our concrete actuality, and any would-be existent that should lack such a feeling, or its ana-logue, would be a piece of reality only half made up.

—William James, *Varieties of Religious Experience*

Are you sure you don't want any?" Hyuen says over the clatter of breakfast dishes and silverware, the gruff rumble of waitresses taking orders and breakfast chatter at the diner in Queens. He digs into the stack of pancakes, part of the Deluxe breakfast which promises three kinds of meat: bacon, sausage, and Taylor ham, a bagel, and a fruit cup that Hyuen has pushed to the side so that he can make room for the side of French fries with gravy he just ordered.

There are autographed pictures above each booth of celebrities Ryan doesn't recognize, their arms around the owner of the diner. The one above Ryan and Hyuen's booth is a guy who has had bit parts in gangster movies. The owner of the diner holds his hands above his head, pretending the guy is holding him at gunpoint.

"No, thanks," Ryan says. He's not sure whether he wishes he

had a gun or whether he wishes he was being held at gunpoint. Either of them seems preferable to seeing his sister on a psych ward. "I'd rather watch. It's like an experiment. How much can one tall, thin man eat in one sitting? Are you sure you're not stoned?" Ryan wishes he was.

The diner is between a check-cashing place and an OTB, on a busy boulevard with lots of traffic. The cab that brought them here stopped in the middle of the road to let them out, causing a choir of horns despite the "No Honking" signs. They're only a few blocks from the hospital where Tommy, aka Seedsucker, said Marguerite was, but once again, Ryan finds himself unable to move any closer.

"Sorry," Hyuen says, sopping up gravy with a fistful of French fries. "I eat when I get nervous, and leaving that message on your father's answering machine made me nervous."

Ryan didn't even ask Hyuen to leave the message. It was Hyuen's idea, as was not telling Bernard via answering machine message about Sam's death. "Not exactly good etiquette," Hyuen said. "I don't care how angry you are at your father." Hyuen is filled with good ideas. It was his idea to accompany Ryan to the diner. It was simply assumed and Ryan no longer feels guilty, just deeply grateful that Hyuen is here, scarfing down his breakfast, because even though Ryan's not hungry, he continues to take his cues from Hyuen. Tragedy is universal. Breathe like the ocean. Keep moving.

"That's a good appetite," the elderly woman in the next booth says to Hyuen appreciatively. Her husband sits next to her silently, sipping black coffee from a chipped cup. The woman's sparse, thin hair is tinted pink so that it matches the parts of her scalp that are exposed. "Why can't you have an appetite like that?" she says to her husband, who harrumphs and continues to look out the smudged window to the street littered with garbage. Plastic bags flutter up into the bare branches of the few trees, which wear metal guards like chokers at the bottom of their trunks. As an ambulance whines by, Ryan imagines that it might take an ambulance to get him out of this booth and down the street to the hospital.

Out of a stream of people making their way along the sidewalk, wrapped in the first scarves of fall, Ryan follows a tall, striking woman, her red hair tied in a knot. She becomes distinct from the crowd as she stops and picks up one foot to examine the sole of her shoe. *Don't squash those souls*. It appears she's stepped in a pile of dog shit.

"People don't clean up after their dogs," the pink-haired lady says to her husband, who harrumphs again. "Aren't people ashamed? Look at that poor woman."

The redhead is swearing, the words clear in the way her lips move—fuck, shit, fucking shit—as she wipes the bottom of her shoe with a sheaf of newspaper. She's balancing on one foot, her other hand on her companion's shoulder, a shorter, squatter man who at first looks like any lucky older guy who has landed a beauty. His eyes are startled with luck, looking off in two different directions.

And then Ryan is hungry after all. He is starving. He wants to bite the back of his father's neck, his father standing there, short and frumpy next to this tall redhead cleaning dog shit off her shoe. Ryan wants to tear his father's flesh from his bones and devour it while his father begs for his forgiveness. But before he begs for Ryan's forgiveness—for naming him after a dead man instead of a mystic, for not noticing that it wasn't Ryan who was the fellow who would give his father some trouble but the other way around, for kicking him out of the house—Bernard will tell him, without even having to be asked, how much he loves Ryan, so much that it has tattooed the shit out of his ratty, tattered, dulled motor of a heart, how if only he was able to show his love, his heart wouldn't be so full of holes. Where's your italicist, Bernard? Ryan will ask, jumping up and down. I retired his ass. Who is the most? You are, Ryan, you are! Bernard will say.

"What are you looking at?" Hyuen asks, mouth full of the sausage he put to the side in order to eat the French fries, but has now returned to. He follows Ryan's eyes out the window just in time to see Bernard pull the diner door, heavy with the late-September wind, open for Bella the redhead who makes a big production of thanking him.

"Thank you, kindest of sirs! However can I repay you? Perhaps with a newspaper covered in dog shit?" She makes faux-worshipping signs in the air with her arms and gestures to the trash can outside, dramatically batting thick eyelashes over close-together eyes that make Ryan a little dizzy.

"Look, there's a lot that's my fault, but the dog shit was not my fault," Bernard says. "You're the one who suggested we come here in the first place."

"My father," Ryan tells Hyuen. "Apparently, I wasn't the only one who wasn't in a rush to get to the hospital. We're a family that has its priorities straight."

"That's your father?" the pink-haired woman says with excitement. "What a coincidence! Did you hear that?" She nudges her husband, who doesn't even bother to harrumph as he holds his empty cup up in the air to catch the attention of the waitress.

"Please put a cork in it," Hyuen says to the woman, who turns to her husband and mouths, *Did you hear that?* to which he replies with another harrumph. "Here," Hyuen says to Ryan, gesturing at his own mouth, and Ryan wipes the drool from the other side of his mouth with his napkin.

"I don't know what to do," he says.

"You don't have to do anything right away," Hyuen says. And though the only thing that Ryan has told Hyuen about his father is how disappointed he was in Ryan, nothing of the circumstances under which he left the train depot, Hyuen makes more sense than anyone ever has, so Ryan watches as Bernard and the redhead sit down and order coffee. He watches as the redhead pretends to hold something in the air between them and Bernard mimics her. Bernard closes his eyes and pretends to sip from the invisible thing he holds and then makes a big production of the invisible thing's tasting delicious.

"Delicious!" he says, sarcastically.

"Don't even try if you're not going to do it right," Bella says, flicking him with the tip of her napkin. "I'm just trying to help you relax, but it won't work if you're not trying."

"Okay, I'll do it again." Bernard reaches for his cup so quickly, he knocks it over. "See?" he says, jumping back as the coffee runs off the table and onto the floor. "I'm a wreck. Don't make me play this game. Real life is hard enough."

Ryan watches as the waitress excuses her way past other customers, carrying a big beach towel. Then Bella turns and looks across the diner in his direction. "What are you staring at?" she asks, and Bernard follows her voice.

For a moment, Bernard stares at Ryan as if he was as estranged from him as the pink-haired lady with her harrumphing husband.

"You're going to have to get out of the booth," the waitress says, pulling Bernard's shirtsleeve. "I'm not a miracle worker."

"Okay, so now maybe you should go over," Hyuen says.

"You don't know anything about this," Ryan snaps. He remembers how small Marguerite felt in his arms those nights he walked her to sleep. He was always amazed that a creature that small contained all of the potential for a grownup life. He wishes he was that small now and Hyuen could carry him right out of the diner.

"Don't yell," Hyuen says.

"I'm sorry." Ryan enjoys the way they are fighting. There's something natural and easy about it, necessary and useful. A different kind of song than *Who is the most?* or *Where is my fucking train?* It's a song Ryan hasn't heard before.

"Don't be sorry, be careful," Hyuen says.

"You're right," Ryan says. "I want to go over there. Okay, I'm going over there. Watch me go. Here I go. Are you ready?" He can't move. "Okay, seriously." He pretends his life has a soundtrack. *Love hurts?* No. Too dramatic. *Take these broken wings and learn to fly?* Too corny. *When things that are so plain turn into an awful pain. He will understand seeking the truth amidst the lying.* George Harrison's "The Art of Dying" seems eminently appropriate, and with that, he's up and walking across the diner, banging chairs out of his way with his hip so they squeak and squeal against the linoleum floor.

"Hey," a hipster with a sharp, pointed goatee wearing a gas station attendant's coveralls says, holding up a fork threateningly to Ryan as he squeezes past. "Watch it."

Bella is in the corner, settling the bill with the waitress away from the spilled coffee, and Bernard has his head in his hands and his hands on the table on top of the coffee-drenched beach towel. He looks up only when Ryan is standing directly over him.

"I got your message," he says.

"That would be a first," Ryan says.

"Your friend's message. This is no time to be a wise ass. Is that your friend over there?" Bernard nods his head in the direction of Hyuen, who stares out the window at the people streaming by on the sidewalk. Ryan doesn't feel like answering Bernard's question. It wasn't the right question. How about, *How are you?* or *Who are you?* He isn't sure what he feels like doing, but it doesn't involve telling Bernard anything he might want to know.

"Ryan," Bernard says. "Come on, why don't you sit down? You're making me nervous."

"Then it's working," Ryan says. Still, he slides into the booth across from Bernard.

"Have a little sympathy," Bernard says, putting his head back into his hands. "Can't you see that I'm falling apart?"

Staring across the table at this man with a beard that has become more salt than pepper, this man who can only look him in one eye, it occurs to Ryan that usually he is walking away from tables where Bernard is sitting. The night Bernard told Ryan that he couldn't continue working at Playland forever, for example. The night Bernard said Playland was exactly that, all play and no work, and you know what that makes Jack. "A really happy guy?" Ryan had said, before he told both his parents to fuck off. He can't remember the last time, if there ever was a last time, he and his father have ever sat down to a meal together alone. All those mandatory family dinners, and it occurs to Ryan that he barely knows this guy.

"Couldn't you see that I was falling apart then?" Ryan is grateful for the background noise of the diner, the clatter of silverware and plates, other people's conversations that don't have to do with dead mothers and lost sisters and father-son reunions. The sound of traffic outside is hopeful, the promise of life elsewhere.

Bernard begins to tear tiny pieces from his napkin and put them in a pile on the saucer next to the half-spilled cup of coffee. There is still a swirl of milk on the top, unstirred.

"A farmer had a young son who wasn't afraid of anything," Ryan says. He pushes the cup and saucer away from Bernard and stills Bernard's hand with his own. "I hated that fairy tale. One night I came home so stoned from Playland that I stood in the driveway and didn't even recognize the house. I stood there, shaking, because I couldn't get that part of that fairy tale out of my head. I wasn't yearning to shudder, I was shuddering. At first, it felt good, like the shaking was taking me somewhere." That night, standing in the driveway as he had on so many occasions, proud in his separateness, Ryan really hadn't recognized the train depot. That night, he hadn't recognized his own hand held up in front of his face. He stood there, his insides fluttering, wondering how it could be that he *was* his body and yet his body was utterly unfamiliar. He lay down by a blackberry bush and fell asleep, hoping to be transported somewhere else. When he woke up, he realized the hope came from being stoned.

"There wasn't anything bad enough I could do to get your attention," Ryan says. "And trust me, I tried. It took Marguerite—and good move, naming her for a mystic to make up for her being an accident—quoting some bullshit you pumped into her about fidelity and love. You know I didn't want what happened to happen."

"I know that feeling," Bernard says. "The way you felt lying there, hoping, in the blackberry bush." Ryan expected his father to interrupt him, but he didn't expect him to agree with him. He can see his future face hidden in the fleshy depths of Bernard's, lurking behind his beard. It's not so bad. He wants to touch that face but thinks better of it. He puts his hand under his leg and sits on it. "I want to be taken somewhere too," Bernard says.

"You can't just switch booths like that," the waitress says, suddenly back with her pot of coffee. She stares at Ryan. "This isn't a free-for-all. I've got to keep the bills straight. Do you all want to sit together or do you want to, I don't know, leave?"

Ryan is grateful someone is telling them what to do next because he hasn't figured out how to tell Bernard about Sam.

"Maybe that's a good idea?" Bernard says. "Leaving? Going to see Marguerite?"

"I let go of her hand," Ryan says.

"Whose hand?" Bernard says.

Ryan stares at the blue formica tabletop between them. Did Bernard see a table made of granite? That Ryan's failure of Marguerite, a story that has been so central to his life for over a decade, is something that Bernard has to be reminded of, or might not even know at all, at first makes Ryan want to bang his head on the table until his brains lie there like the dead barn cat's. See this, Bernard. Then, slowly, as slow as the first swell of a wave as it begins to take shape, a wide-open feeling begins to expand inside his chest. It's the same kind of freedom he felt when he tore off his clothes, first his tee shirt, and then his shorts, and then his underwear in a swift no-turning-back kind of gesture, when he went skinny-dipping with the teenagers on the beach all those years ago.

"Are you all finished?" Bella asks, returning to the table with a glass of ice and sliding back into the booth next to Bernard. She looks at Ryan as she wraps the ice in a napkin and hands it to Bernard. "In case you start your fainting routine. Who are you anyway?"

"His son," Ryan says to the redhead. "Who are you?"

"A friend of your father's," Bella says, apparently unperturbed by finding Bernard's son here in the diner, though her voice is softer, gentler. "Hold the ice to your head," she says to Bernard. She takes the ice wrapped in a napkin from Bernard and holds it to his forehead. "Lean back." She pushes Bernard back in the booth.

Hyuen has danced his way quietly through the masses of breakfasters, and suddenly towers over them all. Ryan didn't realize until now that Hyuen could do his magic dance with the living too. "I'm so sorry about your wife," Hyuen says.

"What do you mean?" Bernard asks.

"You're not being so helpful anymore," Ryan says to Hyuen.

"I'm an idiot," Hyuen says, wincing. "I thought you told him."

"Told me what?" Bernard is tearing the napkin again, using both hands. "Tell me, Ryan."

"How did this become my life?" Ryan asks.

"His wife?" Bella asks. She looks as though she is about to say something and then thinks better of it.

"It was sudden," Ryan says. The look on his father's face tells him he doesn't need to say anything more just yet. He wouldn't need to say everything all at once. Just a little bit at a time.

Bella holds out her hand to Ryan, and he takes it, smooth and kind in his. "So that would be your mother. I'm so sorry." Bernard looks at the floor and the waitress and the shredded napkin.

"Which is why," Bella says, slipping out of the booth and brushing the wrinkles out of her skirt, "this is the end of the line for me." Ryan watches as she takes Bernard's face in her hands as if he was a child, and kisses him on the forehead. She puts the ice-filled napkin on the table and it unfolds so that the ice cubes escape and slide out over the edges and onto the floor.

"Oh, great," the waitress says, walking in the other direction. "You all are a real gift."

"You don't need me around," Bella says. "Trust me. I'll take the bus the rest of the way." She heads for the door, swinging her hips in a way that says, now I'll be gone, then wrestles the door and the wind to let herself out.

"Go," Ryan says, and Bernard stumbles after Bella. Hyuen slips into the booth beside Ryan and stretches his long arm across the back then pulls Ryan a little closer to him. Was it Ryan's imagination, or did Hyuen smell faintly of formaldehyde? He thought of the fern morbiditus, thick-leaved and flourishing. "We'll wait here," he says though Bernard is already out the door.

Out on the street Bella turns around, and with her hands on Bernard's shoulders, she moves him out of the flow of people aflutter with scarves retrieved from the backs of closets, wrapped in jackets that have been packed away for months. "You don't need me around for this," she says. Bernard's not so sure as his head flops back and forth a little. *I like her.* Sam's voice is faint. Bernard will never hear the real thing again. His knees buckle a little.

"Losing," Bernard says in an effort to stave off real life. "It's not hard to master." *Don't do that.* Being an asshole might be the secret to safeguarding Sam's voice. *Elizabeth Bishop was my favorite. Lay off "One Art." Where are your words? Not Marguerite Porette's, not Louise Lateau's, yours. Yours, yours, yours.*

"Be still," Bella says. *She's right.* "There's no moving away from this. I'm not her." *I'm liking her more and more.*

Bernard nods, his arms hanging by his sides, useless. "I know you're not," he says. Don't everybody go at once, he thinks. Not everyone at once. "I knew you weren't."

"You have to go back in there," Bella says. *Going, going, gone.*

"I wanted everything to be different," Bernard says, though he's not sure what he's talking about, whether he's talking about right now or years ago when he found himself walking down the rocky path to the beach with his wife and two children. This is the last time I'll be standing on the street saying good-bye to a beautiful-at-a-second-and-a-third-and-a-fourth-glance waitress, right? But there is no answer. He nods as Bella turns to go but doesn't move. He tries to fill the silence in his mind with the image of Bella's lovely red head bobbing above everybody else's as she expertly maneuvers her way down the sidewalk, around a crowd of people gathered by a street vendor selling chestnuts and another cluster huddled over a man with CDs and books lined up on a brightly colored blanket. Bernard fills his mind with Bella's bobbing red head until, like a life buoy floating farther and farther out to sea, it is blocks and then blocks and then blocks away. Then it turns a corner and disappears altogether. Bernard tries to hold it in his mind, but the firefly flash goes dark, and then it's just him and the September air that smells like charcoal and roasting chestnuts and trash.

Good Mourning, Good Mourning, Good Mourning

The radiator clank, clanks Marguerite out of the stillness of the dark black night. When she opens her eyes, she is struggling up from deep deep down. Her head is bigger than any pot-smasher planet head, and her body is made of rusted metal. At first, through the blur, she doesn't recognize the mute brown dull edges of her old room. Paging Dr. Good man, Dr. Good man, and there is still hope. She doesn't see George Harrison with his relic to test her, and hope has not faded altogether.

Rest, rest, the taller mourning woman sings in the up and down hall. "This is mandatory rest," she sings and, firefly flash, Marguerite's mother's voice sings down the hall of the train depot. *Mandatory family dinner, put your shoes on, put your shoes on, put your shoes on*. For a moment, Marguerite's mother and the taller mourning woman sing together, praying twice.

"Welcome back," says Regina. She lies on her bed, one hand behind her propped-up head, the other smoothing out her nightgown nightdress. She examines a fingernail as if it holds the answers to all the world's mysteries, then nibbles on the cuticle.

"Where've I been?" Marguerite asks. She isn't sure she exists anymore, so she moves her slow gauze-covered hand to her face to make sure.

Regina doesn't answer. She points out the window to the bus stop where two little boys stand on either side of a woman, shooting at each other with plastic guns. The woman has one of the boys' scarves tucked under her chin as she tries to wrap the other around the shooting boy's neck, but he ducks and holds the gun to her face. "Mandatory rest o'clock," says Regina. "You've been gone that long. I thought you weren't coming back."

Pow, pow, the mandatory rest o'clock boys shout as they shoot their plastic guns and dance around their mother. One of them steps out into the street and the mother grabs the back of his tee shirt and tugs him back onto the sidewalk just as a honking car screeches and swerves. The sky above the trash-strewn street, above the cars that zip by, above the bus stop, is far, far away, an inscrutable blue that wants nothing to do with the county of queens below. Marguerite holds her gauze-wrapped hand to her ear to see if it will tell her anything, but there is only pow, pow, and then that is gone too, into the fuzzy black of Marguerite's mind mined with George Harrison's relic.

"I buried my girl," Regina says suddenly, to the ceiling, and she rolls toward the wall, silent, her back to Marguerite, her nightgown nightshirt twisted around her. She lays her palm flat against the wall, as though she is healing it. "She stopped breathing one day. The agency called me and said, 'You can come now.' So many years later, I didn't even recognize her."

Marguerite hears the question in Regina's voice: *Do you recognize this? Do you recognize me?* She slides off her bed, barefoot, imagining the heels of all the socks she ever wore completely unraveled. On her bare non-soul-squashing feet, she walks the short distance between the beds, the nubby carpet tickling the tired souls of her feet. She climbs onto Regina's bed in answer to Regina's question. She squeezes herself into the small sliver of space beside her, her arms stiff, her stomach pressed against the warm wall of Regina's back, breathing in and out, in and out, like the plastic bags in the naked trees outside, in and out like the red weed tide. Here is

my breath, Marguerite offers, here is my breath, Regina says back,
until they are breathing together, until they are one body lying
there, very still but alive.

Days that are actually minutes later, Regina rolls over and kicks
one long leg of secret maps straight up above her into the heavy
charcoal air of September all day long. "Get off my bed, shark girl,"
she says, which isn't necessary because Marguerite is already rolling
off. "Isn't it time we found your heart?"

"It's gone," Marguerite says. She is full of breath and life and
there is no room for anything else anyhow. Besides, she understands
as Regina puts her feet up on the wall to walk them up and down,
up and down, that all of this looking and looking is Regina's being
nice to Marguerite. Her secret maps don't know where Marguerite's
heart is because where her heart is is beside the point. The point isn't
getting anywhere in particular, the point is continuing on.

Marguerite's slow, plodding blood says nothing as she returns to her
own bed and Regina says, "Rest. Might as well. It's mandatory."

Marguerite puts her head down, and the blur that is inside her
head becomes the blur outside, until she wakes from a dream of her
father's fairy tale voice into the rest of the day. "Ah, wife," it said,
years and years ago. "You have taught me what it is to be afraid. And
for that, I am forever grateful." Now her father's voice is in the up
and down hall, looking for my daughter now that visiting hours are
just about to begin, though we came a little early and we apologize
for that but we were in a hurry. "Good mourning," the scary mask
face is saying from the front desk. "Good mourning."

"Look at this," Anna Karenina says. She has escaped mandatory
rest and is out in the hall.

"Mandatory rest!" the scary mask face shouts above the voices.

"Child's destiny has arrived after all," Anna Karenina says, her
voice staying in the same place, not budging. She's forgotten about
her train entirely.

"Who's there?" Marguerite asks as Regina, on her tiptoe feet,
walks to the door, opens it a crack.

"Fifty-seven percent," she says, pointing this way. "Thirty-four
percent," she says, pointing that way.

Then, firefly flash, only it's not a firefly flash, "I am her brother," her brother's voice strong and ready for her tough enough heart, says to the taller mourning woman who sings *wonderful, wonderful*. "And this is her father. We are her family."

Marguerite lifts her head as heavy as the pot-smasher's planet head from her pillow damp from drool. *During almost the entire duration of the ecstasy, Louise remains seated in her chair, inclined somewhat forward, and motionless as a statue. Her bleeding hands rest in her lap.* The piece of paper rubbed thin by Marguerite's fingers is long gone, rubbed into thin air. She puts her gauze-wrapped hand in her lap. *Her eyes are motionless. Her countenance indicates rapt attention: dead to all earthly objects, she is absorbed in the contemplation of some spectacle, which she seems to behold above the region of the earth. . . .* Will they be speechless from wonder? Will they stand stock-still in awe? What if, instead, they could be wonderless, aweless? What if, instead, they put their heads down and rested, content in sleep without dreams?

From his room, the wide-awake, never-sleeping man shouts, "I've had enough of this two-bit operation. A grown man needs naps like you idiots need pig candy."

Thump-thump, even from inside the room, Marguerite can hear her heart in Ryan's shirt pocket. She can hear its gentle, contented thump, thump against the cloth where he's put it for safekeeping. Regina leads her by her good hand out into the up and down hall, where, no firefly flash, her brother holds her against her own heart thump-thumping in his shirt pocket, and it turns out he doesn't have to carry it to the cathedral in Warsaw or the beach. It isn't time for the jelly jar glass; it is time for it to be right here, beating between them. There is no answer to the question she asked with her tongue that night, but there is Ryan holding her good hand and not letting it go. He touches the gauze on her other hand as if she has grown new skin. Her father whispers in the corner with the taller mourning woman. "More powerful than God," the taller mourning woman whispers, and "sea of light?" and Marguerite's father, no firefly flash, really, really here, puts his head in his hands.

"Don't cry," Marguerite says, because Ryan is still holding her hand, not letting go.

Her father puts his hand on her shoulder and says, "Brave, brave girl. Braver than I'll ever be."

Her brother tells her father that yes, she is much braver, and that maybe he should go outside and tell Hyuen they would be down soon.

"No," Marguerite says, holding up her bandaged hand to her father because there's something rising in her and she wants to explain. "Remember? You have taught me to be afraid."

Marguerite doesn't see her father rush for the elevator as she closes her eyes and firefly flash, a bright summer day. Her little-girl bare feet tough with summer calluses in the stubbly field outside their new home, the where is my fucking train depot. There was her favorite cow even though her parents and even her brother, who loved her the most, always said there was no telling them apart and how could she really know, but leave her alone she's only five and even if she couldn't tell them apart, why couldn't they just let her pretend? Her parents working in their studies and Ryan off with the farmer's son for a little while, telling her to stay there with the cows because he would be right back. There was her hand on the cow's big soft head, feeling the big bones in its face chew and chew. Standing there, on a rock in the field, stroking the cow's face warm from the sun, her little body ached for *more*. That's what her father called it. *Don't you want more?* he'd asked her mother when they decided to buy the train depot. That's what her mother called it too. *Doesn't* everyone *want more? Isn't that what life's about?* her mother asked back. *The endless wanting of more?* A conversation of questions. *More.* A little girl on a rock warmed by the sun, holding the cow's face full of chewing bones. Her whole life was still to come, a big, fantastic mystery, but would it be *enough* more? *More! More!* When they walked down to the ocean later that day, when Ryan let go of her hand, when she walked to the edge and then took one step and then another until she was stepping into *more*.

The firefly flash not bright enough for her to see the V of birds chop chopping through the sky clearly enough, to taste the ocean salt she licked off her arm sharply enough, to know for certain whether she walked off the pier or whether she stumbled, but there it is, the desire for more.

"I'm tired," Marguerite says. Her brother nods. That he's heard her words out loud is as important as anything that has come before. This is what's important right now as time stops looping-the-loop and, finally, stands still to take a breath.

"We'll take you home," Ryan says.

"I want to watch," Anna Karenina says, refusing to stay in her room, though the taller mourning woman walks toward her, saying *rest, rest, mandatory rest.*

Is this my life? Are you my beautiful wife?

Firefly flash, her mother's underwater voice in the underwater room made especially for Marguerite, lying back on the red divan as Marguerite sunk deep in the underwater quiet of the bath made the perfect temperature with her mother's weary arm. This is for you. *Where was her mother?* Ryan doesn't hear this out loud, and Marguerite is relieved because she isn't sure she wants to ask it in words yet.

Regina slips out of the room and squeezes Marguerite's arm so that her blood swish swishes in reply. "I am done with mandatory rest too," Regina whispers in Marguerite's ear, "and it is done with me. The pow pow boys are long gone. Mandatory rest o'clock is done."

Regina takes Marguerite's gauzed hand gently, gently in hers. She breathes in, she breathes out, and then twirls away on tiptoe feet. Marguerite watches the warm wall of her back as it moves away down the up and down hall.

"Ease up, three, no two, no none percent," Regina says, brushing the scary mask face's arm off of hers as it tries to stop her. The gesture is already a firefly flash and Marguerite wonders when the flash flash will return it to her.

"See you, sharky girl," Regina says over her shoulder. She is heading for the room with the smoking brains, the scary mask face scurrying after her. Marguerite curtsies low because here in the Queen's county, you should be grateful when your heart finds you.

Regulate and Arrange All Matters so That Souls May Be Saved

The wind blows the top layer of sand so the flying grains sting their ankles as they make their way down to the shoreline. The pier is gone, torn down bit by bit by last summer's huddle of teenagers who pulled the rotting parts of the wood away until the rest of the pier collapsed and floated out to sea. Bernard holds the plastic bag with both hands and Ryan follows close behind him.

Thompson waits up in the dunes, reading aloud from *The Rule of Saint Benedict*. Over the past few days, waiting in the train depot for someone, anyone, to return, *The Rule* has saved him time and time again, protected him from entropy or, more specifically, from heading to a bar. Today, he reads from "The Times of the Brother's Meals." *From Holy Easter to Pentecost, the brothers eat at noon and take supper in the evening.* He reads softly because as Bernard and Ryan left Thompson to head down the slope of the beach, Bernard said, "I can hear you." *Beginning with Pentecost and continuing throughout the summer, the monks fast until midafternoon on Wednesday and Friday, unless they are working in the fields or the summer heat is oppressive.* It comforts Thompson to think about eating at noon tomorrow and fasting afterward.

Though Bernard objected at first to allowing the "hippy porn carpenter" to have anything to do with scattering Sam's ashes, Ryan pointed out that if it hadn't been for Thompson, Sam might have been lying on the kitchen floor for who knows how long. Who was that redhead anyway? Ryan asked and Bernard didn't answer him.

The argument for allowing Thompson to be there was actually Hyuen's, which Ryan has adopted as his own. Ryan, Marguerite, and Bernard stuffed themselves into the car in Queens, and it was Hyuen who made their trip all the way from New York to Rhode Island bearable. Now Ryan is more convinced than ever he should follow Hyuen's lead. He hadn't said a word about it, hadn't made it a discussion, he just put his hand on Ryan's back and looked at him with those steady almond eyes, then climbed in and made it seem as if there was more room in the car once he'd folded himself inside, not less.

"Abraham Lincoln was the first advertisement for embalming," Hyuen said as they started down the road. "After he died, they rode him around from town to town by train so that everybody could see the president. But what they saw was the wonders of preservation after death." Bernard nodded stiffly, and Marguerite stared at Ryan as if trying to determine whether he was really there or not, but Ryan could tell everyone was grateful for the way Hyuen filled the car with his voice. Even when he forced them to play silly license plate games, it was a gift. "Let's see how many other license plates have fallen off their cars," Ryan said, at one point and Hyuen pinched Ryan.

Hyuen is up at the train depot with Marguerite now. Though the hospital claimed they straightened out her medication, they said Marguerite was still somewhat delusional. In fact, the hospital suggested she stay there for a while longer, but Bernard insisted they take her home, that this is what Sam would have wanted. Though Marguerite hasn't asked, Hyuen has decided its too soon to explain her mother's death to her. Bernard and Ryan are relieved there's someone there to make the decision.

While she lies on the bed, Hyuen holds up clothes to her. He has asked her to say "yes" or "no" to each item depending on whether she wants to take it to San Francisco, where her brother has invited her for a visit. So far, she has said yes to everything but her Led Zeppelin "The Song Remains the Same" tee shirt.

She doesn't want the song to remain the same. She wants the song to be brand-new.

Down at the beach, water foams around Bernard's then turns to bubbles and disappears as he stands there waiting, though he's not sure for what.

Behind him, Ryan steps on a jellyfish and jumps back.

"Jellyfish," he says to Bernard. "Did you know the jellyfish's mouth is also its ass?"

Bernard laughs. "Nope." He's still waiting for something to tell him what to do. He clutches the plastic bag tighter still.

Hyuen once told Ryan that jellyfish have an incredibly complex set of genes despite their simple-looking bodies, that they are much more complicated than they appear. Watching his father, Ryan wishes that the exact opposite was true of humans. That, in the end, despite the body's complexities, humans were really very simple. He is grateful that he doesn't know what his father is thinking, that he has absolutely no idea.

Bernard dips a finger into the plastic bag. *Is this my life? Is this my wife?* He reaches in and collects a handful, and the lighter ashes are taken up into the air by the wind. Sam always said she wanted to be cremated because of the way her parents died. Once they moved to the train depot, she liked the idea of being scattered over the ocean they could see from the kitchen window. *This view is so beautiful it could save a life.*

"That's ridiculous," Bernard always said when she told him being cremated would be a tribute to her parents. "It doesn't make any sense," he'd say. "How is being cremated a tribute to your parents death by fire? There's something a little twisted about it."

"A tribute doesn't have to make sense," she said.

You're right, he thinks now. He imagines the dusty rose manuscript on top of the paper towel dispenser, someone stopping to take a leak, then discovering it as he washes his hands. He imagines the someone taking it with him, putting it on the passenger seat of his car to read later. He imagines it lying there, not yet opened; filled with possibility. He hands the bag to his son, who shakes his head no.

"Do it all at once," Ryan says. Hyuen told him the bodies of the people who donate their bodies to science are cremated. A semester's worth at once, piles and piles of ashes on a big barge taken out to sea. This always seemed comforting to Ryan, and he wishes he could have put his mother on a barge like that so she could be part of the pile.

Indeed the abbot may decide that they should continue to eat dinner at noon every day if they have work in the fields, Thompson reads so that he doesn't have to watch. *Similarly, he should regulate and arrange all matters so that souls may be saved and the brothers may go about their activities without justifiable grumbling*. It will be an act of will. He will discipline himself into happiness. He turns and starts up the rocky path. The wind carries the scent of the pine forest to him and he breathes it in deeply. He will keep death daily before his eyes. He will keep death daily before his eyes. He will keep death daily before his eyes.

Bernard turns the bag inside out and shakes it. For a moment, Sam's dust flying upward, Bernard feels it. Something happening outside his body, apart from his pounding heart circulating his blood around and around in endless loops.

When they left the hospital, the taller nurse, the one who told him Marguerite had been quoting Louise Lateau when she burned herself, handed him a book she thought would be helpful. In it he found the passage Sam had forced him to read about the mistakes made in attributing mood disorders to either biological factors or psychosocial ones. Nature or nurture, one or the other. Was that what their daughter had? A mood disorder? It made him think of a stormcloud racing around a courtroom. "You! Mood! Order in the court!" A judge pounding his gavel. So it wasn't only his lousy genes? It wasn't *only* his lousy parenting? He wishes Sam was here to tell him, no, it was *both*, more than the sum of the parts, more, always more, more, but she's rising up and up and up on the wind until she disappears altogether. He shuts his eyes as his wife's dust falls in to the ocean, becoming the salt that washes ashore to cling to the hair on his shins.

It's September again, all month long, and Marguerite is walking through the charcoal smell of fall to catch the bus to school, where she is starting her senior year over. She is no longer in the Queen's County, though she sometimes curtsies to make her brother laugh, to send him a secret message thanking him for tending to her heart. She's not in Kansas anymore either, Dr. so-called so-and-so, not at all. She is in another city altogether, living with Hyuen—the man with the Carol Channing eyelashes—and Ryan, in a city where the hills give way to a view of a different mysterious ocean.

Marguerite stops to lean against one of the pastel houses as the trolley jingle-jangles by, staring at the mystery of this new ocean until her body loses its borders and she becomes the swirling vast blue-green reflecting the sun back to itself. Then she shakes her head until she is flesh again. She takes her medication, in part because Ryan and Hyuen have made her promise. She keeps her promise, the way she kept her other promise to go to spend those long days at the outpatient treatment center. She made them promise her in return: she is allowed to live with them as long as she wanted.

If she concentrates, even through the medicine she can firefly flash her way back to her blood's whisper before it was shushed.

Ryan wears goggles and a facemask as he tenderly scrubs the space where an elderly man, a friendless shut-in with no family, began to disappear into the floor after he was dead for a week. It took that long for a neighbor to notice the smell.

Hyuen sees people like this man in the morgue all the time, people who donated their bodies to science long ago and then outlived the next-of-kin who had been assigned to deliver them to the hospital. At Hyuen's suggestion, Ryan has started a renegade company that cleans up the homes of people who have died unexpectedly or alone, or both. There are no provisions for cleanup after suicides, murder, or for people like this man, dead for a week before anyone noticed.

The place is knee-deep in crumpled newspaper that hides food so moldy it looks like an experiment. Still Ryan feels peaceful. As he reverently scrubs what remains of the man's body from the floor, he feels for a minute as if he is disappearing himself. It's as if he is making space for something else. He hopes that, like Hyuen, what he is doing looks like a graceful, necessary dance. The in and out of his breath against the facemask achieves a certain rhythm, his hand moves in regular, smooth circles against the floor, and through his breath and the smooth circles he feels himself communing with the dead man's spirit. He's explained this to Hyuen, though he knew he sounded ridiculous. Hyuen said it wasn't ridiculous at all, that that was what usefulness feels like, and in explaining usefulness, Hyuen made Ryan feel useful. When Ryan tosses the sponge in the trash bag with the crumpled-up newspapers that date back years, he feels that usefulness.

He lifts his facemask and walks outside into the San Francisco fall day. He hangs his goggles around his neck as he sits on the steps to smoke a cigarette. He watches cars make their way slowly down this back street through mists of fog. He likes the anonymity the fog misty air affords.

Hyuen doesn't like him to smoke at home, which is a pain in the ass. It sometimes drives Ryan a little nuts that Hyuen seems not to have any vices except bossiness. Every night, Hyuen insists they all sit down to dinner, the way Sam did. When he first suggested it, Ryan rolled his eyes at the irony of falling in love with his mother after all. Still, last night, as Ryan watched Hyuen flutter his eyelashes against Marguerite's arm to make her laugh, watched him dance his long-limbed walk to and from the kitchen, carrying plates and instructing Marguerite and Ryan in the art of setting the table, he was able to appreciate it. As the three of them stepped out of the chaos of their days to sit still and calm at the dinner table, Ryan saw what Sam had been fighting for. He takes a long drag on his cigarette as he peels a bit of newspaper off the bottom of his shoe. He, Hyuen, and Marguerite are a family with a different song, a song whose words they are making up as they go along.

Bernard is in the train depot, looking out the kitchen window at the lifesaving view, out to the distant sliver of ocean. A group of cows gather at the fence in the field just below the window, switching their tails at flies. A gopher pops its head up and perches on one of the mute rocks that have once again pushed their way to the surface of the backyard.

It seems right that Sam is a part of that ocean now. It comforts Bernard—it might even make him extraordinarily happy—to think of her as a part of the very ocean she loved to look at. He waits for Sam to make fun of him or disagree, though her voice has been gone for a year now. Still, he can imagine what she would say. *Are you still going on about happiness? Happiness is not the point. Neither is extraordinary happiness nor ecstasy nor the mysterious spectacle Louise observed above the region of the earth. What's so wrong with the region of the earth? If you want too much, you'll float up, up, and up, until one day you'll look down, and those simple connections that offered themselves to you will have become miniature antlike versions of themselves. Small comforts are no small comfort.*

The words aren't as convincing delivered in his own voice, but Bernard's willing to try it. He moves away from the window because if he looks too long comfort is replaced by a sadness so heavy it threatens to drag him to the very floor where Sam died alone. Instead, he goes into the bathroom and lies next to the divan next to the window. Even a year later, he never lies on top of it for fear his body will find the impression of Sam's. *Fairy tale in reverse: A woman who once spoke poetry and now speaks only in frogs.* He lies on the floor and looks at the dust bunnies underneath the divan,

wishing for that notebook of Sam's, which walked off with the
hippy porn carpenter. He wishes for any sign of her at all.

Small comforts that are no small comfort: He just got back from
visiting Ryan, Marguerite, and Hyuen in San Francisco, never easy.
Ryan's tough on Bernard—there are lots of ground rules (Rule #1,
no talk of Louise), but Hyuen's a good referee. Bernard knows that
it's Hyuen who convinces Ryan to let Bernard visit at all. When
Bernard left, Hyuen said, "Ryan told me he misses you." Bernard's
not sure this is true, but that Hyuen would know Bernard would
want to hear it meant something.

Small comforts that are no small comfort: At dinner one night in
San Francisco, Marguerite touched his newly-shaved face and said,
"I like your face. I've never really seen it before." Small comforts
that are no small comfort: Bella called from the acting school in
Connecticut and asked him to come for a visit. "I'm lonely," she
said. "Everyone here's an *actor*."

Bernard gathers a handful of dust bunnies and slowly climbs to
his feet and tosses them in the trash can beside the dead man's bathtub he will never, ever use. He's tired, but he asked the farmer's son
if he could help him out in the fields today. It will be good for him
to get outside, to get a little sunshine the way he always nagged
Ryan to do. It'll do him good to get a view of the depot from the
outside in for a change. He's putting the place up for sale next week.
He thought he wanted to hang on to it, but like his beard, it had
been through too much, and it's also too expensive for someone who
has quit his job and isn't sure what he'll do next.

Small comforts that are no small comfort: the smooth wood of
the "Where is my fucking train?" bench. He runs his hand along
the back of it on his way out the door into the optimistic bright light
of the day.

Firefly flash, flashes of her mother light up the foggy morning of
Marguerite's medicine mind: her mother's hip pushing and pushing
against the window that would never open without a fight, her arm

dancing through the linen closet looking for her inspiration. *Where did it go? Is it underneath the sheets?* Firefly flash, that beautiful weary arm, still up to its elbow, still testing the water, is like a star's light reaching Marguerite years later.

As she waits for the bus, Marguerite reaches up to touch the pompom on her new wool hat. "It's too hot for a wool hat," Ryan said before he left for work, his goggles around his neck. "You're in a warmer place now." He pulled the hat off her head and put it back in the closet. After Ryan left, Hyuen slipped it back onto her head. "Ryan doesn't know everything," he said. The way he touched her cheek reminded her of another phantom tenderness.

Overhead the birds don't chop, chop through the morning air, they just fly. Marguerite's heart is in her chest where it belongs, though some days, today, for example, it beats louder than others. As Marguerite fingers the pompom on her hat, firefly flash, and there is a ghostly outline of the magic sunset hour lady pacing the length of the bus shelter outside the hospital in the Queen's County. The magic hour sunset lady dips her foot into the gutter near the crackly brown leaf-covered drain, reaching up to touch her own pompom history and whoosh, the soul of this someone Marguerite once knew but was careful to never, never step on ghosts on by with her own secret history.

Her blood whispers Good Mourning, Good Mourning, Good Mourning, but to the bus driver and to the other people on the bus Marguerite will say "Good Morning, Good Morning, Good Morning."

Acknowledgments

I am especially indebted to Dr. Augustus Rohling's essay about Louise Lateau, "Louise Lateau: Her Stigmas and Ecstasy" which appeared in the 1879 edition of *The Catholic Review,* translated by Reverend W. J. Walsh. Please see the permissions page for the page numbers on which the excerpts from this essay appear. Also to *The Rule of Saint Benedict*, edited by Timothy Fry, Dr. Edward Strecker's article, "The Continuous Bath in Mental Disease," which appeared in *The Journal of the American Medical Association* in 1917, and *The Varieties of Religious Experience* by William James. Of equal importance in my research and thinking were Ian Hacking's *Mad Travelers: Reflections on the Reality of Transient Mental Illnesses*, and *Manic Depressive Illness*, edited by Frederick K. Goodwin and Kay Redfield Jamison. I would also like to thank Mavis Staples, and the Staples Singers, for their version of "Are You Sure," a song that was integral to the writing of this book.

I would like to acknowledge and express my gratitude to the UCross Foundation, the Gilman School's Reginald Tickner Fellowship, and the Kratz Center for Creative Writing at Goucher College for their support during the writing of this book. Thanks as well to

Lost Lamb Farm and the Bradlee/Pittman/Pinchot family for providing beautiful places in which to write. I am also extremely grateful to my colleagues and my students at both the University of Maryland and Goddard College for their support and inspiration.

My thanks to Emily Auerswald and Bruce Holsinger for their help with research. Many thanks to those people who read various drafts and provided invaluable notes: Jane Barnes, John Casey, Elizabeth Evans, Julia Greenberg, and Timothy Schaffert. My deepest gratitude and affection to Jeremy Shapiro for his keen reader's eye, his wit, and his curmudgeonly tenderness.

Many thanks to Kelli Martin, whose kindness and guidance over the years made this book possible. My agent, Alice Tasman, read countless drafts of this novel and, as usual, went above and far beyond, talking me off the ledge more than once. I am indebted to my editor, Jennifer Pooley, for her insight, her generosity, and her stalwart support.

A special thank you to Jason Tougaw, who first read this book when it was a few fragmented chapters. He has been a tireless, exquisite reader and friend, whose own writing has served as a model of boldness and innovation.

Permissions

About the author

About the book

Insights,
Interviews
& More . . .

Read on

Meet Maud Casey

Carol Cohen

MAUD CASEY made the literary scene early. She was born in Iowa City, where her parents were attending the Iowa Writers' Workshop. "It's sort of ridiculous," she says. "Fortunately, I would apply many years later and be rejected."

In her first years she covered a great deal of ground. Following their time in Iowa her family moved to Vermont. There, she recalls, "our dogs would come home stuck with porcupine quills, my parents made homemade maple syrup, and everyone had ear infections." Next came Rhode Island— "My parents bought a beautiful small island (Fox Island) on the cheap in Narragansett Bay. We lived there except during the winter, when we wisely went to live with my grandmother in Saunderstown—where there was more than a forever-breaking-down generator for electricity."

Finally, at the age of four, she settled in Charlottesville, Virginia.

Asked about her initial experiences as a reader, Maud replies: "I had the good fortune

66 'Our dogs would come home stuck with porcupine quills, my parents made homemade maple syrup, and everyone had ear infections.' 99

to grow up around lots of books—though being a somewhat cowed and anxious kid it sometimes felt as though I was born with a reading list I would never finish. Still, I did love reading (and being read to) and loved books that were part of a series—Thornton Burgess' Old Mother West Wind series with Spotty the Turtle and the Willful Little Breeze was an early favorite."

When did she graduate to headier stuff? "The first adult book I fell in love with on my own (i.e., it wasn't on my parents' bookshelves) was *Sisters by a River*—by the British writer Barbara Comyns," she says. "The first sentence is a run-on that rampages out of the gate with no thought of anything but carving out a voice like no other: 'It was in the middle of a snowstorm I was born, Palmer's brother's wedding night, Palmer went to the wedding and got snowbound, and when he arrived very late in the morning he had to bury my packing under the walnut tree, he always had to do this when we were born— six times in all, and none of us died. . . .' I thought—'You can do *that*?' Who knew?"

She received a BA from Wesleyan University and an MFA from the University of Arizona.

Writing was always something she thought of doing. Her family, after all, could boast a tidy sum of writers—not only her parents, but her sister, several aunts, and a number of cousins. "It's pathological," she says. Daunted by the in-house competition, she did not pursue writing as early as one might expect. "I wrote my first story in a college workshop with the very wonderful Frank Reeve," she says. "He basically said, 'This isn't so great, but keep going'—and I did. Frank was the adviser for my senior thesis, a collection of ▶

> 66 Her family could boast a tidy sum of writers— not only her parents, but her sister, several aunts, and a number of cousins. 'It's pathological,' she says. 99

stories that (years and years and years later) would lead me to my second book—*Drastic*."

Her work history is at once commendable and amusing. She temped for about six years through a riotously-named agency. "Once through a place called Temporama," she says, "until they finally wised up and changed their name." Not unlike novelist Francine Prose (who once worked as a lab assistant in the Bellevue morgue), Maud Casey worked as a secretary in a whole-body donation clinic in the basement of the University of California, San Francisco Medical Center. "The bodies," she explains, "were used by the medical students for research. I took calls from potential donors, and their next of kin calling to notify us that the donor had died. Often— after the initial interview in which I had to ask questions such as *Do you have any infectious diseases?* and *Do you have all your limbs?*—I would find myself involved in long existential conversations about the meaning of life or comforting a lonely eighty-year-old woman whose husband and friends had died. I was twenty-one and just out of college." She continues: "Near the end of the job (it lasted for months—one of those long-term temp situations) I went upstairs to the morgue to watch one of the donors be embalmed. I felt I needed to pay my respects to an actual body after talking to all these disembodied voices over the phone. It freaked me out, but I was very moved by the donor's generosity and by that proximity to death. One time a potential donor came by in person—that was a little awkward."

After graduate school she moved to New York City. She continued to temp, worked for

"'Near the end of the job I went upstairs to the morgue to watch one of the donors be embalmed.'"

a year as a counselor in a domestic violence shelter, and for three years as an administrator at the Lee Strasberg Theatre Institute.

Maud moved to Baltimore in 2002 to be the writer-in-residence at the Gilman School. In 2004–2005 she was the writer-in-residence at the Kratz Center for Creative Writing at Goucher College. She has also taught fiction in Goddard College's MFA program and at Illinois Wesleyan University, Wesleyan University, and the University of Arizona.

Does she bring to her profession any peculiar habits? "I'm a very nerdy writer," she says. "I write early in the morning. I always wanted to be a late-night swaggering type but I just can't pull it off. I write on my iBook G4—which is white and has developed these palm-shaped stains from where I rest my hands in a very unergonomic fashion. I've opted to treat these 'Shroud of Turin' stains as something magical rather than as something unhygienic and gross."

"My humor has occasionally been mistaken for bitterness," she said (in an *EightDiagrams.com* interview). "I won't name any names—but let's just say that a particular anonymous review of *Shape (The Shape of Things to Come)* referred to it as a 'bitter little novel.' I'm still planning on getting a T-shirt made that says 'bitter little novelist.' "

Her stories have appeared in *The Gettysburg Review, The Threepenny Review, The Georgia Review, Beloit Fiction Journal, Prairie Schooner, Shenandoah,* and *Confrontation.* Her book reviews have appeared in the *New York Times Book Review, Salon,* the *Washington Post Book World, Elle,* and the *San Jose Mercury News.* Her essay ▶

> ❝ ' I write on my iBook G4— which is white and has developed these palm-shaped stains from where I rest my hands in a very unergonomic fashion. ❞

Meet Maud Casey *(continued)*

"A Better Place to Live" appeared in *Unholy Ghost: Writers on Depression* (edited by Nell Casey) and in the Modern Library volume *Out of Her Mind: Women Writing on Madness* (edited by Rebecca Shannonhouse). Her essay "The Rise from the Earth (So Far)" appeared in *Maybe Baby* (edited by Lori Leibovitch). She lives in Washington, DC, and has taught in the MFA program at the University of Maryland, College Park since 2003. ◯◯

Maud Casey on Writing *Genealogy*

THIS IS A WORK OF FICTION THAT GREW (in part) out of my interest in a real woman—a nineteenth-century Belgian mystic named Louise Lateau. I owe much of this book to a happy accident of research (that, and an agent who twice refused to let me give back the advance during writer's block—round two *and* round three). While looking into the history of the categorization and diagnosis of mental illness, I was reading a terrific book by Ian Hacking called *Mad Travelers*. It's about a nineteenth-century *fugueur*—the mad traveler of the title. His name—incredibly enough—was Albert Dadas, and he worked for a gas company in the Bordeaux region of France. He became infamous for wandering the countryside—often ending up as far afield as Constantinople, Moscow, and Algeria in a trancelike state. He'd arrive and wouldn't know how he got there. In that book was a passing reference to Louise Lateau. It was that passing reference that led me to a wacky essay in the 1879 *Catholic Review* written by a German doctor named Augustus Rohling.

Louise Lateau had (among other fascinating qualities) stigmata and fasted for twelve years—then died at the significant age of thirty-three. One of Charcot's disciples, Desire Bournville, studied her. Lateau became the focus of an inquiry by the Belgian Royal Academy of Medicine. No one could really get to the bottom of her—but watching Rohling try in the course of the essay really fascinated me. Rohling's essay argues that Louise Lateau was a vessel of God. In that way, his analysis ▶

> ❝ I owe much of this book to a happy accident of research (that, and an agent who twice refused to let me give back the advance during writer's block—round two *and* round three). ❞

Maud Casey on Writing *Genealogy*
(continued)

is part of a larger argument going on in the nineteenth century between rationalist psychology (Freud is said to have made a derisive remark about Louise Lateau once— dismissing her stigmata as hysteria), hard science, and religion. As a born worrier, I was worried at first about using a historical figure—particularly as I excerpt Rohling's essay in my novel. I wanted her to seem *real,* but I also wanted her story to help shape the stories of my made-up characters. The possibilities of the collision between this woman who had existed in the world and the Hennart family who (until now) existed in my head—running rampant and behaving very badly—really excited me.

Something goes on between the lines of Rohling's essay that fascinates me—between the lines of sections he includes on a scientific analysis of Louise (essentially lengthy discussions of plasma and blood vessels), the scrutiny of her by the Catholic Church, and the accounts of her ecstasies. Louise, described by Rohling as "totally devoid of imagination" and "simple, and upright," was anything but. "Whatever was going on," she seems, in fact, wild with passion and imagination. And here is where I made the leap that novelists are wont to make. There's a lot of religious iconography in the delusions of the mentally ill—Louise's ecstasies struck me as similar to manic episodes or psychotic breaks. William James (in *The Varieties of Religious Experience*) talks about the way religion exists "not as a dull habit" but as an "acute fever." Religious fervor and insanity sometimes look alike— hearing voices, hallucinations, and feelings

" Religious fervor and insanity sometimes look alike— hearing voices, hallucinations, and feelings of transformation and transcendence. "

of transformation and transcendence. In a story I'd been working on, also called "Genealogy," the seed I'd written about a character who suffers from manic depression and her father. In the novel, that daughter became Marguerite and her father became Bernard.

The idea was not to romanticize mental illness or to dismiss Louise's spirituality (or worse—to chalk it up to a chemical imbalance that might be cured by the pharmaceutical-du-jour), but rather to consider those things religion and madness have in common—a striving to reach beyond oneself and an impulse toward ecstasy. It seems very human—that desire for more, for bigger, for meaning, for feelings that knock you over or knock you out. It created an interesting echo when I lay Marguerite's mental illness and Louise's ecstasies side by side. While Bernard (the father in *Genealogy*) is unable to face his eighteen-year-old daughter's mental illness, he becomes consumed with this article about Louise Lateau—which happens to focus on her teenage years and the beginning of the stigmatas. Marguerite, in turn, conflates her own experience with that of Louise. So Louise became what Italo Calvino would call a "magic object" in the novel—a connecting force that brings the family together, narratively speaking.

It was important to me to retain the flavor of the essay—which is why I decided to use excerpts from the essay itself. There's a beauty in the language, particularly in the rare moments when Louise is allowed to speak for herself. At one point Louise says to ▶

> " It seems very human—that desire for more, for bigger, for meaning, for feelings that knock you over or knock you out. "

the president of the Episcopal Seminary of Tournay (who has arrived at Louise's family home to investigate Louise's ecstasies), "It fills me with such a lively sense of the presence of God, that, from the contemplation of his greatness (and) of my own littleness, I feel at a loss whither to turn that I may hide myself." In many ways, all of the Hennarts are after that feeling of littleness in the face of something greater than themselves. While none of them find religion in the traditional sense, they all find *vicarious* religious experiences. It's one of the things they've bequeathed to each other— a genealogy that goes beyond blood and beyond genes. Sam finds Thompson's St. Benedict; Bernard finds Louise Lateau and her ecstasies; Ryan worships at the feet of music he loves but can't really play; and Marguerite teeters on the edge of reality— absorbing it all.

" While none of the Hennarts find religion in the traditional sense, they all find *vicarious* religious experiences. It's one of the things they've bequeathed to each other—a genealogy that goes beyond blood and beyond genes. "

10

The Hennarts' Reading for Ecstasy List

"Louise Lateau: Her Stigmas and Ecstasy: An Essay Addressed to Jews and Christians of Every Denomination" by Dr. Augustus Rohling (New York: Hickey & Co., Publishers, Booksellers and Stationers)—appeared in 1879 in *The Catholic Review* (available from Amazon Booksellers).

The Complete Grimm's Fairy Tales.

The Complete Poems 1927–1979 by Elizabeth Bishop.

The Blue Estuaries: Poems 1923–1968 by Louise Bogan.

Creating Mind by John E. Dowling.

Madness and Civilization: A History of Insanity in the Age of Reason by Michel Foucault.

The Rule of St. Benedict edited by Timothy Fry, OSB.

Mad Travelers: Reflections on the Reality of Transient Mental Illness by Ian Hacking.

The Varieties of Religious Experience by William James.

Manic-Depressive Illness by Kay Redfield Jamison and Frederick K. Goodwin, MD.

An Unquiet Mind and *Touched by Fire* by Kay Redfield Jamison.

Collected Poems by Robert Lowell.

Transforming Madness: New Lives for People Living with Mental Illness by Jay Neugeboren.

The Hennarts' Reading for Ecstasy List
(continued)

"Mood Stabilizers in Children and Adolescents" by Neal D. Ryan, MD, Vinod S. Bhatara, MD, and James M. Perel, PhD. *Journal of the American Academy of Child and Adolescent Psychiatry*, vol. 38, no. 5, pp. 529–536, May 1999.

In the Night Kitchen and *Where the Wild Things Are* by Maurice Sendak.

"The Continuous Bath in Mental Disease" by Edward Strecker. *The Journal of the American Medical Association*, vol. 68, p. 1796, 1917.

Have You Read?
More by Maud Casey

DRASTIC: STORIES

Meet the college graduate working in a whole-body donation clinic; a young woman obsessed with Benedictine monks; a middle-aged woman who becomes a stand-in talk-show guest; unlikely friends who meet in a domestic violence shelter; a young girl and the father who stole her away to escape his wife's mental illness; and a graduate student from a suburban family who believes her physical connection to the world is deteriorating. Maud Casey explores how we survive modern crises of loss and love in tales of emotional and geographic nomads. Some of these characters teeter on the brink of sanity and a netherworld of delirium. Some grapple with a grief so tempestuous it threatens to paralyze them. Some just want a sign that they have left their mark, their scent on someone, somewhere—and that someone is better for it. These simple gestures of optimism and vitality, gorgeously rendered, make *Drastic* an unforgettable collection.

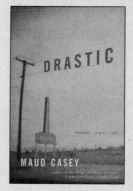

"Casey's language is remarkably consistent, her voice and tone entirely, refreshingly unaffected. The book's humility is what sets it apart from other tales of disaffection. There's a deliberate tenderness in Casey's handling of her characters, instead of the usual deadpan, the too familiar irony."   —*Washington Post*

THE SHAPE OF THINGS TO COME: A NOVEL

Isabelle, a woman in her thirties without any of the trappings of a *grown-up* life, has just been fired from her job at a San Francisco phone company. Returning to the midwestern suburb of her childhood (Standardsville, Illinois), she contends with her dating single mother, a neighbor who once appeared on *The Honeymooners,* and an ex-boyfriend. She also becomes a *mystery shopper* for a temp agency—posing as a variety of potential tenants for newly built suburban communities to access their exclusive services.

Enchanted by the possibilities of disguise, Isabelle spins a web of lies that keeps the world at a distance—until she unearths long-kept secrets that force her to rethink everything she thought she knew.

"Casey is a stand-up philosopher posing the most vexing questions about human existence while satirizing the materialistic ways we find to hold our despair at a distance. . . . [S]he's funny and inventive on the subject of sex, and she empathizes with the least of her characters, especially office workers."
                    —*New York Times Book Review*

As Contributor

UNHOLY GHOST: WRITERS ON DEPRESSION
edited by Nell Casey

"These essays address depression with notable sanity and stylistic elegance, exploring the debilitating conditions that fall under the depression umbrella more strongly than any single memoir could" (*Entertainment Weekly*).

Maud Casey's piece, "A Better Place to Live," appears in this unique collection of twenty-two essays about depression—a collection edited by her sister, Nell Casey. In the spirit of William Styron's *Darkness Visible, Unholy Ghost* finds vivid expression for an elusive illness suffered today by more than one in five Americans. Unlike any other memoir of depression, however, *Unholy Ghost* includes many voices and depicts a most complete portrait of the illness. Lauren Slater eloquently describes her own perilous experience as a pregnant woman on antidepressant medication. Susanna Kaysen, writing for the first time about depression since *Girl, Interrupted*, criticizes herself and others for making too much of the illness. Larry McMurtry recounts the despair that descended upon him after his quadruple bypass surgery. Meri Danquah describes the challenges of racism and depression. Ann Beattie sees melancholy as a consequence of her writing life. And Donald Hall lovingly remembers the "moody seesaw" of his relationship with his wife, Jane Kenyon. Among the book's additional contributors

15

Have You Read? *(continued)*

are Russell Banks, Chase Twitchell, Edward Hoagland, Darcey Steinke, and William Styron.

With an introduction by Kay Redfield Jamison, *Unholy Ghost* allows the bewildering experience of depression to be adequately and beautifully rendered.

Don't miss the next book by your favorite author. Sign up now for AuthorTracker by visiting www.AuthorTracker.com.